WHEN YOU WERE ME

WHEN YOU WERE ME

ROBERT RODI

KENSINGTON BOOKS
http://www.kensingtonbooks.com

KENSINGTON BOOKS are published by

Kensington Publishing Corp.
850 Third Avenue
New York, NY 10022

All Kensington titles, imprints, and distributed lines are available at special quantity discounts for bulk purchases for sales promotion, premiums, fund-raising, educational, or institutional use.

Special book excerpts or customized printings can also be created to fit specific needs. For details, write or phone the office of the Kensington Special Sales Manager: Attn. Special Sales Department, Kensington Publishing Corp., 850 Third Avenue, New York, NY 10022. Phone: 1-800-221-2647.

Library of Congress Card Catalogue Number: 2006939881
ISBN-13: 978-0-7582-1533-8
ISBN-10: 0-7582-1533-9

First Printing: June 2007
10 9 8 7 6 5 4 3 2 1

Printed in the United States of America

*The author owes
a nearly inexpressible debt
of love and gratitude to
Haven Kimmel, Christopher Schelling,
Augusten Burroughs, Tim Sommer,
and above all,
Jeffrey Smith.*

Part One

Jack

Chapter 1

That it began with Sharon was no surprise. Pretty much every shock or trauma in Jack's life had begun with Sharon. He and Jimmy used to call her "the hellhound." She was their junior by a decade, but they lived in a kind of quailing awe of her. She might do anything, and usually did. Their father's first heart attack, for instance, occurred when he learned Sharon had hospitalized one of her seventh grade classmates—pushed him behind some collapsible bleachers and tried to close them on him. (She was apparently provoked by a disparaging comment about Adam Ant.) The second heart attack followed some dozen years later, when Sharon called home at a quarter to three in the morning to say she was flying to Riyadh with a handsome Saudi architect whom she intended to marry. She showed up at Intensive Care the next morning, trailing an aroma of distillation, and reassured Dad that not only was she was still in town, she didn't even remember making the call, and had only the haziest recollection of meeting anyone even remotely Arab. Then she said "Excuse me," turned her head, and projectile-vomited all over his I.V. drip.

So any phone call from or about Sharon was as likely as not to involve high cardiovascular risk. But this time the hammer blow came, not from what she had done, but from what she had become.

"A grandmother," she repeated, as Jack had apparently asked her to do. He couldn't remember doing so. He was busy trying to blink away the cottony white film that had descended over his eyes when he'd heard it the first time.

"You're—" he stuttered. "You're—"

"A *grand-muth-ur,*" she said yet again, enunciating as if to an idiot. "For God's sake, what's with the mealy mouth? You knew Kari was pregnant. I told you at Thanksgiving."

Jack looked for a place to sit down, but he'd answered the phone in the foyer so there was no chair. Improvising, he slid his back down the wall and squatted on the floor.

"I know, I know," he said. "But . . . it's like, 'My niece is pregnant' is one thing. 'My little sister's a grandmother' is . . . I dunno. Something else."

"It's the same damn thing, fathead." She'd never had any respect.

"No it's not, it's not remotely the same. The perspective is completely different. I mean . . . my God, since when are you even old enough?"

"I'm forty-three, Jack. You'd know that if you bothered sending cards."

"You don't send *me* any."

"Well . . . no. I picked up that bad habit from you. You were supposed to be a *good* influence on me, see?"

"As if anyone on the planet could've influenced you."

"Don't try to shirk the blame. All my failings are really your fault." Her tone was light, bubbly; she was clearly ecstatic, and was enjoying teasing him. Why? . . . Why was she so giddy?

Oh, right—*the baby.*

"Boy or girl?" he asked.

She hooted. "I'm impressed, it took you just under two minutes! I was betting you'd forget to ask at all."

"Boy. Or. Girl," he repeated, unamused.

"Girl," she said. "Six pounds, four ounces, with little apple cheeks you could almost eat."

"That's . . . wonderful. Seriously, I'm a little freaked out, but I'm so happy for you, Sharon. You and Bert both. And of course Kari and Steve. Congratulations all around."

"Thanks. We're all delighted."

A longish pause followed. Jack knit his brow; Sharon wasn't usually the kind who let that happen. When confronted with any silence, she was only too happy to fill it.

"Well," he said, "umm . . ."

"You're not going to ask her name, are you?"

"Oh, Christ! Sorry. What've they chosen?"

She giggled. "I *knew* you'd forget."

"Just tell me the name, Grandma."

"Jocelyn Cassandra."

"Pretty. Family names?"

"Jocelyn was Steve's mother. So you'd think my name would be in there too, but no, Cassandra is from some character in a book Kari read as a kid and never got over."

"You're kidding . . . *I Capture the Castle?* Dodie Smith? . . . I *gave* her that book!"

"Well, thanks a lot. What are you doing poisoning my daughter's mind?"

"I gave you the same damn book when *you* were ten. You just never opened it."

"Yeah, well, I was never much of a reader."

"Few juvenile delinquents are."

"Hardy-har. Anyway, you *have* to fly out and see us now. Be introduced to the baby you apparently helped name."

"Of course, of course. I wouldn't *dream* of missing the christening."

"Well, a dream's the only place there'll be one."

"Oh, Sharon, come on! It's just a little sprinkled water. And then all the gifts!"

"No, they've decided. Neither of them is religious. And it's fine with me. I mean, can you see me walking into a church? Place would burst into flames."

"Hey, that should've been my line!"

"Beat you to it, didn't I? . . . Seriously, Jack, do come and see us. We miss you."

"Soon, I promise. Meantime, my love to Bert."

"And mine to—" She stopped herself. "And mine."

Jack turned off the phone but remained seated on the floor a while longer. *"And mine to Harry,"* she'd almost said. Caught herself just in time. For God's sake, he and Harry had split almost a year ago. And she had the nerve to mock *him* for forgetting things?

With a groan, he got to his feet and placed the phone back in its cradle. He looked up at his reflection in the little gilt-framed mirror that hung above the cherrywood stand.

Your baby sister is a grandmother, he told himself. *And that makes you . . .*

He stopped short, unwilling to admit the word. *Old,* he thought. *Old, old, old.*

He leaned into the mirror and ran his hand across his surprisingly unlined face. Despite a receding hairline, he didn't *look* old. People routinely guessed him ten years younger than he was.

Except, he thought, tugging at the still supple skin around his eyes, *ten years younger is still old enough to be a grandparent. Damn you, Sharon.*

As he continued probing his face, he noticed a few liver spots—not on his face, on his hand. They were lurking sheepishly beneath the sandy hair splayed across his knuckles. *Old man hands,* he thought.

"All right," he said aloud, "enough." If there was anything more pathetic than an aging single gay man, it was an aging single gay man minutely assessing himself in a mirror. He turned resolutely away and headed back to his bedroom to dress.

But as he padded down the hallway, he couldn't resist giving his pectorals a squeeze, if only to reassure himself that they were still there, and still impressively cut. "And I've got the blood pressure of a man half my age," he said, seemingly to Nelly, who was curled up on the sheets he'd tossed aside when he woke up. But Nelly, who in dog years was even older than he, was plainly sound asleep.

Chapter 2

It was unusual for Jack to have to dress in the morning. Ordinarily he had no place to go, no reason to get out of bed at all. Not since he'd sold his public relations agency, Ackerly & Associates, to the larger, multinational HDG Corp., for a sum of money so extravagant it took him several weeks to realize, *I never have to lift a finger on my own behalf ever again.*

But in the two years since, Jack had learned that this wasn't quite so felicitous a condition as he'd thought. He'd been working since his teens, in business for himself since twenty-four. With his career now ended, he was left with but one directive: to do whatever he wanted. To this day, he had absolutely no idea what that was.

Accordingly, he tried to fill his calendar with whatever he could, which, at his level of achievement usually meant boards and committees. This morning he was scheduled to attend a meeting of the board of directors of the Tealight Theatre, a small, quirky, often distressingly snide company that specialized in putting on nude re-enactments of 1970s sitcoms. They were currently into a mildly successful run of *Welcome Back, Kotter* episodes, but were excited to have recently been granted the rights to re-stage *Mork and Mindy* (largely by neglecting to mention the bare-ass aspect to the copyright holders; their philosophy was, "It's easier to get forgiveness than permission"). The company had lately come up with some new ideas to increase its draw, one of which was audience participation—meaning that before each show, someone who had paid for the privilege of ogling naked people making fools of themselves was forcibly drafted into joining them. This innovation had been wildly successful at driving people away, which had in turn put increased pressure on the board to find new sources of funding—which is, Jack had learned very quickly, the sole *raison d'être* of any board, anywhere.

Still, Jack liked having somewhere to go this morning—a reason to put on a Dolce & Gabbana suit, a reason to skip breakfast—a reason to shave, for Christ's sake. But he dreaded the actual meeting. He wondered what he had to do to get on the board of something slightly more prestigious; say, the Court Theatre, or Hubbard Street Dance. He knew the answer: *show them the money.* So far, he'd raised exactly five thousand dollars and change for Tealight, which wasn't exactly the kind of booty that would prompt other organizations to clamor for him. It was a classic Catch-22: he had to raise money to graduate from Tealight-caliber organizations, but that meant raising money for Tealight-caliber productions. Jack, whose idea of theatrical subversion pretty much ended at *The Boys In the Band*—if not *Mrs. Warren's Profession*—just didn't feel the requisite passion to oblige.

Traffic was terrible this morning; Lake Shore Drive was moving at the speed of a suppurating wound. Jack had forgotten the soul-shriveling tedium of commuting; and yet he'd done it, day in, day out, for a quarter of a century. How had he borne it? . . . He turned up the CD he'd selected for the drive, *The Easy Way* by the Jimmy Giuffre 3, but even the cool, muted chords of his favorite Fifties jazz combo couldn't quite hold his attention.

Well no wonder, he could hear Harry saying. *That's not even music. It's, like, "noodle-noodle-noodle." You want something to take you out of yourself, you need Bonnie Tyler, man! "Total Eclipse of the Heart."*

"Yes, of course," he said aloud, "how stupid of me. The Eighties being *so* much more relevant and useful than the Fifties."

I didn't say that, he imagined Harry retorting. *I was quite clearly talking about the differences between two specific pieces of music.*

"But your conclusion is based on your pathological adoration of the world in which you came of age, and your equally fierce loathing of any era before you were born."

Am I on the couch now? . . . Did you get your license to practice psychotherapy when I wasn't looking? I wish you'd told me, I'd have thrown you a party . . .

And that's how it started—another imaginary sparring match with Harry. When they'd broken up, ten months before, the actual dialogue had been minimal; Harry had said, "Listen, I just feel we've reached the end point here; I mean, have we ground to a halt, or what?" and Jack had straightened his spine and channeled Margaret Dumont, loftily replying, "If you expect me to help you bail out of this relationship, or God forbid beg you to stay, I'm afraid I'm going to have to disappoint you." After that they'd been terse and matter-of-fact with each other, speaking only about the practical aspects of their breakup, who was keeping what and what was owed to whom for whatever.

That's only because, after twenty-four years with the man, Jack knew *exactly* why Harry was leaving. He'd known for some time, but wouldn't—couldn't—address it. Too proud, perhaps, or simply too aware of his inability to fix the problem; or possibly, probably, just plain angry at Harry for being such a cliché.

"Ah, fading youth," he said now, a little sarcastic trill in his voice. "You're forty-two, handsome, fit, successful, much loved, and completely at liberty to do whatever it is you want with your life. You're richer, healthier, luckier, and freer than just about anyone else on the planet. Statistically, the people who rate higher than you in the equation don't even register as a blip. But ah me! You've got laugh lines, so your life is a tragedy. You've got a middle-aged gut, so the world can offer you no consolation. You're not a fresh young twink anymore, so all that's left for you is the grave. And all of this is, of course, my fault. Because I plucked you out of circulation when you were just nineteen, I'm the one who's made you this way. Intellectually, you know that's not true, but in your heart it's what you believe. So go ahead, pull up stakes and flee as fast as you can. Put me behind you and hurl yourself back onto the party-boy circuit. You'll get your youth back that way. Of *course* you will."

Jack realized he was tailgating the Taurus in front of him; its jittery driver kept looking at him in her rearview mirror, clearly concerned by his dogged proximity, and by the look of open rage on his face.

He forced himself to calm down, to prevent his anger from consuming him. Especially since such anger would scarcely have any impact; at the first strong word, Harry's shields would go up, and he'd go defensively deaf. And in fact, things weren't as simple as Jack had been making them out to be, anyway. The reality was more ambiguous, as reality usually is.

"See, I went through it myself," he said now, his voice gentler. "I know you think I didn't, but I did." He smiled, which Harry would perhaps find condescending, but it was meant to be warm, avuncular; an older man passing along his wisdom to a younger one. "It's tough to grow old. It's the toughest thing any of us will ever have to do. Suddenly, your own body betrays you. You look in the mirror, and all you *see* is betrayal. You try to run for a cab, and your knees seize up. You try to read a book, you fall asleep. And if your own slow decline isn't bad enough, there are all the young turks infiltrating your world, living life with the same intensity you used to. Bad enough to have to look at them, but then they start snapping at your heels, going after everything you worked so hard for—your job, your status, your goddamn identity.

"Still, I think I had it easier," he continued, as he inched up on the Taurus, taking care to brake a good three feet from its bumper. "I mean, there I was, growing old, struggling to accept it, to learn to live within the law of diminishing returns—and right beside me, in bed with me, I had a strapping young buck. Nine years younger, and filled with all the sap that would rise in me no longer. I could accommodate myself to middle age, because I could reach out and *feel* youth, literally hold it in my hands, whenever I wanted. Just take a revivifying hit off of your beauty and vitality— hell, the sheer *heat* you gave off, even when you were asleep.

"But you . . . you don't have that. Here you are, all these years later, going through your own midlife crisis, and instead you're joined at the hip with someone *even older*. Someone whose hair is thin and whose blood is thinner and whose feet are always cold, who can't help reminding you of all the wilting and flagging and fading yet to come. I don't blame you for wanting to get away. Honestly, I don't. Go on, go, as far as you can! Drink from the cup of youth till they force it out of your hands. Go, with my *blessing*."

Traffic opened up before him, and he had to snap himself out of his reverie in order to shift into gear and accelerate. It was only when he was cruising towards the Grand Avenue exit that he realized he'd done it yet again. Why was it, every time he had one of these imaginary confrontations with Harry, he never ended up justifying himself and reducing Harry to penitent tears? Why did he never right the great wrong done to him? Why, in his own revenge fantasy, did he always *lose?*

Chapter 3

A light rain was falling by the time Jack reached Orleans Street, so he pulled into one of the Self-Park garages that cropped up every few blocks. It would've been faster to leave it with an attendant somewhere, but Jack was constitutionally unable to hand over the keys to his precious Porsche to someone he had never met before. Once, Harry had convinced him to do just that, when they were running late for a restaurant reservation; Jack had just slipped in a CD—Dexter Gordon's *Our Man In Paris*—and the first cut ("Scrapple From the Apple") was playing when they got out of the car. After dinner, when the attendant returned it to him, he noticed that the CD was now on the *final* cut ("Like Someone In Love"), which to Jack just plain spelled joyride. He cursed himself for not having noted the mileage, because Harry only laughed at his CD "proof"—as he always seemed to be laughing at him, at the end.

Unfortunately, in the extra time it took him to park, the weather had worsened, and he had to dart three blocks like a civilian under sniper fire, zigzagging for cover under awnings, the el tracks, the occasional carbon monoxide-choked tree. It was futile, of course, and he arrived at the meeting with his suit smelling distinctly of damp wool.

Several of the other board members had already assembled; younger by decades, they clustered in a corner comparing their newest consumer electronics purchases—ever-smaller personal stereos and telephones, by now so diminutive they were effectively useless to someone like Jack, whose failing eyesight could scarcely discern whether he was looking at a cell phone, a camera, or a tin of Altoids.

Jack seated himself instead next to Robyn, whose last name he had unfortunately let slip away; in fact it was something of an achievement that he managed to recall her *first* name. He was notoriously bad at that sort of thing, and had more than once fallen into close friendship with a colleague whose name he never quite knew until, embarrassingly late in their relationship, a third party would enter their sphere and require them both to introduce themselves.

Robyn was somewhere in her late thirties, early forties; the lacquered sheen she wore prevented any more accurate pinpointing. She was a professional woman of the kind Harry used to call "invulnerably single." Her hair, dress, makeup, and body language all conveyed an image of unquestionable authority, if not outright mastery; she looked *threateningly* glamorous, as though she had all the world beneath her Nicole Miller-shod heel. And yet her eyes glittered with naked desperation, and when she opened her mouth to speak, she really gave the game away: she started half a dozen sentences at once, which then bumped and collided with each other as she labored to bring at least one of them to conclusion. In short: despite her carefully applied demeanor, this was a woman hopelessly, pathologically, even terminally unsure of herself.

"*Something's up,*" she murmured, grabbing Jack's forearm as he settled in next to her.

"What do you mean?" he asked.

"It's the kids—more clannish than usual, they—when I

walked in it was like—well, you know, they're never exactly friendly, but at least—it's the *whispering,* you get the feeling—oh, Jack, your beautiful suit, the *rain*—"

Her verbal logjam was even worse than usual. She must indeed be seriously rattled; and a cursory glance at the younger board members revealed very *un*-cursory glances cast back at *him.* He felt himself physically stiffen, as though steeling himself against being pushed from a plane.

He was still in the grip of this first flurry of alarm when Theo Orsula entered, followed by his slight, carrot-topped wife and a preening young dark-skinned man in a suede coat and a scarf, as though this were a mild day in midwinter, or a production of *Doctor Zhivago.* Theo was the company's general manager, his waifish wife the business manager, and the dark-skinned man—introduced as Paul Rashimudden—was, it turns out, the new artistic director.

As Paul Rashimudden lowered himself into his chair, with such gravity and deliberation that this might be his coronation, Jack picked up a definite gay vibe. He scrutinized him for any further evidence to support this hunch; but then Paul unexpectedly turned and met his eyes, and screwed up his face with—well, *distaste* is the only term Jack could think of. Like he'd gotten something foul lodged in the back of his throat. The message was clear: *It is impertinent of you to look upon me.*

Burly, balding Theo called the meeting to order and got right to the first item of business. "We think Paul's tenure is a fresh start for Tealight, and accordingly we've decided to shake things up in the rest of the organization as well. Which, as some of you may have guessed, includes this body. I feel we need some new faces here, some fresh ideas, a renewed perspective on our common goal." With a theatrical flourish, he turned and said, "Jack, Robyn, I'm grateful for everything you've done for us, and we'll always count you as friends of Tealight Theatre. But in this new era, we think we'd be better off with a board of directors who could bring . . . well, a revitalized commitment to our mission."

Your "mission"? Jack wanted to say. *What mission is that? Recycling the disposable flotsam of crap culture by smearing it with two-bit burlesque?*

He bit his tongue; but the fact that this thought, these words, had come to him at all, meant of course that Theo was right. Jack wasn't really behind the Tealight Theatre; he never had been. He'd cynically viewed this as a stepping stone to more enviable boards on which he might serve, and he'd finally been caught out.

Accordingly, he rose from his chair, extended his hand and said, "I understand, Theo. I wish you all the luck in the world."

Robyn floundered next to him, her eyes darting from Theo to Jack, uncomprehendingly, as though they had been bleating in whalesong. "What? Does that—Jack, what is he— Are you saying you're—Is he firing us? Is that what he's— What did we do to—"

Jack took her by the arm and gently pulled her to her feet. "It's all right, Robyn. It's just the wheel turning. Out with the old, in with the—"

"Young," muttered Paul Rashimudden. There was a snicker from one of the other board members. Jack felt it like a body blow.

Numbly, he guided Robyn through shaking Theo's hand and then helped her make as graceful an exit as possible, an endeavor made vastly more difficult by her sudden uncertainty as to which way was, in fact, up. At one point Jack momentarily took his hand from her shoulder and she immediately walked into a potted fern.

In the elevator, she astonished him by dissolving into sobs.

"I'm sorry," she wailed as she dug through her purse for a tissue. "It's just that—well, rejection, you know, it never gets any—I mean, I've never been any good at—*God,* you'd think at *my* age, but that's the whole—I didn't even *like* that crummy theater, so why am I—oh, fuck, this is *just* what I need." Her car keys had fallen out of the purse, and when she'd bent to pick them up everything else spilled out, too. Jack leaned down to help her just as she was shifting to her other knee, and as a result they bonked heads.

Jack yelped in pain, then clasped his forehead and laughed. It was just what they needed after all the awkwardness and the tension. Robyn sucked in a few watery guffaws herself, as she hastily refilled her purse.

"Listen, can I treat you to breakfast?" Jack asked, feeling an almost paternal pity for her.

She was back on her feet now, examining her makeup in a compact mirror. "Oh, thanks, sweetie—no, no—I mean, *yes*, but not today, maybe next—I mean, my mascara *alone*, it's—I'm okay, really, I'm going to be just—Friday, maybe Friday, can I call you?"

"Sure, whenever. And hey," he said, giving her a broad wink. "It's all right. It's not the end of the world. It was just the board of a lousy theater company. We're both better than that."

She looked at him through her little raccoon mask of sodden sorrow, and suddenly she seemed calm . . . in fact, the picture of serene resignation. "I wonder," she said. "I'm forty-five, Jack. If there were something better, I probably would have found it by now."

The elevator doors opened and she marched out, her head once again held high, her stride that of a warrior, a conqueror.

But the only thing she'd vanquished had been Jack, who was so startled by her parting words—delivered without a stammer or tic—that he went momentarily rigid. It wasn't till the elevator started closing again that he snapped back to life, knocked the door back open, and staggered out into the lobby.

Chapter 4

What had shaken Jack about Robyn's observation was its implication that every life formed an arc, and that after a period of accumulation, achievement, accumulation, achievement, one reached a plateau after which nothing could be expected but decline, diminishment, decline, diminishment. Clearly Robyn felt that her firing from the Tealight Theatre Board of Directors was part of her arc's declension; that, at 45, she really had nothing to hope for but more of the same.

When Harry left him, Jack had put the best possible spin on the matter. They'd had their problems, problems that had expanded like mold to stain the good parts of their life together; so he'd felt primed and ready for a clean start, a new, sparkling fresh stage of his life. But if Robyn was right, he was fooling himself; the stage of life he was entering was its denouement. Things would now begin to fall away from him with remarkably regularity; he'd already lost his lover and a fair amount of hair, and now his position on the Tealight board. And he'd replaced them with . . . what, exactly?

The rain was still pelting the sidewalk when he reached the lobby door—in time to see Robyn shut herself into a cab. Well, at least the girl knew how to treat herself right. She may be going down, but she was going down in comfort. Jack had had a momentary impulse to shuffle back to his garage, hands in his pockets, ignoring the rain as it assailed him— like a character in a movie who was feeling deep despair. He shook this off as silly; as long as he was this close to the Loop, and since he suddenly had his morning free, he might as well do a little shopping. He hailed the next cab and told the driver to take him to Michigan Avenue, to Tiffany.

Minutes later he found himself at the gift counter, buying a silver teething ring for his new grand-niece. Even better, the clerk attending him was adorable; mid-thirties, hair of silken jet, a cleft in his chin and a deranging smile. Jack had asked that the teething ring be engraved, and the clerk now produced an order form and a pen. "What would you like?" he asked.

You, thought Jack, but he said, "Just the name. 'Jocelyn Cassandra.'"

The clerk looked right at him and said, "Pretty." With just enough ambiguity that if Jack wanted to, he might fool himself into thinking he hadn't meant the name.

"Spelled in the traditional manner?" the clerk asked as he filled in the form.

Jack came up short. "I suppose so," he said. "I mean, I *hope* so. I'd hate to see them saddle the kid with some creative spelling, filled with multiple S's and double N's and a silent E at the end. Or God forbid, an accent mark."

The clerk looked up and laughed; it was like a gust of fragrant summer. *Was* he flirting? . . . Jack had no idea. It had been so long since anyone had flirted with him. It would be awful to leap to the wrong conclusion, to make a fool of himself. And yet . . . he kept thinking back to his epiphany of thirty minutes earlier: *I'm tired of things dropping out of my life. I want to bring something in.*

His mind worked feverishly as he gave the clerk his name and telephone number. He considered saying, *And now may I have yours?,* but thought better of it.

"Very well, then, Mr. Ackerly," said the clerk, giving Jack a copy of the form, "we'll give you a call when the ring is ready."

Jack cleared his throat. "How long does engraving usually take?"

"Anywhere from two to three weeks; but if you need it sooner, we can—"

"No, no, it's fine," he said. Then a thought occurred to him. "Although . . . perhaps sooner *would* be better. I'll have to check. Do you have a card, so I can call you if that's the case?"

"Certainly," the clerk said, and he produced one from his jacket pocket and handed it to Jack, who looked at it. It said, CARLO JENNINGS, SALES ASSOCIATE.

"Interesting," said Jack. "'Carlo,' not 'Carlos.' Are you Italian?"

"Partly," said Carlo. "I'm named after my maternal grandfather, who was from Alba."

"My grandmother was Italian," said Jack, grasping at any reason to keep the conversation going.

"It's funny, a lot of people do think my name is spelled wrong," Carlo said. "They'll point to the card and say, 'Oh, look, they forgot the S.'"

"Well, it's an unusual name," said Jack. "I can't think of a single famous Carlo."

"Not since Bergonzi, no."

"Oh, you're familiar with Bergonzi?" said Jack. "I'd have thought you too young for that."

"Not too young for great singing." Carlo flung another of those inimitable smiles his way.

"So . . . you're an opera buff, then?" Jack's mind was working feverishly.

"Thank you for not saying 'queen,'" said Carlo with a laugh.

"Actually . . . me too. And, as it happens, I—well, I hope you don't think I'm being inappropriate or forward or anything—but I'm a season ticketholder at the Lyric, and I've got two seats for *The Makropulos Case* next week, and my date has bailed out." Bailed out ten months earlier, in fact, taking some of the furniture with him. "I don't suppose you'd care to join me—no pressure, no expectations. But Karita Mattila is the lead." He waggled his eyebrows and smiled.

Carlo's smile wilted a little. "Oh—wow. You're really very kind to offer. But . . . that's Janáček, isn't it? . . . I'm sorry, I don't really go for that grim Czech stuff. I really only like *bel canto*. Call me a vulgarian, but if it doesn't have hit tunes . . ." He shrugged. "I'd be a lousy companion. But thank you, really. Very generous of you."

Jack felt this rejection the way Robyn had felt it from the Tealight board. He made some witty, dismissive remark, then deliberately added some comment about the teething ring to close the conversation on an official note, and turned away with a feeling that he was swimming, not walking. He somehow managed to make it down the escalator and out into the street where, alas, it was still raining.

What the hell is wrong with me?, he asked himself as he waved down another cab. *It's nothing personal. The guy just doesn't like Janáček.*

And in fact, by the time the taxi dropped him at the parking garage, he'd quite convinced himself that the long-dead composer was solely to blame for his failed pickup.

Chapter 5

All the same, two days later he found himself in his therapist's office.

"Well, Jack," said Alan, "what's troubling you?"

"What do you mean?"

He smirked. "Come on. Every Tuesday, like clockwork, you call to cancel your regular appointment. The only time I see you is when you ring up out of the blue like this and beg me to 'squeeze you in,' and that's invariably because something's eating you."

Jack settled into his chair. He and Alan were both seated on the same side of Alan's glacial mahogany desk. Alan sat with his hands folded over his knee. A pen and a notepad were at his elbow, as always, but to this day Jack had never seen him pick them up.

"Well, then, all right, something *is* eating me."

"Do you want to talk about it now?"

"You're awfully brusque today, doctor." 'Doctor' is what Jack called him when he wanted to tweak him a bit.

Alan—lean, patrician looking, and seemingly imperturbable—wasn't easily tweaked. "Well, we do seem to go through this little dance every time."

"Then maybe this little dance is something I need."

Alan shook his head. "Other people, maybe. Not you. You're one of the most self-aware, self-actualized people I've ever met."

"So, why am I here?"

"Exactly. Why are you here, Jack?"

Alan kept a little sculpture kit next to the client's chair. Its base was a magnetized block, atop which rested of a pile of thin metal chips. You could mold the chips any way you liked and the charge of the magnet would hold them in place. Jack suspected that Alan drew some inferences from the way his clients played with the chips—whether they simply fidgeted with them, or tried to form them into something recognizable—and he was determined to thwart such judgment by ignoring the kit altogether. Alas, sometimes he found himself idly stirring or piling the chips without realizing he was doing it . . . as in fact was the case just now. He quickly plucked his hand away and dropped it into his lap.

"It's old age," he said, almost tossing it off as an aside.

"You're worried about growing old?"

"More like wondering if I already have."

"I see. How old *are* you, Jack?"

He lifted his gaze just long enough to meet Alan's eyes. "You don't know?"

"If I did I wouldn't ask."

"Surely it's in my file."

"Would you like me to go get the file? Would that be easier than you telling me?"

"Oh, no, no. I didn't mean that. I'm just surprised you don't—" He realized he was beginning to babble. "Fifty-three, I'm fifty-three."

"And you think fifty-three is old."

"It is," he said. "Isn't it?"

"Am I the one who makes that determination, Jack?"

It sometimes annoyed him the way Alan insisted on repeating his name. But he tried to quell his pique, since expressing it might lead Alan down some other, useless path. "Of course you don't make that determination. But I'd like your opinion so that I can weigh it against the others I've gathered."

"And what others are those, Jack?"

His face flushed. Of course he hadn't gathered any others. Why was he talking this way? . . . "My sister is a grandmother," is all he said.

"Ah."

"My *baby* sister."

"She's younger than you?"

"By a decade."

"And because you've learned she's a grandmother, you've concluded you're old."

"No, no," he said. He noticed he was fiddling with the magnet set again and snapped back his hand. "I already knew I was old. But because I've learned she's a grandmother, I've concluded I'm *not young.*"

"What's the difference?"

"I don't know."

Alan regarded him for a moment in silence. "Take a guess."

Jack shrugged and sat back in the chair, gazing at the ceiling as though looking to heaven for inspiration. "I suppose . . . when you're young, you have so much opportunity."

"What particular opportunity do you feel you've lost?"

"The . . . I . . ." He ground to a halt, then caught his hand in the act of creeping towards the sculpture kit again. "I suppose just the *concept* of opportunity. Limitless opportunity. Of having time to explore it all."

Alan frowned. "That's a little more abstract than the kind of thing that usually brings you in here, Jack."

Stop saying my name, he wanted to snarl. But he realized that his very irritation was a sign Alan was prodding him in the right places.

"I've been working since I was seventeen," Jack said. "I

owned my own company at twenty-four. I made my first million at twenty-nine. I mean, I'm proud of that, I have no problem with that, but . . . you know. It came at a cost."

"What was the cost?"

"Oh, I don't know," he started fidgeting with the chips again; this time he let himself continue. "Never knowing what else I could have done with my life. Maybe I could have taken up the guitar and—"

"You can still take up the guitar, Jack."

"Yeah, but—maybe I could've been a pop star, or something."

"You could still be a pop star."

"Well . . . sure, but the odds are against it. And, I mean . . . I'd be a fifty-three-year-old pop star." He corrected himself: "Fifty-four or fifty-five, by the time I learned to play."

"Why is that less desirable than being a younger pop star?"

"What, are you kidding?"

"You don't pay me to kid, Jack."

"Well . . . the freedom, the money . . ."

"You'd have those at fifty-five, wouldn't you?"

"Yes . . . but . . ."

A small, telling silence. *"But . . ."* Alan prodded.

"What good are money and freedom to someone my age?"

Alan raised an eyebrow, then recrossed his legs. He had the look of a cat who'd steadily stalked a mouse and was now ready to pounce.

"What good," he said quietly, "are money and freedom to someone *younger* than you?"

Jack dropped the chips and pushed the whole kit away. "You can *get laid,*" he said, with more than a little bravado. Alan may have cornered him, but he wouldn't respond by cowering.

"And is that what you want to do now?"

"Yes." He was only mildly surprised to hear himself say it.

"And you think you can't have sex at fifty-three?"

"Sure, I can have fifty-three-year-old sex."

"And that's not as good as twenty-three-year-old sex?"

"I wouldn't know."

Alan raised both eyebrows. It was the most pronounced expression of alarm Jack had ever witnessed from him.

"It's true," Jack said. "I was a virgin till I was twenty-five. I only had three, uh, *encounters* before I met Harry, and then I was pretty much monogamous for twenty-six years."

"Jack," said Alan, "do you think it possible that what's bothering you isn't growing old, but . . . *regret?*"

"How do you mean?"

"I mean you never experimented sexually when you were younger. You never dated. You never sowed your wild oats."

Jack grunted. "Could I be that shallow?"

"It's not shallow if it's bothering you."

Jack cupped his hands over his knee and waited a moment. "Aren't you going to tell me I can sow my wild oats at fifty-three?"

Alan grinned. "I don't think you'd believe me."

"I sure as hell wouldn't." He released his knee and leaned forward again. "So, what do I do?"

"What do *you* think you should do?"

"I don't know. That's why I'm asking you."

Alan gave him a you-know-better-than-that frown. "I don't dispense advice, Jack."

"Then what good are you, *doctor?*"

Alan sighed, but remained mum.

"Look, just give me *something,* here."

"All right. I suppose . . . if I were you, I'd allow myself to grieve, then move on."

"*Grieve?* It's not like my dog died, Alan."

"But your youth has. Jack, I swear to you, there's no one alive who doesn't believe his or her youth wasn't wasted."

"But mine really *was*." He noted a whining tone to his voice and cleared his throat.

"Jack . . . aging is something we all face. Saying goodbye to youth and its unfulfilled promise is something we all have to do."

"Unless we die young."

"Well, you didn't. And I can't believe you wish you had."

Jack sighed. "No, course not."

"Look, it's not quite been a year since your breakup, it's only natural you're feeling sexual longing. But you've misplaced it. You're fixated on some kind of idealized sex you think you missed out on as a youth, but it's just that: an idealization. It wouldn't have been like that."

"I guess I'd prefer to know that firsthand."

Alan sighed and raised his palms. "I've got nothing else for you, Jack. You're an intelligent man. You'll work through this."

"As I careen towards the grave."

"Jack . . ."

"I know, I know. I'm sorry. I don't really expect you to have some magic way of turning me twenty-three again."

"If I did, I wouldn't. We *earn* our lives, Jack, day by day."

He rose from his chair. "Okay, that's sounding a little too embroidered-on-a-pillow for my taste. I'm leaving before you go all Rod McKuen on me."

Alan got to his feet. "Who's Rod McKuen?"

He sighed. "No one. Never mind."

They headed for the door, and as Alan showed him out of the office Jack turned and said, "Do you mind if I ask how old *you* are?"

"Why is that relevant?"

"It's not. Just humor me."

Alan hesitated, as though weighing whether he ought to play along, then said, "I'm thirty-four."

Jack nodded. "Okay. Thank you."

"Does it make a difference?"

"It shouldn't." He shook Alan's hand and said, "Thanks again," then headed across the reception area towards the elevators.

"It shouldn't," he muttered as he pressed the call button. "But it *does*."

Chapter 6

With Harry out of the picture, Jack had relied on his friend Walt to be his opera date. This was something of a desperate measure for Jack, because Walt's taste in music theatre was rather less refined than his own—he'd seen *Wicked* eight times and sobbed at seven of them—and at the opera he invariably fell asleep during the first act. *The Makropulos Case* got him before Scene 2, and in fact Jack felt himself nodding as well; despite the electrifying presence of Karita Mattila, all the back-and-forth about court dates and hidden documents didn't quite make for riveting drama.

During the interval, Jack treated Walt to a glass of champagne to bolster them for the second act. Walt took a sip and said, "Mm! *Geshmak.*" He had recently discovered that one of his great-grandmothers was Jewish, and now peppered his conversation with Yiddish as though to the manner born.

They were on the mezzanine of the great gilded box that is the Lyric Opera House, and so went to the railing to survey the crowd milling in the lobby below. It was the same anything-goes sartorial stew served up at any twenty-first-century cultural event, with tattered jeans brushing up against haute couture, sneakers next to stoles, goth at peace with gowns. There was a middle-aged man in a top hat, tails, and spats; another in what appeared to be leather fetish gear.

"So let me see if I've got this straight," Walt said, folding his arms over the railing (and nearly spilling champagne on a dowager below). "This *yefayfiyeh*, this Emilia Marty—she knows all about this inheritance case and the letters signed by Ellian MacGregor, because that's who *she* is, right? . . . She's the same person a hundred-whatever years later, but she hasn't aged?"

Jack tossed back a mouthful of champagne. "It certainly appears that way. We'll find out in Act Two."

"Oh, come on, what kind of *eizel* do you think I am? It's obvious that's where they're going with it. It's just the *dumkops* on the stage who haven't picked up on it yet—that *yatebedam* Prus. Does he become her lover?"

Jack had to laugh. "You've got a pretty good grip on the story for someone who slept through most of the first hour."

"Yeah, well, sorry about that, what can I say, I'm all *far-mutshet* after my week. Plus, you've got to admit, the music's not all that exciting."

"You don't like Karita Mattila?"

"Oh, yeah—she's a real *krassaveitseh*, and what a voice! I just wish they gave her something to *sing*."

Jack nodded. In truth, *Makropulos* was the kind of music drama he admired more than liked. Much as he hated to admit it, he was a lot like Carlo, the clerk he'd met at Tiffany; he went for the big hit tunes, the showstopper arias and duets. This was more like a sung play, all dissonance and dialogue.

As he recalled his conversation with Carlo, he felt something—almost a kind of psychic pull—draw him out of his reverie. He focused his eyes on the people below him . . . and there, incredibly, was Carlo himself!

He stood bolt upright, as if he'd been caught staring. But Carlo hadn't noticed him; he was busy sipping cocktails and chatting with another young man, who, like Carlo, was decked out in what looked like very expensive club wear. The other man's hair was crested into a trendy "faux hawk," a look Jack had always found utterly ridiculous.

Walt said, "So, *nu?* Something the matter?"

"I—no—it's just, I just spotted someone I know, that's all."

"Oh, goody, who?" Walt said, scanning the crowd with interest. An inveterate gossip, he always preferred watching the people in the house to watching the performance on the stage.

"No one, really. Just—the one there—guy in the black-and-white Moschino shirt, talking to the redhead with the hair like a rooster."

Walt spotted him. "Oooh! Nice. Some former fling of yours?"

"No, nothing like that," Jack insisted. "He waited on me at Tiffany last week."

At that moment Carlo turned and looked up at the mezzanine. Jack panicked and turned away at once.

Walt clicked his tongue. "Pardon me, *neshomeleh*, but unless he caught you shoplifting, there's no cause to be so *shemevdik* around a shopboy."

Jack sighed; concealment was useless. "I asked him out," he said. "Asked him to this very performance, actually."

"To which you'd already asked me, *chutzpenik*," Walt said. "Never mind, go on."

"I knew you wouldn't mind. Anyway, he turned me down. Said he didn't like this kind of thing."

Walt gave a low whistle. "And yet here he is with somebody else! *Oy.*"

"I'm sure there's a perfectly reasonable explanation."

"Of course there is."

"Is he still looking this way?"

"No."

Jack turned back towards the railing, just as Carlo looked up again. He ducked behind a pillar.

"Sorry," said Walt. "He really wasn't looking when you asked me."

"I know, I know."

"He's not looking now."

Jack sighed. "This is silly." He handed Walt his champagne flute.

"What are you doing?"

"I'm going to say hello to him."

"What? *Bist meshugeh?*"

"I didn't get this far in life by *not* facing my fears, Walt."

"Fine, fine," Walt called after him as he moved away. "I'll just wait here for you."

Jack could hear his heartbeat over the murmur of the crowd as he made his way down the staircase and across the lobby to where he'd spotted Carlo. His pulse started to thrum and his mouth went dry. But his legs continued to carry him. It was a matter of sheer will. He *would* do this; he *would* face his fear. He always had.

He came up just behind Carlo and was about to call his name when two other young men appeared and warmly hugged both Carlo and his companion.

One of them said to Carlo, "Hey, hon, glad to see you here!"

Carlo said, "I'm glad to *be* here. I've been desperate for tickets, but the whole run's sold out. It would've *killed* me to miss La Mattila! Though it's too bad poor Jerry's fogged in in Toronto."

"Yeah," said Carlo's companion, "well *I'm* glad you were able to take his place at the last minute. I hate goin' to these things alone."

"Honey," Carlo said, "you say the words 'Karita Mattila,' I guarantee you I drop *everything*." They all laughed a bit and the topic of conversation shifted to something else.

All of Jack's courage flushed right out of him. How could he now go up and tap this young man on the shoulder? What could he possibly say to him? *Oh hi, I don't know if you re-*

member me, I'm the ancient old troll who couldn't even get you to 'drop everything' for La Mattila.

Humiliation clinging to him like an ill-fitting second skin, he skulked back upstairs, where he found Walt holding two empty champagne flutes. "Sorry, I got thirsty."

"Never mind," he said. "You ready to go back in?"

"You didn't talk to the clerk. I was watching."

"No, I didn't talk to the clerk. You ready to go back in?"

Walt shrugged, then followed as Jack turned back towards the theater door. "Fine," he said as he slipped the empty flutes onto a tray. "Be that way . . . *farbissener.*"

Chapter 7

They settled back into their seats. Jack was obviously too upset to talk, so Walt busied himself with a close reading of the program book till at last the lights dimmed and the conductor returned to the stand, amidst polite applause.

As the action of the opera resumed, Jack found himself unable to pay attention. His mind was a whirlwind of conflicting emotions. Remorse, certainly; he *should* have spoken to Carlo, should have put the callow young man on the defensive. There would at least have been satisfaction in that. But he also felt a kind of shame, an embarrassment at his own naiveté; why had he ever flirted with the boy in the first place? Had he really thought he had a chance? Why couldn't he accept that he was middle-aged now, and of no interest or use to anyone half his age? It was a kind of perverse vanity, of the sort that kept him glancing at his reflection in store windows. Glancing, but not seeing, apparently.

But his predominant emotion, surprisingly, was rage. At first it was vast and undirected; if he'd had a lever at his side that would detonate a bomb at the earth's core, he would happily have thrown it. There wasn't a molecule of the whole miserable planet that meant a damn to him right now.

Yet as his roiling blood cooled, the anger narrowed in focus and settled closer to home. It was all his own doing, he realized. He had set himself up for this fall; spent years doing so. When he was younger—when he was *young*—when the opportunities for pleasure were plentiful, when carnal love was without responsibility or consequence, he had rejected it, spurned the sexually spendthrift spirit of his generation and instead girded his loins for labor, devoting himself to productivity and profit. Now, thanks to his ambition and industry, he had freedom of a different kind. Time and money, elusive goals to his contemporaries, were to him available in quantity. He could do whatever he wanted.

But alas, there was only *one* thing he wanted to do, and despite being free to do it, he couldn't. He wanted to frolic. He wanted to cavort. He wanted to *play*.

And he was fifty-three years old.

Gradually he resigned himself to his dilemma, and the action on the stage began to draw his attention. Though even this seemed to mock him. Emilia Marty, the woman whose father had given her eternal life, had tired of the endless passage of the years. She couldn't feel her youth anymore—could feel nothing. Jack couldn't imagine this; couldn't conceive of ever growing tired of endless opportunity, infinite possibility, and the firm flesh and hot blood to meet it head on.

Soon, he found himself gripped; despite its lack of hit tunes, the opera worked itself to a gorgeous, devastating climax in which Emilia Marty, before her assembled accusers, renounced her claim to a tedious immortality. In a paroxysm of exquisitely orchestrated agony-slash-ecstasy, she died.

The curtain fell; the lights went up; the audience broke into warm applause. Jack clapped along, although his mind was elsewhere—mired somewhere between the story he had just seen and his own midlife predicament.

Suddenly Walt nudged him. He looked up to find that all around him, his neighbors had got to their feet. Karita Mattila had come out for her bow, and was being fêted with a standing ovation.

Jack rose as well and joined in the hosannahs. Walt surprised him by calling out, *"Brava!"*

La Mattila extended one knee and lowered herself, gazelle-like, into a posture of divine submission. Her arms were piled high with flowers. She plucked one from its bouquet and flung it toward the balconies. A little ripple of appreciation pealed from above.

Jack couldn't take his eyes off her. An undeniably ravishing woman, but—it was so odd—under the full house lights, she looked fully forty.

As was their habit, Jack and Walt stopped at the Four Seasons for a drink afterwards. But tonight, one drink became several.

"Eternal youth," scoffed Jack as he lifted his tumbler for its last swish of single-malt scotch. "I'd settle for being young *once.*" He licked his lips, set down the glass, and signaled the waiter for another.

"You were young once," said Walt. "I've seen pictures. Hot little thing, too. *Shain vi di zibben velten.*"

"Well, that's just the tradegy of it," Jack said. He shook his head. *"Tragedy.* I didn't *do* anything with it. I mean, you sowed some wild oats, didn't you?"

Walt chuckled. "Enough to keep Quaker in business through midcentury."

"Right!" said Jack, jabbing his finger in the air. "See, *that's* what I missed out on. That's the part I skipped!"

Walt shrugged and said, "Too late now," then finished his own drink.

Jack glared at him, suddenly feeling genuinely capable of mayhem. "Well, that's a fucking insensitive thing to say."

Walt looked up, a bit shocked by Jack's reaction. "Sorry," he said. "Didn't mean to piss you off."

"Well, you did!"

"*Es tut mir bahng!* What am I supposed to say? 'It's okay, Jack, you'll get another chance'?"

It occurred to Jack, with one of those great epiphanies that come only to the very drunk, that this was *exactly* what Walt was supposed to say. It was what he'd been waiting for *someone* to say.

He also realized that he was speaking this out loud.

Walt said, "You want to be *young* again? That's what you want? What, are you *meshugeh?*"

"Yes. I am. So sue me."

"What, like in the opera? . . . A secret formula, written down in Greek? Is that what you're looking for?" Walt's tone was inching towards mockery. Jack bridled.

"No, of course not," he said. "I mean, yes." The waiter appeared—a young waiter, with burnished skin and hair like copper wire—and leaned between them to set Jack's new drink on the table. "I mean," Jack said, "look at this boy. Just *look* at him. What wouldn't you give?"

The waiter paused in mid-hover, eyes wide, at a complete loss. Walt leaned into him and explained, "Not to do you— to *be* you."

The boy visibly relaxed. He smiled and said, "Two full-time jobs and student loans up the patootie? You have my *permission* to be me."

"You don't mean that," Jack called after him as he walked away. Heads turned his way; Walt had to shush him.

"I can't help it, Walt," he said. "I just want to be young again!"

"Try Vitamin E. Just keep your voice down."

"I don't mean *look* young. I mean really, honestly *be* young."

"Jack, my dear, I think we'd better get you home."

And Jack realized at once the wisdom in that. Within a matter of minutes, he'd plumbed a new depth: not only was he a hideous old troll, he was now a hideous old *drunken* troll.

"Get me a cab," he told Walt as he guided him toward the elevator. "And tell the driver there's an extra twenny in it for him if he drives me straight into the lake."

Walt laughed. And that's the last thing Jack could remember . . .

Chapter 8

. . . until the voice of the cabbie awakened him. "Buddy! *Buddy!*"

He'd crumpled into the back seat like a marionette set carelessly on a shelf. Straightening up, he looked out the window and saw he'd arrived home. He fumbled for his wallet, but the cabbie stopped him: "Your friend already paid. He also says to tell you, go straight to bed."

Jack said something noncommittal in reply, then got out of the cab with all the grace of a load of laundry being dumped from a hamper. The cab pulled away and Jack shambled up to the front gate. Then somehow he had to find, extract, and insert his key in the door. This operation consumed a surprising amount of time, during which Jack cursed audibly, causing at least one young woman to cross the street rather than pass too near him.

When he got inside he lunged for the elevator and pressed the call button, then leaned against the wall and concentrated on breathing. The lobby was all awhirl, things that danced at the edge of his vision darting away when he turned to focus on them.

He briefly fell asleep on the way up, and when he woke up June Kraml was in the cabin with him. He felt a jolt of alarm and stood up straight.

"Evening, Mrs. Kraml," he said in as neutral a tone as he could manage. "You're up late."

The old woman looked at him with rheumy eyes. "You smell like a distillery," she sneered.

"Ah, that would be from the drinking!" he said with what he thought charming joviality. But Mrs. Kraml appeared to think otherwise. She scowled, turned away from him, and did not return his wishes for a good night when he exited the elevator on his floor.

He let himself into his apartment with only marginally greater ease than he'd gained access to the building, and when he swung open the door there was Nelly, smiling at him and wagging her tail—with, it must be said, a telling look of anxiety on her weary grey face.

So much for going straight to bed. Jack had parental duties to which he must attend. Nelly had been alone for several hours, and must now be walked.

Locating and affixing the leash proved to be an ordeal of almost Olympian difficulty, but eventually he got her out the door and onto the elevator, and then before he knew it he was outside again, breathing in the crisp night air. Nelly instantly commenced reading the canine scents along the parkway, analyzing the information they conveyed, and occasionally leaving her own comment before moving on.

This street, Jack thought, proud of himself for the sheer brilliance of the analogy, *is the neighborhood dogs' very own message board.* He smiled. *The dog blog.*

Pleased with himself, he tried to build on the metaphor— something about urine being a *lingua franca*—but he was too drunk for the finer points. His mind was operating only along the broadest lines.

He let Nelly lead him where she would, mesmerized by the avid way she sought out certain aromas and then lingered over them; possibly a new dog's announcement of his arrival? Or a territorial dispute between two males that

Nelly was following like the story of a scandal in the morning *Tribune*? . . . Clearly she was a "reader" of taste and discretion, because there were several occasions on which she sniffed out a certain odor, only to lose interest in it as soon as she found it. Jack supposed it was like eagerly flipping to the film section of *The New Yorker* only to find the movie under review to be the new Mike Myers.

Finally, Nelly seemed to run out of both piss and interest, and she looked up at Jack. And he turned and looked up at the street. Which was not one he recognized.

"Well, goddammit," he said. "Where've you taken me, girl?"

Nelly cringed a bit, as though sensing the blame being laid at her feet; then she turned and started back the way they'd just come.

Jack shrugged. "Seems as good an idea as any." He was aware that he was still speaking aloud. He knew he should stop doing that, but didn't seem quite able.

Nelly led him past a particularly seedy row of Z-grade businesses—a dry cleaner, a shoe repair shop, a currency exchange—all closed for the night. Then they came to a storefront proclaiming FORTUNES TOLD–TAROT READINGS, whose window was decorated with faintly Egyptian looking symbols—hieroglyphic-looking eyes, for example, and a crudely painted ankh—and which looked in on a ouija board, a crystal ball, and a framed photo of Pope Benedict in which the pontiff looked a bit out of sorts, as well he might in such company.

Someone was locking up the store. A big woman, Latina, with gales of gorgeous blue-black hair cascading down her back. She wore more jewelry than anyone Jack had ever seen before, and from what he could tell not an ounce of it was quality. Her shawl, however, appeared to be real silk, albeit fringed.

"Excuse me," he said to her.

She turned to him. "Sorry, closed," she said.

"I can see that. I just want to know, can you tell me how to get to Division Street?"

Her eyes flashed in the dark. "You live there." It was not a question.

"Yes, I do."

"And you're lost."

Dear God, was the woman trying to impress him with her mind-reading abilities? "I'm overwhelmed," he said flatly. "How do you do it." And *that* wasn't a question, either.

She smiled at him. "There *is* something I can do for you," she said. "You want something."

"Yes. Directions to Division Street."

She shook her head. "Something else."

Jack was just drunk enough to bite. "Well, yes, as a matter of fact, I'd quite like to be twenty-three years old again," he said, perhaps a bit too ferociously. "Either that, or a simple finger in the right direction, and I am in your debt, madam."

She smiled and bent down to scratch Nelly's chin; the dog had crept closer to her, sniffing curiously. Then she looked up and said, "She doesn't like it when you leave her at night."

Jack shook his head. "What? . . . Who?"

"Your girl here." She gave Nelly a final pat and stood up again. "And no, I can't help you."

"You don't know where Division Street is?"

"Behind you. Six blocks, then left for two more. I meant the other thing."

"Well, thank you anyway. I appreciate it. You have a good night, now." He turned to go.

"But there's someone who can."

He looked over his shoulder. "I beg your pardon?"

"There's someone who can. Help you achieve what you long for."

"Ah. And who might that be?"

She shook her head. "I don't know. I see her in your future, though. She's very clearly there. But you have to find your way to her. She won't come to you."

Jack forced a smile onto his face and said, "Well, I'd better get right on that. Thank you again for all your help. Good night."

He flicked Nelly's leash and led her back up the street. When he'd gotten safely out of earshot he gave Nelly a conspiratorial look and muttered, *"Cuckoo."*

Nelly remained noncommittal.

Chapter 9

Perhaps inevitably, he awoke the next morning with a killer hangover. He lay in bed some forty minutes, moaning and groaning and wishing the sun would go away and bother some other planet. Eventually his bladder forced him from his haven under the sheets. Nelly, who lay atop the blanket, stretched out to fill the space he vacated.

After he'd finished in the bathroom he shuffled to the kitchen to make coffee. He was surprised to find the lights still on, a bottle of Pinot Noir open and nearly drained, and a filmy wineglass on the table, along with an open phone book, an empty bag of pretzel sticks, and, rather incongruously, his shoes.

He immediately cast his mind back to the night before, but the last thing he could recall was walking Division Street with Nelly. He had no memory of arriving back at the apartment, none of opening a bottle of wine (which under the circumstances was just shy of lunatic), nor of searching for a phone number.

With no small trepidation he crept over to the table, took his shoes from its surface and set them on the floor (first things first), then peered at the book. It was open to the pages listing NUTRITION CONSULTANTS . . . NUTS & BOLTS . . . NUTS–EDIBLE–RETAIL . . . What the *hell*?

He sat down and read on. OBJECTS D'ART (he chuckled at the misspelling) . . . OCCULT SERVICES . . .

Oh.

Right.

From within the recesses of his tannin-addled consciousness emerged the dim memory of sitting here last night, pouring glass after glass, reflecting on the magic "youth formula"
of the opera and the ridiculous prophecy of the Latina fortune teller—and how it all somehow coalesced into a "What
the hell" moment that led him to seek out a solution right then
and there, with the only tool available to him. The goddamn
Yellow Pages. It was almost funny—the thought processes of
a typical drunk.

He wondered if he'd actually phoned anyone; but there
were only three OCCULT SERVICES listings, and one of
them was for a bookstore. He doubted he'd have actually
reached anyone even if he had dialed them up. A narrow escape . . . he'd seriously have to watch his alcohol intake
from now on. He wasn't twenty-five anymore.

He felt a sudden pang. Why did everything have to come
back to *that* particular point?

The phone rang; its shrillness shredded his brain like let-
tuce. He lurched up, grabbed the handset before another
shriek could occur, and said, *"Hello!"*

"Hello?" A woman's voice. "Good morning, Jack. Didn't
wake you, did I? . . . I waited till after ten."

"No, I'm . . . I'm sorry, who is this?"

A giggle. "It's Fancy."

Fancy Northcotte. Christened Nancy, but still bearing her
childhood nickname. His personal assistant for more than
twelve years. She'd taken early retirement when he sold the
agency; she couldn't imagine working for anyone else. And
theirs had been a blissful relationship; Fancy, some dozen
years older than he, had been a kind of professional mom to
him. She'd handled everything for him, anticipating his every

need and desire. No problems, no miscommunications, no questions asked.

"Fancy," he said, genuinely glad to hear from her. "How are you? How's the life of leisure?"

"Oh, I manage to keep busy," she said, a tinge of merriment in her voice. "Got the garden, my book club. And I'm training for a half-marathon."

"You're kidding," he said. "That's wonderful. You always were a go-getter."

"Mm-hm," she said. A pause, then, "You don't remember calling me last night, do you?"

He actually felt his face blanch. "I . . . I called . . ."

"Me, yes," she said, clearly enjoying this. "You did seem a bit . . . muddled at the time." Jack wanted to die. "Anyway, you asked a favor of me—'You're the only one I can depend on, Fancy old girl, never let me down'—and I'm just calling to follow up."

Oh, God, thought Jack. *What did I ask her?*

"I was out last night," he said, lamely. "With Walt. You remember Mr. Neurath? . . . You always said he was a bad influence."

"Mm-hm," she said noncommittally. "And how are you this morning?"

"Never better," he lied. "Tanned, fit, ready to rumble."

"Oh good. Anyway . . . you asked me to look into something for you. A little out of my usual area of expertise, but I so enjoy a challenge. And the Internet certainly comes in handy, doesn't it?"

"Fancy, you're not obligated to do anything for me, I shouldn't have asked y—"

"Tut tut! Already done. Now, there doesn't actually seem to be anything like an actual potion to restore lost youth—"

Oh, God, thought Jack. *I want to die. I want to seize up and die right this second.*

"—though apparently there are some unscrupulous so-called magicians who will sell you just about anything you ask for, you have to watch out for them, they're all complete charlatans. I've gotten all this from a certain Mr. Ravencroft, though I strongly suspect that's not his real name; he's the head of an actual coven of witches out in the suburbs, near Arlington Heights, and he seems to be a straight shooter, all things considered."

"Fancy, I have to stop you right there, I—"

"Oh, don't please, I can't remember the last time I had so much fun. Anyway, Mr. Ravencroft doesn't think you'll find what you're looking for, but he gave me the name of several occult practitioners in the Chicago metropolitan area who come with his highest recommendation though of course no guarantee."

"This is very embarrassing, Fancy."

"Mm-hm. Anyway, I have three names for you, if you want to jot them down."

"Fancy, I . . ." He paused. The words of last night's fortune teller barreled back to him, unbidden: *I see her in your future, though. She's very clearly there. But you have to find your way to her. She won't come to you.*

He gulped, then said, "Is one of them a woman?"

"Yes," said Fancy. "A Francesca LaBrash, up in Andersonville."

Jack sighed. "Oh, all right. Give me her number."

Chapter 10

Jack sat in the Foxglove Café in Andersonville, sipping coffee and reading a free "alternative" newspaper. The cover story bewailed the plight of a poor, elderly artist whose life's work—a series of murals on the back of her building, which she had painted over the course of three decades—was in danger of being lost to the avarice of a developer who planned to raze the structure and build horrid new condominiums in its place. Jack read the story with a growing sense of bewilderment; even the photo of the building conveyed its utter ruin. What was the developer expected to do, spend millions shoring it up for the sake of a bunch of naïve tableaux on its crumbling exterior? How could he ever hope to recoup that kind of investment from a small, squat, six-unit residential building? Shouldn't the journalist have instead directed his scorn at the artist, who either stupidly or willfully chose an ancient and crumbling medium on which to bestow her legacy . . . ?

But he realized he was in enemy territory, and so kept his tsks to himself and simply folded the paper shut. Opinions such as his were clearly treasonous here. The Foxglove Café was, he was glad to read on the wall, a Nuclear-Free Zone, but this prompted him to wonder which cafes in the city weren't. Was there perhaps a missile silo lurking beneath his corner Coffee Tea & Thee . . . ?

He scanned the crowd. All around him people proudly displayed their grey and brown drabness, shapelessly heaped with layers of clothing whose cheapness they would have been only too proud to proclaim. Everything in this place, from the homemade lace curtains to the handwritten menus, seemed to boast of clunky craftiness; as if to be chic were to be toxic, and style nothing more than oppression. In his silk trousers and Gucci loafers, Jack felt like Louis XVI in the shadow of the scaffold.

He was here, of course, to meet Francesca LaBrash; it was her neighborhood and she could walk here, which suited her because she didn't have a car. But if she lived so close, why was she twenty minutes late . . . ? Jack's doubts about her were increasing.

The doubts had begun when he'd phoned her. She'd been chirpy and bright, *chatty* even, and she spoke dizzyingly fast. Not at all what he'd expected of a witch. She also said things like "yipes" and "okel-dokel" which somewhat undercut Jack's already struggling faith in her occult powers. In fact, after he'd arranged this rendezvous with her, he'd phoned the Ravencroft fellow—first name Archie, it turned out—and asked if he was quite confident in his recommendation of her.

"Oh, absolutely," Ravencroft had said; "as I told your colleague, she's a natural. Came late to the craft, in her thirties, but took to it like no one I've ever seen before. She simply has an innate understanding of cause and effect, of energy flow, of probability, that are years beyond even me. Some people instantly pick up languages, Mr. Ackerly. Others immediately comprehend even the most complex mathematical equations. Francesca is like that with magick."

And so he had kept his appointment with her. But was she keeping it with him . . . ?

Just when he was telling himself that this was all a ridiculous endeavor anyway, what was he thinking, he should just get up now and save himself some dignity—there was a commotion at the front door. A middle-aged woman with a grey pageboy and a calf-length plaid skirt had tried to enter the café in some haste, but the strap of her large wicker bag had caught on the door handle and yanked her back, causing her to lose one of her shoes. She fell back against the door, which re-opened, and when it re-opened the woman fell down on her rump, ripping the strap right off of the bag, out of which now tumbled a large package of kitty litter, which broke on the sidewalk and spilled its contents far and wide.

"Oh, *nertz,*" said the woman, and Jack thought, *Francesca.*

A few very busy moments later—after several helpful souls had come to her aid and she had pulled herself together, without ever once pausing in her rapid-fire declarations of *Thanks, gosh, thank you, jeepers, such a klutz*—she took a seat across from Jack, not quite as flustered as he'd imagined she'd be. Perhaps this kind of thing happened to her a lot.

"Oh, well," she said with a perky smile, "what are you gonna do? Caca happens. And it's no use crying over spilled litter. Oooh," she said, an idea occurring to her, "I littered litter! Get it? It's *litter* . . . and it's *litter!* I made a funny!"

Jack forced himself to smile, and something in the zip code of a chuckle fell past his lips.

"Anyway," she said, placing the wicker bag on the floor and fondling its broken strap one last time, "gosh, it's a shame about this bag, anyway I'm sorry I'm late, the 36 bus just took forever, I don't know why, traffic wasn't that bad, I asked the driver what the problem was several times but he wouldn't even look at me, the old poop."

Jack scowled. "I'm sorry; I thought you lived just a few blocks from here."

"Mm-hm," she said, stuffing a piece of flatbread into her mouth. It crumbled over her lips and dribbled into her lap.

Jack shook his head as if to clear it. "Then . . . why were you on the 36 bus?"

She looked at him as though he was stupid. "I was coming *from work,*" she said. "I'm on *lunch.*"

"But if that's the case we could've met closer to your off . . ." Jack stopped himself, deciding to pursue the matter no further. He felt too much like Alice talking to the Red Queen.

A waitress came to the table, wearing an olive-drab sleeveless T-shirt, a dirty apron, and grey woolen kneesocks. Jack had to turn away with a shudder. Francesca ordered a green tea, then turned back to him and said, "Well, Mr. Ackerly—"

"Oh, call me Jack."

"All right. Is that your name?"

Jack blinked. "Why else would I—" *No, no,* he cautioned himself; *that way lies madness.* "Yes, it is."

"Well, all right then!"

They stared at each other for a few awkward moments; then Jack said, "You were saying?"

"Pardon?"

"You were just saying something."

"I was?"

Jack took a breath and repositioned himself in his chair. "You said, 'Well, Mr. Ackerly,' and I said, 'Call me Jack.'"

"Mm-hmmm," she said tentatively, as if only just following him.

"So . . . I interrupted you."

She turned her head slightly and gave him a dubious look, then suddenly clapped her hands and said, "Oh, yes! Yes, of course! So sorry, Mr. Ackerly."

He started to say *Call me Jack* again but quickly swallowed the impulse; just let the woman get on with it.

"Anyway," she said, "I did some preliminary research into this youth business of yours, and I have a couple of things to go over with you." She bent down and started rummaging through her bag. And kept on rummaging. And rummaged further. At one point she said, "Like trying to find the prize in the Cracker Jack," and then a moment later, "Hey, I made another funny!" This time Jack attempted no polite smile.

Eventually she sat up and gripped the small of her back. "Oooh! Curse my lumbago!"

"You have lumbago?" Jack said.

"No, just a twinge," she said. "It's an expression . . . who was it used to say that? Mister Magoo? *'Curse my lumbago!'*"

Jack shook his head. "I can't help you."

"Anyway, it doesn't matter, I don't need no stinkin' notes, I'm a professional." She put her elbows on the table. "The upshot is, Mr. Ackerly, there's no real way to restore lost youth. Which I pretty much suspected, because if there were, *everyone* would be using it, wouldn't they?" He nodded; this was something he hadn't considered. His estimation of her rose just a bit. She went on, "There appears to be a way to retain *existing* youth, but you're already beyond that, and besides it involves harvesting the blood of young virgins, which is why no one's used it in years and years and years."

"Right," said Jack. "Not enough virgins."

She slapped the table and pointed at him. "Now *you* made a funny!" A few heads turned her way. Jack made a mental note: *Make no more funnies.*

She leaned across the table. "There *is* another possibility," she said. "Though it's not anything I've read about, I sort of made it up myself. A little brainstorm, don'tcha know. 'Necessity is the mother of invention,' and all."

Much as he hated to admit it, Jack was intrigued. Clearly the woman was several dimes short of a dollar, but he'd come all this way to meet her, why not hear her out? So he said, "Go on," but had to wait while the waitress presented Francesca with her tea, and then through Francesca's laborious and ultimately disastrous attempt to extract honey from a plastic bear.

When she'd sufficiently cleaned up, she continued. "There's no way, as I said, to restore your lost youth, but I'm fairly certain there's a way to give you someone else's."

Jack blinked. "What do you mean?"

She sipped her tea and flapped her hand in front of her mouth. "*Hot,*" she gasped; then, more hoarsely, "I'm pretty sure I could transfer your personality into a younger body."

"*Whose* younger body?"

"Anyone's," she said. "You find someone the right age, whose look you like, I can put you right into his head. Make you him."

"And what happens to *his* personality?"

"It goes into *your* head. It's a swap." She took another sip of tea, then waved into her mouth again.

Jack sat back and looked at her. He was speechless—suddenly chastened, as if he'd pursued this silly project just a shade too far. Even if it *were* possible, the idea of assuming an entirely new identity . . . it wasn't what he wanted. There was something . . . unwholesome about it. Something messy and decadent . . . *degenerate,* even.

"Let me think about it," he said, because it was more polite than simply saying no.

But in fact, he would think about little else for the next several days.

Chapter 11

He went about his business as usual—or rather his lack of business, his life being at present devoid of any real purpose—but at his core he felt subtly altered. That's what he had hoped, when he'd let himself pursue an occult solution to his midlife crisis; he'd counted on it being a kind of therapy, a prolonged bout of play-acting that would help exhaust his longing for lost youth, and leave him healthily and happily restored . . . laughing, perhaps, at his temporary derangement and the absurd things he had done under its influence.

Well, he *was* restored, in one sense; he now accepted, if with sadness, that he was wedded to middle age . . . at least until the onset of *old* age, which he preferred not to contemplate at the moment. He had also reconciled himself to having spent his youth austerely—terminology he much preferred to saying he had "wasted" it—and now looked for solace in the great spiritual texts (though with limited success; for instance, he found himself arguing with Aquinas).

Yet despite this he remained profoundly unsettled. If it was true, as Socrates asserts, that the unexamined life is not worth living, could it be equally true that you can examine it too thoroughly? . . . Most of the foolery that Jack had en-

gaged in the past few weeks could be easily dismissed as a
kind of spring fever; but not the moment—the fleeting but very
real moment—when he had actively contemplated Francesca's
offer. When, briefly, he had seriously considered "swapping"
his body for that of a younger man.

The more he thought about it, the more distasteful it was
to him; he wanted to expunge it from his memory. And yet,
maddeningly, it seemed an hour couldn't pass without him
reflecting on some thorny new problem posed by the idea:
for example, real estate. Would he, in a younger man's body,
be able to stay in this apartment? Or would he be forced to
assume fully the younger man's identity, inheriting all his
material possessions along with his flesh and bones? Would
he end up living in a one-bedroom flytrap while his former
body remained housed in the lap of luxury . . . ?

When he found himself too actively working out the means
by which such problems could be managed, he stopped himself and tried to think about other things. Nelly, for example, and her recent bout of incontinence. The vet, presuming
a urinary infection, had prescribed antibiotics, but Jack was
well aware that her kidneys might simply be failing; she was
a very old dog.

And yet even such practical rumination led him back to
the forbidden topic. What, he wondered, would happen to
Nelly if he swapped bodies *and* apartments with someone
younger? . . . He might be willing to let his thirteen-room
condominium go, but not his thirteen-year-old pet. She
would have to come with him. But would she understand? . . .
Would she even recognize him, if he were encased in new
skin? . . . Or would she prefer to stay with her old master's
body, identifying him by his look and his scent, not understanding—*incapable* of understanding—that he was no longer
in there . . . ?

And so he continued to torture himself. He was resolute;
he told himself repeatedly that he would never, *could* never

do such a thing—take another man's life, robbing him of decades to satisfy his own selfish desire for a do-over at callow youth. And of course, it almost certainly wasn't even possible. Why, then, couldn't he stop *thinking* about it . . . ? It was some flaw in his nature, something primal and greedy that kept hungering for life and didn't care if it was someone else's. It was a beast inside him, and it frightened him, and he couldn't make it go away.

Physical exertion helped; pushing himself to the limits of his endurance seemed to quiet his roiling brain. And so he began running—a mile at first; then two, then three—soon he was up to five. With his iPod strapped to his biceps he could literally pound the pavement, Dinah Washington or Miles Davis blaring into his head, and keep rational thought at bay for an hour or more.

He was on the final leg of one such run when, turning to examine his reflection in an antique store window (he liked how he looked when he was running; a dozen years younger at least), he bumped into a customer coming out of a Starbucks and knocked the man's coffee out of his hand.

He said, "Oh, oh, sorry, sorry," and then, "Let me buy you a new one," before remembering that he had no money on him.

"It's all right," said the man—young, cruelly handsome, with cheekbones like the white cliffs of Dover—as he crouched down to fetch the cup. "I was almost finished." He got up and tossed it into a nearby trash bin, then smiled at Jack and said, "Seriously, it's all right."

Jack yanked out one earbud so he could hear what the young man was saying, but he bobbled it and it fell to his waist. He had to grope for it while it dangled before him, and it evaded him the first few times, and when he looked up again Harry was there.

Standing right next to the handsome young man he'd assaulted.

Harry, of all people.

"Well, look at you," Harry said, holding his own Starbucks cup. "Training for the marathon, or fleeing the police?"

"Neither," said Jack, still abashed but making a valiant attempt at lightness. "Just stalking you. You weren't supposed to notice."

"Well if that's the case," said Harry, draping an arm around the young man's shoulder, "you don't wanna go careening into my date. Dead giveaway."

His date. Harry's *date*.

The young man extended his arm. "Brian Isley," he said. "Since I apparently have to introduce myself."

"Hey, looked to me like you'd already met," quipped Harry. "At fifteen m.p.h."

Jack shook his hand and said, "Jack Ackerly."

"Pleased to meet you, Jack," he said. Jack waited for him to add, *I've heard a lot about you,* because wasn't that customary in these situations? . . . But Brian didn't say it. He didn't give any indication that he'd ever heard of Jack at all.

Some more pleasantries were exchanged, but Jack could barely hear them. He was too busy gazing at Harry, who looked younger and happier and healthier than ever—Harry in new, younger clothes, with a new, younger hairstyle and his bronzed arm around the shoulder of a new, younger boyfriend.

Finally Jack said, "Listen, can't let my heart rate drop," and plugged the earbud back in. He waved a quick goodbye before resuming his run, at a rather faster trot than before. He felt an absolute compulsion to get as far away as possible, as quickly as possible.

When he looked in the store window again, he saw himself through Brian Isley's eyes: a sad, flabby, middle-aged man, drenched in sweat and sagging beneath the weight of his years.

Despite the iPod's siren lure, his mind veered off again—this time, with clear intent.

And by the time he got home, he was thinking, *There's nothing really so awful about swapping minds with someone younger . . . not if it's consensual . . . not if both parties agree . . .*

Chapter 12

Which is how he came once again to be seated at a table in the Four Seasons' bar—this time at four-thirty in the afternoon, with the sun still streaming through its windows.

He'd come to see the waiter from his last visit—the one who'd said, about Jack, "He has my permission to be me." Drunk as Jack had been at the time, that had stuck with him. He had it in mind now to try and draw the young man out a bit more, learn how serious he had been. And possibly, maybe—if all went well—proposition him. Make him an offer he'd have to take seriously. "Here it is, my boy; I'll add a quarter million to your bank account if you'll only add a quarter-century to your age." Who wouldn't be intrigued by an offer like that? . . . The only problem was, Jack couldn't imagine himself actually saying it. It was like something from a bad TV show.

He was quite nervous; and he was a man whose nerves were the envy of all he knew. He was almost enjoying the strange sensation of being uncertain of himself, even a little afraid. It was like visiting a foreign country, albeit one where you didn't know the language and couldn't stand the food.

A different waiter approached him—a slender man clearly on the wrong side of thirty—and asked his pleasure, and he could think of no good way to say "I'm waiting for another server," so he ordered a sparkling water. Every atom in him cried out for a vodka and tonic, but he wasn't about to risk *that* again. The waiter returned dutifully and swiftly—there being almost no one else in the bar at this hour—and Jack nervously took a handful of peanuts from the table, then sat back on the sofa and nursed his drink while he waited.

The waiter—*his* waiter—showed up half an hour later, after Jack had felt obliged to order another water and a small plate of quesadillas—and at the sight of him he almost hid himself, as though guilty of something. He caught himself in time, and busied himself instead by tearing his damp cocktail napkin into little soggy strips. He kept an eye on the waiter, watched him move about the bar; he seemed to move with power and grace, and Jack thought, *That's fine, that would do just fine for me.* Then he wondered how much of that grace was natural, and how much of it was learned behavior that might disappear with another driver behind the wheel.

And once again he was struck by the absurdity of what he was doing. If only he hadn't run into Harry. If only he hadn't run into Harry like *that*. If only he hadn't gone to that damn opera and gotten ideas. If only he hadn't gone to that damn opera and seen Carlo. If only Sharon hadn't become a grandmother. If only he hadn't been such a frigid little prig in his twenties. *If only . . .*

The waiter sailed by his table twice and Jack's heart pounded like a tom-tom, but he said nothing; his voice in fact quite dried up. He thought, *What the hell?* and ordered the vodka tonic. Thus emboldened, he waited for the waiter to come by again.

Which he did, thrice more. And Jack remained mute every time.

It was now ten minutes to six. Jack realized he wasn't going to talk to the waiter. For some reason, he had no problem entertaining faintly obscene fantasies of mind-swapping as long as they were confined to his own head—or were shared with a stranger who was clearly a lunatic. He could even let himself almost *believe* in them, within the buffered little zone in which he kept them. But to bring them out in the open like this . . . actually present them to someone in the real world . . . someone young and beautiful, whose scorn would show so openly on his face, and would flay him like razor wire . . .

No, no. That just wasn't going to happen. He signaled for his bill, paid it with his AmEx, left a generous tip, and then got up to leave, cloaking himself in the dignity of someone who had no embarrassing obsessions or science-fiction beliefs, and it was a little depressing to have to admit to himself that this was a disguise. But after tonight, he could put it all behind him. The shock of seeing Harry again, Harry and his new young beau—that had driven him as far down this path as he could or would go, and now that he knew that, he could relax and welcome back mental health.

His bladder demanded his attention on his way out, so he detoured towards the men's room. And when he swung open the door, there was the waiter at the sink.

Something must have shown in his face, because the waiter saw it in his reflection and inched a little bit farther away.

Jack said, "Oh, hi." He hadn't meant to say anything, but out it came anyway.

The waiter looked up and with a noncommittal smile said, "Hi," then finished washing his hands and turned off the faucet.

Jack went to the sink farthest from him, plucked a tissue, and blew his nose loudly. The waiter dried his hands on a towel.

Jack thought, All right, this is silly, and said, "How's that second job going?"

The waiter looked up at him, surprised. "Pardon?"

"Don't you have another job?"

"Yyyyes." Said warily.

"You mentioned it the other night," said Jack, fiddling with the faucet. "I was here with a friend? . . . You probably don't recognize me, because I'm sober now."

The waiter nodded in a way that seemed to say, *Oh, are you?*

Jack said, "It was a little embarrassing. I kept pointing to you, and it was like I was coming on or something, but really I just wanted to switch places with you. Which my friend then explained."

"Right," said the waiter. He tossed the soiled towel into the wastebasket.

Jack lathered up his hands. "And then you said, if I remember correctly—and maybe I don't—that because of your two jobs and—and something else—that I had your *permission* to change places with you."

The waiter nodded. "Yeah, well," he said smiling as he inched towards the door. "It can be a grind."

Jack turned and looked at him. "I don't suppose you really meant it."

Maybe there was something too earnest in Jack's tone that frightened him; but the waiter quickly grinned and said, "You have a good night, now," then pushed open the door and essentially fled.

Jack stood motionless for a while, his hands under the running water, and stared at his face in the mirror. The lighting was particularly harsh in here. He looked wizened and drawn; he looked seventy.

The sun was still dawdling above the horizon as he drove home. He was embarrassed and angry with himself, and he was taking it out on the drivers ahead of him, none of whom were going anywhere near fast enough to please him.

He was also taking it out on himself.

"Here are the things I resolve," he said aloud. "I resolve

to accept life as it is, and not to whine or pout or sulk about how it ought to be or should have been.

"I resolve to place youth and sexuality in their proper perspective and to not allow the long-lost allure of either to derange me any further.

"I resolve to have no more to do with witches, warlocks, wizards, astrologers, magicians, or anyone with three cups and a walnut.

"I resolve t—oh, for the love of Christ, *go,* will you, the light's as green as it *gets.*"

He leaned into his horn, producing an extended wail of aggrieved outrage, and still the Dodge Dart ahead of him hesitated, its elderly driver uncertain as to whether he was really *meant* to cross this intersection.

In a fury, Jack threw his car into reverse, backed up twenty feet, then shifted into gear again and lurched into an alley. As he hurled down its length, sailing by multiple mute garage doors and disdaining to pay heed to the speed bumps, he said, "I resolve to forge closer ties to my family because they're really all I have left. I resolve to finalize plans for my old age, as it will be here soon eno— *SHIT!*"

He slammed on the brakes. Just as he was careening towards the alley's end, a bicyclist appeared at its mouth. Jack's tires squealed, the young cyclist looked up in horror, the car skidded, Jack jerked the wheel, the car spun out—

—and the back end clipped the bike. Its rider was thrown from its seat.

Part Two

Corey

Chapter 13

For a few moments he couldn't recall what had happened. He was staring up at the sky, and it seemed almost as though he was falling into it—he could feel the pull in his head, his stomach. Then he felt the grit of the road beneath him, the bite of concrete in his arms and legs, and he realized he was in fact earthbound. He tried to get up; his head swam, and a sharp pain in his side made him yelp like a puppy.

Someone was looming over him now; older guy, a wild look on his face. Saying something . . . "Are you okay? Are you all right?" Corey's eyes refocused, and he saw the Porsche just beyond, the driver's door hanging open. *Been hit,* he thought. *By a car.* He had enough presence of mind to add, *And some car!*

"You shouldn't move," said the man, who, Corey noticed, was wearing Gucci loafers and no socks. *God, how George Hamilton,* he thought.

"I'm all right," he said. He tried to get to his feet and the pain in his side flared up again. He made a face.

"Let me take you to a hospital." Gucci guy again.

"No, no," he insisted, on his feet now. He looked around him, aware that he was missing something . . . what? Oh, yeah. "Where's my bike?"

The old guy pointed. Corey turned, and saw his two-year-old Motobecane a totally shocking distance away, just lying in the street. "Well, *shit*," he said.

He hobbled over to it—he'd hurt his knee, probably landed on it—while the old guy followed him, babbling away about *sorry, so sorry, sure you're okay, shouldn't you be wearing a helmet, take you to see a doctor*. Corey picked up the bike; it was a little beat up but it looked rideable.

The old guy was still yammering away. Why was he so freaked out? "Am I bleeding, or something?" Corey asked him.

"No, no. But you may be in shock."

"Just had the wind knocked outta me," he said. "I'm fine."

In truth, what he was, was embarrassed. The guy was right, he *should* have been wearing a helmet. Also, he'd been going the wrong way down a one-way street, which the guy seemed not to have noticed yet. For some reason, Corey was desperate to get away before he did.

Corey mounted the bike; it wobbled a little beneath him. "I'm good," he said. "Just took a tumble."

The old guy reached into his pocket and brought out a thin leather wallet. What, was he going to give him *money* now . . . ?

"Look," he said, producing a business card, "at least take my contact info. In case . . . well, I'm just very sorry. All my fault. Anything I can do . . ."

At the most basic level Corey realized that yes, in fact it was the driver's fault; but *he* was the one who'd gone ass-over-teakettle, *he* was the one who'd been made to look awkward and vulnerable, lying on the street with his limbs splayed like a rag doll. Every instinct compelled him to get away, to flee this humiliating scene, and *fast*.

"Thanks," he said, taking the card and stuffing it into his pocket. "Um . . . bye."

He grasped the handlebars—causing another sharp twinge in his flank—and began pedaling. The wheels wobbled more noticeably; they must've been knocked slightly out of alignment. But he kept going, pushing himself—till he realized he wasn't headed anywhere but *away*. Where had he been going before the car hit him . . . ? He couldn't recall.

He stopped the bike and put his left foot down to balance himself. When he released the handlebar and stood upright, he was almost toppled by a shrill scream of agony in his side—far worse than what he'd felt before. *Delayed reaction,* he thought. Gingerly, he lifted his shirt and examined his skin.

Unbroken, unblemished; as though nothing at all were the matter.

Strangely, his knee was now bruising up terribly, going all purple and yellow below the hem of his shorts—but he felt only a slight discomfort there. His *side,* however—with no outward show of harm—was virtually crippling him.

Wherever he'd been going, he'd be better advised to head home now. Put some ice on his knee, and what—a heating pad on his side? . . . That's what his mom would've done for a pulled muscle. Is that what this was—a pulled muscle? . . . And did it really even matter, since he didn't own a heating pad . . . ?

He started out again, but the pain was simply overwhelming. Each time his leg came up from pedaling, it was like a volley of daggers in his side. He had to quit after only a few blocks and set the bike against a convenience store wall. He realized then that he was crying—that it hurt so bad, his face was actually slick with tears.

A hefty lady in a housedress came out of the store carrying a flimsy bag that valiantly strove to contain two liters of Vanilla Coke. As she was getting into her battered blue Pontiac Montana she saw Corey.

"You all right there?" she asked.

Corey nodded; but the woman was just enough like his mother, and his defenses were sufficiently down, that he quickly followed with, "I got hit by a car and now I can't ride my bike 'cause it *hurts*."

The woman looked at him a moment. "Where's the driver?"

Corey made a kind of empty gesture behind him. "I told him I was okay."

"Hell if you're okay." She was being stern with him. Clearly *somebody's* mother.

"I didn't know how bad it was," he said, and he snuffled up a wad of mucus, willing himself to cry no more.

The woman nodded; all three of her chins jiggled. "Well, we're gettin' you to a hospital. You just hop in." She nodded toward the passenger door.

"I can't," Corey said. "My bike."

"Lock it up," the woman said, only mildly exasperated. "You can come back for it."

Corey didn't really want to go with her, but he was so grateful to have someone take charge that he did what she said. He set the crippled Motobecane in the store's bike rack and fixed it there with its big black Kryptonite lock. Then he got into the woman's car and sat beside her.

She shifted into reverse and looked over her shoulder as she backed into the lot. "Let's see now," she said as she put the car in drive, "nearest hospital to here's Children's Memorial, I think."

"But I'm not a child."

"Well, they ain't gonna turn you away from the emergency room for that."

The mention of the ER made Corey realize suddenly how swiftly events had overtaken him. He wished he could rewind, redo it all—but of course he couldn't. And he couldn't exactly dis this woman's generosity, now that he'd accepted it.

"This is very nice of you," he said, the last of his tears drying.

She smiled at him and patted his hand. As she pulled into traffic, she said, "Oughtta be wearin' a *helmet*."

Chapter 14

She pulled up the emergency room drive and dropped Corey at the entrance. He thanked her fulsomely and even planted a kiss on her cheek, but resolutely refused her offer to accompany him in, which she accepted with what appeared to be relief; she'd clearly only offered for form's sake.

The glass doors slid open as he approached, but he entered only far enough to trigger them to close again. Then he lurked in the vestibule, craning his neck so he could watch the Pontiac Montana roll out of sight. When its taillights had receded into pinpricks, he snuck back out and stood for a moment in the gloaming, wondering what to do now.

He certainly wasn't about to check himself into the ER. He wasn't feeling *that* bad. The pain in his side had abated during the drive, and besides, what could a bunch of doctors do to treat what was almost certainly a pulled muscle? Nothing he couldn't do himself. What they *could* do was bankrupt him with exorbitant hospital fees. Without health insurance, it would be criminally stupid—not to mention cowardly—to run into their high-priced arms over a simple little fall from his bike.

The thought of benefits caused him to remember where he'd been headed before the accident: to a job interview, at a tavern on West Armitage. Well, he'd have missed that by now. Maybe if he called and explained, they'd let him re-schedule . . . ? No, no; it would only come across as a lie—"I was hit by a car," yeah, *right*—and only confirm the ill feeling he'd have caused by not showing up at his appointed time.

Thinking of the time, he took out his cell phone to check its readout: 6:43. His friend Frida would surely be home from work by now. If he walked a few blocks east, he could catch the Clark Street bus, switch to the Broadway at Diversey, and ride almost to her door on School Street. He thought of calling her to let her know he was on his way, but he hated wasting air time. And anyway, he didn't have a backup plan, so it was this or nothing. He set out walking.

By the time he reached Clark he was in shrieking agony. As usual, two nearly empty buses pulled away simultaneously as he approached, and it was a small eternity before another ambled up, choked with passengers. Corey was by now nearly doubled over with pain; when he climbed aboard the bus he trembled like a very old man.

After a few minutes a pair of students got up to disem-bark; Corey slid into their seat as they vacated it. A mor-bidly fat man plummeted down next to him, breathing like a marathoner just past the finish line. Corey shut his eyes and let his temple rest against the cool glass window.

The bus made maddeningly slow progress, stopping every two blocks to let on or off a seemingly endless procession of young thugs, thin grey alcoholics, and Polish cleaning ladies. By the time he reached Frida's corner, it was past 7:30.

When she opened the door, she had to wave away an acrid haze before she could see him. "Baby!" she said, her voice slightly strangulated, and then she coughed. Of course there was a joint in her hand. Frida smoked far more dope than anyone Corey had ever known. "Come on in! What's the matter? You been crying?"

He took a deep breath and then plunged into the marijuana-fogged apartment. He'd never really gotten used to it; nor to how the aroma of burning cannabis threw into such ironic contrast all the dainty, old-lady furniture Frida had inherited from her great-grandmother. An entire Victorian house's worth of high-backed chairs, end tables, rosewood hutches, and china cabinets had all been crammed into her one-bedroom flat.

"Matter of fact I *have* been crying," he said as he squeezed past her dining room table towards her huge velvet sofa. Her tabby cat, Aorta, was curled up there, and gave Corey a don't-tell-me-you're-sitting-*here* look. Corey, not giving a damn, plopped down onto the nearest cushion, which squeezed the adjacent one into the air, sending Aorta flying. Landing on all fours, she turned, glared at Corey, then went off in a huff.

Frida squeezed through the furniture to join him. A big girl with long black hair, she worked as the receptionist at a Gold Coast salon. When there was down time, the stylists amused themselves by working on her; as a result, she nearly always looked spectacularly made-up—*showgirl* made-up. Tonight she seemed to have a lacquered skein over her face; Corey wouldn't have been surprised to find little eyelets by the ears holding an elastic band, as for a Halloween mask.

"What's there to cry about?" she said as she sat beside him, curling one pudgy knee beneath her. "You're not even seeing anyone. Unless you've managed to speed through a whole relationship arc since we talked two days ago."

He'd done this deliberately—held off telling her his news, knowing she'd tease or mock him. Now, he could really lay on the guilt.

"I was hit by a car," he said. "A Porsche. Threw me right off my bike."

Her cartoon-like face registered cartoon-like shock. "Omigod, baby! Are you all right? Omi*god*."

"Actually, I think I'm a little fucked up. You got anything for pain?"

She offered him the joint, but he refused it. A year earlier, after a harrowing few months in the throes of crystal meth, he'd foresworn party drugs of all stripes. He simply didn't trust himself.

"Oh, come on," she said. "It's therapeutic. Medical marijuana."

"Just any pills you've got would be great," he said.

She pushed herself to her feet again, squeezed back into the living room, and shimmied over to the corridor leading to the bathroom. "Did you get the Porsche's license plate?" she asked en route.

"Didn't need to. Guy stopped, got out, did the whole apology thing."

"So did the police arrest him?" She was out of sight now; just the lazy haze of smoke indicating where she'd gone.

"No police," he said. "I thought I was okay, so I just said forget it."

Sound of a medicine cabinet banging shut. "You said *what?*"

"It didn't hurt so much just then," he said. "It's gotten worse ever since."

She reappeared and began the sideways slide back. "So, this guy drives off, leaving you fucked up, and you don't even know who he is or how to get in touch with him?"

"No," he said, humbled. Then, "Oh, wait—yeah, he gave me his card."

She sat back down beside him and said, "Here. Take these." When he opened his palm, she dropped three different-shaped pills into it.

"What are they?" he asked.

"Couple different things. One of them should work. Where does it hurt?" Before he could answer, she noticed his knee. "Oh, Christ, never mind. Kind of apparent."

"Actually, that's not so bad," he said. "Looks way worse than it feels. It's my *side* that's killing me. Right under the armpit and down about eight inches. Must've pulled a muscle or something." He looked at the pills. "Anything to wash these down?"

She got up again, now warmly solicitous. "Could use some ice for the knee, too," she added. As she squeezed herself through to the kitchen, she said, "Listen, baby, you just call that guy. Hit him up for some cash."

He blushed. "I don't need any cash."

"You don't know that. You said it yourself, you're fucked up." He heard the refrigerator open and close. "You're gonna need *some* kind of medical attention."

"They can't do anything for a pulled muscle," he insisted.

"They can give you pain pills."

"*You* can give me pain pills."

He heard the hum of the open freezer. "I mean a prescription, idiot."

"I don't need a prescription. Just a couple doses to get over the initial discomfort."

She reappeared with an open bottle of Grenache and a dishtowel filled with ice. The joint dangled from her fingertips. "Have it your way," she muttered.

Corey downed the pills with the Grenache, then made a face and said, "Terrible stuff."

"I know. I won't even cook with it."

"But you'll give it to a friend in need?"

"Medicine isn't supposed to taste good." She placed the ice pack on his knee and made him hold it there. "And how else am I supposed to get rid of it? Been in my fridge for, like, *years.*"

Corey felt his gorge rise, and was on the point of snarking at her for serving him ancient swill; but he held his tongue because he wanted something else from her. "Listen, I was also hoping you could drive me home. Or at least back to where I left my bike."

She grimaced. "Right now? Tonight?"

"Well . . . yeah. I mean, I do *live* there."

She sighed. "All right, fine. It's just . . . I got this great parking space right out front, and if I move now I'll never find another one when I come back. I'll have to drive around for, like, forty minutes just to find a spot six blocks away."

"*Pleeease,*" he said, making doe eyes at her.

She sat back and took another long toke. "Look," she said after she'd exhaled, "why don't you just stay here? I mean, you shouldn't be alone anyway, in case you go into shock or something."

"I won't go into—*Jesus,* why does everyone think I'm gonna go into shock?"

"Plus, I can give you more pills if these wear off, and if you're *really* fucked up in the morning I can drive you to a hospital. If you're not, I'll drop you at home on my way to work. 'Kay?"

"I don't know," he said. "You got anything to drink besides the Grenache?"

She grinned. "It can be arranged."

"Then I guess it's a deal."

The joint was now nothing more than a smudge of black against her yellowed, calloused thumb. She flicked it into an ashtray and said, "Great! We can order a pizza and watch a movie! Any preferences?"

He considered this a moment. "Sausage and black olives. As for the movie . . . anything but a comedy. Kinda got the whole 'side-splitting' thing goin' on already."

Chapter 15

After a half-dozen glasses of Three-Buck Chuck, Corey felt amazingly better. So much so that he and Frida ended up dancing on her dining-room table to Scissor Sisters, till the neighbors' pounding on the walls rendered them shy and giggly, and reduced them to admonitory shushes for each other. When the adrenaline wore off, they found they were too wasted to finish the film Frida had rented, in which Meg Ryan and Melanie Griffith played tragically estranged sisters who inherit a Christmas tree farm from their uncle. Corey was the first to give up on it; Frida, perched over a bong, remained deeply involved with the story a while longer—though, in typical stoner fashion, she talked over all the dialogue. "Look at her clothes! I said *look* at them, baby. I ask you, how many bitch corporate lawyers do you know who wear white satin Balenciaga hoodies?"

"Not one," Corey said through a yawn, neglecting to add that he in fact knew no bitch corporate lawyers of any kind.

Because of his injury, Frida insisted he take her bed, which he was equally insistent he not do; he couldn't seem to convince her how vastly, incomparably better he felt. In the end it was easier simply to give in.

But when he awakened the next morning—to her gentle prodding, as she craned over him wearing only her bra and panties, shocking the sleep from him with her looming, fleshy femaleness—he could barely move.

"Chop chop," she said, pulling on a chemise as she exited the bedroom. "Gotta be out the door in twenty minutes."

Corey didn't think he could make it out of *bed* in twenty minutes; but he made a heroic effort and somehow got into his clothes. He declined Frida's offer of instant coffee, and tried to convey just how terrible he felt and how courageously he'd forced himself past the blinding pain to get dressed *just for her* . . . but it was a different Frida this morning: brisk, efficient, unsympathetic—a Frida intent only on meeting her professional responsibilities. Corey had seen many of his friends in this mode, shrugging off the bliss and intimacy of the night before to focus their energies on grim commerce. He'd never been able to manage such a transformation himself. Which is probably why he continued to lurch from one dead-end job to another.

In the car, Frida continued to ignore his obvious pain and instead launched into a harangue against her longtime boyfriend, Julio, whom Corey had never met. In fact, no one had met Julio; a few of Frida's friends were even convinced he didn't exist. But Corey believed in him; there was no way a woman would tell such cringingly humiliating stories about a man she herself had made up.

"You remember when he invited me up to his cousin's summer house in Michigan City?" she said this morning as she leaned over the steering wheel and wiped away the accretion of several days' smoke from her inner windshield. "And then he told me the trip was off 'cause his cousin got sick?" The light changed to green and she lurched the car forward again. "Well guess what, I found out he *went up there anyway.* He *lied* to me, baby. Lied right to my face! Well, over the phone, actually, but it's the same thing. And get this: *he took someone else!* I don't know who yet, but you can bet your ass I'm on the case . . ."

Despite his searing pain, Corey had asked her to take him

to the convenience store where he'd left his bike. He wasn't nearly up to riding the two miles home, but neither did he want to leave his most valuable possession on naked display in this predatory fucking city.

As well he might not . . . for when they reached the store, there were three bikes in its rack, and none of them was his. Corey kept examining them one by one, as though this were all a trick of the light, and a sudden shift in perspective might reveal his longed-for Motobecane. It just didn't seem possible it wasn't where he left it.

"Well, that's it," Frida said when he got back in the car. "You *have* to call now."

"The police?" he asked, not comprehending her.

"Oh, them if you want, fat lot of fucking good it'll do you. No," she said, pulling back into traffic, "the Porsche guy."

"Why? *He* didn't take my bike."

"No, baby, but he hit you and you're fucked up and you couldn't ride the bike so that's why it was stolen, and also you need medical attention and drugs and those cost money. How much is in your checking account?"

"None of your business."

"Less than a thousand?"

Corey felt a flush of shame. When had he last had more than a thousand? "Possibly," he said.

"And you don't have any job lined up?"

He fiddled with the cuticle on his thumb. "No."

She sighed. "Baby, it's been, like, a month since the last one."

"I know, I know . . . but things are improving a little. At least now they'll give me a reference."

"You're kidding! I thought you were fired with extreme prejudice."

"I was, but the old lady had a change of heart and dropped the lawsuit. She admitted the floors were very slippery that day, plus she said she'd been planning on new dentures anyway. So all the restaurant has to do is pay her cleaning bill and I'm off the hook."

"Be that as it may, this is do or die time," she said as she rolled down her window to dump out a stale latte that had been in her cup holder overnight. "You're, what, twenty-six? . . . You've got no job, no prospects, no assets, no cash. You're looking at a big fucking pothole in the road ahead."

He scowled. "So, what, I'm supposed to extort money from this Porsche dude?"

"It's not extortion! *He hit you!* What the fuck is wrong with you that you don't *get* that?"

He shrugged his shoulders. "It's a guy thing."

"Yeah, well, get over it. This driver, how old is he?"

Corey shrugged. "Forty, fifty, sixty . . . something like that."

"Right. Ancient old dude, possibly already senile, driving around in his Porsche, getting' down to Billy Joel while talking to his accountant about his retirement plan—we're talking a fucking *menace.* They should just take your license away when you get that old. But no, no, they let guys like him keep on driving even after they've got hearing aids and colostomy bags, because they *pay.* The just throw money at whoever's in charge and suddenly they're back on the road, all nice and legal and legally blind."

"I'm not sure that's how it works," he protested, but she was in full flow.

"And *then* one of them hits someone like you, a young guy barely getting by, trying to scrounge out *some* kind of sad subsistence-level existence in a fucking brutal fucking world, and you end up totally fucked and you miss a job interview and your bike gets stolen on top of it, and what happens? . . . *You're* the one who feels guilty? While Harrison Ford goes driving off into the sunset? How the hell fucked is that?"

"I never said I felt guilty. I just feel . . . I dunno. Stupid. *Embarrassed.*"

"Hon, embarrassed is for when you forget someone's

name. *Pissed off* is for when they slam their fucking import car into you."

He persevered in arguing with her, but in vain; and it was with some relief that he left her on the curb in front of his apartment building, and waved feebly as she drove off to her other life, in which she was a *receptionist* and was *paid for her labors*. This still seemed wildly exotic to him. Every job he'd ever had, he'd approached with nothing more than the hope of staying beneath the radar for five or six weeks before he was inevitably noticed and fired. The cosmos, alas, had seldom played along.

Chapter 16

Corey got home early enough to steal a newspaper from the lobby mail drop, and so spent the day lying on his bed, nursing his injury and flipping through the classifieds. The sight of all those columns of job openings always nurtured a tremulous hope in him, but as he went through them one by one the hope wilted, shriveled, and died. There just wasn't anything remotely for him. Each position called for a particular variety of "experience," and the only kind he'd had was of circuit parties, drugs, and marathon sex. That had been enough to keep him in jobs five years ago, when he'd been a cute young twink; and even though he was still young, still hot, and still willing, he was less so than the hordes of twenty-year-olds who had swarmed onto the scene after him and grabbed all the hat-check and busboy and other cute-young-twink jobs. Sometimes Corey thought he might reasonably graduate into a more mature man's career, like mixing drinks; but all the bars he knew already had their star bartenders, who held onto their posts with all the tenacity of studio-era movie divas. And Corey couldn't bear the idea of starting out in some grimy dive, mixing brandy Alexanders for middle-aged queens and being pawed by fat forty-year-olds.

Frida had given him more pills—it was a mystery where

she got them, but he knew better than to look a gift horse in the mouth—and he took them periodically throughout the day, which resulted in quite a bit of napping. When he finally got up again, it was near dusk. He was feeling less pain than before, and in fact was well enough to realize he hadn't eaten all day. He checked his refrigerator, finding nothing there but a jar of pickles, a nearly empty bottle of orange juice, and assorted ancient condiments. He settled for the pickles and the juice, which was slightly off.

He'd have to spring for some food soon, if he was going to survive. As he munched on the pickles, spilling brine onto his bare legs, he checked his bank account. It was even emptier than the fridge. He really had to get a job *this week.* It was imperative. As it was, he had just enough funds to pay the rent and utilities and pick up a very few groceries besides. And that was only if he didn't go out *at all.* He would have to forego, absolutely and definitely, any nightlife of any kind, period, end of story. He'd just stay in and watch television like a normal American. That was all there was to it. He was *resolute.*

A few hours later he entered Bar Sharona, a former lesbian hangout that had slowly been overtaken by gay men. The dreamy earth-mother nudes still hung on its walls, which provided the perfect note of gay-male irony. Corey was willing to buy his first beer or two, by which time he'd ideally have found someone to treat him the rest of the night.

He surveyed the crowd. Aside from Kent, the dazzling bartender—who gave him a little leering nod when he entered—the prospects were underwhelming: Lots of older guys lurking against the wall like wolves, trying to look casual but with the darting, desperate eyes that gave their game away; little clusters of giggling boys, thrilled at the prospect of being naughty; a couple of regulars, the guys who always seemed to have a stool, who always seemed to have the *same* stool.

Then Corey found him. *The One.* Craggily handsome dirty

blond having a beer with a gangly, balding companion. Corey had seen this configuration many times before. Hell, he'd been part of it himself, with his jug-eared buddy Tyler. The idea was, a hot guy takes a goofy-looking friend out with him so that he has someone to hang with and—if he manages to hook up—someone he can ditch with no repercussions. Because the goofy guy will *always understand*. And will always be happy to play the hapless chaperone again, any time, any place.

Of course, that meant Corey was at a disadvantage. For him to approach this guy would be to admit that he was interested. And like all hot guys—like Corey himself, in the same position—the man would use that leverage to make Corey *work* for his score. He'd pretend not to return the interest; he'd pretend to have to be *persuaded* away from his fish-faced buddy.

But Corey knew the way around that. The key was the goofy friend—the friend without any guile or attitude, who would be only too happy to have some strapping young buck come and talk to him. And so Corey headed over.

"Hi," he said to Fishface—ignoring the hottie next to him completely.

Fishface turned. "Well, hi yourself!" he said, smiling.

"Corey," he said, extending his hand.

"Mike," said Fishface, shaking it. Then, nodding to his friend, "This is Adam."

Corey gave Adam only the most glancing of nods, then turned back to Mike. "I'm just heading to the bar," he said. "Can I get you something?" This was how it worked, see; he'd treat the ugly guy to a drink, chat him up, flirt; but somewhere in the process he'd start sending signals to the handsome friend, who, tired of being ignored, would then butt in and try to claim Corey's attention for his own. Advantage: Corey. He'd get the guy, with no loss of power or control. *Genius,* really.

But instead of gleefully accepting Corey's drink offer, Fishface Mike just gave him a mysterious smile. Corey couldn't really read it, and it made him uncomfortable. Mike then turned his head slightly towards Adam, as if to make sure he was getting all this; after which he looked back at Corey and said, "Thanks, hon, but actually we're just heading home."

"So soon?" said Corey in his most flirtatious manner. "It's just shy of midnight. What, you gonna turn into a pumpkin or something?"

Mike cackled. "No, but we've got dogs to walk. And we're a little worn out; we only just stopped in for a drink on our way home from a really *looong* opera. *The Makropulos Case;* maybe you've seen it?"

"The—what? . . . No, I—I haven't." Corey was flustered. What was all this "we" business?

"Well, we recommend it," said Mike, *"conditionally."*

Adam craned his neck in and said, "Really just for Karita Mattila. She's amazing."

Mike gave him a poke and said teasingly, "Nuh-uh, this one's mine!" He turned back to Corey and explained, "He's jealous 'cause the hot guys usually only want to talk to *him.*"

Corey was putting two and two together, but he couldn't bring himself to believe it made four. "Y-you two are a *couple?*"

Mike nodded. "Five years now," he said. "But if he doesn't start picking up his dirty laundry, we won't make six. If that happens, can I call you?"

Adam rolled his eyes and tugged Mike's sleeve. "Come on, hon," he said. "Dogs're waiting."

"Oh, you can't *stand* it, can you?" said Mike, his voice dancing with glee. "Now the shoe's on the other foot, you're just *beside* yourself."

Adam responded by grabbing Mike by the arm and physically removing him from the scene. Mike waved back at

Corey and said, *"Arrivederci,* sweetheart! Thanks for the memories!"

Corey watched the bickering boyfriends make their exit, his jaw hanging on his chest. He then shook his head in disbelief and headed to the bar.

Kent came over to him, drying his hands with a towel. "Hey, who died?" he said.

Corey shrugged. "I don't understand the world anymore."

"Well, you've come to the right place. Couple drinks, it'll all be made clear to you. Either that or it won't, but you won't care."

"I can't *afford* a couple of drinks," he said, propping his chin in his hand. "One's my limit tonight."

Kent cocked his head at him. "Hard times?"

Corey nodded.

He winked. "Tell you what. I can't have my regulars looking like sad sacks. You're on my tab tonight. We'll fix you right up."

Corey's eyes opened wide. "What? . . . Are you kidding? No, no I can't let you do that!"

"It's my pleasure," he said with an incandescent smile. "Course, I'm not *totally* being a Good Samaritan, here." He leaned in close and stage-whispered, "I'll expect a show of gratitude later." And before Corey could react, he headed off to mix him a cocktail.

Corey sat, dumbfounded for the second time in just ten minutes. Was Kent—Bar Sharona's star bartender, the object of lust for every man who passed through its portals, the barjack so hot they practically bussed gay men in from Iowa to see him—was Kent trying to *pick him up* . . . ?

Well, then! Things were looking up . . . and in a *big* way.

Chapter 17

Kent's shift didn't end till two, so Corey had to sit and wait a bit; he also had to summon all his reserves of self-control to keep from drinking too much. It would be a disaster to get smashed tonight, of all nights. He wanted to remember *everything*. So he sl-o-wly sipped his cosmopolitans and watched the courting rituals going on all around him, the coy gavottes and the lusty flamencos that accelerated into fevered dervishes as the final call drew nearer. He felt something close to pity, especially for the ones who tried to engage him in eye contact: Poor, sad schmucks. If only they knew whom he was going home with tonight!

When the lights went up and the last stragglers were turned out (some finally pairing up literally as they passed through the door), Corey was left alone in the sudden, silent brightness, and it was like a bucket of cold water in the face; the little realm he thought he knew so well, this tiled terrain of murky, musky manhunting, stood revealed in an entirely new aspect: a drab little industrial-looking box. (And not, alas, scrupulously clean.)

When Kent reappeared he'd donned a shirt over his trademark tee, had slicked back his hair, and was wearing an expensive watch—one of those gaudy, bulky gold ones you saw on people like Donald Trump. Corey arched an eyebrow.

More surprises were to come, as Kent led him out back to his car: this year's Audi convertible. The top was down, and as Kent pulled into the alley and sailed towards the street, heedless of stray cats or pissing bums, Corey felt the air whip deliciously through his hair.

"Feeling any better yet?" Kent asked as they sailed up Halsted Street.

"Mmm," said Corey luxuriously. "I could get used to this."

"World gets you down, nothing beats bein' kissed by the wind."

"Believe me, I'm sold."

Kent placed a hand on Corey's thigh. "So what's the trouble anyway?"

Corey sighed. "It's complicated," he said, wanting to confide in Kent, but not wanting to begin some whining litany lest he ruin the mood. "Comes down to being twenty-six and not having much going on."

Kent gave his thigh a squeeze. "Hey, listen. I've been there. Believe me, it gets better. My life's been fucking *golden* since I turned thirty. I wouldn't go back for anything."

"You're *thirty?*"

"Thirty-one," he said, sliding his hand a little farther up Corey's leg. "Just trust me, kid. It'll work out for you. You *do* got it goin' on. Fact is, I've had my eye on you for months now."

Corey turned to him in surprise. "You never said anything."

"Never had the chance." He tucked his hand into the fold between Corey's leg and crotch. "You were always on a mission. Couple of drinks, a few friendly words, then *wham,* I'd see you hustlin' some hottie out the door."

"I guess I can't deny it." He smiled. "Nice to be the hustlee for a change."

Kent gave Corey's growing tumescence an appreciative grope. "Yeah, I can tell it agrees with you."

They ended up pulling over about ten blocks on and engaging in some serious face-mashing; but they were soon snapped out of it by catcalls from a group of ski-capped youths on the sidewalk just beyond. Flushed and excited, Kent sat up, adjusted his cock and balls, then grabbed the wheel and roared back into traffic.

He escorted Corey to a sleepy neighborhood in Old Irving Park, then down an alley and into a dark, warm garage. When they got out of the car they immediately lashed into each other again, but after bumping several yard implements off their hooks they regained control and headed for the house.

As soon as Corey saw it, across the moon-silvered lawn, his jaw dropped. "You live *here?*" he asked, as he eyed the charming little bungalow.

Kent took him by the hand and led him toward it. "It ain't much," he said, "but it's home."

It may not have been much to him, but to Corey—who didn't know *anyone* who didn't live in a cluttered apartment—even this humble little cottage seemed palatial. The notion of walls that weren't shared was extravagant beyond belief to him. He imagined hearing no one else's music . . . smelling no one else's cooking . . .

And then, inside. The first thing that struck him was the acrid odor of ciagarette smoke—worse even than at the bar. Which was strange, because he didn't figure Kent for a smoker. But this thought was quickly dislodged by the sight of all the furniture on display. Even in the dark, he could discern its tasteful silhouettes—could see that it was all arranged as though actual adult human beings might really live here, and host other human beings for activities other than fucking. He felt as though he'd suddenly been phased into another dimension . . . one that existed adjacent to his own, and had been invisible to him till now.

But that's all the time he had for observation, as the biological imperative overwhelmed his curiosity. Within minutes, he and Kent had tumbled into a bedroom, stripped naked, and begun devouring each other like hyenas.

When their carnal ferocity at last exhausted itself, Corey lay on the bed beside Kent, who seemed by the tenor of his breathing to be lightly drowsing, and wondered what was expected of him now. Ordinarily he'd get up, get dressed, and either walk home or hail a cab. But walking was impossible at this far a remove from civilization; likewise, he couldn't afford a cab, even if he could manage to find one in this eerily quiet residential nook. Easier just to stay where he was; but he wasn't entirely comfortable spending the night. He'd never been very good at morning-after chitchat, and was especially shy of having to do this with Kent, whose lifestyle was so vastly, incomparably beyond his own.

Was this what it meant to be a bartender? . . . Your own house, a flashy car, a thousand-dollar watch, and who knew what else? . . . And it wasn't as though Kent had gone to seed, either. God knows the man was still sizzling hot. And over thirty! Maybe there was hope after all. Perhaps Corey had been too quick to dismiss bartending as a career. He could actually see himself living this kind of life. And it wasn't as though he was qualified to do very much else.

He wondered how long it had taken Kent to get this far. Well, maybe that was something he could ask him in the morning, as they sat down to poached eggs or Cream of Wheat or whatever people who lived in actual houses ate for breakfast. Maybe Kent could even be his mentor, and he could repay him with services rendered. Kind of like the way he'd heard it was in ancient Greece, where older guys would shepherd younger ones into manhood in return for a little ass.

His mind meandered along these lines a while longer, and such happy thoughts might even have wafted him off to sleep . . . but alas, as the effects of alcohol and sexual adrenaline ebbed away, he was left with the return of the sharp pain in his side, as well as the urgent call of a full bladder. He got up, winced in discomfort, and made his way toward the door, arms extended like antennae lest he walk into anything unexpected.

The hallway was even darker than the bedroom. He felt his way along the wall, assuming that he'd soon come to a door, and that the door would open onto a bathroom. And indeed his fingers did eventually ripple across a doorframe, upon which discovery he dropped his hands and fumbled for the knob, then noisily turned it and swung open the door.

Immediately, something didn't feel right. He couldn't see a thing, but he could *hear* too much space for a bathroom; the silence resonated too expansively. Also, the stench of cigarette smoke was very much stronger here. Still, he couldn't be absolutely certain it wasn't a loo till he checked, so he groped for the light switch, and when he found it, flicked it on.

What stood revealed was in fact *not* a bathroom; it was another bedroom. And in the bed lay an old woman, her hair in curlers, her face alert with fright, the covers pulled up under her chin, and the whole of her trembling with terror.

"Whoops," said Corey.

The woman began to bleat like a sheep. Corey was momentarily mystified, till he realized that this was how screaming must sound after decades and decades of a three-pack-a-day habit.

Suddenly Kent was by his side, frantically tying a robe around his waist. He jerked Corey out of the doorway, looked in and muttered, "Sorry, Ma," then closed the door gently and heaved a weary sigh.

Corey said, "I was just looking for the bathroom."

Kent, somehow managing to look both distracted *and*

numb, said, "This way," and gently pushed him in the opposite direction.

After a few paces, Corey looked up at him and said,
"You live with your mother?"

Kent let slip a disdainful chuckle. "What, you think I can
afford a house of my own? I'm a goddamn *bartender* . . ."

Chapter 18

Later that day Corey got a call from his friend Tyler, who said, "Are you all right? I just heard you were in a car accident."

Corey sighed over his lack of privacy. "You talked to Frida, right?"

"No, I heard it from Sam."

"Who's Sam?"

"The guy in my Pilates class? . . . The one you picked up two years ago?"

"*That* guy? *He* knows I was in an accident?" God, Frida must've told the whole town."

"He said you're hurt."

"Well, I *did* get thrown off my bike. But I think I just pulled a muscle in my side."

"So you're okay?"

"Basically. It still hurts a lot, except when I drink."

"But I mean, otherwise . . . I was just worried, is all."

"I'm sorry. I should've called, I guess." He had an idea. "What are you doing tonight? You free for dinner?" Tyler always picked up the check; it was a lingering habit from seven years earlier, when he'd had a mad crush on Corey and done everything possible to please him.

"I'm free, sure," Tyler said, but there was an edge of hesitation in his voice.

"So . . . we're on, then?"

A pause. "I guess I could. I'd like to. I'm just a little strapped for cash."

Corey felt his dinner slipping away. "We could go someplace cheap," he said, grasping to keep hold of it.

"All right, then. La Bocca?"

Corey blinked. That's what Tyler considered cheap? . . . La Bocca della Verita was Corey's idea of *swank*. "Perfect. I'll make the rezzy for eight." This had always been Corey's sad little fiction: that by phoning the restaurant and reserving a table, he was making a contribution equal to Tyler's picking up the check.

He was late arriving, because he'd forgotten that his bike had been stolen and he'd have to walk all the way to Lincoln and Wilson. Tyler had already been seated at a table outside on the sidewalk, and had broken into a bottle of wine. As Corey approached, he stood to greet him—and kept standing, higher and higher, till he'd folded out to his full six feet and four inches. He enveloped Corey in a hug—which, given Tyler's bony, gangly frame, was sort of like being embraced by a coat rack—and then the two friends sat down.

"Have a little liquid painkiller," said Tyler, filling a new glass with a lovely auburn Brunello.

"Mm, thanks," said Corey, and, taking it up with a nod, he added, "cheers." He swallowed a mouthful, then said, "But the pain's not so much an issue right now. I took a Vicodin before I left the house."

Tyler sat back, his mouth open. "Okay, so I guess we should talk while you still can."

"It's just one pill," he protested, a little petulantly.

"One pill *plus* the wine," Tyler sneered. "So you're self-medicating?"

"Nnnno," he said, as if to an idiot. *"Frida* is medicating me."

"Oh, *well,* then, that's all right." This wasn't going well. They'd only just sat down, and already they'd lapsed into a tiff. But he couldn't really blame Tyler; he'd been the only one to stand by Corey during the worst of his crystal crisis, when it hadn't been remotely easy to be his friend.

Fortunately the waiter chose this moment to check in. He was young and olive-skinned, with coral blue eyes and squid-ink hair. Both Corey and Tyler sat up a little straighter at his arrival.

"Good eefening, gentlemen," he said. Hint of a Mittle-european accent. *Even better,* thought Corey. *Means uncut.* "Can I tell you about tonight's specials?"

"You can if you want," said Tyler, "but we know what we're having." They always ordered exactly the same meal every time they came here; it was one of their little rituals.

"Ferry good," said the waiter, and he poised his pen over his pad. "Wheneffer you're ready."

"We'll split the carpaccio, and then we'll both have the ravioli anatra."

"Ferrrry good," he repeated more deliberately as he jotted this down. Then, with one quick yet telling glance at Corey—eye contact established!—he sauntered off again. Tyler—poor, gangly, jug-eared Tyler—watched him go with undisguised longing.

Now that the tension had been broken, Corey decided to start over with a new topic—one which was of no small interest to him. "So you say you're strapped for cash?"

Tyler sighed. "Yeah. Pain in the ass."

Corey raised his glass to him. "Join the club," he said. "Haven't got two nickels to rub together."

"It's a special feeling," he agreed as they clinked glasses.

"So, what's the problem?" Corey asked after a mouthful of wine. It was a lovely vintage, warm and full, and he was feeling expansive. Misery really *did* love company. "They not paying you enough?"

"Hm? . . . Oh, no. Everything's fine there. Got a raise, even. And a staff."

This caught Corey by surprise. Tyler worked in the human resources department of a medical supply company—something which struck Corey as so crushingly, stupefyingly dull that he'd never really asked him much about it, or listened very attentively when he spoke of it. He'd always just assumed it was a grunt job, like the ones Corey himself always seemed to land. But if he'd been given a raise . . . and a *staff* . . .

"Just two people," Tyler added now, as if reading his mind. "But they both report to me, so . . ." He trailed off with a shrug.

Corey absorbed the shock; then he told himself that in some ways, this actually made things more reassuring. If Tyler, working steady and earning serious wages, could find himself hard up, then Corey could scarcely be too severe on himself for being in the exact same predicament. His equanimity restored, he said, "So, job's fine then. What's the problem?"

"I'm buying a new condo," said Tyler with a scowl. "In fact I close Thursday of next week. But the thing is—"

"Whoa, whoa, *whoa,*" said Corey. "You're buying a *new* condo? . . . I thought you *rented.*"

Tyler shook his head. "I swear, Corey, meth just wiped your memory clean. I bought my place *five years* ago. With the bequest from my grandfather's will, remember?"

There was a brief flicker in the gaseous murk of Corey's addled recall. "I think maybe I do," he said. "Just."

"Anyway, I've got a buyer for the place, but she doesn't have financing yet. Which means I have to close on my new place before I've actually sold the old one. Which means I won't have the *funds* for the new one yet, so I have to take out what's called a bridge loan, to cover the interim period. And, I mean, I don't know how long that's going to be. And the interest, it just keeps climbing the longer the loan goes. If my buyer doesn't get her ducks in a row soon, this could really end up costing me. It's a bite in the buttocks, I'll tell ya. I'm losing sleep."

Corey had lifted his wine to his lips, but not drunk any; he was frozen in place, as though hit by a whammy. This was so vastly—so *incomparably*—different from his own financial complaint that any fellowship he might've felt had not just evaporated, it had pretty much exploded. He didn't even understand what Tyler was *talking* about.

He slowly put the glass down and tried to collect his thoughts. "When," he said, and he realized his voice was about an octave higher than it should be. *"When,"* he began again, lowering it to a more suitable baritone, "did you even start *looking* for a new place? You never said a word to *me* about it."

A flash of guilt crossed Tyler's face. "I know, I know," he said. "It was just a whim. I got myself a Realtor and started checking out what was on the market. Fell in love with the first place he showed me. Crazy, I know, but I put in a bid, and the seller accepted it. So here I am, buying it, and a month ago I wasn't even *thinking* of moving."

Corey started to feel dizzy. He'd been installed in his grimy little garden apartment for eight years now. The idea of moving even his few worldly goods out of it was huge beyond his capacity to imagine. That Tyler—who'd accumulated much more than he ever had—would treat all this in so light a fashion, making Olympian decisions on the spur of the moment, and juggling vast sums of money—money that existed only on paper, money he'd never even *see*—it was all too much.

Corey had always regarded Tyler as something of a sidekick. Years earlier, when they used to do the town, trawling the clubs and bars and discos together, Tyler had hero-worshipped him. That was because wherever he went, he'd been the object of attention and desire, even of outright competition between would-be suitors, while Tyler—awkward, pipe-cleaner-limbed Tyler—had looked on in abject devotion. Corey had never had any reason to think that would change. And yet here they were, Tyler having crossed some invisible boundary, quietly undergoing some rite of passage that Corey, in his indolence and pleasure-seeking, had clean missed.

He cleared his throat and said, with great difficulty, "Tell me about the new place." He just wanted to get Tyler on a talking jag, so that he could nod politely and pretend to listen while secretly reevaluating his entire life.

Tyler was only too glad to comply. "Oh, it's *gorgeous*," he enthused. "Big, long railway apartment, turn of the last century. Eight rooms, three bedrooms, one's going to be a home office . . . are you listening?"

"Hm?" Corey had caught sight of their waiter, who was just approaching with a plate of carpaccio. *That's ours*, he thought. *And he's mine*. He straightened up again and said, "Yes, of course. Go on."

"It's on the top floor," Tyler resumed, "so there's a skylight in the kitchen and the master bathroom." The waiter arrived at the table and placed the carpaccio between them. "Cathedral ceiling in the living room that opens onto a teak deck . . . I'm gonna put a big Weber grill out there, for summer. Master bath has a sauna . . ." He trailed to a halt and looked up at the waiter, who still loomed over them.

"Fresh pepper?" the waiter asked.

"Mm," said Tyler.

As he worked the grinder over the carpaccio, the waiter said, "That your new place you're talking about?"

"Well—as of next week, it's mine."

"Sounds luffly," he said, withdrawing the grinder and flashing Tyler a flirtatious smile. "You're really *bait* now."

"Oh, go on," said Tyler, blushing.

The waiter shook his head. "No, I'm serious. Nothing sexier than real estate." He paused. "Anything else I can get you gentlemen?"

"Not right now, no," said Tyler, still blushing.

After beaming one last smile at Tyler, the waiter melted away.

He hadn't looked at Corey even once.

Chapter 19

The *ravioli all'anatra*—being duck ravioli in a cream sauce—was sufficiently decadent to send Corey to the gym next day. He'd slacked off since his accident, but he couldn't do so forever; already he felt a slight thickening in his waist, and wasn't about to allow himself to bloat. So it was time to get back in the saddle.

In recent months he'd had to give up his membership in the pricey men's gym to which he'd belonged since moving to Chicago, and instead take his workouts for cheap at the YMCA. The change had deeply affected him. From prowling the low-ceilinged, testosterone-infused atmosphere of the Uptown Gym & Sauna, he'd been reduced to ambling behind tired old non-English-speaking men in dingy T-shirts, waiting for his two minutes on ancient Nautilus machines.

Today, however, his two minutes were reduced to approximately two seconds. He'd no sooner settled himself into the vertical press and attempted to push its weight bar away from him, than his torn muscle blinded him with a vivid splash of agony. It seemed he must have cried out, because when he looked up all other eyes in the room were turned on him, and some bloodhound-faced man in black socks and flip flops asked if he was okay.

No less frustrated than humiliated, he retired to the showers, but there was little to console him there. In the old days, he'd liked to finish his workouts with a refreshing communal grope in the steam room; but the only men who ever used the steam room here looked as though they'd died in it, and not recently.

He showered, changed, and headed home, not even minding that it took him twice as long to walk as it had to go by bike. He had no place he needed to be, nowhere he even wanted to be; he was, he realized, becoming one of those lost men you often saw on city streets, shuffling along without purpose, eyes focused on something entirely internal, unaware of wind or rain or the jeers of children, and trailing an aroma made offensive less by the stench of perspiration than by that of despair.

When he reached his building he found Ignacio in the lobby, emptying his mailbox. Corey gave a little sigh of exasperation; he never liked running into Ignacio—the man was well past thirty, increasingly obsessed with preserving what youth he had left, and possessed of the nervous air of someone who doesn't really believe he exists unless someone, *any*one, is looking at him. He'd also, unfortunately, taken a lascivious interest in Corey and never lost an opportunity to pester him with sophomoric innuendos, which Corey supposed was his clumsy way of coming on to him.

Ignacio stood at attention as Corey came in, and put on a maddening little smirk. "Well! Hel-*lo*, stranger. Who you been up to?"

"Morning, Ignacio," said Corey, bypassing his own mailbox. There'd only be bills he couldn't pay, and those could just sit there, for all he cared.

"Don't *you* sound worn out, honey?" Ignacio said. "Someone keep you up all night? . . . And if not, are you taking applications?"

"I'm fine," said Corey, inserting the key in the vestibule door.

"Or maybe," said Ignacio, undeterred, "you're a little put out by the news. I know *I* am."

Corey had by this time cracked open the door and was ready to push his way through. *Don't ask,* he admonished himself; *just don't ask.* But he heard himself say, "What news?"

Ignacio couldn't have been more pleased at halting him in his tracks. He grinned like a cat who'd cornered a sluggish mouse. "Oh, you haven't seen it yet? . . . They slipped a letter under everybody's door. Probably did it just after you went out."

Corey wasn't about to beg to be told. "Well, I'll just go up and read it, then," he said, and he swung the door open and passed through.

"Building's going condo," Ignacio called after him.

He turned, and stuck out a foot to keep the door from swinging shut again. "What?"

Ignacio nodded vigorously. "Been sold to a developer," he said. "We're all being sent packing."

"How long?" Corey asked, not even caring that resignation and defeat colored his voice.

"They're doing the rehab in stages," was the reply. "Starting with the front units. So unfortunately, you're first out." He smiled. "Me, I'm in the back, so I've basically got all summer. Tell you what, if you have trouble finding a new place, you can come crash with me. For however long it takes." He actually darted his tongue over his lips.

And it was the measure of Corey's complete surrender to the bludgeoning of fate that he said, "Thanks. I'll keep that in mind." And that he meant it.

He trudged down the short flight of stairs to his apartment, unlocked the door, and entered. Knowing he would soon be forced out, he looked at the place as if for the first time.

He'd often joked that it was just one step up from a crack

den; but by any objective measure, that was exactly on target. Its carpeting was stained and mildewed, its walls discolored and flaking, its ceiling warped and bowed. His furniture was nothing more than a ragtag assemblage of his friends' college castoffs. The couch, for instance, had been Tyler's; he remembered joking, as he took it from him, "Maybe now these cushions'll see some action!" But the joke was on him; for now Tyler was talking about his cathedral ceiling and his teak deck, and it had been a long time since the couch had seen any "action" beyond spills from salsa jars.

The plain fact was, Corey hadn't had anyone back here in more than a year—had avoided it, he now realized, because he was embarrassed by the place. Everything in it was chipped or peeling or stained or torn; there were no books and only a few CDs, all gone rogue from their jewel cases, scratched and smudged and carelessly strewn atop a clumsy stereo system that hailed from deep in the last century. The kitchen was bereft of cookware, utensils, anything that might mark a dwelling as being civilized, not savage. The whole place was squalid; it was a hovel.

And he now found himself in the unenviable position of seeing it for what it was, while at the same time realizing it was all he had. He'd devoted his life to a chimera: to sexual pleasure, the most fleeting of all diversions. He'd poured years' worth of care and labor into both his person and his persona, turning his flesh into an irresistible vehicle for desire, his manner into an open invitation. He'd cavorted, he'd frolicked, he'd made a profession of promiscuity. He'd given himself over to the never-ending chase, not caring that whenever he caught what he was after, he held it but a moment before it slipped from his grasp. And here he was, after a decade of his single-minded pursuit, left with nothing but lurid memories.

He had no education; he had no career; he had no money, no property, no assets, no hope. He'd lost his job, his apartment, his only means of transport, and all of his illusions. He sat on the couch—on the jetsam of someone else's discarded life—and faced, for the first time, the sheer yawning abyss of his life. Its depth was profound, and he was caught in it, and there was no way out.

Or . . .

. . . or *was* there?

Did it matter, now that he'd abandoned everything else, whether he sacrificed his last scrap of self-respect? . . . Could he, now that he'd been cast so low, bring himself to do what he wouldn't even consider mere days ago?

He went to his desk—"desk," he now noted, being his delusional term for the rusting card table atop which he dumped his mail, receipts, spare change, and his second-hand laptop—and sorted through the scattered bits of paper till he found it.

He picked it up and looked at it; fine ivory stock with, he now noticed, raised characters. *Quality.*

JOHN G. ACKERLY, it read. And then a phone number.

No title, no company name, no cell or e-mail or other contact info. He felt a spasm of anxiety in his stomach. Could he really bring himself to confront the kind of man who was so utterly self-confident, so beyond the need to boast of affiliation or constant availability, that he would hand out a card like this?

He dialed the phone and held it to his ear. With each ring, he found himself hoping there'd be no answer . . . or failing that, that the connection would default to voice mail, and he could hang up with impunity.

"Hello?" said a deep male voice.

Corey cleared his throat. "Um," he said. "Hi. Is this John G. Ackerly?"

A pause. "This is Jack Ackerly. Who's calling?"

"Oh right, I—uh—this is Corey Szaslow? I know you don't know me—well, you do, but not my . . ." He was babbling. He took a breath and started over. "I'm the guy who you hit.

With your car? The guy on the bike? . . . Anyway, you said if I needed anything, I should call you. Well, it turns out, okay, I know I said I was all right, but I was a little premature." *Premature.* Corey patted himself on the back for pulling that word out of thin air. "Turns out I'm actually, uh, I actually need some medical attention and some, uh, some other consequences, that . . ." Damn, he should've rehearsed this. Would he never learn? He let the sentence die and forged ahead. "I'm calling because I don't have insurance or anything and I can't afford any treatment, so—so what I'm asking is, I'm wondering if you'll be as good as your word. If you'll help me out." The tone of his voice had gotten progressively more pleading; he thought he'd better stop while he was ahead.

There was a long pause. Then Jack Ackerly said, "Certainly I'll honor my word. You wouldn't be in any difficulty if it weren't for me, so I'd be only too happy to help you out of it." Another pause, this one slighter. "Do you have a figure in mind?"

Of course Corey didn't have a figure in mind. Corey never had a figure in mind. Frantically he tried to imagine what kind of sum he could reasonably extort from this guy that would get him not only a doctor's care, but a new apartment, possibly a new bike, and a little money to live on as well . . . Was three grand too much? Would he balk at that? Or was the guy so decent—he certainly *seemed* to be—or possibly so afraid of being sued, that he'd go as high as five or six? Even *ten?*

"I don't know," Corey said. "Um—can I get back to you?"

"By all means." Another pause. "Although . . ."

Uh-oh. He'd been found out. Somehow, Jack Ackerly had heard the blatant desperation in his voice. "Although . . . what?"

"I wonder if you'd be willing to discuss a more . . . permanent arrangement with me."

Corey blinked. *What the hell?* . . . "I don't know what you're talking about."

"No, of course you don't. There's no way you could. But . . . if I told you there may be a way for you to end your money troubles for good, would you be interested in hearing about it?"

Corey blinked again. "Does it involve something kinky?"

Jack Ackerly laughed. "I wouldn't call it kinky, no. A bit out of the ordinary, certainly."

Corey frowned. He could easily have handled kinky. That it was something else put him back on shaky ground. "Well . . . I guess I'd be willing to *hear* about it."

"All right, then! When are you free to meet . . . ?"

Part Three

Jack, Corey

Chapter 20

"So, that's it," said Jack. "I know it all sounds a little unorthodox, if not plain crazy, and like I said, I doubt it'll even work. It's just an experiment—a kind of therapy, really. I'm trying to work through some issues. I don't expect you to understand fully . . . but, I, uh . . ."

His throat dried up and he had to abandon the sentence. The boy, Corey, sat across from him, utterly stone-faced. What was he feeling? . . . Fear? Scorn? Pity? Panic?

Finally, he spoke. "So, it's sort of like the Vulcan mind meld?"

Jack blinked. "I'm sorry?"

"On *Star Trek,* when Spock puts his fingers on a dude's temples, and he gets this major flood of his memories? . . . Sort of like that, only it's both ways, and it *sticks?*"

Jack considered this a moment. "Not too far off, I guess."

"Soooo . . . I'd be you, and you'd be me. Is that it?" His tone was completely neutral. Jack couldn't read him at all.

"Yes. As I said earlier, you'd take over my life as Jack Ackerly. You'd inhabit my body, live in my apartment, and have access to all my goods and assets—with the exception of some funds I'd transfer over to your name, so that I'd have something to live on when I took over *your* life."

Corey remained impassive, and after a lengthy silence said, "I'd be *you,* then. I'd be *old.*"

Jack winced, but immediately recovered. "Wellll . . . you'd be fifty-three." He paused. "Fifty-three and *rich.*"

Corey sat back in the overstuffed chair and sighed; even so, he wasn't showing his hand. Jack had absolutely no idea what was going on in his head.

He took another sip of his vodka-and-tonic. He'd invited Corey to meet him at Four Seasons' bar—wanting, he supposed, to confine as much as possible of the narrative of this semi-sordid pursuit to a single location. That way, if it all came crashing down around him, as seemed likely, he'd only have this one spot to avoid thereafter, to keep from being reminded of the entire embarrassing affair.

He took advantage of the conversational lull to give Corey another sizing up. The boy was a bit older than he'd have liked; he guessed twenty-six, twenty-seven. And while undeniably handsome, and in very fine shape—his tight T-shirt showed off his ripped abs, and his shorts his sculpted calf muscles—he seemed a shade . . . well . . . *seedy.* It was something in his ice-blue eyes; something in his manner . . . and, yes, now that he'd had a second look, something very subtle about the look of him. His cheekbones, for instance, were ideally pronounced; but the sunken cheeks beneath them seemed to owe less to diet and discipline than to incipient destitution.

But that wasn't necessarily a bad thing. Jack realized that the only type of young man who would agree to his proposition, was one who really *had* hit rock bottom—who had nothing to lose. He couldn't help wondering what had brought Corey so low; after all, the boy was handsome, articulate, in good shape, fairly well-mannered, and possessed of no small degree of self-confidence. Jack had spotted him the moment he entered the bar, and seen his look of momentary dismay as he realized just how much he was underdressed; a look which subsequently transformed itself into steely resolve as he set his jaw, straightened his spine, and strode on in, brazening it out.

Their introduction had been terse; the boy had a firm handshake and a wary eye. Jack, nervous himself, had waited only to order drinks before plunging into the matter at hand, sensing that Corey didn't have the patience to wait through the usual conversational preambles.

Explaining his proposition, Jack again became aware of how absurd it all sounded when spoken aloud. Never mind, this was the last of it; after tonight, he would pursue this folly no further. He'd actually already given it up, after his last humiliating visit to this very bar; but Corey's phone call, several days later, had seemed to be fate dangling one last chance at him—as though having tested his forbearance, and now rewarding it.

Corey shifted in his chair and grunted a little, then put his bottle of beer on the table and said, "I just have one question." He looked Jack in the eye and said, *"Why?"*

Jack nodded; he'd anticipated this. "Personal reasons," he said. "I'd prefer to leave it at that. Though it shouldn't be too hard to imagine why someone my age would want to be young again."

"Way I see it," said Corey, "you're healthy, you're rich, you still look pretty good," and here Jack felt himself blush at the unexpected compliment, "and I'm presuming you don't have some kind of fatal disease or whatever . . ."

"No, of course not," Jack interjected. "I'm not trying to sell you tainted goods." Then, muttering: "Well, a few nasty allergies, but other than that . . ."

"Right, then; you've got a perfect life. You've got everything. So, big deal, you're old. I mean, what the hell. Everybody gets old."

Jack grimaced. He hadn't counted on being grilled by this kid. "I know that. But I feel . . . like I've *always* been old."

Corey cocked his head, as though unable to understand this.

"I was always in a hurry, see," he explained. "Couldn't wait to make a name for myself, forge a career, build a business, make an impact. I wanted power, I wanted authority—all right, yes, I wanted money, too. And I went after them with all the zeal of youth. But that's the *only* way I was ever youthful. I never . . . well, to put it plainly, I never had any fun."

Corey lifted his jaw, as though reappraising him. "Ah."

"I don't mean, like, skiing holidays or anything . . ."

"I know," said Corey. "You mean fucking."

Jack blushed again. "Well . . . yes and no."

"How 'no'?"

He shifted in his seat. "All right, *yes,* then. But . . . I mean, just saying 'fucking' . . ." He actually lowered his voice while pronouncing the word, and Corey gave him a superior smile. ". . . it's so reductive. What I'm talking about is the feeling of limitless possibility; the chance for endless renewal, the feeling that every man you meet is a potential new world to conquer . . ."

Corey raised an eyebrow. "Oh, you're gay?"

Jack was brought up short. He'd grown so accustomed to having everyone know this about him that it seemed odd to have to confirm it. "Yes; I would've thought that was obvious."

Corey shrugged. "My gaydar's a little off for guys your age. Though now that I think about it . . . the Gucci loafers with no socks was pretty much a giveaway."

"I'm not wearing Gucci loafers."

"You were when I first met you. When you hit me."

Jack cocked an eyebrow. In the immediate aftermath of a disorienting, potentially crippling accident, this boy had noticed his designer shoes. There seemed no reason now to ask if *he* was gay. Which was a load off Jack's mind. He suspected that even the most desperately needy heterosexual would think twice about selling his body if he knew it would be used for the seduction of other men—in the same way certain people are loath to sell their houses to a buyer who wants to gut the kitchen and dining room.

"Be that as it may," Jack said, trying to return to the subject; alas, he found he couldn't remember what it was. "What were we just talking about?"

Corey shrugged. "Doesn't matter." Scooting forward, he sat on the edge of the seat and said, "Look, boss, you seem like a standup guy. I mean . . . I don't have any psychopath alarms going off in my head, and believe me, the life I've led? . . . I've had to develop a *serious* early-warning system. Matter of fact, you seem kind of . . ." He groped for the right word. ". . . well, don't take this the wrong way, but, sad."

"*Sad?*" Jack blurted, surprised and a little offended.

"Step out of yourself a minute," Corey said. "Give yourself the once-over from where I sit. Then tell me I'm wrong." Jack's jaw hung open; he couldn't think of a reply, and Corey blazed ahead. "I'm just saying—well, I can't really give you an answer now. Because, like, what you've just told me is so freakin' looney tunes that my first instinct is to cut and run. But, like I said, you're an okay guy. You've got sincere eyes."

"I do?"

Corey nodded. "So, there's this, like, total disconnect between the way you come across, and the crazy shit you're talking here. And, okay, I can't lie, it's true I've driven my life into the ground, and the idea of jumping ship to some kind of millionaire existence that's already up and running is pretty goddamn appealing. Even if it means doubling my age. But, I mean . . . not being *me* anymore? . . . How the hell do I even start to think about that?" Jack began to speak, but Corey held up a hand and said, "No, boss, wait; I'm just saying, meeting you has been the weirdest fucking thing that's ever happened to me, which, believe me, is saying something. I'm not even a hundred percent sure I should still be talking to you. So I want some time to think about it."

Jack turned his palms up in submission. "Absolutely. I never expected you to make a snap decision."

"Just two things, though: first, I'd like to get some medical attention. *Before* I make up my mind." He gestured towards his black-and-blue knee.

"Of course," said Jack. "I'll set you up with my G.P. Get you fixed right up." *And ready for me to move in,* he thought.

"Second," Corey continued, "you say this whole crazy scheme probably won't even work. Yeah, well, no kidding. But, okay—what happens then? If your witch pal craps out on you, do I just get sent home with a thank-you and a handshake? Seems to me if I'm willing to do this, I should get something out of it, whether it goes down as planned or not."

Jack nodded. "Like I said, just before the . . . uh, procedure . . ." He wasn't brave enough, even now, to say *spell*. ". . . I'd transfer a significant sum of money into your bank account, with the idea that that'd be what I'd live on once I became you. But if I *didn't* become you, the money would still be there, under your name. I wouldn't be able to reclaim it. So it'd be yours to keep. How does that sound, as a consolation prize?"

Corey looked at him sideways. "How much is 'a significant sum'?"

Jack bobbed his head back and forth and said, "Oh, four, five hundred grand. I'd have to see what was liquid at the time."

Corey stared at him for what seemed a very long time. Then he took a deep breath, stood up, and said, "Right, nice meeting you," and extended his arm.

"Pleasure's mine," said Jack, shaking his hand. "And listen, I'll give you a call as soon as I've set up a date with my doctor."

Corey nodded, a bit glassy-eyed. He turned, blinked a few times as if readjusting his vision, then headed out of the bar.

Sharp kid, thought Jack as he signaled the waiter for the check. And the thought was a comforting one. He wouldn't relish the idea of handing over his body to some clueless idiot. Corey might lack business acumen in the strictest sense, but he had cunning; he had an instinct for survival.

Jack was struck by how seriously he was suddenly taking all this, and immediately he was assailed by conflicting reactions—hope and scorn, elation and dismay, alarm and dismissal—largely expressed in repeated volleys of the simple interrogatives, "What if this doesn't work?" and "What if it does?"

He decided that since Fate had dealt the hand, he'd let Fate play it out, and made a serious effort to debate the thing no further.

This was easier resolved than done; but he found playing the stereo in his car very, very loudly was a help.

Chapter 21

One June afternoon when Corey was eight, he lay propped on his arm on the living room floor watching an episode of *Doctor Who*. During one of the talky parts he sat up to shake his arm, which had gone tingly, and noticed his mother seated on the sofa. She was wearing her coat, which was strange. She patted the spot next to her and dutifully he got up and went to join her. He stretched out across the cushions and lay his head in her lap, and while she stroked his hair he brought her up to speed on the story, filling her in on the motivations of the various characters and describing in no uncertain terms what he would have done to make the whole production "less fakey." She listened quietly, speaking only once. Eventually her gentle stroking rendered him drowsy, and he fell silent and stared at the television in a kind of trance. This was broken only when his Aunt Ginger entered the room sobbing, and told him that his mother had been killed in a car wreck while out running errands. Corey said, "But she's right here," then sat up and saw that he was lying there all alone.

The memory of that day, that moment, had never left him. And it was why, against all reason, he wasn't more skeptical of what Jack Ackerly had proposed to him. He knew—he had seen for himself—that there was an uncanny flipside to

cold reality. And while Jack had stressed that the "procedure" probably wouldn't even work, Corey wasn't so sure.
He had a healthy respect for the paranormal and suspected
that Jack did likewise, and that his repeated disclaimers to
the contrary were more an attempt to convince himself,
rather than Corey, that he was still a rational man.

So while Corey was elated by the idea of signing on for
some kind of voodoo ceremony and having it fizzle, leaving
him hundreds of thousands of dollars richer and yet still
himself, he didn't dare depend on it. If he went forward
with this bizarre arrangement, he'd have to be prepared to
accept the intended consequences: that at the end of it, he
would be permanently lodged in someone else's skin. He
tried to imagine no longer being young . . . no longer being
himself . . . and he couldn't. It defeated all his powers of
conjuration.

To be sure, the idea of becoming Jack Ackerly wasn't so
horrid in itself. The man wasn't unattractive; he seemed extremely well preserved, and what signs there were of age
came across more as distinguished seasoning than encroach-
ing decrepitude.

And then there were Jack's millions; certainly *they* added
to his appeal. But they were also problematic. Corey had
gotten to know himself very well in the past few years, and
one of the more unpleasant things he'd learned was that he
was deeply susceptible to addictive behaviors. To make it
worse, he was also a world-class rationalizer. How would
such an excessive character as his respond to never having
to say no? . . . If he was honest with himself, he'd have to
admit that one of the major factors in beating his meth
habit was simply not being able to afford it anymore. What
if that were no longer an issue? . . . What if there were no
longer a risk of hitting bottom, because he was so goddamn
high up that "bottom" wasn't even a concept anymore?

He sighed and looked out the window. He was on the el,
riding home as the sun sank spectacularly, hurling bolts of

scarlet and orange skyward like cries for help. But he was too inwardly focused to notice any of it. He repositioned himself on the hard plastic seat; the way the damn thing was designed, it was impossible to get comfortable. And this moment of torture led him to set aside his fears and think, *On the other hand . . .*

He imagined a lifetime—a shortened lifetime, to be sure—of riding only in cabs. Or better yet, limousines. Or putting himself behind the wheel of whatever monstrously expensive German sports car caught his fancy that month. He imagined dining out every night, ordering anything he liked from the menu and not even looking at the price. He imagined traveling, cavorting through London, Paris, Prague . . . skiing at Gstaad, sunning at Ibiza. He imagined having a whole closet filled with this season's couture: Prada, Versace, Dolce & Gabbana . . .

But this last thought brought him back to the crux of the matter—since the back on which those clothes would rest wouldn't be *his*.

With a little freeform symphony of shrieks and squeals, the train pulled up to his stop. He grabbed a pole and swung himself up to his feet and then through the hissing doors, all in one fluid motion.

He crossed the platform. The air was still warm, and he felt his skin prickle. Suddenly his stomach began to fuss and kick, like an infant newly awakened, and he realized he was quite hungry. True, he'd snarfed down nearly an entire dish of mixed nuts at the bar, Jack having nibbled only a few before noticing Corey's ravenousness, after which he'd sat back and let Corey have it all (another reason Corey had judged him a standup guy). But now he badly needed some more substantial fare.

He trudged down the steps onto Irving Park Road. He was tired, and he still had nearly a mile to walk. Suddenly the sheer, grinding *want* of his daily life bore down on him, and he wondered how he could possibly turn down any means, however aberrant, however absurd, of easing it.

As he approached the first intersection, a car jumped the light and almost hit a pedestrian, who glared hard at the windshield and flipped the driver the bird.

Seeing this, Corey suddenly made a connection: his mother had been killed in a car accident. Now, he himself had been hit by a car; but instead of killing him, it had hurled him into a second chance at life—a kind of rebirth.

Was his mother responsible? . . . She'd shown herself capable of acting from beyond the material realm. Could this be her way of making herself known to him again? Or was this just his hunger and exhaustion talking? . . . He probably shouldn't think too much on it. He might get all worked up and start crying in public, or something equally mortifying.

But he couldn't help remembering the one thing his mother had said to him, that last, impossible afternoon on the couch. Which was, "What kind of man will you be?"

Corey, eight years old and obsessed with the exploits of heroes, had told her he was going to be the kind that helped people.

He realized now that perhaps his only hope of ever honoring this promise was to do it as Jack Ackerly.

Chapter 22

Jack had waited till they were just blocks from the doctor's office. "Listen," he said, "there's something I have to tell you."

Corey didn't react with alarm; in truth he seemed almost not to have heard him. He was still running his hands over the dashboard, the seat, the interior trim. The first thing he'd said, after getting in the Porsche and emitting a low whistle, was, "So is this part of the package?"

"You get the car along with everything else," Jack had answered.

Corey shook his head. "Man, you are *crazy.*"

"Yes, and well aware of it, thanks."

"You got a garage to park it in?"

"No, I leave it on the street. For God's sake, Corey."

The boy had looked sheepish. "I guess that was a stupid question."

"I'm sorry. I know this kind of living isn't what you're used to. But you'd better get familiar with it, and fast, because it's coming your way."

"Only too happy to," Corey had replied. "So, tell me about the car."

And Jack had done so, to the best of his knowledge, till he'd grown bored with himself and with the boy's exuberant materialism, at which point he'd directed him to the glossy owner's manual instead. That had absorbed him for a while.

"I said, I have something I have to tell you," he now repeated.

Corey looked up. "Hm?"

"It's about this visit to Dr. Guptil." He turned a corner and he could see the medical complex looming above Damen Avenue. "Of course he'll check out your injuries, but I've also asked him to run a full physical on you. That includes a blood test, the works."

He held his breath a moment, waiting for the boy's outraged objection.

But Corey just shrugged, and said, "Whatever," then turned back to the manual.

Jack raised his eyebrows in surprise. "You understand, he'll be checking you out for *everything*," he said. "All the standard STDs, including HIV."

"Mm-hm," said Corey, hovering over the page describing the stereo system.

"I know you might consider it an invasion of your privacy," Jack continued, unwilling simply to abandon all the arguments he'd spent so much time practicing, "but when you consider that you've already agreed to sell me your body, that I will in fact be living in it—well, privacy simply isn't an issue. It's like, if I were buying a house, I'd hire an inspector to check for faults and damage."

Corey remained nonchalant. "Right. I get it."

Jack shrugged and gave up; though he was almost disappointed to have been ready for a fight, and not gotten one. He pulled up before the door of the med center. "After you're done here," he said, "we'll go out and get you a new bicycle."

Corey closed the owner's manual and looked at him. "Daddy's reward for a good little boy, huh?"

Jack was taken aback by the comment. He couldn't tell if

its intent was hostile or teasing. Corey's mouth was twisted into a slight grin, but it could easily be interpreted as derisive.

"Not at all," he replied. "But I just though—well, you'd mentioned—and it *is* my fault, so . . ." He was starting to babble, and paused to gather his thoughts. "And really, the bike is for me, more than you. I could buy one on my own, but I don't know anything about them. Whereas, if we go together, you can help me make a selection." Corey was still smiling at him. "And then, of course, use it yourself till—well, till I—"

"Till you switch bodies with me," said Corey. "You seem to have a lot of trouble saying that. Even though it's what this is really all about."

Jack felt his face flush. The boy had nailed him. "I guess that's true."

"You sure you're ready to do it? Even though you can't even say it?"

"Oh, I'm sure," said Jack. But secretly he wondered, *Am I?* And then, as always, *Of course I am. Plus, it's not like it's going to work, anyway.*

Corey replaced the manual and—still smiling mysteriously—said, "All righty, then."

"Yes," Jack repeated. "All righty." It was a phrase he'd never used in his life before. He wondered if he should practice using it; it might come in handy when he met people who knew Corey. Help convince them that that's who he was.

Corey grabbed the door handle in preparation for letting himself out of the car; then turned and said, "So, when's your turn?"

Jack looked at him. "My turn for what?"

"For *your* complete physical."

Jack hadn't expected this. He muttered a bit, then said, "Well, Dr. Guptil's been my G.P. for a number of years. If you ask him, he'll show you all my records."

"I doubt that. Unless you call and tell him to."

"I will. I'll do it right now." He pulled his cell phone from his breast pocket.

Corey put a hand on his, stopping him. "Don't bother," he said. "I'm not sure I could trust him."

Jack was astonished. "What do you mean? He's a respected professional, who—"

"He's your doctor," Corey said, interrupting him. "How do I know you and him haven't put your heads together to fool me into thinking you're, like, totally healthy? When, really, you've got leprosy or whatever."

Jack felt the first stirrings of anger, but he managed to quell them. "If that's an issue for you, by all means, find a doctor you personally trust, and send me to him. I'll be happy to put your mind at ease."

"Nah," said Corey, his grin growing into a smile. "Just fucking with you. Way you go about all this—like it's a business transaction. Kind of cute." He opened the door.

"But . . . it *is* a business transaction," he said as Corey stepped out of the car.

Corey peered back in. "If you say so, boss." He shut the door and gave him a wave, then entered the building.

Jack drove off, and found himself slightly rattled by the exchange. What had Corey meant by that last little jibe? . . . The boy, in many ways so uncouth, so unworldly, had a disconcerting habit of reducing things to their essence. He'd called Jack on his reluctance to name the agreement between them, and now had twitted Jack for treating that agreement like a negotiated contract. In fact, Jack *had* considered making the whole thing legal by drawing it up for their signatures, but he doubted any attorney would do it for him, nor any court in the land recognize its validity.

He wondered if, at Corey's level—at *street* level, as it were— it was a matter of survival to say what you mean, even though it chafed or abraded. Could Corey, for this reason, see something about their arrangement that he couldn't? . . . Certainly it was much more than a business transaction; it was a fundamental and revolutionary shift in the core identity of each of them. It realigned everything from their skin and bones to their names and fortunes. It was, in fact, a conscious attempt to thwart nature, to thwart time, to thwart fate.

But . . . it was *also* a business transaction. And details mattered.

God damn it, they *did*.

A light rain began to fall. Jack switched on his wipers, then shook his head clear. The climatic interruption was just enough to bring him out of his inner debate and place him back in the hardscrabble world. He dispelled all discordant thoughts and turned his mind, instead, to bicycles.

Chapter 23

If Corey had unnerved Jack, Jack had unknowingly repaid the favor. In fact, Corey's slightly disparaging remark about Jack and his "business arrangement" was not, as Jack thought, the result of some clearer, street-honed perception; it had come from simple fear and insecurity. The number of aspects and angles to this affair seemed to multiply by the day, and Jack appeared to be on top of all of them. Corey, his head spinning, could only feel a growing sense of panic; when he'd toyed with Jack about having a physical, and said to him, "Way you go about this—like it's a business transaction"—his aim hadn't been to put down him or make him feel foolish; it had been to make *himself* feel more in control. I can't worry about anything like that, he was trying to convey, because either this works out for us or it doesn't, and none of this preliminary crap is going to be what determines that.

Which was more or less how he felt. But then why was he still going along with it? . . . He wondered as much, while Jack's doctor prodded him and poked him and peered into his ears and throat and anus. He realized that, despite his increasing agitation as his agreement with Jack became ever more solid and real, he was far *more* agitated by the prospect of staying in his own skin and continuing to inhabit his shattered ruin of a life. Just the idea could start him hyperventilating. He began to do so now, while seated on the examining table, and had a time of it persuading Dr. Guptil it was just a case of nerves.

The succeeding few days passed uneventfully, until Jack called to tell him he'd been given him a clean bill of health. "So I guess we can go ahead and do this thing." He sounded brisk and officious; Corey listened carefully for evidence of fear or doubt, but his own heartbeat blocked up his ears. "I've contacted Francesca—the witch I told you about—and put her on alert. Probably all that's left to do is the house tours."

"The *what* tours?" Corey had asked, sitting bolt upright.

"Excuse me, *apartment* tours," Jack corrected himself. "Whatever." Corey felt his throat dry up. Jack must have inferred something was wrong. "What's the matter? Certainly you want to see the place you'll be living, before you actually have to live there."

Corey managed to emit a guttural noise that sounded vaguely affirmative.

"Well, same here," Jack continued. "Look pretty funny, wouldn't it: me in your body, wandering around your building, trying to find which door is yours."

"You're not living *here*," Corey blurted.

"Only temporarily," Jack said. "Till I find a bigger place to move into."

"Listen, boss, do yourself a favor, get the bigger place right now. You don't want to stay even one night in this place."

Jack was taken aback. "But . . . what about all your stuff? I'll have to take possession of it in order to move it."

"I'll move it for you. Right into a Dumpster."

"You've got *nothing* you want to pass on to me?"

He thought hard. "Really, just what I'm standing up in." It was a humiliating admission. But better to say so upfront, than endure the embarrassment of having Jack Ackerly set one foot in this mildewed hovel.

Jack sighed. "Well, okay. I'll take your word for it." Another pause. "*Nothing?* Not even kitchenware?"

"Not even a flyswatter. I live in a dump, okay? It's the reason I'm even *doing* this. I mean, come on." He was tugging at the flap of hair over his ear—a nervous trait; he'd had it since childhood. He wondered if he'd still do it when he was in Jack's body . . . and whether, if he did, he'd find himself pulling the hair right out.

Jack said, "All right, I guess that makes sense. But you should really come get acquainted with *this* place. See where everything is. Plus, I'll have to show you how the security system works; don't want you triggering any alarms while you're entering your own home. And I'd better walk you through my archives: previous IRS returns, real estate transactions, various business contracts that are still in play—it's a bit of a complicated life, I'm afraid. But I have good people running it for me. All you really have to do is know where everything's filed, and who handles it. I'll print out a master list for you."

Corey felt panic well up in him again. He said, "Mm-hm," somehow splitting it into three syllables.

Jack didn't notice; he kept chattering on, eventually asking Corey when he'd like to come by. "How's tomorrow? That work for you?"

"Shum," said Corey.

"Great. I've got some matters to wrap up early, so let's make it around eleven. I'll take you to lunch afterwards. We can talk through all the final details."

"Yibb," said Corey.

Jack gave him a cheery goodbye and rang off. Corey remained cross-legged on the couch for a good ten minutes, listening to his heart, which was galloping like a team of reindeer. Eventually he reasoned that activity was the best means of quieting his nerves, and decided to take a cue from Jack: he'd devote himself to wrapping up whatever affairs needed wrapping, before he became somebody else.

He fetched a pad of paper, whose pages bore a Days Inn logo—Corey had snatched it from the bedstand after tricking with one of the hotel guests—and a leaky ballpoint pen. He poised the pen over the paper, and he thought.

After a few moments, he wrote down, *Cover story.* And a few moments later, he crossed it out, because he couldn't think of anyone for whom such a thing would be necessary. He had no job and hence no colleagues. His only family was his Aunt Ginger, who was living in Santa Monica and with whom he hadn't spoken in years; and even if she did suddenly decide to renew ties with her nephew—well, it had been so long since she knew him at all, that to her, Jack-as-Corey would seem no stranger or more suspicious than Corey himself would have.

As for his friends . . . well, he'd had many in his life, and was fully aware of the fickle nature of even the closest relationships. His best buddies ten years earlier were people who had since faded almost completely from his life. So, eventually, in the ordinary run of things, would Frida and Tyler and the others. Knowing this made it easier for him to abandon them now, a few years early—if that; Tyler, he recalled, had already begun drifting away from him. For the same reason, there was no need for him to invent some elaborate story about why they would suddenly be seeing less of him; after a short period of hurt or confusion, as Jack's "Corey" slipped out of their lives, they'd forget about him and move on.

So there seemed to be nothing of a personal nature for Corey to bring to closure. He tried thinking more practically. What about his utilities? Should he cancel them? . . . No, because Jack would want to transfer his existing accounts to whatever new apartment he chose for himself.

Eventually he was forced into another embarrassing admission, if this one only to himself: there was nothing in his life that required his attention. He could step out of it, and let someone else step in, with as few repercussions as if he were giving away a favorite shirt.

Feeling dull and heavy, he lay down his pen and went to bed.

Chapter 24

Corey was twenty minutes late, which was annoying. Jack kept tidying, plumping pillows and squaring chairs to the wall, and wondering why; obviously the boy was coming from an environment so squalid that Jack could have left newspapers and dog hair over every square inch of the place and still impressed him. Possibly he didn't want to risk the place looking untidy, lest the prospect of having to clean it scare him off. But that was ridiculous; if the boy was ready to abdicate his very identity, how spooked could he be by the prospect of a little light housekeeping?

Finally, the doorbell rang. Jack checked the monitor and saw that it was indeed Corey out front, staring up at the place with a maddeningly blank look. He'd chained his new bicycle to the wrought-iron fence; Jack would have to have a word with him about that.

No. No, he wouldn't. Because soon the bike would be his, and the fence would be Corey's, and never again the twain would meet.

He spoke to Corey over the intercom, instructing him to take the elevator up to six, and then buzzed him into the building. Nelly, having heard the doorbell and now the buzzer, came into the foyer, wagging her tail in anticipation of a guest.

There was a knock on the door; Jack opened it, and Corey entered, his armpits dark and his hair damp against his forehead. At first Jack thought this must be nerves, but then he remembered the bicycle, and the humidity of the day.

"Come on in," he said with a grand gesture.

"Jesus," said Corey, "I need sunglasses first! . . . How many windows you got in the place? God *damn.*"

"You can count them when you live here," Jack said.

And suddenly there was Nelly, nosing Corey's crotch. Corey dropped to one knee in response, scratching her head and nuzzling her and saying, "Oh, hey, hey there, who're you, boy?"

"Girl," said Jack. "That's Nelly."

"Hello, Nelly girl, who's friendly then?" Nelly's tongue slurped across Corey's cheek and flicked between his lips. Corey made a face and laughed. "Whoa, there! Nelly gets down to *business,* doesn't she?"

"She's anybody's bitch," said Jack. It was his standard quip for these moments.

"She's great," said Corey. "*This* is great. I always wanted a dog!"

"Oh, now, wait," Jack said, "don't get the wrong idea. Nelly comes with me."

Corey rose to his feet. "Oh, come on, boss, this is her *home.* You don't wanna take her away from it!"

"She's lived several places with me already," he said. "Another move won't throw her."

"Another master might."

Jack still had no reply to this, so he said, "She's a very old dog. Lots of medical issues. Lots of *medications,* all timed to the minute. It's best if she comes with me, no matter what I look like. And you're better off getting a younger dog anyway. You can, now. Two or three, if you like."

Corey pouted a little and gave Nelly another scratch. Jack slipped behind him and shut the door, then said, "Let me show you around."

"Okay," said Corey. "Come on, Nelly! Come on, let's go look around!"

Jack led Corey from the foyer into the sunken den. "As you can see, the layout's pretty open. This is the main living area. The fireplace is gas, unfortunately; I'd have preferred wood-burning. But you make concessions."

"Where's the TV?"

"Media room's down that corridor," said Jack, pointing. "Stereo's there, too, but it's hooked up to speakers in here, for entertaining. Master bedroom's across the hall. My office is there, next to the garage elevator; guest room and bath are just beyond."

Corey looked around and blinked.

"Let me show you the kitchen," Jack said. "There are two ovens, but one of them's tricky."

"Actually, I just need to sit down for a minute," Corey said. "This is all a little much."

Jack felt a flicker of pity. He didn't have to heart to say so, but most of his things were in storage; in moving to this apartment after his and Harry's breakup, he'd considered that he was paring down to the bare minimum. But to Corey, it all seemed extravagant excess.

Corey sat in the closest chair and took a few deep breaths. His hand unconsciously started caressing the intricate tooling of the armrest. Eventually he realized what he was doing, and looked down at it. "Nice," he said.

"All the furniture in this room—most of the furniture in the place, actually—is custom-made. It's Lorenzo Meagher—possibly you've heard of him? No?—a wonderful designer and artisan, and a very good friend." He shifted his weight to his other foot. "As long as we're on the subject, I should point out I'm taking a few of these pieces with me. Moving them out today, actually."

Corey looked up. "You found a place already?"

"A transitional one. Empty apartment in a building I own.

Which, soon, *you'll* own. I trust you won't kick me out."
He laughed. Corey just stared. "Anyway, it's unfurnished,
so I don't have much choice. I've already emailed Lorenzo
and ordered replacements for everything I'm taking. You
won't get them for a while, of course, but it'll be worth the
wait. And you can cancel it if you'd rather go for another
style here."

Corey sighed. "Man, even your furniture is complicated.
I can't wait to get into the finances."

Jack smiled and sat on the arm of a couch. "It may seem
complicated, but it's all in order. And you can always call
me if you have a question or get confused."

Corey sat silently, still rolling his hands over Lorenzo
Meagher's woodworking. Finally, he said, "Can I have a
Coke or something?"

"Pepsi alright?"

Corey grimaced. "You're one of those, huh?"

Jack laughed. "Sorry. Always have been."

"Whatever. Long as it's not *Diet* Pepsi. Like drinking battery acid."

"Wouldn't know," said Jack merrily as he headed for the
wet bar on the far side of the den. "Never tried battery acid."
He bent down beneath the bar, opened the mini-fridge, and
produced a can of soda. Standing up, he found Corey staring at him oddly.

"Something wrong?" he asked.

The boy shook his head, the paused and said, "Can I
ask . . ."

Jack waited a moment. "Can you ask what?"

Corey looked embarrassed. "It's just . . . remember when
I was seeing your doctor, and you told me, if I asked, you'd
agree to be examined too?"

Jack popped open the can; a little breath of sweet car-
bonation tickled his nose. "You changed your mind? You
want to do that now?"

"Sort of."

Jack took a tumbler from the rack and plopped some ice cubes into it. "Not a problem. You have a doctor in mind?"

Corey shook his head. "No doctor."

Jack looked up. "Pardon?"

"Just me," Corey said sheepishly. "Sorry, but . . . well, I want to see what I'm getting into. *Literally.*"

Jack cocked his head. "I'm not following you."

Corey shyly flicked a finger at him. "I want to see what you look like."

Jack stepped from behind the bar, arms outstretched, and said, "Well, here I am!" Then, another look at Corey's wide, pleading eyes, and he understood. *"Oh."*

"I hope you don't mind."

"No, no," he said with too much bravado. "Why would I mind? . . . Makes all the sense in the world, actually. I'll just . . . uh . . ." He looked around helplessly for a moment, then said, "Excuse me."

He stepped back behind the bar, feeling that such modesty was ridiculous at this stage of the game, but unable to help himself. He fumbled with his belt—why were his fingers suddenly so thick and unresponsive?—and unbuckled his trousers. He kicked off his shoes, peeled off his socks, and let his pants drop to his ankles. Stepping out of them, he gave Corey a sidelong glance, then peeled off his boxer briefs. Naked from the waist down, he concluded by pulling his polo shirt over his head and draping it across the bar.

He felt a sudden chill, which was absurd; the day was tropical.

He stepped out from behind the bar and into Corey's view. He realized he was sucking in his stomach, then thought, *What's the point of that?* and let it go. Reminding himself that he was the kind of man who faced his fears, he didn't lurk demurely by the bar, but strode straight over to where Corey was seated, to give him a better look.

"Well?" he said, turning around to better display himself, and resisting every urge to camp it up. "Think you could live with it?" He corrected himself. "*In* it?"

Corey's visage was, as usual, unreadable; damn the boy, where had he acquired such a poker face? . . . Undoubtedly it was the result of years of cruising, never wanting to convey too much desire, too soon. Not that that was a problem in this case.

At least, not for Corey. But something strange was happening to Jack. He'd never been in a situation quite like this one: naked, before the appraising eyes of a near stranger. Like he was a piece of merchandise; which he supposed, in one sense, he was. But the surprising—and altogether disconcerting—thing, was that Jack found it rather *exciting*. He felt the unmistakable onset of tumescence.

He tried to turn away, but Corey said, "No, don't. That's . . . that's really kind of what I wanted to see."

This had the effect of arousing Jack even more, so that within moments he was at full mast.

"Don't want to buy the car without checking out the motor, huh?" he said, resorting to camp at last, to hide his awkwardness.

Corey only nodded. "Something like that."

A moment later, Jack said, "All right, that's enough," and scampered back to the bar. He struggled back into his clothes, slipped on his shoes, buckled his belt, then washed his hands at the sink and, finally, grandly, finished pouring Corey's Pepsi, which he now brought to him. "Ice is a little melted, sorry," he said.

"Never mind," said Corey, and he took an appreciative sip.

Jack sat in the chair opposite him. "Just for the record, that was one of the more unusual situations I've ever found myself in."

"Sure to be a few more before all this is over," Corey said, and he smiled.

"So," said Jack, his pride unable to restrain him, "what's the verdict?"

Corey held the tumbler high and said, "Very refreshing!"

"Ha, ha, ha," said Jack impatiently. "You know what I mean."

Corey shrugged. "You're in pretty good shape for a guy your . . . Well, let's face it. Fifty-three could mean *anything*. But I'm actually really relieved." He made a blatant nod towards Jack's nether regions. "You've got good raw material. I think I can work with it."

There didn't seem anything to add to that, so Jack took him to the front hall and taught him the security codes.

Chapter 25

Jesus Harry *Christ* that flabby old *wreck* of a body!
Corey pedaled faster and faster, as though he might somehow escape the image of Jack naked—leave it flapping in
the wind behind him, obscured by his dust.

Jack *dressed* well, he had to hand it to him. All those designer shirts and tailored slacks really disguised the shape-
lessness underneath. Corey never, *never* would've guessed.

He took a left turn at Wellington and the pebbles on the
road almost wiped him out; he lurched his weight in the opposite direction and pulled himself upright again, just in
time.

All right. *Okay.* Time to get control of himself. Did he
want to have another accident, here?

Yes, YES, he *did*, he *wanted* that. An instant death would
solve *all* his problems.

But maybe not that way; even in this extremity of distress, he didn't like the idea of being torn apart by a half ton
of razor-sharp metal.

What about the painkillers Dr. Guptil had given him . . . ?
What if he went home, stretched out on the sofa, and downed
them all, one after another? Would that be enough to gently
carry him off as he slept? . . .

He reached a stoplight and had to brake abruptly. As he

waited at the corner for the signal to turn green, he had a moment to catch his breath, and to tamp down the roiling panic in his head.

The first thing to remember was, he didn't have to go through with this. He'd signed nothing; and such was the nature of their agreement that Jack could scarcely sue him if he backed out now. He'd be laughed out of court. If Corey just started, from this moment on, pretending he'd never even met Jack Ackerly, Jack would be helpless to do one damn thing about it. He'd be stuck in his dumpy old body in his gorgeous zillion-window apartment forever.

Except . . . Jack had really been decent to him. He'd gotten him medical attention, bought him a new bike, even given him some cash to pay his more pressing bills. And he'd never even put the moves on him. Corey had expected that, wasn't quite sure how he'd handle it; but he never had to. Jack seemed to have no designs on Corey's young, lithe body.

Except, he *did*. Designs of an entirely different kind.

The light changed. Corey pushed the bike forward and resumed pedaling, at a more reasonable pace.

Fine, then. Jack was after his body. But even then, he'd conducted himself unimpeachably. He'd proposed the swap matter-of-factly, put no pressure on Corey to agree to it, promised nothing that he couldn't deliver. Despite the highly questionable, if not objectionable, nature of the entire enterprise, Jack had been, throughout, that rarest of creatures: a gentleman.

And he seemed to bring out a similar streak in Corey, as well. That's why he hadn't been able to say to him, "You're old, you're fat, and your erection is nothing special." He couldn't even bring himself to hint it. Poor Jack, standing there at attention, allowing himself to be judged, laying himself open for scorn or derision but hoping, no doubt, for better—it had been almost pitiably endearing.

And, really—*was* it such a bad body? . . . As Corey had

said, fifty-three could mean anything. At the Y, he'd seen forty-year-olds who were first-class disasters: folds of fat like molten wax, rashes and patches disfiguring the skin, great collapsing planes for faces. Jack was an Adonis by comparison. He had muscle as well as fat; his chest was broad, his arms big. So what if he had a thick waist; Corey could slim it down with a few weeks of diligent gym-going. Certainly he'd have plenty of leisure time to devote to the task. It's not like he needed to work, what with all of Jack's millions at his disposal.

Corey zipped across Halsted Street and came within sight of his building. He eased up on the pedals and coasted past the barrier of parked cars.

What, he reflected, what was the point of having a hot body, anyway? . . . Corey had devoted his life to just that, and to reveling in the erotic opportunities it had brought his way. The result had been ruin, years evaporating behind him with nothing whatever to show for them. So *what* if he were middle-aged and liver-spotted with a 36-inch waist and an uninspiring hard-on? . . . It wasn't like he was going to be living his old life. The whole point of this switch was to *escape* his old life. To give *Jack* the chance to be young and beautiful and sexually adventurous, while Corey tried . . . something else.

Maybe that was the problem. He still hadn't chosen what that something else would be, and so, emotionally, he was still clinging to his old priorities.

And that, he now realized, was because he was still nursing a tiny hope that the swap would fail. That Jack's witch would just flame out, leaving Corey still Corey, but several hundred grand better off.

He carried his bike through the vestibule and down the stairs to his apartment door, fumbled for the keys, and let himself into the little rat's nest he now found it difficult to call home.

He fetched a Red Bull from the fridge and plopped down

on the sofa. He sipped slowly and listened to his heart slow down after his exertions.

He knew—he'd already told himself—that he couldn't go forward with this arrangement if he were counting on it to fail. That was a recipe for serious disappointment, or worse. He had to be prepared to honor his part of the agreement— to *become* Jack Ackerly—and, intellectually, he was prepared to do just that.

Emotionally, though . . . emotionally, he wasn't there.

He realized he had to do something—something proactive, something beyond mere words—to persuade himself that he *was* there. Something that, once done, couldn't be undone.

He finished off the Red Bull while wondering what that might be. The closest he came to an answer was, dragging all his belongings to the Dumpster. Beginning with his bed. That was as close to a ceremonial goodbye to his current life as he could imagine.

But he was more than a little drained by the day's events— his crash course in Jack's life and affairs, his confrontation with the reality of Jack's flesh—and couldn't bring himself to lift a finger. Besides, it's not like the place had to be vacated for a new tenant, anyway. Renovators would be gutting it. Let *them* move the furniture, when the time came. There wasn't anything Corey really wanted here that wouldn't fit in his backpack. A couple of high school yearbooks, some photos of his mother, a few scraps and momentos of old friends and lovers.

And just like that, he realized what he had to do.

He got up and collected all the things he'd just named— the several cherished artifacts of his otherwise arid twenty-six years—and put them into an old cardboard box still lying around from a UPS delivery some months before. He taped up the box, addressed it to Jack Ackerly, and deliberately left off any return address.

The next morning he took it to the Post Office and had it

sent at the Media Mail rate, which the clerk told him might take several days. By which time, presumably, *he* would be the Jack Ackerly who received it.

Feeling much more serene than he had in weeks, he stood outside in the brilliant sunlight and flipped open his cell phone, intending to call Penny's Noodles; he was in the mood for some carryout Pad Thai to celebrate his emotional break-through.

But the phone surprised him by ringing before he could dial. He pressed TALK and held it to his ear. "Hello?"

It was Jack. He'd set a date with the witch. The day after tomorrow, two in the afternoon. Did that work for Corey . . . ?

Corey's stomach trampolined, and suddenly the world went white.

"Bish," he said.

Chapter 26

Jack heard, for the first time, the panic in Corey's voice, and after hanging up he asked himself whether his eagerness to relive his youth was betraying him into haste. He'd thought he was proceeding with admirable thoroughness and deliberation; but clearly Corey felt rushed. Certainly the boy might not relish the idea of stepping out of his smooth, young skin—that was to be expected; but he might equally find the idea of stepping into Jack's identity intimidating. Had Jack *really* prepped him enough . . . ?

After all, Corey was only twenty-six and lacking in so much experience of life. Did Jack really expect him to become instantly the kind of man who was at ease in the cosmopolitan circles in which he traveled? . . . Jack, of course, had earned his way into those environs; he had perhaps forgotten how forbidding they could seem from the outside. And no number of attorneys, advisers, or consultants would be sufficient to quell Corey's premonitions of inadequacy.

No, the only solution was to have Corey actually encounter these people firsthand; observe them in their natural habitat, and by this means learn that they were every bit as venal, shallow, and insecure as anyone he'd ever met in the gay *demimonde*.

And so Jack decided to throw a party for all his closest friends.

It was terribly short notice, of course; among ordinary people, that might have doomed it to failure. But Jack's set had more liberty than others; they could free themselves for a spontaneous invitation without much trouble. Also, Jack knew very well that, however discreet he'd been about his current turn of mind, he was even so the subject of gossip; Walt, if no one else, would have seen to that. So his spur-of-the-moment cocktail party would have an added appeal: all those who had been talking about him behind his back could come to his house and get a good look at him, infer what they liked, and murmur their conclusions to each other while he was across the room.

And Corey could see it all.

But not as a guest; he didn't want to introduce him to his friends. That would draw too much attention to him, and he didn't want people observing too closely Corey's manners, gestures, and habits of speech, lest they grow curious when those same affectations occurred, later, in Jack.

No, Corey would be staff. He'd wear a little jacket and a bow tie and circulate among the guests with trays of hors d'oeuvres. And every so often Jack could take him aside, put names to faces, and explain who everyone was in relation to his life.

It was a fine plan; Jack was proud of himself. But if he was going to keep his appointment with Francesca—and he didn't want to reschedule; setting an initial date with the scatterbrained witch had been trouble enough—it had to take place tomorrow. That was a tall order; he needed a caterer, sufficient alcohol for his invariably alcoholic guests, a uniform for Corey . . . in the end, he put it all in Fancy's hands. She was delighted to come to his aid again, and—just as he'd presumed—plainly intrigued by the idea of his throwing a party so soon after the drunken episode he'd subjected her to over the phone. (He wondered if she might've let slip that story to Walt, or anyone else; but no. Not Fancy. She was as solid as earth.)

The only thing left for him to do was to invite the guests. He made up a list—twenty persons in all—and commenced calling them. Invariably he was connected to their voice mail; but that was fine, it enabled him to recite the same short, chatty message each time—having some people over for a drink tomorrow, just a spur of the moment thing, a lark, he hoped everyone was free to drop by, no need to RSVP, just show up if you can.

So immersed was he in all this activity, that almost an hour had passed before he realized he hadn't yet told Corey. He phoned the boy immediately and explained him what was required of him. Corey agreed—if with no great enthusiasm—and everything was set.

Fancy arrived first, of course, all briskness and efficiency, Corey's uniform draped over one arm and a gaggle of hired hands behind her toting crates of champagne and liquor, which Jack directed them to deposit in the storeroom. Fancy hung the uniform in the guest closet and gave Jack a hug; she was a small woman but of ample dimensions, and when she enfolded him in her embrace he was momentarily dizzied by the scent of lavender. He hadn't realized how much he'd missed her.

Corey arrived thirty minutes later, and then had to go back outside again because Jack didn't want his bicycle hooked up to the front gate. He allowed him to bring it inside and put it in the storeroom as well. Corey looked awkward and shy, but Fancy took him under her wing and he couldn't but warm to her genteel bossiness. She had him dressed and ready just in time for the food to arrive, after which she spirited him away to the kitchen to help the caterer—a young girl just starting out, leave it to Fancy to find someone so ready to oblige—and arrange the trays. Everything was Asian; there were skewers of satay coated in peanut sauce, Chinese-spiced beef rolled up in cabbage leaves, ginger-scented wontons, and the like. Not, perhaps, the ideal food to wash down with champagne, but given the time constraints, Jack would've felt petty to say so.

With everything seemingly under control, Jack felt comfortable retiring to his room to dress. In reality, he merely exchanged one casual ensemble for another, but there was something about the ritual that made it seem necessary. Also, it gave him time to settle Nelly; she'd been happily agitated by all the comings and goings and had worked herself into a fit of barking. Jack couldn't have that during the actual party, so he brought her back with him, settled her on the bed with a basted rawhide as a treat, and stroked her neck till she quieted down.

Robyn was the first guest to arrive. Jack was a little dismayed by this; he'd only invited her out of lingering pity for her over their mutual firing. But he didn't know her all that well, and despite being characteristically dressed to kill—in a lethal red cocktail dress that slashed across her right shoulder like a wound, and pumps with toes so pointed Jack found himself moving out of their way, lest they accidentally bring him to harm—she was uneasy and apologetic. "Did I get the time right? I thought you said—wasn't it six? I could've sworn you said—I could come back later if you're not—Oh, Jack, how much do I love that shirt, it's just—No really, I'll just walk around the block until—"

Jack managed to get a glass of champagne into her hand, and after a few sips she visibly relaxed. They made small talk for a few minutes till Walt arrived, making a typically melodramatic entrance: "What, *farshnoshket* so soon? I've got catching up to do! Give me a glass, already!"

As Jack filled a flute for him, he introduced Robyn: "A colleague of mine from the Tealight Theatre board."

"Well, *ex,*" said Robyn. "What I mean is—Oh, Jack, I'm not telling tales out of school, am I, because—Pleasure to meet you too, any friend of Jack's is—I'm sorry, I didn't catch your—"

"Walter Neurath," said Walt, extending his hand. "Now, tell me all about yourself, including every sordid detail about your association with this lousy *parech*, here."

Robyn began to comply, and Jack thus felt it safe to start edging towards the door, the better to meet the next guests. But he'd only gotten a few inches away when Walt interrupted Robyn by calling out, "Oy, Jack, remind me to tell you later, I saw your *nishtgutnik* ex-husband the other day."

Jack smiled back at him. "It's all right, Walt, you don't need to tell me every time you run into him."

"I know, it's just he looked completely *narish*, running around dressed like a man half his age. He's gone *meshuggah*, you ask me."

"I don't have to ask you, you always tell me."

"Well, you know how he is better than anyone. Always clinging desperately to youth. The way he acted when we were all in Key West, *gedainkst?*"

Robyn was beginning to look uncomfortable. This was so typical of Walt; he'd meet someone new, flatter them with his attention, then, when they'd begun to open up to him, he'd turn away and start a conversation with someone he already knew—peppered with exclusive references the newcomer didn't share. And if he could also manage to tweak his older friend into the bargain, that was a bonus.

"He's not like you, Jack," Walt said, his eyes glittering. "He doesn't know how to grow old gracefully."

Jack felt his face burn at this clear reference to his unfortunate confession in the Four Seasons bar after *The Makropulos Case*. Walt was really a terrible person; Jack couldn't imagine why he remained friends with him.

Robyn, no longer able to endure being so pointedly ignored, asked Jack where she might find a restroom, and then headed off in the direction he sent her.

Walt sidled over to Jack and said, in a lower voice, "So,

what's the story with that *tsatskeh* anyway? The way she talks, I mean—all *fartshadikt*. Someone leave her out in the sun too long, or what?"

Jack couldn't think of a civil answer to that; fortunately, Corey chose that moment to enter with the first tray of food. At the sight of him, Walt's focus completely shifted. One of his eyebrows raised into a high arch, and as Corey approached he visibly sucked in his stomach.

At that moment the next guests arrived, and Jack felt himself quite free to greet them.

Chapter 27

"The heavy-set guy in the madras jacket," said Jack in a low voice, "is Gary Mahlanki. He was my right-hand man when I had my P.R. firm. After I sold up, he formed an agency of his own with his wife, Carol—that's her to his left, dribbling plum sauce on her Escada jacket. They're pretty well connected, so they can usually get you tickets to concerts or ball games that are sold out everywhere else. Good people to know. Just be warned, he has the most offensive breath on the face of the planet. Like he's storing dead mice in his cheeks."

"Yeah, I sorta found that out on my own," said Corey, who had been avoiding that end of the room ever since.

"Aaaaand I think that's about it," said Jack, scouring the room one more time. "Anyone I've missed?"

Corey shook his head. Over the course of the evening, Jack had managed to familiarize him with every one of these people, all of whom were major players in his life—and would, presumably, continue to be after Corey took it over.

"Well, then, any questions about anybody?" Jack asked.

"Just one," Corey said. "How do I get the Yiddish guy to stop grabbin' my ass?"

Jack rolled his eyes. "I don't think you can," he said.

"You'd have to be a whole lot older and a whole lot less attractive to manage it."

Corey almost said, *Tomorrow I will be,* but caught himself in time.

He took his empty tray back to the kitchen, where Adriana, the caterer, was patiently arranging sesame chicken wings on a platter for him. Robyn leaned against the refrigerator, smoking. She'd come back here earlier in the party, ostensibly to offer a helping hand, and when this was gently declined had stuck around anyway. Corey soon guessed that she didn't know any of the other guests and was too timid to do anything about it; which was wildly at variance with the character projected by her clothes, which screamed Bitch Goddess Who Ate the World.

"So anyway," she was saying to Adriana, who quietly gave the impression of listening while really just getting on with her work, "I just feel that it's not—Possibly you disagree with me, don't be offended, I'm only saying—Well, I can only really speak from my own experience, can't I, because who else is—Those are really delicious, by the way, what are those little black things, are they some kind of seafood or—My point is, unless you're really going to put it out there, you're just not ever going to—I mean, I'm not saying I've *never* put it out there, just—"

Adriana handed Corey the new tray and he left the kitchen again. In the corridor he ran into Fancy, who said, "Is that woman still smoking in the kitchen?"

"Yes, ma'am," said Corey.

"I asked her not to. I can taste it on the food, and if I can, so can everybody else."

Corey nodded, and Fancy stormed past him.

As he wove through the little throng of people, Corey paid acute attention to who was saying what. Franklin Demarest, Jack's Porsche dealer, was describing the vacation house he'd just bought in Steamboat Springs; it was the same subject he'd been droning on about the last time Corey had made the circuit of the room. He'd felt a little stab of envy, then; but now he noticed that Demarest was visibly boring all three of the people he'd cornered. Also, that his suit didn't fit properly; the back of the neck jutted away from his shirt collar, creating a gap big enough to plunge a flagpole into.

He moved on, passing Jack's tax attorney, Judith Addison-Madison, and his insurance broker, Lois Kohr. They were discussing with relish the more hideous details of a mutual friend's botched cosmetic surgery. Lois Kohr had the kind of shrill, staccato laugh that killed merriment in every other person within earshot; but that was all right, since Judith Addison-Madison nursed no sense of humor anyway. If she had, she'd have noticed that hyphenating her maiden and married names turned them into a singsong denomination straight out of Dr. Seuss.

Corey had been very reluctant to meet these people; he'd imagined them to be lofty, superior sorts, and their conversation to be of nothing but their world travels, their fabulous houses, and their epic divorces. And he hadn't been far wrong; but what he hadn't foreseen was that they were also human beings. They exhibited odd quirks, inadvertent boorishness, and unfortunate lapses of taste; some were having bad hair days, some had fat in inconvenient places, and some talked far too loudly, getting even louder as they continued to drink. Their shoes may have been expensive, but when they crossed their legs you could still see the wear and tear on the soles.

He'd been frightened of these people—afraid that, once he was among them, his inadequacy would radiate from him—but now he thought he might be able to handle them. They were really just like everybody else he'd ever met; seagulls on a beach, running back forth across the sand, shrieking in delight and in outrage, and getting into tugging matches over whatever bits of garbage they found.

As he made the rounds of the room again, gaining confidence with every step, he found himself back in the vicinity of Gary and Carol Mahlanki, the public-relations couple. Martin Raice, one of those stocky, red-faced men in their sixties who still manage to retain acres of wavy, bouncing-and-behavin' hair, was just shaking the Mahlankis' hands and introducing himself. "I don't know how we haven't managed to meet before this," he said, "given all the soirées Jack's thrown over the years."

"He has a pretty wide circle, our Jack," said Carol, still seemingly unaware of the blob of plum sauce on her jacket that made her look as though she'd been shot point blank.

"I especially wanted to talk to you about my wife, Lisa," and here Martin nodded across the room to a very young trophy wife, whose filmy, strapless cocktail dress was held up only by the points of her nipples, which had apparently been cosmetically enhanced to function like thumbtacks. He turned back to the Mahlankis and said, "She and a friend have put together a line of couture sunglasses for dogs, and they could use some professional help building awareness. Not just of the product, but of the whole neglected area of canine eye protection."

Corey thought, *A girl like that could shit on rye bread and you'd hire a P.R. firm to help her sell it, you poor sad patsy,* but he kept a smile on his face and extended the tray towards him.

Martin and both the Mahlankis availed themselves of chicken wings without ever once looking at Corey. Gary Mahlanki popped his in his mouth, and, after quickly sucking off most of the flesh, said, "That's a very intriguing proposition, Martin, and I'd like to talk to you about it further. But my gut tells me that Mahlanki & Mahlanki is *exactly* the firm to help you turn this into a vital, energetic brand . . ."

Unfortunately, the more Gary spoke, the more his toxic-waste breath escaped him, and Corey beat a hasty retreat before the cloud of acrid funk could weave its nearly visible fingers around his head. He turned away just as Martin

Raice, too, took an astonished step backwards, his eyes filling with tears as though he'd inadvertently walked into a cloud of mustard gas.

Continuing his rounds, Corey came upon Martin's wife Lisa as she spoke earnestly to a young buck in leather pants who, while certainly no more than thirty-two or thirty-three, managed to project a full half-century's worth of sleaze.

"So, you're absolutely certain," he was saying to Lisa, "even though I've promised the whole session would be the *ne plus ultra* of tastefulness?"

"I don't know what that means," said Lisa, shaking her head and sending her golden curls dancing around her dimples. "But the answer is still no. I'm an executive's wife"—she pronounced it *ugg-ZUCK-yuh-tiv*—"so I absolutely will *not* pose nude." After a beat, she added for emphasis, "Not ever again!"

A moment later Corey once again entered the sphere of Lois Kohr and Judith Addison-Madison, who were *still* greedily picking over the story of their friend's surgical mishap. Judith had in fact worked herself into a frenzy of wild conjecture: "What I *hear*," she said, "is that this is actually the *second* surgery, and its sole purpose was to fix the original one, which no one was supposed to know about, and which just went *completely* awry."

Lois gasped. "You mean . . . thank you, sweetheart"—This to Corey, as she plucked a wing from the tray he'd presented to her—"You mean the way she looks now, that's the *repair job?*" She nearly swooned with pleasure. "Whatever can the original damage have looked like?"

Suddenly they were interrupted by a third woman, whom Jack had earlier pointed out to Corey as Rita Danilov, his travel agent. Rita's face had prompted Corey to do a double-take: she wore a permanent look of alarm, as though she'd just lifted her head to discover a basketball coming at her. And there was something about her nose that edged, just slightly, towards the not-quite-bipedal. Corey's mind had flashed immediately to Dr. Zira in *Planet Of the Apes*.

By the way Lois and Judith fell dead silent when Rita joined them, Corey inferred that it was in fact *her* botched surgery that had been providing them such a gratifying wallow. This supposition was only confirmed when each of them air-kissed her and, in voices a full octave higher than they'd been just seconds before, told her how absolutely wonderful it was to see her. "Have you lost *weight?*" Lois trilled, and Judith chirped "Love your *hair*—ten years younger!"

"What have you two been gabbing about?" asked Rita, as she too helped herself to a wing from Corey's tray.

Lois said, "This lovely weather," unfortunately at the same time that Judith said "Angelina Jolie," which resulted in a small, embarrassed pause, then a flood of backpedaling. When Corey left them, Rita was listening politely while nibbling on her hors d'oeuvre, her lips disturbingly working diagonally instead of up-and-down.

Eventually the guests, much the worse for drink, began to depart, and after the last one had gone Corey changed back into his street clothes and returned to the kitchen. Jack was polishing off the dregs of a bottle of Veuve Clicquot while Fancy helped Adriana pack up her things.

"You taking off?" Jack asked.

"Well," said Corey, nodding at the countertops, which were crowded with soiled dishes and champagne flutes, "I thought I'd help clean up." He'd forged a kind of bond with Fancy and Adriana, the way people behind the scenes often do.

"Don't be silly," said Jack, who seemed a little inebriated himself. He slapped him on the back and said, "We've got it covered. You go enjoy your last night!"

Corey saw Fancy give him a puzzled look, and thought it best to retreat before any uncomfortable questions found their way to him. He fetched his bike from the storeroom and was on his way to the door when, on a hunch, he went to the front window and checked out the street below.

Sure enough. Just as he'd suspected.

He went back to the kitchen, where Fancy gave him another very pointed look. Jack wasn't there.

"Where'd he go?" he asked.

Fancy regarded him for a moment, then nodded towards the bedroom.

Corey crept down the hall and knocked on the door, which, being partially open, swung further so from the pressure of his rapping; and there was Jack, seated on the bed, petting Nelly, who was clearly glad to have him back at her side.

Corey entered and sat on the bed as well, and scratched Nelly beneath one ear. She leaned blissfully into him. "Listen, Jack," he said, "you got a back way out of here or something?"

Jack, now clearly sleepy from drink, said, "Hm? Why?"

"That Yiddish guy is parked out front. Waiting for me."

Jack laughed. "Good old Walt."

"Yeah, well. Good old Walt's not good enough for my last night as me." *Or any other night, in any other body,* he added to himself.

Jack said, "You can take the garage elevator, and leave through the alley."

"Thanks," said Corey, and with one last rub of Nelly's muzzle he got up to go. "See you, then."

"Right," said Jack. "See you."

He paused for a moment; there ought to be something more to say, since the next time they met, only a matter of hours hence, they'd be . . . well, on the verge of becoming each other.

But he couldn't think of anything that didn't sound trite or insincere, so he quietly retrieved his bike, took it down to the building garage, and rode away into the night.

*   *   *

By one o'clock he was out on the prowl again. Again, and for the last time . . . unless—no, no going back to that, no more hoping for failure. He'd committed, he was ready, he would accept all the consequences of his choice. He would, at least for once in his life—once in *this* life, before he abandoned it—be a man.

He'd intended to go out with a bang . . . no pun intended. Hook up with a hot guy, maybe two, and stay up all night working through his entire repertoire. A "one for the road" kind of thing; replay the greatest hits before bringing down the curtain and breaking up the act.

But somehow, he couldn't get himself into the right frame of mind. There was a kind of weight on him now; something seemed physically to be holding him down, preventing him from ascending to that level of carefree carnality that had always propelled him through his adventures like a hound in heat. It didn't feel oppressive, this weight; in fact, it had a comforting familiarity. What was it? . . . Possibly nothing more than his sense of himself. He was unable—or perhaps merely unwilling—to set aside his awareness of all that was Corey Szaslow, for the evanescent pleasure of being no more than a collection of impulses—the sum total of his lusts.

He took a long, last look around the strip, the geography of which had served as the setting for so much of his own personal mythology; and as he took his leave of it, it was less with nostalgia and fond regret, than with a kind of anthropologist's eye: the low, dark storefronts, the come-hither lights, the rhythmic thud of dance music pulsing through the doors, the haze of cigarette smoke, the bitter tang of testosterone; and above all, the bodies—hundreds of them, punished into perfection, lashed into fashion, strutted and thrust and paraded in all directions, offered up for appraisal, available on condition, but always in motion, moving on, moving in, making moves, moving on again.

It seemed, strangely, to be more fitting to leave the scene as an observer than as a participant. What he wasn't allowing himself to acknowledge, was that tomorrow's turning point was in a way a redundancy: already, somehow, he had become a different man.

Chapter 28

Typically, the boy was late for the most important appointment of his life, and as a result Jack had to endure a half-hour wait in Francesca's garden apartment, sipping tea (a purple, viscous blend he couldn't identify and was afraid to inquire about) and trying to avoid the bits of cat fur wafting everywhere around him. Given the room's airtightness and greenhouse warmth, he couldn't begin to imagine how they managed to find air currents to ride, but they were riding them right into his face.

As he waved a tuft away, Francesca, who was otherwise busy painting a red pentagram on her hardwood floor, caught him in the act and became immediately apologetic. "Oh, gosh, what can I say, the cats, yes. It's awful, the way they shed. I ought to brush them, really. Tomorrow, yes; tomorrow I start doing that. Spa treatments twice a week. Brushing, nail-clipping, teeth."

"It's fine," Jack said, as the tuft lazily darted around his head like a punch-drunk wasp. "It's just, I'm a little allergic." He was characteristically understating the case; in truth, cat fur played merry hell with his sinuses.

"Oh, well," Francesca said brightly, getting back down to painting, "not for long, anyway. Be breathing through someone else's nose tonight."

The fur fluttered down now and settled squarely on the surface of Jack's tea. *With my luck, he's allergic too,* he thought, setting the cup down and gently shoving it away from him. He felt something slink seductively past his calves, and said, "How many cats you got here, anyway?"

"Just the thirteen," Francesca trilled happily as she scooted around the floor, laying down a wide red circle that encompassed the pentagram. "Jizzy, Winkle, Bo-Bot, Curly, Ashtoreth, Spanky, Luvums, Itch, Osiris, Pantagruel, Bingo, Hathor, Lollipop, and Razor."

Jack had been mentally tallying, and now raised an eyebrow. "That's *four*teen."

Francesca squatted back on her knees and looked up in alarm. "Uh-oh," she said. She started counting them herself again, silently mouthing their names as she held up a finger for each.

At the idea of a baker's dozen feline fur factories secreted in the nooks and crannies all about him, Jack felt his sinuses prickle and swell and his eyes begin to itch. A big, messy sneeze snuck up on him; he was barely able to fetch his handkerchief and get it in place before it sloppily exploded.

Meanwhile, Francesca's paintbrush, now held loosely at her side, started dripping on the floor. "Oh, hey," Jack said as he tucked the handkerchief back in his pocket, "watch out there."

"Dag*nab*bit," she said, jerking the paintbrush up, which only sent globules of red flying across the length of the apartment. "Mother *Macree!*"

As she fussed over the mess, Jack looked at the pentagram itself, which was drying very quickly, and in a duller, darker shade than it had been going down. He had the sudden and awful suspicion that it might actually be blood, and not for the first time wondered if he'd gotten in over his head.

He nodded at the pentagram and said, his voice breaking slightly, "I-is that what I think it is?"

Francesca nodded brightly. "Mm-hmm! Good ol' tempera paint." She climbed out of her crouch. "*Dang* these middle-aged knees."

Jack looked closer at the pentagram. "*Tempera* paint?"

"Gosh, yes," she said, on her feet now and smoothing out the lap of her blouse. "Water soluble. Cleans up a treat." She looked at him with an arched eyebrow. "You didn't think I'd use anything *permanent*, did you? . . . I mean, I may be a witch, but I'm a witch with a security deposit."

"No, no, I . . . no." Jack really had no idea how to talk to this woman. And his sinuses were clamping shut like a Venus flytrap. A few minutes more and he'd have to breathe through his mouth, like a village idiot. Where the hell was Corey?

Francesca moved over to the coffee table; as she did so, the shoulder of her blouse slipped, revealing her bra strap; the left leg of her slacks rode up her calf; and the button of her sleeve hooked onto her waist and untucked her. She was like a living embodiment of the principle of entropy; whenever she moved, she seemed to dissolve into a shambles.

She plucked up the teapot and waggled it at him. "Refill?"

"No thanks," he said, pushing the cup even farther away. "Wired enough already. So, the pentagram . . . that's, what, like, to summon spirits or something?"

"Oh, gosh sakes, no," she said with a laugh as she poured herself a cup. "No spirits lending a hand here today! We're strictly do-it-yourselfers." She set down the pot and joined him on the sofa, seating herself uncomfortably close to him. The weird intensity she projected was awkward enough from across the room, but up close it was like being mugged. She seemed ready at any moment to grab him and start eating him whole. And as he'd feared, he *was* now breathing through his mouth, which he very much hoped she didn't interpret as sudden sexual excitement.

"No," she continued after a sip, "a pentagram is just, like, a kind of conduit for arcane energies. It sort of *pulls* them from wherever they're active in the area and holds them there till I'm ready to use them. The principle is sort of like—well, you know those fluorescent bug zappers? Best I can describe it."

He looked at the pentagram. "So you've, what, got a bunch of mystical mosquitoes piling up in there right now?"

"Something similar," she said, sipping her tea again. She sipped very noisily. Slurped, really. This close to his ears, it set Jack's nerves jangling. "More like lightning bugs."

The doorbell rang and Francesca jumped up to man the intercom. As she did, the naugahyde cushion she'd vacated emitted an enormous sigh. Jack wanted to say, *I know how you feel.*

"Hull*yew*," cooed Francesca into the speaker, pulling her blouse up over her shoulder again; as if in compensation, one of her socks went limp around her ankle.

"It's Corey Szaslow," came the breathless reply.

Francesca buzzed him into the building—a sound that resembled a chain saw bisecting an automobile—and moments later Jack heard the boy's light tread on the stairs. From the swiftness and increasing volume it was clear he was loping up two or three steps at a time. Jack couldn't help smiling. *Soon,* he thought, *those legs will be mine.*

Then, for the first time, something clutched his heart and squeezed: a terrible realization that he was about to cross the line to genuine profanity—in the old, ecclesiastical sense of the word: the farthest extreme from the sacred. He had dared to treat the human body, the human *mind,* as commodities, to be sold or traded, and he was here to put the seal on the deal and close out the contract. What had he been thinking? . . . How had he *dared?*

Then came the knock on the door, jolting him out of his sudden fear. It flowed right out of him as though he were a sieve. And then he had another, equally surprising epiphany: *This isn't going to work.* He supposed he'd never *really* believed it would. He'd followed it through because . . . why?

It amused him? . . . Was it only some tawdry little fantasy he enjoyed entertaining to the fullest, before the inevitable disappointment? . . . Or was the awful truth no more than this: he had nothing better to do with his time?

Francesca swung open the door and Corey entered in one big gush, all arms and legs and excuses. "Oh, hey, nice to meet you, sorry I'm late, it's, like, okay, I biked over here and I thought Ainslie goes all the way through but it doesn't, it runs smack up against the tracks, so I had to keep going north to find a road across, and then suddenly I was in this cul de sac and I didn't, like, know *where* I was, I was all turned around, and then there was this *dog* . . ."

He was breathing heavily—panting, really—and there was something wild about his eyes. And Jack had his third epiphany in as many minutes: *He's lying. He got scared, and just kept riding around on his bike, hoping he'd find some way to talk himself out of this.* But he hadn't. And here he was. Which was all that mattered.

But . . . *why* did it matter? . . . If this whole silly scheme was doomed to failure anyway, why care whether Corey showed up or not?

Jack was momentarily perplexed by the contradictory workings of his mind. He found himself wondering whether that mind would work any better once it was housed in a much younger brain. He could only hope.

Corey stepped forward, flashing his dazzling teeth, and shook his hand. "Hey, boss," he said. "Good to see you! Though I guess I'll be seein' a *lot* of you, from now on." He laughed, just a touch hysterically.

"Only in your mirror," quipped Jack. As Corey moved past him, he got a whiff of the boy's sweat—strong enough to infiltrate even his allergy-blocked nasal passages. And he thought: *First order of business will be a hot shower.* The thought of being alone with Corey's naked body—*truly* alone, in the sense that it would be *his* naked body—gave him a strangely erotic thrill, quelled only by a sudden constriction of his throat. How much more cat dandruff had he gulped out of the air in speaking just those few words?

"All right, then," said Francesca as she began busily lighting candles. "Hate to rush you, but we *are* running late and I've got a past-life regression seminar in forty minutes." She shook out the match, then tossed it towards an ashtray and missed; it landed on a little pile of paper napkins and started a small fire. "Oh, jeepers," she said, with barely a trace of alarm. Then she calmly picked up Jack's unsipped cup of tea and dumped it on the flames.

Crisis averted, she turned with a smile and said, "Take a seat, each of you, on opposite sides of the pentagram."

Corey slipped his backpack off his shoulders and said, "Do we need to take our clothes off, or something?"

"Only if you'd be more comfortable, snooks," she said, and she lowered herself to the floor; somewhere on her, a seam audibly burst.

Jack sat opposite Corey, and they locked eyes. Jack shrugged and smiled, as though this were just some crazy scene they'd stumbled into, and not something they'd spent weeks meticulously setting up.

He noticed again how attractive Corey was, and felt another momentary erotic charge. It was strange; he'd never allowed himself to see Corey in any such light while they were negotiating this arrangement—but now, here, at the moment he was taking possession of it, he could only congratulate himself on his good luck: his new body was *hot*.

Then he remembered that he *wasn't* taking possession of it because this was all a ridiculous sham, and he grew embarrassed and confused, and averted his eyes.

Francesca turned on her stereo and a great discordant chorus of scraping strings emerged from the speakers. She turned and said, "Kronos Quartet playing Jimi Hendrix. I like that kind of fusion for my background music; the sonorities of the old world, the energy of the new."

"Who's Jimi Hendrix?" asked Corey.

Francesca frowned. "Well. Maybe not *that* new." She patted him on the head. "Check your LP collection when you get your new body to your new home."

Jack felt a flush of embarrassment. He *did* have Hendrix LPs at home. Though it would take Corey some time to find them; they were buried deep in his storage locker in the basement, along with the other detritus of decades past— decades he would soon be shedding.

If this worked. Which it wouldn't. *Couldn't.*

Could it?

Maybe his inability to adhere to either belief or skepticism was simply a matter of not sufficiently understanding the mechanics involved. Right now this was all just voodoo hoodoo, so of course he couldn't believe in it. But if he knew more . . .

He cleared his throat and said, "So, how does this work, exactly? You said we're not invoking any 'spirits,' so . . . what exactly *are* we invoking?"

"Nothing," said Francesca as she lowered herself to the floor between them, at the high point of the pentagram. "We're just rearranging energy flow, is all."

"Sounds like New Age bullshit," said Corey. Immediately he flinched at his own rudeness. "Sorry."

"Never mind, lovebug." She turned back to Jack as she unscrewed a jar of herbs and powders. "See, consciousness is a funny ol' thing: it exists, but it's not physical; it's more like electric impulses, though even that's an oversimplification. Theoretically, we should be able to convert anyone's consciousness into digital pulses and store it in a computer. Well, that's what I've heard anyway." She started sprinkling the herbs in a crescent formation before her. "What we're doing here is something similar. The pentagram has bound up some of the earth's magnetic energies here, using nearby geomantic webs—though 'nearby' in this sense might, depending on a host of factors, mean ley lines in Europe or

China; magick really isn't an exact science—not like chemistry, or astrology." She screwed the lid back on the jar. "Anyway, I'll do the same thing with *your* consciousnesses in a moment: unbind them from your physical bodies and send them as energy patterns into the pentagram. From there they'll shoot back into the geomantic web, probably run around the earth a couple of times before barreling back up here, in the opposite direction. That's the theory, anyway— or a gross oversimplification thereof. I've never actually done anything like it before, so I guess we'll all find out together."

Corey raised an eyebrow. "So you mean . . . there really *is* a chance it won't work?"

"There's *always* that chance, angel pie."

Jack smiled; it was the *aha!* moment. Francesca had just prepped them for failure; so when nothing happened, she could legitimately claim it was due to inexperience, not to fraud. Never mind. He'd pay her anyway.

Looking back at Corey, he couldn't but notice the slight smirk of relief on his face. As much as the boy seemed to want this . . . he also didn't want it. Did Jack feel similarly conflicted? Was *that* the source of his ping-ponging credulity?

Francesca lit a match. A large orange cat snuck up behind her and nuzzled her; she nudged it away and said, "Not now. Mommy's *working*." Then she shut her eyes and began rhythmically muttering in a strange language.

"Latin?" asked Jack during a pause between phrases.

"Danish," she said, eyes still shut. "My first husband was from Copenhagen. I *could* do it in English, but this way helps me really concentrate on the words." She went back to incanting. The match was burning down, threatening to singe her fingers; she appeared not to notice. Jack caught Corey's eye; Corey caught Jack's. Wordlessly they expressed their concern.

Still Francesca kept reciting her spell. Her focus, if anything, deepened.

The match burned down to her fingers. She didn't cry out.

"Should we do something?" whispered Corey.

"I suppose," said Jack. "I don't want her to hurt herse—"

Before he could finish, Francesca's eyes flew open, and she flung the match onto the crescent of herbs. It exploded into bright flame.

Jack had to admire the show she was putting on; not only would he pay her, he might even tip her. But then the whole matter was rendered moot, because something now slammed into the building, knocking him over on his back. He thought it must be an earthquake. *But there are no fault lines in Chicago,* he reminded himself.

His next conscious thought was, *Terrorism!*—and then the floor opened up and swallowed him whole, and he was falling—into water?—*something* was all around him, pressing against him and also passing over him. He was utterly disoriented and tried to breathe—if he could breathe, he *couldn't* be underwater—but he didn't seem to remember how. He couldn't see anything, either . . . which was funny, because it wasn't dark; it wasn't exactly light, either; it was like an absence of the whole *concept* of a visible spectrum—which was clearly ridiculous because his eyes would have to register that absence as *something,* and—and—

—and suddenly he realized how funny it was to be having a metaphysical quandary like this when he was clearly either falling to his death or drowning to similar effect—except he didn't feel like he *was* falling now—and he couldn't quite tell down from up—or even left from right.

I can't orient myself, he realized with dismay; *can't get myself straight*—and he was sufficiently himself to chuckle at the unintended pun.

And then he started spiraling like a top; or at least that's how it seemed, though he felt no evidence of actual movement, no friction, no centrifugal force, just a continual circular reordering of everything around him, swifter and swifter and swifter and swifter yet—

And then he felt something grow beneath him—or above

him, he couldn't tell—that pressed on him, with greater and greater force until he felt he might just pop like a pimple—

And then he popped like a pimple.

Up he went, ascending in a kind of arc, across what he couldn't say—it wasn't sky, surely—but he was traversing *something,* moving faster and faster—

And then he hit the mountain.

Hard.

If it *was* a mountain.

If he was *he.*

He felt a thick haze of jumbled sensations; like when he'd been accidentally clobbered by a baseball bat at fifteen, and everyone had stood over him saying *Are you okay? Are you okay?* but he couldn't see them, and couldn't speak even if he could—he'd been knocked clear out of himself and had had to scrabble back in, clawing at his consciousness as at the lowest rung on a ladder—

And then that memory gave way to a sensation: cold.

And another: the smell of wax.

He opened his eyes.

He was sprawled out on Francesca's pentagram, one cheek pressed against the floor.

"Are you okay?"

For a moment he thought this was an echo from his recent memory; but then Francesca repeated the question, and he sat up to answer her.

He looked to his left; but she wasn't there.

"I said, are you okay?"

The question came from his right. He jerked his head in that direction, and there was Francesca, sitting placidly as before. Which was a kind of miracle—whatever had slammed into the building had knocked her clear across the pentagram.

He looked beyond her, and noticed something even stranger; the whole *apartment* had apparently been knocked for six. Everything that had once been over *here,* was now over *there.*

Then he heard the moan; and he looked across to see . . .

. . . to see . . .

. . . himself, to see himself.

Jack Ackerly.

Rousing himself from what looked like a two-day drunk.

And then he realized that the *apartment* hadn't inverted.

He had.

He was just looking at it all from a different angle now.

Corey's angle.

He held up his arms.

Young arms; rippling with veins and sinew.

Hairless arms, pink and strong.

And his hands . . . so large . . . the nails in need of clipping . . .

And then something rubbed up against his back and wrapped itself around his waist. He looked down into a pair of yellow feline eyes.

But . . . he was *breathing.*

He was breathing *just fine.*

"Oh . . . oh my *God!* W-what did you *do* to me?"

He snapped his head up and looked at himself—or rather, at Corey, in his discarded body. And his old face was there, twisted up in panic and rage; his old hands clutched his old throat, which now coughed up a globule of phlegm, which his old mouth spat on the floor.

"I SAID WHAT DID YOU DO TO ME?" The face was twisted with desperation and anger. It frightened Jack that he might ever have looked that way.

"Don't panic," he said calmly. "It's just an allergy attack. I'm . . . or rather, you're allergic to cats."

"Feels like I'm fucking *dying!*" Corey rubbed his eyes.

"Don't do that—don't rub them!"

"They itch!"

"Yes, but if there's cat dander on your hands you'll just make it worse."

Corey moaned, gasped, and then sneezed. He looked up helplessly; Jack knew what he was feeling—the familiar post-sneeze drip of dislodged mucous.

"There's a hankie in your pants," he said helpfully.

Corey reached into the pockets of Jack's old trousers and produced the handkerchief. Almost instantly, he flung it on the ground. "It's *soiled!*"

"Well, yes," Jack said. "I used it just before you came in."

Corey gave him a *What-the-fuck-is-wrong-with-you* look and said, "You don't offer someone a *used* handkerchief!"

"I didn't offer it, it *belongs* to you. And whatever gunk is in there came from *your* nose."

"No, no," said Corey, his new face red and swollen. "It came out of *this* nose, sure, but *before* it was mine. That filthy rag has nothing to do with me." He got to his feet, weakly. "You might've *warned* me I'd feel this way."

Jack breathed in. His lungs felt like they could hold *gallons* of air. "I guess I never realized how bad off I was before."

"Thanks, boss, that makes me feel *so* much better." Corey stumbled towards the door. He nodded at Francesca and said, "Sorry, thanks for everything, but I gotta get clear of this place."

He flung open the door and raced out.

Jack jumped to his feet (his *new* feet!—And how *quickly* they responded!) and ran after him, calling out, "Car's parked on Argyle, in front of the Starbucks—keys are in your pocket! Oh, and I always keep allergy pills in the glove compartment—but don't take more than two at a time!"

The pounding of Corey's feet on the stairs ceased with the creaking open of the front door.

Jack ran back into the apartment and flung open the window overlooking the street. As his old body staggered down

the sidewalk away from him, he called out, "Oh, yeah—
You're allergic to shellfish, too!"

Corey waved back at him, almost in dismissal, and turned
a corner.

And he was gone.

Taking quite a bit of what used to be Jack with him.

Jack turned away from the window, feeling a peculiar
blend of elation, excitement—and unexpected sadness.

Francesca was still cross-legged on the floor, before the
burnt remnants of the crescent of herbs. She looked at him.

He looked at her.

"Ssss-so," she said warily.

He cocked an eyebrow. "So," he said.

"So, I'm inferring . . . that it worked?"

It was a few moments before Jack realized he had to take
a leak. His new body had to pee out something he himself
hadn't drunk in. It was a weird thought, and it made him
giddy. As he swept down Francesca's dark little hallway, he
could smell himself; and the rank aroma of sweat that had
so offended him, when he'd detected it earlier in his old
body, now seemed strangely satisfying. He couldn't breathe
in enough of it. He lifted his lithe young arm and inhaled
deeply of his armpit. He almost purred in pleasure.

In the bathroom, he examined his face in the mirror. It
was so beautiful . . . so smooth, untouched by worry or weari-
ness or decades of disappointment. He opened his mouth and
inspected every tooth. Perfect, perfect. He wondered how
long it would take Corey to discover he now had a rather
large dental bridge in the back of *his* mouth. He hoped the
boy wouldn't think he'd deliberately withheld that; there'd
just been insufficient time to tell him *everything*.

He stood back a moment and admired the sudden splen-
dor of himself. Of his *new* self. The self with which he would
live all the excitement, all the adventures, all the romance of
the golden years he'd missed.

And then, inevitably, he looked down at the bulge between his legs. He reached his hand into his shorts and gripped his new equipment. It hardened up at his touch. He aimed it at the bowl and let the urine surge out of him while it still could—before his erection stopped the flow entirely. He managed to empty himself almost completely before he was left holding a mammoth young prick, all poised for action. It was such a beautiful thing—so young and vital! . . . It was almost more than he could bear to tuck it back into his shorts. But to stand here in Francesca's chintzy old-lady bathroom playing with himself was just too creepy an idea to consider.

The door swung open a bit and for one panicked moment he thought Francesca was going to intrude on him; he managed to zip himself up just in time. But it turned out to be just one of the cats. It slipped through the opening it had made and entwined itself between his ankles.

He reached down and stroked it. "Yes, puss," he cooed. "I can pet you now. Doesn't bother me a bit. Puss, puss, puss! . . . Why, I could even *get* myself a little pussy if I wanted to."

He found himself giggling at what he'd just said. In point of fact, pussy wasn't at *all* what he wanted to get.

He hoisted the backpack over his shoulders again (though not really again—they hadn't been *his* shoulders the last time it had hung here), and thanked Francesca anew, adding that she should mail him her bill.

"Sure, sure, no problem, my pleasure," she said. "Really, it would've been almost worth doing for free. I mean, hel*lo,* the bragging rights *alone!* Can't wait to see the look on Pansy Wetherall's face, the big fat Druid fishwife."

Jack gave her a wink as she opened the front door for him. "You give her hell, Francesca."

"If only I could . . . *literally,*" she said wistfully. "But what am I saying, she's probably got a time-share there already."

Jack stepped out into the hall and realized Corey hadn't told him where he'd left his bike.

"Just one more thing," said Francesca behind him.

He turned. "Hm?"

"Well, I'm obliged to say this. Rules and Ethics Committee thing. The spell is new, but it's not quite permanent yet. You can reverse it if you want to. Though it's a pretty awful process."

"Don't worry," he said, "I won't want to."

"You have about three months, is all," she said. "Till the Fall Equinox. After that, it's too late. You understand this? . . . Don't nod, say 'Yes, I understand.' I have to put it in the form that you said it."

"Yes, I understand," he said. He felt the strength coursing through his legs. If he couldn't find the bike, maybe he'd just *run* home.

"All right, then, sweetums. You have a nice one." She waggled her fingers at him and shut the door.

And Jack Ackerly breezed down the stairs and into his new young life.

Part Four

Jack (Corey)

Chapter 29

It took Jack ten full minutes to find where Corey had left his bike, and several more to locate, in the numerous pockets of his cargo shorts, the key to its Kryptonite lock. But with the sun beating down on his wheat-tressed head, the sweet summer air filling his ample lungs, the blood coursing through his veins like a rousing chorus of "Oklahoma"—well, it might've taken him twice, three times as long, and never annoyed him. During the search, a few dozen people passed him on the street, and so buoyant did he feel, so brimming with youth and promise and possibility, that he felt like bellowing "Hello!" to every one of them, tossing them a smile, encouraging them to embrace the day. But he'd lived long enough in the city to know exactly how this would be perceived.

The ride back home was a somewhat harrowing enterprise; it had been a long time since Jack had been on an actual bicycle, as opposed to the stationary bikes at the gym, and he was a bit out of practice when it came to maintaining his balance. Also, the legs and trunk he had to work with were as new to him as the bike itself. But once he got up and going, the sheer momentum made him giddy—and despite two rather nasty spills (caused by his inability to resist glancing at his reflection as he sped past storefront windows), he managed only to scrape an elbow; which, despite hurting like the dickens, only made him more splendidly aware of the new body he was wearing. Each stab of pain was like a pinch that didn't wake him—reminding him this could not be a dream.

He reached his new apartment building, and seeing it through Corey's eyes was like seeing it for the first time. He had been here just this morning, to drop off Nelly before heading over to Francesca's; at which time it had occurred to him that it might not have been the best idea to take a third-floor apartment in a building without an elevator. Nelly, in her old age, had largely lost the ability to maneuver stairs, and Jack had had to carry her up all three flights, seriously winding himself. Now, however, he laughed at the inconvenience of toting his bike the same distance. With young, supple muscles like these, what did it matter?

Even so, he'd worked up a pleasant film of sweat by the time he reached his door, and his breath was slightly labored. It was exhilarating, this feeling of lifting, doing, *breathing*. He slipped his key into the lock and heard the jingle of Nelly's collar as she padded towards the door in anticipation. Good old Nelly; despite his delight in all that was new for him (and *of* him), it was a comfort to know his best friend would still be there to greet him when he came in.

Except . . . when he swung open the door and rolled the bike in, with his usual "Hello, girl!" on his lips, Nelly stopped short and stared at him. Her tail drooped. She seemed almost to peer behind him, as though checking for someone else. Then she looked up at him, gave him a polite smile and the merest formality of a tail-wag, and kept her distance.

He set the bike against a wall and crouched down. "Come on, girl. It's me. I told you this was going to happen, remember?" She stared at him noncommittally. He reached up and fetched her leash from the telephone stand. "You wanna go for a walk, old girl? Huh? Walk?" He waggled the leash before her face. "Walkies?"

Nelly was usually eager, if not downright wild, to walk, so her reticence was a little frustrating. But Jack managed to persuade her to allow him to buckle her up, and they set out together.

At the top of the stairs he tried to pick her up, and she went rigid and refused, wriggling out of his grasp. When he tried harder to hold onto her, she actually bared her teeth at him.

"For God's sake, girl," he said, "aren't you supposed to have some kind of mystical dog sense that lets you recognize me? I mean, you've known me for years! Is a body really all I was to you?" She gave him a look that might have said, *Is that really all you were to yourself?*

Humbled, he gave up and let her descend the three flights on her own. This took an achingly long time and pretty well exhausted her, so that by the time they made it outside she wasn't up to much more than a stroll to the corner and back, during which time she obligingly voided her bowels and bladder. Jack had hoped to walk farther, into the heavily gay business district a block or so away, and use her as an icebreaker to meet his new neighbors (and potential lovers). But Nelly was refusing to cooperate; he wouldn't be able to use her as a crutch.

Fine, then. The way he looked—the way he *felt*—he didn't need one.

Back inside the building, Nelly reached the bottom of the stairs and balked completely; she wouldn't even attempt the first step. Frustrated, Jack muttered an obscenity, swept her up under one arm, and loped up all three flights before she could realize what was happening and object. When he set her down before the door, she was so dazed she almost fell over.

She was back on form when he tried to give her her pills. She required quite a battery of them—steroids, antibiotics, antivirals, anti-inflammatories—and while mere hours before, she had allowed Jack to push them gently down her throat, she now resisted him mightily. What a difference a new hand meant! He fought her with all the force of his own will for several minutes—prying her jaws apart and telling her, "You—WILL—take—these"—but once again, he ended by ceding her the victory, and was forced to embed each pill in a little chunk of *pâté de fois gras,* with which he'd fortunately stocked the refrigerator just that morning, and which Nelly consumed with no small delight.

By this time, he was sweaty, tired, and well lubricated with dog saliva. He'd nurtured an erotic expectation of his first shower as Corey—being alone, in that body, naked under jets of hot water, rubbing himself with soap, exploring the crevasses and crannies he'd only briefly glimpsed as yet—but by the time he actually made it under the showerhead, it was all he could do to get himself creditably clean before collapsing.

It had, after all, been an eventful day, and it had taken its full toll on him. He tumbled into bed, then rolled over and set the alarm for 11:30. He wasn't about to miss his first night on the town. And he fully intended to score.

His last thought, as he drifted off, was, *Do people still say "score"? . . .*

Chapter 30

By midnight he was on Halsted Street, reeling from the sight of so many lean, lanky, hungry-looking young men, and from the knowledge that now he was one of them. Everything about everyone seemed to shout sexual availability; a lock of hair falling across a forehead—a leather cord tied around a wrist—a disdainful flick of a cigarette into the gutter. On this dim-lit terrain, thick with musk and sweat, there was no detail of a man that lacked a context; and the only context possible was seduction. How many nights had Jack driven down this strip, looking out from his car window, like a middle-class tourist on a Kenyan safari, gazing in wonder at the wildlife beyond his reach, but not daring to let its gaze meet his? . . . And yet, he always saw men his age—even older!—milling among the lithe young gods, their desperation seeming to give off a scent that parted the crowds ahead of them like a cow-catcher on a locomotive. Jack had known, should he try to enter this world, that he would cut no less sorry a figure than they; and so he had always held back, content merely to look, then drive on.

But now, here he was—his fine young form on virtual display in his sleeveless microfiber tee, his low-rise jeans, and his flip flops. His hair—so thick! so wonderfully aromatic!—hung loose around his shoulders, and everything about him was as louche as he could wish it. He was utterly confident that tonight, he would not go home alone. Tonight, he would initiate himself into the sexual rites he had disdained so many decades ago. Tonight, at long last, he would fuck for the sake of fucking.

He entered a bar—he wasn't even quite aware of which one; he simply followed the crowd of men like a fish in a current—and was immediately engulfed by the seismic bass of the sound system. Ordinarily, something like this would drive him out the door in seconds, but tonight he realized its function: such powerful, hypnotic noise crowded out sentient thought, suppressed any stirring of individual identity, and drew everyone into a communal rhythm, to which the only possible response was animal.

Within seconds—*seconds!*—Jack spotted him. *The one.* His choice for the night. A tall, gaunt, but tautly muscled young man—no more than twenty-two or twenty-three—with deep, dark eyes like vortexes, and the kind of blue-black jaw and chin that connoted at least two shaves per day.

And what's more, the man's eyes were on him, too.

Jack played it cool. He bought a beer. He checked out the crowd. He wandered the labyrinthine bar, going from room to room, enclosure to enclosure. And he made no attempt to hide an occasional turn of his head, to see whether his chosen mate was following.

He was following. And he made no attempt to seem otherwise, either. Each time Jack turned to look at him, he boldly met Jack's eyes. The spark of carnal energy that passed between them was almost overpowering. Jack felt everything, all the matter of the world, converging in his groin. He had never been so aware of his genitals. They seemed alive as never before, sensitive to every step he made, all their nerve endings suddenly as receptive as TV antennae. For the first time in his life, Jack understood the vulgar phrase, "I thought I was going to come in my pants."

Eventually, after two more beers and several more tantalizing rounds of cat-and-mouse, Jack summoned his courage and approached his predator.

"Hey," he said.

The man grinned at him. "Hey."

Jack felt dizzy with anticipation. What next? Invite him home? . . . No, no. Too soon. Buy him a drink! That's it!

He nodded at the man's near-empty bottle. "Another one on me?"

The man cocked his head, as though thinking it over. "What the hell?" he said. "That's a good first step."

Jack blinked. He didn't know what to make of this. "Well, okay then," he said. He jerked his head towards the bar and said, "I'll be right back. Don't go away."

"Isn't that my line to you?"

Jack, confused, knit his brow. "Sorry?"

He shook his head. "No, *I'm* sorry. I shouldn't have said that. Look, if you want to make things right, that's great. I'm not gonna come down on you. I'm not bitter."

"Bitter?" said Jack. He had a sudden, unpleasant sensation that something wasn't quite right here.

"Well, yeah," the man said. "You avoid me for six months, you don't answer my calls, what do you expect?" His eyes grew wilder, and Jack took a step back. "Fine, I know there's two sides to every story. I know I came on too strong. So you sail in here tonight like nothing happened, you get it all going again—okay, fine. I'm all for it. Buy me another beer and treat me right, yeah, sure. Everything's forgiven." He leaned into Jack. "Just *don't fucking ditch me* again, okay?"

Jack contemplated a response, but instead chose to rely on his instinct, which was to turn, head out the door, and go directly home as quickly as possible.

Back in his apartment, he locked the door behind him and didn't even turn on the lights, but skulked about in the dark, peering out at the street from behind his curtains to make sure he hadn't been followed. When Nelly came up behind him and nudged the backside of his knee, he nearly jumped through the roof.

"I'll walk you tomorrow," he whispered to her when he'd recovered. "Feel free to shit on the floor if you can't wait that long. I give you permission."

It occurred to him for the first time that it might not have been a good idea to have taken on the identity of someone with as much sexual history as Corey.

That night, as he lay in bed, alone and wide awake, he was tormented with doubt.

What have I done? he asked himself.

What am I doing?

And even more troubling, *Who am I?*

He tossed and he turned, but answers remained elusive.

Chapter 31

Humbled by his first foray into the gay meat market, Jack stayed home the next night. He told himself it was more important at this point to re-bond with Nelly (or bond with her for the first time; he wasn't sure which applied, in his unusual condition). Also, there was still plenty to do around the apartment; he'd barely begun to unpack. So he ordered a pizza and spent the evening hooking up his flatscreen TV, his DVD player, his TiVo, and the various other elements that comprised his home entertainment system. It was a long, frustrating task, involving much cursing at the several manuals; he'd never been good at this kind of thing. Harry had been the one with a knack for it. Even when they split up, Harry had been kind enough to disassemble all Jack's components and color-code the cables and plugs, so that Jack could easily put it all back together when he got to his new digs.

Alas, Jack had left that system in place for Corey and had gone out and bought a whole new one for himself. He also had a brand-new toolbox, filled with a full complement of shiny, just-purchased wrenches, screwdrivers, pliers, and the like. There was something about all these new goods and implements that filled him with hope. Predictably, he ended up surrounded by gaping boxes, shredded plastic wrap (which Nelly kept sneaking off with), scattered instruction sheets, and pizza gone cold because he was too focused on his task to remember to eat it. And for all his labors, he still had a stereo that wouldn't play, speakers that wouldn't speak, and a TV that aired only snow.

Interestingly, he found relief from the frustration in frequent and furious masturbation. There was something about this body that seemed to demand that kind of attention. Jack could just remember, back in his own twenties, having had a similar compulsion, visiting the bathroom several times a day to find quick, orgasmic relief from the relentless intensity of living each day. In those days, *everything* had seemed to give him an erection: the smell of coffee, the bounce of an elevator, the breeze. Now it seemed he was again to be so afflicted.

Later, after walking Nelly and clearing his head in the cool night air, he had a small electronic epiphany, and was able to make the proper connections to get at least the television up and running. Satisfied with this initial victory, he threw himself on the new sofa and did some channel-surfing, as he consumed a few leaden, chilly slices of his dinner.

He came across Paola Molinara on CNN; the fiery cultural critic was discussing some recent California sex scandal that had ended in murder. "People delude themselves," she said in her pile-driver manner, "into thinking that sex is this happy, hippie, purely physical activity with no psychological consequences. This is just wrong, okay? There's a reason our parents' and grandparents' generations had all those oppressive rules; they were there for our protection. I'm not saying roll back the clock, no, I'm all for free love, but free love *without illusions*. Sex is a powerful force, it's a primal drive that we have to strive to control; we have to take charge of our own sexuality, our own sexual behavior. We have to take responsibility, like adults. This idea that people can go and fool around with whomever they like and then walk away, because la-di-da, it's just sex, that's playing with fire. We see it time and again, there's a dark side to sex, and we ignore it at our own risk. In some cases, the risk of our lives."

Jack flipped to the next station—Animal Planet—and watched for a few minutes as a cat walked a tightrope with a parrot on its back—but Molinara's remarks stayed with him. She had a point; his misadventure of the night before was a perfect illustration. He'd thought he could just swagger into a bar, fix his gaze on someone, then take him home and ravish him. He blushed to think how foolish he'd been, how cocky and arrogant, asssuming it was all so easy. Of *course* it had blown up in his face, and he'd had to turn tail and run home, like a small animal scampering to its bolt hole. He'd have to be more careful from now on; more prudent, more selective.

And yet, and yet—*God*, he was horny! How many times had he got himself off today, and he was *still* ravenous for the real thing. Had he been like this before, back when he was first in his twenties? . . . He was suddenly and profoundly impressed by the sheer force of will it must have taken to sublimate his raging libido and funnel the energy instead into commerce and industry.

He was just about to doze off before the still-blaring television, when his cell phone rang. Scrambling back up from near-slumber, he fumbled it open and answered it—before realizing that it could be no one he knew; he'd yet to give this number out.

"Hey, it's Tyler."

Jack felt a flash of recognition. Corey had written out—by hand, on notepaper, which Jack had found endearing—a list of his closest friends and their identifying attributes; Jack had only glanced at it, because, as he'd told Corey, he'd probably be concentrating on making a new circle of friends, with whom he'd have more in common. He had, in fact, folded Corey's list into quarters, put it somewhere, and forgotten about it.

"Hey, buddy," he said jovially now, as he struggled to re-member what Corey had written about this Tyler.

"Hey, buddy, yourself," came the reply. "I can only as-sume you didn't check Caller I.D. before picking up, or you wouldn't have answered."

"Well, now, that's just not true." He sat up and used the remote to mute the TV.

"It's absolutely true," said Tyler. "I can hear it in your voice."

"No, I just woke up, is all."

"Exactly my point. You woke up and grabbed the phone out of instinct, without checking to see if it's the guy whose calls you've been dodging for, like, ten days now."

"Dude, you're way paranoid," said Jack, and he realized it was the first time he'd ever used the word *dude*. He hoped it didn't sound as awkward as it felt on his tongue.

"*You moved,*" said Tyler. "I went by your building today, to see if I could corner you at home, and I discover you've been fucking *kicked out*. There are workers gutting the en-tire building. You're living somewhere else now, and you didn't even tell me."

"Well—it all happened so fast."

"This has *not* been happening fast," said Tyler. "You've been weird with me ever since that night at La Bocca, when I told you about my condo. You realize we've talked, like, exactly once since then?"

"Look, I'm in a strange place right now . . ."

"Jesus! That's what best friends are *for*. How many strange places have I seen you through, anyway? . . . Like, ninety?"

Best friend? . . . Corey hadn't mentioned any best friends. In fact, he'd assured Jack that he'd have no trouble shirking all his old circle; that none of them would even much notice if he slipped quietly out of their lives. Why had Jack taken that at face value? . . . Why hadn't he recognized that, as a result of Corey's life degenerating to the point at which he'd seriously consider Jack's proposition, he might also have fallen prey to some seriously low self-esteem? . . . *Of course* he had people who cared about him; who didn't? Jack had been stupid and naïve.

But the question now was: what to do about it?

"Look, Tyler," he said, "I . . . just give me some space, okay? I just need a little time to sort through some stuff."

A pause. "Why?"

"*Why?*"

"Yeah, *why?* . . . Now, go on and tell me it's none of my business, Corey. I goddamn dare you to."

Jack had been about to do that, but now bit his tongue.

"We go back, like, a dozen years," Tyler said. "You know me better than anybody else. I thought that meant something."

"Maybe it does," said Jack. "We'll find out, when I come through this . . . this *thing* I'm in."

"Which you won't tell me about."

Jack took a deep breath. "Sorry. Can't."

"Screw 'can't.' *Won't.*"

"Fine, whatever you want to believe . . ."

An audible click; then nothing. Tyler had hung up.

Jack sat back, still holding the phone, and let out a sigh of relief. That had been much harder than he'd anticipated; still, he'd got through it. It was clear, however, that he'd better figure out some way of dealing with Tyler; the man obviously wasn't going to go away.

The phone buzzed again; Jack checked the Caller I.D. this time.

Tyler again.

Not going away, indeed.

He couldn't very well not answer, so he flipped open the phone. "Hello?"

"It's not just me," said Tyler immediately. "There's Steven, and Frida, and Jorge and Kevin and Perry . . . shit, you think we all haven't been talking to each other? You pushed *all* of us out of your life."

"Honestly, it's not like that . . ."

"Honestly, it is. And you know what? . . . When you push someone, you can get *pushed back*."

Another click. He'd hung up again.

Jack stared at the phone a moment and said, "Whoa."

It had no sooner left his ear than the phone buzzed again.

"I'm sorry," said Tyler. "I didn't mean that. Just know, okay, that you're hurting people you don't have to hurt. Right? Because whatever it is you're going through, we *want* to go through it with you."

"Tyler, I—"

"No, no"—something slightly strangulated in the voice; was he crying?—"When you're ready. Just . . . we'll be here. *I'll* be here."

And he hung up yet again.

Jack was still reeling when the phone blared to life once more; and this time, he felt a flash of irritation.

"All right, Tyler," he said, "I get it. We'll talk soon, but meantime could you jus—"

"This isn't Tyler," said a gruff, older man's voice. "This is Gordon Hearn."

Jack knit his brow. "Who?"

"Your ex-landlord. Got a call from my contractor today, his crew says your apartment's still loaded up with your crap."

"Nnnno," said Jack, "I moved it all to the Dumpster." Hadn't Corey said he was going to do that?

"Hell if you did," said Gordon Hearn. "It's all right where you left it, like you were still living there."

Jack sighed. "Well, I'm *not* living there, and I don't want any of that stuff, so feel free to just throw it out."

"Oh, great, thanks," said Gordon Hearn with acid sarcasm. "Any other little jobs you want me to do for you, while I'm at it?"

"What's that supposed to mean?"

"It means I'm not your fucking janitor, and neither is my

contractor. He's in the construction business, not garbage disposal."

"I understand that," said Jack. "But how hard can it be to just move a bunch of old furniture out of the way?"

"Couldn't say," said Hearn. "You tell me tomorrow, after you've done it."

Jack shook his head. "I'm certainly not going to do that."

"Then you certainly will be getting a bill for the removal, from me."

"I won't pay it."

"I got a lawyer says you will."

Jack was just about to top that—*Don't threaten me with lawyers, I've got an entire firm on retainer, whose most junior partner could eat your boy for breakfast*—before he realized how ridiculous that would sound coming out of Corey's mouth.

He weighed his alternatives—which took little enough time, since he had none—then sighed. "I'll be there tomorrow," he said.

"Damn straight," said Gordon Hearn.

As soon as he rang off, Jack turned off the phone before it had a chance to summon him again. He got up to brush his teeth, then turned back and popped its battery out for good measure.

Chapter 32

The next morning Jack reluctantly dressed for his task. He'd bought some sharp new clothes for his new body the day before, but he couldn't bear the idea of wearing them for actual physical labor; the only choice remaining was the T-shirt and cargo shorts Corey had had on when they'd made the switch, and those—sweaty, threadbare and more than a little smelly—Jack had actually tossed in the trash. He retrieved them now and pulled them back on, a little sneer of disgust on his face.

He hadn't even bothered to shower; what was the point? He'd soon be getting dirty again. He said goodbye to Nelly— who was still treating him very coolly—then grabbed his bike and trotted down the stairs. It amazed him anew, the sheer vitality in these young limbs. The bicycle, while cumbersome, was no burden at all to him; except for having to beware lest he scrape the walls at the landings, he might have been able to forget he was carrying it at all.

The morning was sweet and cool. He swung his leg over the bike, mounted the seat, and set out for Corey's old apartment, which wasn't much more than a ten-minute ride. He'd been there once before, when he picked up the boy for his appointment with Dr. Guptil; but he hadn't really looked at the place—he'd been too busy looking at Corey.

He found it again without much trouble, even though it appeared somewhat different, with a façade of scaffolding out front. Looking at it now, he saw that it was bigger than he'd recalled; it must boast fifteen, twenty units. He had no idea which had been Corey's.

After locking the bike to a signpost, he realized all he had to do was check out the door buzzers; since there'd been no new tenant after Corey, his name would still be up there, with his apartment number following. But alas, this proved optimistic; for it seemed that Gordon Hearn had left it to the various tenants to supply their own buzzer inserts, which meant that most of them were just names scrawled on scraps of paper, and some were simply empty. Corey, of course, was one of those who'd never bothered.

The mailbox, then. His name would have to be on that. Jack loitered around the door until someone exited the building; then he slipped in while the door was open.

The vestibule was small and dark and smelled of both insecticide and cooked cabbage. Jack approached the rows of tall, battered aluminum mail slots; sure enough, each bore a name and the corresponding apartment number. Jack began searching for Corey's.

He hadn't yet found it when someone came in and said, "Well, well, *well*. If it ain't who it is."

Jack turned and saw a strange man smiling at him. Not unattractive either; mid-thirties, long, lank hair, a two-day stubble. Nice muscles—if a little too pumped for comfort. By his demeanor, this was clearly someone Corey knew, so Jack smiled and said, "Hi."

"Returning to the scene of the crime, eh?" said the man, and he came over to the mailboxes and opened one of them. "Can't imagine why. Unless it's unfinished business with yours truly." He wagged his eyebrows at Jack.

"Actually," said Jack as the man retrieved his mail, "I just came by to move my furniture out. The workmen won't do it. I was basically threatened."

The man turned and put one hand on his hip. "Oh, you just left your old crap behind, huh? . . . My, my, my, must've landed yourself quite a sweet new sitch. No wonder you didn't take me up on my offer to crash at my place for a while. Still, you might've at least said something. 'Thanks, but no thanks.' Or just, 'Goodbye, Ignacio, nice knowin' ya.'"

Ignacio, thought Jack. He couldn't remember any Ignacio from Corey's little list of acquaintances. Again, he found himself wishing he'd read it more closely.

"Sorry," said Jack. "It all happened kind of fast."

Ignacio shrugged. "I get it. You don't owe me nothin', sport. Though I'm sad to see you go. Ass like yours doesn't come along every day." And he gave Jack's buttocks an appreciative leer.

Jack blinked. Was this . . . a *come-on?* . . . It couldn't be. He wasn't showered, he was wearing filthy old clothes . . .

. . . and yet, he was twenty-six years old and hot. Did details really matter?

Ignacio tucked his mail under his arm and said, "I don't suppose there's any chance of a goodbye kiss?"

Jack, taken off guard, said, "Well . . . I don't know. Maybe."

Ignacio's eyes popped open *"Maybe?"* he said. "What do I have to do?"

Jack thought for a moment. He'd never wielded power like this before; or if he had, he hadn't realized it. Was it really ethical, to employ it for his own gain?

On the other hand, wasn't that the whole point? Wasn't that why he'd done all this?

He gave Ignacio as alluring a look as he could manage and said, "Help me move my stuff to the Dumpster."

Ignacio said, "Sugar, you are *on.*"

He took Jack by the hand and led him into the building, down a staircase and past a boiler room to a garden apartment. This neatly solved Jack's problem of finding Corey's place; and a problem it certainly would have been, tucked away as it was in the basement.

The sound of hammering and sawing filtered down from above. The light was dim and gray, and he and Ignacio stood by the door to the apartment.

"Well?" said Ignacio.

Jack looked at him. "Well, what?"

"Well, aren't you going to let us in?"

"I don't have a key."

Ignacio raised an eyebrow, then touched the door with his foot. It swung open.

They looked at each other and laughed, then entered.

"So," said Ignacio exultantly, "I finally enter the lion's den!"

Jack looked around him in increasing dismay. It was clear that there had been workers in here already; most of the light fixtures had been removed, and cords sprouted from the ceiling like nose hairs; bits of plaster covered the floor so that it resembled a parade route, littered by confetti. But this new disarray couldn't mask the more enduring, more depressing dinginess of what Corey had left behind: a dilap-idated, dirty couch; a hideous coffee table with a crack in its veneer; mismatched chairs, their cushions split like a boxer's lip. It was worse than any fraternity house he'd ever known, and that was saying something. How was it possible to live this way? . . . At *twenty-six,* for God's sake?

Ignacio, however, seemed not to be dismayed by the sight; in fact, he was positively chipper. "Let's get to it, shall we?" he said, grabbing a tilted floor lamp and heading out the door. Who could blame him, Jack thought? He was looking for-ward to his reward.

In short order they had moved everything except the bed—which, in truth, was little more than a futon on a frame. Stand-ing over it, sweating, grimy, panting, Ignacio looked at Jack and said, "Well, then. This is it."

It was the kind of remark that could be interpreted in any number of ways. Jack—buffeted by thwarted lust, confu-sion, exhaustion, and a kind of existential despair—chose the first that occurred to him. He grabbed Ignacio by the back of his hair, and pulled him in for a deep, startlingly hungry kiss.

Ignacio, taken by surprise, lost his balance and fell onto the futon, pulling Jack after him. The frame broke underneath them, but they barely noticed.

Afterwards, Ignacio's air of triumph was insufferable. "I always knew I'd nail your ass one day," he said as he got up and stretched. "Admit it: you knew it too. You *liked* teasing me. You had every intention of giving in one day, but God forbid you'd ever show it."

As they dressed, Jack looked at Ignacio with a clearer head and thought, *He's not really all that attractive.* He was, actually, more like a parody of an attractive man. A jigsaw puzzle of an attractive man, with one or two pieces missing, and another from a different puzzle set altogether, pounded in where it didn't want to fit.

And as Ignacio continued to croon about the inevitability of their fusion, Jack realized, by degrees, what he'd done: he'd lowered himself to sleep with someone Corey had judged unworthy of him.

Corey, it seemed, had lived in squalid surroundings, but had been scrupulous about how he used his body. Jack had done just the opposite. Which was worse?

While he was considering this, Ignacio scampered off without helping him move the futon.

Jack had now had his second lesson.

Three strikes and you're out, he told himself.

After laboriously junking the futon and mattress, Jack went back to the apartment to make sure he'd cleared everything, and found that in Ignacio's haste to be away he'd left his bundle of mail on a bookshelf. Jack took it to the Dumpster and used it to garnish Corey's old belongings.

Okay, he thought. *Time to get it right.*

Chapter 33

Three nights later he found himself at Bar Sharona, an establishment he hadn't tried yet, but which Corey had mentioned in passing. After striking out the two previous evenings, things appeared to be looking up. He'd turned a few heads as he walked in, and even the very hot bartender winked at him, which did wonders for his confidence.

After the disaster of his first attempted pickup, Jack had decided that—given his new youth and beauty—he'd take the passive approach, and let someone approach *him*. He'd read in some tawdry advice column that "The treasure doesn't do the hunting," and though he felt a bit silly thinking in those terms, it seemed to be the safest course for him right now. So for the past two nights he'd showered and shaved and dressed in whatever clothes so hugged his form that in the right light they actually seem not to be there at all, then taken a seat at the bar, and waited. Nursed three, four beers, casting simmering glances at any eyes that dared meet his, and inviting anyone who was interested to approach him. For two nights running, no one did.

Tonight he decided to add a smile to the repertoire, just to make himself less forbidding. True, there was something inherently anti-erotic about a smile; but Corey had nice teeth—*Correction,* thought Jack; *I have nice teeth*—and what could it hurt . . . ?

It hurt nothing, and in fact brought him a nearly instant result. After only twenty minutes, a sweet young freckled man, with a lovely cleft in his chin and tufts of down on the back of his neck, sat on the stool next to his, swung it around so that he was facing the crowd, and said, "So, you're not like, weird or anything, are you?"

Jack looked at him and laughed. "I beg your pardon?"

"Sorry, I'm just in town for two nights, so I'd really hate to waste a lot of time running down someone who's gonna turn out to be all deep-dish at the end of it."

"Is that what you're doing? 'Running me down'?"

"Yeah, I got a gift for the apt phrase, don't I?" He extended his hand. "Ryan."

Jack shook it and said, "Ja—Corey."

"Ja Corey," said Ryan. "What are you, some kinda vanilla rapper or something?"

"It's Corey," he said, sheepishly. "But . . . uh, some people call me Jack."

Ryan looked at him. "So, you *are* weird."

Jack laughed. "You say you're from out of town?"

"Atlanta. Can I buy you a drink, Ja Corey?"

"I'm good right now," said Jack, indicating his nearly three-quarters-full bottle of Rolling Rock. "You don't have a Southern accent."

"I've only been South a couple years. I was born in New Hampshire."

"You don't have a New Hampshire accent, either."

"Would you know one if you heard it?"

Jack had to admit he wouldn't.

Ryan looked at him and grinned, and Jack couldn't help grinning back. Somehow, he'd fallen into an easy, friendly banter with this charming man; and there was a delicious undercurrent of seduction to add spice to the proceedings.

"What do you do in Atlanta?" Jack said after a swig of beer.

Ryan shrugged. "I handle media relations for a highly successful beverage company which shall remain unnamed," he said. "I may be a wage slave to the great corporate Satan, but don't force me to admit it out loud."

"Media relations, huh?"

"Yeah, it's at least half as glamorous as it sounds. Mainly I take calls from reporters who ask me to repeat what I've already sent them in a press release. Someday I want to send one out with the line 'Your mother clubs baby seals for crack money' buried in the second paragraph, just to see if anyone actually reads that far. What about you?"

Jack blinked. "What *about* me?"

"What do you *do?*"

"Well . . . not much lately. But I had my own P.R. firm for about fifteen years. So I've sent out my share of press releases."

Ryan stared at him. "So, you started your own firm at—what, seven?"

Jack blushed. "Oh—I was just trying to be funny. Saying 'fifteen years' like it was forever or something. I should've said 'a thousand.'" He paused. "I've got one of those senses of humor other people don't get."

Ryan just looked at him, his mouth slightly open.

"All right, I'm weird, I'm weird," Jack said. "You had me pegged right from the start."

Ryan smiled. "Actually, I have a rule of thumb," he said. "The guys who'll admit they're weird, are never the guys who really are."

"You have a lot of experience in that area, then?"

He rolled his eyes. "Don't we all? I could tell you stories . . ."

"Feel free. I'm a good listener."

They smiled at each other, and Jack had the exciting sensation of the rest of the bar receding to the distant horizon.

Ryan said, "Let me get a beer first," and as he swiveled back to the bar he put his hand on Jack's knee. Jack felt a jolt, as from an electric current; he almost lifted into the air.

After a few minutes trying to get the bartender's attention, Ryan turned and said, "Who do you have to fuck to get a drink around here?"

Jack said, "It's pretty busy tonight." Summoning all his courage, he said, "We could go someplace quieter."

Ryan looked startled. "Really? . . . You'd—you'd be okay going somewhere else?"

"Why not? I'm not wild about this place, or anything."

He sat back and looked at Jack with a smirk. "All right, Ja Corey. What's with that?"

"What's with what?"

"'*I'm not wild about this place.*'" He leaned closer. "Look. I've got a confession to make."

Jack felt the air around him grow close. "Uh-huh."

"I come to Chicago four, five times a year. I usually hit this bar at least once. And every time I've been here, I've seen you. Usually with someone. In fact, *always* with someone." His eyes bored into Jack's. "I told myself, if I ever had an opening with you, I'd grab it. Even so, this stool was free for ten whole minutes before I could work up the nerve to come and talk to you."

"That's very . . . flattering ," said Jack.

He put his hand on Jack's thigh. "And now you say you're willing to walk out here, at—what—not even midnight? . . . With hours to go till closing? And with *me?*"

Jack placed his hand on top of Ryan's. "Sure," he said. "Unless you want to stay here and *talk* about it some more."

Moments later, they slid off their stools together, to the gasped delight of a pair of heavily cologned young men who instantly took their places.

Chapter 34

Jack spent the night at Ryan's hotel, then woke up with a start at just after six, remembering he hadn't walked Nelly the night before. Devastated by guilt *(I never forgot Nelly when I was me,* is how he rather tellingly phrased it to himself), he tore out of bed and dressed in a fury. With Ryan looking on, rubbing the bridge of his nose in confusion, Jack blurted out the reason he had to bolt.

"Well," said Ryan, "I've heard a lot of morning-after excuses, but this one gets an A for originality."

Jack whirled and said, "Jesus, I'm feeling guilty enough, don't make it worse by doubting me."

"Who said I doubted you?" Ryan said in a tone that implied he doubted him very much.

Jack, half dressed, waved one of his socks towards the window. "You don't believe me?" he snarled. "You want to come along? See for yourself?"

"Love to," said Ryan, and for a moment he and Jack just looked at each other, a little surprised at the left turn they'd just taken.

"Fine," said Jack, "but for God's sake get dressed quick. I'll go get us a cab. Christ, my poor girl's probably been crossing her legs for *hours.*"

Actually, the poor girl hadn't bothered; perhaps sensing

she had the excuse of great age—and also perhaps not caring so much what she did to this new apartment, because
who was its owner to her?—she'd left a tidy little pool of
urine on the kitchen floor, and an almost perfectly coiled little black turd. She looked placidly up at Jack as he and Ryan
burst into the apartment.

"Well, this is a hell of a first impression," said Jack as
they surveyed the damage.

Ryan corrected him. "*Second impression.* Your first was
just fine."

Jack looked at him, and thought, *I'm glad he's leaving tomorrow, because oh my God, I don't want a boyfriend yet.*

Ryan offered to walk Nelly while Jack cleaned up, and
Nelly agreed to be walked by him with an air of distinct
condescension. By the time they returned, Jack had finished
the operation and was about to step in the shower. Ryan
took only minimal persuasion to step in after him.

They spent the rest of the day together and had dinner and
then spent the night together, in Jack's bed, which he was
delighted to be breaking in for the first of what he hoped
would be many similar encounters. The next morning, he
offered to take Ryan to the airport, and Ryan said, "Do you
have a car?" and Jack, thinking of the Porsche, said, "Do I
have a car!" and then a moment later caught himself and had
to mutter, "No."

So Ryan called a taxi and for a moment Jack considered
riding with him, but then he realized how peculiar that
would seem; plus, he really *didn't* want a boyfriend, and
clinging to Ryan while he tried to board a plane was not the
best way of conveying that.

In the days that followed they chatted on the phone several times, and Jack had his first experience with phone sex.
(*Not for me,* he decided. He'd waited too long for the real
deal, and wouldn't settle for anything less.) The phone calls
gave way to Instant Messaging, with gradually decreasing

intensity; and soon they were simply emailing each other a few lines every week or so.

But by that time, Jack had already moved on.

Jack's day-and-two-nights with Ryan spectacularly boosted his self-confidence. This was exactly what he'd been craving: this bonding with other men, sacrificing his own beauty to theirs, consuming each other, commingling on every level, from ardent flesh to radiant spirit. He felt so exhilaratingly *male,* so ecstatically part of a vast, loving, encompassing brotherhood of masculinity.

And yet . . .

Exhilaration is tiring; ecstasy short-lived. And modern life, with its multitudinous demands on attention and time, is relentlessly reductive. As a result, Jack soon whittled his experience with Ryan down to something more manageable—more merely physical. Dicks and ass, in essence. And during the ensuing weeks, while he shopped for a car, managed his new investments, cared for Nelly, and mused about what he might do with himself when the clubs weren't open, he pursued dicks and ass with great focus and energy. The bed that had borne Ryan with such grateful relief, now bowed under the weight of his many successors, dizzying in their variety—tattooed, goateed, pierced, or gap-toothed; some black, some white; some bald, some shaggy—and yet all comfortingly alike in their litheness, their leanness, their chiseled, sculpted anonymity.

In the steam room at his new gym, Jack sat sweating one day, recovering from a workout (one of the few he'd undertaken since inheriting this body). He was reflecting on the previous night's three-way, the results of which had been less than satisfactory. He could remember, just a few months past, when the idea of a three-way was so powerfully arousing, he couldn't risk admitting the thought in public lest he derange himself; now that he'd taken part in a few, he found the mechanics so complicated that it almost wasn't worth the effort. Trying to salvage the experience in retrospect, he strove to remember the way he'd first felt about his new sex life, about the rapturous communion it seemed to provide him with the eternal, pulsing sexuality of the men he bedded, the feeling of having tapped into some great well of thrumming gay male identity that bound him, in a whirling orgasmic nexus, to every other men-loving man alive.

And at that moment he happened to glance at the guy next to him: a large, sweat-slicked, red-faced man of no less than three hundred pounds, with stubby fingers and disturbingly tiny feet, who not only met Jack's glance but fixed it with a welcoming leer. While Jack balked, horrified, the man slid aside his towel to reveal what looked like a fuzzy cinnamon roll between his legs.

Jack turned away, appalled; and in that moment all thoughts of sacred kinship to his gay brethren evaporated for good.

Chapter 35

Jack soon found something to do during the day: sleep.
Despite the vigor with which his new body brimmed, he
discovered that it wasn't inexhaustible; there was a limit to
how much it could endure in a single night. Once he realized this, he recalibrated his nighttime adventures until he
found the equation that, for him, represented perfect har-
mony: the maximum number of hours he could party, com-
bined with the minimum hours of sleep that would allow
him to get up and start the whole process all over again.

His new apartment bore the signs of this arrangement.
Laundry piled up, the kitchen developed a permanent, gritty
skein, and bags of garbage lined the back corridor. The place,
he realized one day, was starting to look like Corey's. But he
dismissed that notion; he wasn't Corey, he was perfectly
able and willing to deal with this . . . eventually.

After awakening one morning to find Nelly carrying a
dead mouse across the living room, he broke down and
hired a cleaning service. Two middle-aged Polish women arrived, carrying all their own solvents, and whipped the place
into shape. Jack was so pleased he engaged them to return
every Wednesday morning. He'd briefly thought he might
find some hot young Polish studs to do the same job, then

reflected that this would probably be less a solution to the problem than an exacerbation.

Freed now of all responsibility save to his libido, Jack was living in full the life he had so covetously imagined for himself. If it seemed, at the moment, empty of feeling, even on occasion empty of sensation, he forced himself to recall what life had been for him, in his fifties, without any scandalous past to look back on. His current adventures, he reasoned, would ripen in memory; he was laying in a store of randy reflection to look back on, when he hit fifty again.

And not all of those moments occurred between the sheets. One night, his hot pursuit of a broad-shouldered redhead at a bar called Moxie's was·interrupted by a tall, handsome, dark-skinned man, with more than a faint aura of self-congratulation. He stepped into Jack's path and boldly asked his name.

Jack recognized him, but couldn't place·him; not until he swept the tail end of a dark burgundy scarf over one shoulder. *Paul Rashimudden,* thought Jack. *The Tealight Theatre's artistic director . . . and the snotty little fascist who made the crack about me being old!*

Jack smiled up at him and said, "Corey, my name's Corey."

Paul looked him up and down, as though he were considering buying him, and said, "Corey what?"

"Szaslow," said Jack.

Paul pursed his lips, as though in intense thought, then shook his head. "I don't know the name," he said. "I thought you might be among the actors I've worked with over the years."

Oh, for God's sake, Jack thought. *What a fucking line of shit.* But he played along, widening his eyes with excitement and saying, "Oh, you're in the *theater?*"

Paul's eyes fell momentarily shut and he smiled. "Guilty," he said.

Jack moved in closer. "Would I have seen anything you've been in?"

"Oh, I'm not an actor myself," he said; "I'm the artistic director for a small repertory company. Actors, I think, tend to look more like *you*."

"*Me?*" Jack gushed. "I really look like an *actor?*"

Paul nodded. "As I said, I took you to be one. Are you *sure* you've never been on the stage?"

"God, no, I'd remember *that*," said Jack with a laugh. "I've always sort of wondered what it'd be like, though."

"Well," Paul said, and he placed an arm behind Jack and gently ushered him into a dim corner, "perhaps we might talk about that. I might be able to help you realize your dream."

"*Seriously?*" Jack said. He hoped he wasn't playing it too broadly; he had a strong urge to laugh at himself. Paul, however, was eating it up. Maybe he really *was* an actor.

"Yes, seriously," Paul said. "I have certain . . . connections in theatrical circles. I could introduce you, help you with auditions . . . *mentor* you, so to speak."

"You'd do that for *me?*"

"I'd be quite glad to do it for you."

"Wow, that's really generous of you!"

Paul leaned in and whispered, "Well, I'm certain you can be generous in return."

Jack said, "Oh, sure! I'll do whatever you want!" After a small pause, during which Paul's eyes darkened with lust, Jack added, "So long as long as it's nothing like, y'know, having *sex* with you or anything." Paul's face froze. "I mean, sorry, I realize you probably weren't even thinking that. I shouldn't be so paranoid. I've got to remind myself not *every* old guy I meet is on the make."

Paul managed to mumble a few more syllables, none of which quite made sense in conjunction with any of the others, before making what was clearly a desperate escape.

Suffused with a sudden, serene sense of fulfillment, Jack emitted a little sigh, then turned back to the bar to obtain another beer.

As he reached into his pocket to draw out some cash, he felt his cell phone vibrating. He hadn't heard it ring in all the noise. He pulled it out and looked at the illuminated Caller I.D. It was a number he didn't recognize.

His guard down, he flipped the phone open and said, "Hello?"

It was a woman; he could barely hear her, what with the din, but it seemed she was crying. "Baby?" she said. "Why've you been ignoring me?"

"I'm sorry," Jack said, heading towards the back of the bar, by the restrooms, where the music was slightly more muffled. "Who's calling?"

This produced a fresh squall of tears. "Thanks a fucking lot!" she burbled.

Jack searched his mind for a woman's name—any woman's name—on Corey's scrawled list of friends. "Frida?" he conjectured, timidly.

"Yeah, Frida, you fucking dumb shit," she said, barely intelligibly. She was definitely crying.

Jack squeezed into a corner by the pay phone—a near relic these days. He wondered if it even worked. Once he was out of the path of the many pilgrims to the porcelain, he said, "Are you all right?"

"Fat fucking lot you care," she bawled. "Haven't heard from you in *weeks.*"

From this vantage point, Jack could see well into the bar—and now spotted the redhead he'd been tailing earlier; the boy stood in the middle of the crowd, looking intently about him. Jack felt sure he was looking for him—that he was mystified by the sudden disappearance of the man with whom he'd been so pleasurably playing cat and mouse.

Scalded by irritation, Jack said, "Look, Frida, I'm not putting up with this. You obviously called because something's wrong. Either tell me what that is, or hang up. We can discuss my abandonment of you some other time." *Like never,* he thought.

No reaction; he thought the connection lost, and said, *"Hello?"*

"You're a heartless bastard."

"I'm hanging up now."

"Tyler was right, you've gone cold."

"Bye, Frida."

"Julio's left me."

"I'm leaving you." The redhead was moving towards the door.

"He's been seeing someone else for, like, eight months."

"Then eight more hours won't matter." He moved back into the crowd. The redhead was near the door now. A pair of bleach-blonds darted past him, shrieking so that he couldn't hear Frida, and he said, "Sorry, did you say something?"

"I said, *I'm going to kill myself.*"

Jack sighed in defeat. He supposed he'd enjoyed enough of the benefits of being Corey that he might now gracefully submit to some of the drawbacks.

"I'll be right over," he said.

"Thank you."

"Just . . . remind me of the address."

A fresh squall of sobs.

Chapter 36

The closer he drew to Frida's apartment, the more irritated he became. And when she opened the door to admit him, he was slammed in the face by a wall of acrid marijuana smoke; he faltered back a step, coughing.

"Sweet baby Jesus," he said when he was again able to speak; tears ran down his cheeks. He took a handkerchief from his pocket and held it over his nose.

"Don't be so melodramatic," said Frida, who—from what Jack could see through the smoke—was a very ample woman indeed, with a figure like the Venus of Willendorf and a face like The Joker on *Batman*. "It never fucking bothered you before."

Jack waved a little path through the murk ahead of him and tried to scurry through it before it closed up again. *Have to have these clothes dry cleaned*, he thought, *or maybe just burned*.

He came up against a dining room table, rather closer to the front door than a dining room table ought to be. He looked up and saw that this was because there was no dining room. There was in fact only one room of any kind, and it looked to him like an antique shop: a whole estate's worth of Victorian furniture and artifacts was crammed in it, with only narrow passageways providing access from one side to the other. All that was missing were price tags.

"I take it you don't vacuum much," he said as he squeezed his way towards the center of the room, where a small clearing in the bric-a-brac promised at least space enough to sit down without his knees in his chin. As he shimmied towards it he caught sight of a tiny kitchenette, and adjacent to that a small corridor with a door that must open onto a bedroom. If it could open at all: Jack imagined a four-poster bed and an eight-foot mahogany wardrobe pressing against each other in a room designed for a wicker hamper and a fold-out futon.

He arrived at a beaten mule of a sofa, and momentarily froze when he saw a cat perched upon it, its knees tucked under it; then he remembered he didn't have to fear his old allergic triggers and he relaxed. He even made an attempt to pet the thing; but it darted away as soon as he came within arm's reach. He shrugged and sat down.

Frida followed him, talking the entire way. He'd been so bewildered by the surreality of her apartment that he only just now tuned in to what she was saying. ". . . works in a flower shop, which is the bitter fucking irony, he was in there to get something for my birthday, but instead of picking out flowers be picked up the florist, which is, like, a special kind of heinous, if you ask me, and what do you even *say* about a woman who'd set her claws in a guy *while he's buying flowers for another woman,* how low can you possibly get, that's, like, the bottom of the ocean where the pressure kills everything but ugly flat scavengers . . ."

She sat down beside him on the couch, and as her cushion depressed, his raised up a few inches. He almost lost his balance and had to grab on to armrest. "What are you, high or something?" she asked as he set himself right.

He shook his head in disbelief. "What if I were? *You're* in a position to judge?"

She took one last hit off the tiny black ember of a joint she had left, then flicked it into an ashtray. "Just for that I'm not sharing," she said, putting her lighter away.

"Don't be ridiculous," he said. "I could fail a urine test just from *breathing* in this place."

She looked at him and said, "Why are you being so cruel? Have you really changed that much? I call you with the worst crisis in my life, and you're all—"

"Wait," he said, raising a hand to interrupt her. "Just wait one little second. You're talking about a *breakup*. You're talking about something that happens every goddamn day, to people everywhere, every age, every class, every income level—*everyone* goes through this. And you're telling me you can't handle it?"

She reddened. "We'd been seeing each other for almost five years!"

"Five, schmive. Imagine living with someone for twenty-six, *there* you go. *That's* a breakup. And yet some people manage to get over it just fine." But a little self-critical voice in his head piped up: *Oh, do they?*

Frida's nostrils were visibly flaring. "Why did you even come here? If you can't be supportive and listen to me and help me through this—"

"I came because you threatened to kill yourself," said Jack, his voice growing louder. "Which, by the way, is a cheap ploy, don't ever do it again. It's degrading to both of us."

"It wasn't a ploy!"

"Hell it wasn't. No one who's really contemplating suicide talks about it. They just do it."

"So you're saying I should've just quietly stuck my head in the oven?"

"Like there was any chance of that! . . . And stop willfully misunderstanding me. You know damn well what I'm saying. I'm saying be honest with yourself, for God's sake. Don't play out these ridiculous, humiliating scenes. Stand on your own two feet. Be a woman instead of a stupid, self-centered girl."

She was crying again now, but this time they were hot, angry tears. "This is what I get? . . . You ignore me, ignore our friendship, for *weeks,* then when I need you the most, you come barging in here and turn on me?" Her voice had grown frighteningly shrill; her cat skulked out of the room in alarm.

Jack wasn't even slightly intimidated; to him, this girl was a joke. "I'm not barging in, you insisted I come over. And I wouldn't be here if I didn't feel I had *some* responsibility to Corey's friends."

"Oh, so you refer to yourself in the third person now, hm? *Very* mature."

Jack blushed at his mistake, but didn't let it daunt him. "Only the truly immature comment on other people's maturity."

She rose to her feet. "I want you out of my house."

"That's where I want me, too." He got up as well, then gestured towards the door. "Shall you go first, or shall I? . . . Because it pretty much has to be single file, doesn't it?"

She was seething. "After everything we've been through . . . I will *never* forgive you for talking this way to me. You, who know me better than anyone . . ."

"Oh, that's bullshit, I've just *coddled* you better than anyone. I don't do that anymore. I've grown up, time for you to do the same."

She'd now come so unglued that a little bubble of mucous was quivering from one of her nostrils. She was on the point of hysteria. "Fine, I'll grow up. Fat and ugly and alone. But never mind, as long as *you're* having fun!" She was screeching now, like an angry macaw.

Jack rolled his eyes. "Oh, brother, here we go . . ."

Her mascara was running; it looked like an oil slick on a birthday cake. "Ha! Yes, fine for you, Mr. Fucks Anything! *Sneer* at someone who's afraid of never being loved again!"

"Afraid?" he scoffed. "You're *making sure* you'll never be loved again. Look at you, hiding behind a screen of make-up, burying yourself in an apartment stacked to the ceiling, like the goddamn barricade in *Les Miz*. You couldn't possibly put more obstacles between yourself and the rest of the world. Wake up! Wake up!"

Since she still showed no signs of moving, he took it on himself to head for the door. When he reached it, he turned around; she hadn't moved, nor was she looking at him; she was standing, trembling; *quaking*, really. Jack waited for some parting shot, some asinine girlish riposte—he would've been happy to give her the last word, the poor, sad thing—but none came.

He quietly left, shutting the door behind him.

Later, at home, after masturbating yet again, he felt the tension flow out of him as through a sieve. And lying in bed alone—which actually felt rather nice for a change—he reflected on the scene with Frida, and was less pleased with his handling of it. He'd been irritated, put-upon, and horny, and he'd let her feel the full force of all that. A girl who was his friend!

Except, she *wasn't* his friend—she was Corey's. The fact that Jack had never met her before made it disturbingly easy to hold her in disdain. There was nothing even close to affection to temper him showing it.

But there was something more that bothered him, that pricked his consciousness as he tried to fall asleep. Finally, just a few moments before he drifted off, he was finally able to articulate it:

Who was I really yelling at?

Chapter 37

Jack's funk only deepened as the days ensued. What he'd considered at the time no more than a dose of cold water in Frida's face, he came to view in retrospect as pitiless cruelty. The woman obviously had her share of issues, had just been dumped by her longtime lover, and had reached out to a dear friend for comfort—only to find that that friend had changed the rules of their relationship without telling her. Worse, he'd gone to her own house to spew his bile at her, leaving her nowhere to retreat, no place left to feel safe. He'd invaded her turf and attacked her. What must she be feeling now . . . ?

His guilt put a pall over his sex life, and since his sex life was basically his only life, he found himself more than a little adrift. Nelly still hadn't warmed to him; she continued to resist his attempts to hold her or play with her, and flat out fought him when he tried to feed her her pills; more than once her jaws clamped down on his fingers, just shy of breaking the skin—*so far.*

Jack took refuge in reading—Evelyn Waugh's *Vile Bodies*, an old favorite—but the book conjured up images of the first time he'd delved into it, during a trip to the Amalfi Coast some twenty years earlier; one of his and Harry's happiest holidays together. Somehow, despite his now being beautiful, desirable, and young again, the memory was an unsettling one; what was renewed life, sexual pleasure, and freedom from responsibility, if he lacked—as horrifyingly clichéd as it sounded—someone to share it with? . . . Thirtysomething Jack, tucking his gut into linen trousers and holding Harry's hand after a lazy dinner in Ravello, had it all over the new twentysomething Jack, tucking his fifty-three years into skin half his age and hurling himself into a chain of empty ecstasies.

One morning he awoke to find a great smear of bloody diarrhea across his living room carpet. It actually took him a full, panicked minute to locate Nelly, who was hiding listlessly behind a couch, whether from guilt or depletion, he couldn't determine. He picked her up and raced down the stairs to the garage, then placed her gingerly in the backseat of his new Saab convertible and drove like fat on fire to the vet's office.

Three hours later, having left her secured to an I.V. drip and obtained reasonable assurances that she would survive the episode, Jack got back in his car, started the ignition, pulled out into traffic, and drove exactly one block before being overcome by emotion. He pulled up beside a fire hydrant, threw the gearshift into Park, and draped himself over his steering wheel to sob uncontrollably.

What have I done, what have I done, what have I done, he thought, over and over again, until the words lost coherence, drifted free of meaning, and he was able, with only a little effort, to pull himself together and drive the rest of the way home without a thought of any kind daring to cross the minefield of his mind.

He found, to his great surprise, a cellophane-wrapped package sitting in the lobby, bearing a card with his name on it. He tore open the wrap and peered beneath it; there was a basket of chocolates—chocolates in profusion; chocolates of every imaginable permutation.

He carried it upstairs, delaying opening the card so that

he might enjoy the pleasant sensation of wondering who'd sent it. He filed through the list of his recent conquests—the Tims and Kyles and Michaels and Victors who had passed over, around, and underneath him like a musky wave—but none of those encounters had resulted in anything close to the kind of connection that would inspire someone to send him a present. By the time he reached his door, he had, rather depressingly, come to the conclusion that there was no one in his life who *could* have sent this. It must be someone from Corey's past, not his. But Corey hadn't hinted at anyone capable of doing this.

Finally back inside, he plucked the card from the basket. He considered saving it as a reward till after he'd cleaned up the mess Nelly had made, but he couldn't bear the suspense; and the chocolate itself would serve as well for that purpose. In an agony of anticipation, he opened the card. It read:

> *Dear boy,*
> *Thank you so much for everything—I love you!*
> $\qquad\qquad$ X O X O
> $\qquad\qquad$ *Frida*

This was, suffice it to say, a surprise.

It's not that Frida's was the last name he expected to be attached to a gift of this nature; it's that her name had never even entered his head at all. She was so far off the list as to have been nonexistent.

At first he thought the note might be sarcastic—that her "thank you for everything" might be her way of saying "thanks for nothing"—but in that case, she'd scarcely have attached it to an extravagant gift basket, would she?

He set the card aside and got down to cleaning up Nelly's mess, which was a considerable effort, requiring a full bottle of Nature's Miracle, and even then there was a lingering stain. He'd have to hire an honest-to-God carpet cleaner to come in and give it a real steaming. But . . . should he do that now, or wait? Nelly would be home within the next day or so; who was to say there wouldn't be another episode?

Plagued by indecision, bored by his freedom, and missing his dog, Jack found himself—amazingly—calling Frida. He hadn't intended to; he'd resolved to have no more contact with her, since the discrepancy in their feelings for each other (she loving him as a longtime friend, him dismissing her as a foolish girl he'd only just met) brought out the worst in him, and at her expense; but her note, and the accompanying chocolates, were indications that his mistreatment of her hadn't been as damaging as he'd thought. He was eager to get himself off the hook; and hence, he phoned.

"I'm glad you like it," said Frida when he thanked her for the basket; "it's mainly dark chocolate, you know—the kind that's actually good for you, 'cause it's got antioxidants. Remember that article we read . . . ?"

"Yes," Jack lied. "But . . . listen, Frida, I'm a little surprised. I didn't think we parted on very good terms."

"Oh, not at *all*," she said with a laugh. "In fact, you know what I did after you left? . . . I swear to God this is true. *I turned on my oven.* I was actually going to do it—I was going to kill myself, just to get back at you! Fortunately, at the last moment, just as I was opening the stove door, I caught a look at myself in the glass? . . . And I was like, *I don't even know who that is.* Big old sloppy mess. And I realized I was, like, completely out of control. And I thought about it, and I realized you were right about everything. You were a one-man intervention, baby! You were Mr. Tough Love!"

Jack felt a surge of relief. "I'm very glad to hear it. But, listen, I've been thinking it over, and I really was out of line, the way I came down on you, I didn—"

"No," she interrupted. "No, baby, I won't hear it. Whatever you said, I needed to hear. I had to have someone kick me in the ass and say, *Grow up.* I mean, for God's sake, I was with

Julio for *five years* and he refused to meet any of my friends. Refused to meet my parents, refused to spend holidays with me, refused to see me more than twice a week. Even refused to spend the night at my place, even *once*. What the hell was I thinking? That I was gonna have a life with that piece of crud? . . . And you're right, he brought me down, he gave me L.S.E., he—"

"L.S.E.?" Jack asked.

She snorted. *"Low Self Esteem,"* she said impatiently. "We've only been saying it for a hundred years, baby."

"Oh, right," said Jack, backpedaling; "I'm—I just—I had to put my dog in the hospital today, I'm a little upset, it's—"

"You have a *dog?*" she trilled. "Baby, for God's sake! What's going *on* with you? Tyler said you'd moved, now you have a dog . . ."

Jack clenched his fist and smacked himself in the head. Why couldn't he just learn to shut up? He was getting drawn farther into this woman's life, and he didn't want to. "I just—I've made some changes, is all."

"Honey, I think that's great, but I don't get why you've cut out all your friends. I'm sorry, I'm not trying to whine or be clingy or anything, but . . . you know I love you."

Jack was taken aback. Corey had assured him his friends wouldn't miss him, wouldn't bother to seek him out—but here was Frida using the L word. He felt a stab of guilt; he'd traded his life for Corey's, not knowing Corey was selling his short; if the boy had known the truth about himself, about the love he inspired, would he have been so quick to leave his old life behind?

"I know," said Jack; it was all he could muster. "I'm sorry."

"You don't have to apologize," she said. "Just . . . well, don't be so quick to move on without us. We can all move on together, you know. It's better that way."

He sighed. "Of course, of course."

"Fine. Will you come to dinner on Saturday?"

He balked. "Wh . . . sorry, what?"

"I know it's a shock. I've never had anyone over before because, well, A, Julio would never agree to be there and it was embarrassing to do it without him, and B, where would anyone sit? . . . But now I'm Julio-free, and I'm having a bunch of the furniture put in storage, plus I bought a recipe book, and I'm going to have a real honest-to-God grown-up dinner party. *Please* say you'll come." When he didn't reply right away, she said, "There's gonna be a surprise!"

Jack felt his dread lessen; he'd always been intrigued by surprises. And after a moment's reflection, he realized it had been weeks since he'd been to a real dinner party—not since his old life, in fact. He was overcome by a sudden longing for the simple joy of friendly conversation . . . light, convivial chatter, spiced by occasional laughter. An evening devoted to companionship instead of abandon, mutual amusement instead of mutual climaxes.

"Yes," he said, "sure I'll come."

And thus his new life took a new turn.

Chapter 38

Jack may have had a fondness for surprises, but the next day brought a nasty one. After having resettled a weak but improved Nelly at home, he left her to rest, and, restless himself, made his way into the warmth of the day, with the idea of soothing his anxiety about his dog with a little therapeutic fucking.

There was a lazy, mildly sweltering breeze that seemed to stir up sexual heat. Everywhere he looked, shirts clung damply to torsos, outlining musculature; or else were doffed completely, stuffed into a back pocket, allowing golden chests to gleam with moisture. Jack appreciated the way a thin film of sweat would spread from shoulder to shoulder, the occasional droplet meandering lazily down to the navel and beyond. Soon he felt the familiar stirring in his loins. Boldly he took off his own shirt and tucked it in the waistband of his shorts.

He headed up Broadway, his eyes alert for the alert eyes of others, and whenever he matched glances with someone else he instantly apprised the desirability of proceeding further. He'd actually got quite good at this.

Soon he met the gaze of a tall, shaven-headed Adonis, pectorals rippling like Hercules beneath a sleeveless tee and, endearingly, sporting a Bamm-Bamm tattoo on his biceps, and he knew he'd found his quarry. He passed the man by, then turned and looked after him.

He, too, turned and looked back; then continued on his way.

Jack followed.

The city street became a jungle, humid, dense, torrid with tension and alive with pursuit—and hot. Oh, *so* hot. The man was alone; that made it easier to maneuver. He wouldn't have to separate him from any friends before closing in for the kill.

He didn't turn back again, which Jack kept expecting; but somehow that made it all the more tantalizing. He must be aware of Jack; couldn't *not* be aware of him, after the pointed look they'd exchanged. He was deliberately teasing him, toying with him. Jack felt every nerve ending tingle with expectation. When he finally nailed this one, he'd have earned it.

Three blocks on, the man slowed, then stopped outside a small delicatessen. Jack thought, *Here we go*—but no; he didn't look back. He entered the store. Jack stood rooted to the sidewalk, his brow knit; what was going on? He'd yet to see someone pull a feint like this. If it was intended to ratchet up the sexual tension, it was a little too calculated. He felt a pinprick of irritation.

But he was still Jack Ackerly—never mind the body he inhabited—and he would not give up. He moved into the shade of the awning and waited.

A few minutes later the man came out again, toting a small carryout bag. He didn't, as Jack expected, look around to see where Jack had gone, but casually headed back the way he'd come.

Before indecision could take hold of him, Jack stepped up to him and said, "Hey."

The man, looked at him, his head slightly cocked, and said, "Hey."

Keeping pace with his prey's long strides, Jack said, "I'm Corey."

The man laughed. "Hello, Corey."

They walked in silence for a few moments, then Jack, annoyed that the guy was missing his cues, said, "And you are . . . ?"

The man stopped, bringing Jack to a halt as well. He said, "Look. I, uh . . . thanks, and everything, but . . . not interested."

Jack squinted. "Sorry," he said. "I thought we had a moment back there."

The man laughed again. "Yeah, well."

"You *did* look at me."

"That I did." He gestured at Jack's stomach. "But honestly? . . . I was thinking, 'Dude, put your shirt on.'"

Jack was thunderstruck. He didn't even hear the man's parting words as he sauntered off again.

Jack turned and looked at his reflection in a storefront window. Well . . . it was true, there was a little more belly than there had been when he'd inherited this body. He hadn't been as scrupulous about gym attendance as he should've been.

Suddenly he recalled a previous remark, uttered as he passed a coterie of queens at a bar a few nights earlier—one of his increasingly common unsuccessful nights out. The remark—"Look out, it's Sasquatch"—had mystified him at the time, and he'd assumed it simply wasn't meant for him (but if not, then for whom?).

Now, he noticed with a start how furry he'd become. In his old life, he'd never had much body hair; so when Corey's chest had started sprouting fuzz, he'd actually been excited. Having grown up in the Fifties, he equated a hairy chest with manliness, and couldn't imagine why Corey had ever shaved it.

Now, however, looking at his reflection, he saw himself

as if for the first time: a half-naked, paunchy, hairy man—
he even had hair on his shoulders!—invading a herd of
smooth, lean, taut young gods.

But . . . Jack was still young, still virile, still *twenty-six,*
for God's sake. A little deviation from the norm shouldn't—
couldn't—matter to anyone.

Could it . . . ?

Bewildered and embarrassed, he headed home. Nelly was
sleeping soundly, so Jack snuck into the bedroom, chose the
most flattering lighting possible, and examined himself
minutely in the mirror.

It was true, it was all true; he'd grown thicker around the
middle, and was quite dramatically hirsute. The solution
was simple: a drastically amped-up gym regimen, and immediate body waxing.

But . . . *but* . . .

He sat on the bed, not even bothering to suck in his
tummy roll.

The truth was, he kind of liked himself this way. He
looked . . . solid. He looked *real.* When he took off his clothes,
he appeared excitingly *naked.* As opposed to all those perfectly sculpted boys, whose nakedness seemed like just another elaborately constructed ensemble.

He wouldn't be untrue to himself. He wouldn't succumb
to body fascism.

And honestly, he was tired of being judged by his appearance alone. His recent dealings with Frida were still very
much on his mind. He'd come to realize that he'd connected
more with her, on a simple human level, than he had with
anyone he'd actually had sex with.

And what was the point of all this sex, anyway? . . . Finally,
now that he'd outgrown it—by at least two waist sizes, apparently—he wondered what he'd been thinking. Like Frida
clinging to a boyfriend with whom no future was possible,
what kind of future was *he* imagining? . . . Sex was a carni-

val ride: wild, joyous, thrilling, but it left you in the same place you started.

Jack felt the blow of a staggering epiphany:

He wanted a relationship.

He wanted, in fact, what he'd had with Harry. But that, he knew, came once in a lifetime.

His shoulders slumped, and he felt the urge to cry, but he refused; he willed himself not to. He reminded himself, for the second time today, that he was Jack Ackerly.

But . . . what did that *mean?* . . . What did it mean to be Jack Ackerly, when he couldn't even *call* himself Jack Ackerly?

He lay back on the bed and sighed.

And then the answer came to him, as easily as though it were written out on the ceiling.

It was true that what he'd had with Harry was once in a lifetime . . . but he was now in his *second* lifetime. He could, if he wanted, have it again.

In fact—daring thought; exciting, frightening thought—he could have it again *with Harry*.

He sat back up, his mind reeling. He recalled the last time he'd seen Harry, when he'd run into him with his new young boyfriend. Harry was obviously into younger men these days; and Jack now fit the bill.

He got up and took a new look in the mirror. Even with a few extra pounds and shoulder hair, he was, he decided, about three times as hot as Harry's new beau. What had he called himself? . . . Brian? Brian Isley.

Jack ran his hands over his flanks and thought, *Watch out, Brian Isley. Jack Ackerly's a-comin'.*

Chapter 39

If he had wondered, in distress, what it meant to be Jack Ackerly, having a project reminded him. Jack took to strategizing his reconquest of Harry with all the confidence, deliberation, and laser-like focus he'd historically shown in his old life whenever he'd gone after something he wanted.

Actually, it proved ridiculously easy to arrange a meeting with Harry. He knew him inside and out, and could not only predict his behavior but arrange conditions so that he'd perform as desired, like a lab rat.

Harry had a Wicker Park gallery, the Harold McGann, at which he showcased the work of two or three young artists at a time. Jack called the gallery and, speaking to the receptionist, Kiyo, said, "Hi, my name's Luke Frears, I represent an artist out of Detroit, Laura Jameson, who's making quite a name for herself here. I'm looking to show her work in Chicago, and Brenda Maloney recommended I call you. Would it be possible to arrange a meeting with Mr. McGann?"

It was a beautiful performance of a carefully constructed trap. Brenda Maloney was, Jack knew, someone with whom Harry dealt frequently, so her name would carry some weight. Also, Kiyo hailed from Detroit, and Jack had often heard her insist that the city was very hip; she would, he reasoned, be only too happy to book time for Harry to examine the work of a Detroit artist. That the artist in question was also female was just insurance; Kiyo was an ardent feminist.

Sure enough, Kiyo gave Jack—or rather, "Luke Frears"— an hour on Thursday morning, beginning at ten o'clock.

Jack drove to Wicker Park at the appointed hour, but instead of making his way to the gallery, he headed to the coffee bar across the street, where he bought himself a double espresso (an indulgence which his new body, unlike his old, could easily endure) and stationed himself by the window.

How many times had Jack received a call from Harry that began, "Hey, babe, had an hour free so I've run across the street for a latte. Just thought I'd check in while I'm at it . . ." Jack was betting that that his habits hadn't changed.

And sure enough, at 10:15 he appeared, exiting the gallery in a bit of a huff (he didn't much like being stood up) and turned up the street towards the coffee bar. Jack smiled in triumph.

And then his smile wilted. Something wasn't tallying with his vision of victory. He'd imagined Harry striding boldly up the street and back into his life; but . . . Harry shuffled. Harry looked a bit stooped; his eyes were downcast. Harry . . .

. . . Harry looked *old*.

Was it possible that the man who had left him because of his advanced years was now succumbing to middle age himself? . . . Or had Harry remained unchanged, and it was only Jack's increasing comfort in Corey's young body that now made Harry look decrepit in comparison?

Certainly the clothes he was wearing weren't much help. Harry dressed far too young for his years, and the discrepancy made him appear even older.

But then he swung open the door to the bar and entered, and as he passed Jack got a glimpse of the vivid green of his eyes, and he thought, *He's still Harry*. And by extension, still worth it. His heart began to thrum a bit.

Harry ordered his latte—with, as ever, "three shots of

vanilla, please," a quirk that had used to annoy Jack terribly; so childish, to ruin good coffee with all that syrup—but listening to him order it now, he was surprised to find it endearing, as though he were hearing an old song he'd never particularly liked, but which brought back memories of a happier time.

Then, as he always did—as Jack knew he would—Harry took a seat by the window.

Just a table away from Jack's.

He took out his phone, flipped it open, and punched in a number, then put it to his ear and after a short pause said, "Oh, hey, babe. Only me. Got blown off by an art rep, so I'm taking a break for coffee, thought I'd check in and see how your day's going. Try you again later."

Jack felt a sudden, jealous cramp; it was exactly the call *he* used to get. Now directed, presumably, towards Brian Isley.

But he couldn't waste time being envious or bitter. He had one last card to play—the *pièce de résistance,* the final bait for his trap. He opened a hardcover book—a biography, *Grace Coolidge: American Calpurnia*—and made a great show of being immersed in it.

And he waited.

Soon he became aware of Harry's eyes on him. He didn't look up . . . not yet. Let Harry spend a few more minutes studying him, taking in his golden gorgeousness. Prolong the moment . . . stave off the inevitable . . . untillllll—

—*now.*

Jack lazily raised his head, caught Harry in the act of watching him, then smiled and returned to the book. He could actually feel the tension as Harry worked up the courage to speak.

Finally, he said, "Enjoying it?"

Jack looked up again. "Sorry?"

Harry nodded at the book. "I said, are you enjoying it?"

Jack looked at it, as though a little embarrassed at being

caught with it, and said, "Oh, yeah. It's—well, I'm liking it, but then, I'm always a sucker for a First Lady bio."

Harry's eyebrows rose. "No kidding? Me too."

Jack brightened and said, "Really? . . . Have you read this one?"

"Oh, yeah," he said, showing off a bit; "it's pretty good. But then Grace Coolidge is a damn good subject; hard to go wrong with her. Tremendously popular, and extremely stylish; she was the first real fashion trendsetter in the White House. And there wasn't another one till Jackie. Actually, she's sort of the Jackie of the first half of the century. That's one of my problems with the book: its title, *American Calpurnia*. I know what it's getting at—that Grace was as big an asset to her husband as Caesar's wife was to him—but Calpurnia was a stately Roman matron. The comparison doesn't say anything about the dazzling star quality Grace had. She was sort of Calpurnia *and* Cleopatra, all in one."

Jack felt a little twitch of indignation. That, in fact, was *his* line—which he'd tossed off two years before, when Harry had first cited his problem with this biography, while reading it in their marital bed. But what was worse, Jack's exact words had been, "So what you're saying is, she had Calpurnia's virtue and Cleopatra's verve," and Harry had laughed and clapped his hands. Now, Harry was passing off Jack's wit as his own—and *not even getting it right*.

Jack swallowed his resentment and, pretending to be rapt, put the book down and stared with admiration. "That's a good way to put it," he said; "you have a way with words. But listen, wasn't Grace also the first president's wife to be formally called First Lady? . . . 'Cause I can't find that in here."

Harry, excited, shifted his chair a little closer and said, "No, actually that was Lucy Webb Hayes, Rutherford's wife, a few decades earlier. She was wildly popular too, a great Washington hostess—despite being an abolitionist who wouldn't allow alcohol in the White House. They called her 'Lemonade Lucy.'"

Jack laughed, but not at the anecdote. It was so wonderfully easy to get Harry to parade his useless knowledge. He said, "Wow, you really *do* know your First Ladies!"

Harry blushed. "Yeah, it's sort of my hobby. I've got shelves of biographies at home; there's scarcely a First Lady I'm missing." He smiled. "My ex used to tease me about it, but . . ." He shrugged. "We all have our quirks."

Jack felt a momentary sting at this mildly unflattering reference to his old self, but managed to hold his look of rapture. "I could probably learn a lot from you," he said, and he extended his arm. "Corey Szaslow, by the way."

"Harry McGann," he replied, taking Jack's hand. They shook, and when Harry tried to pull away, Jack held on for just a nanosecond longer than was necessary; he was sending a signal, and by the look on Harry's face, it was received loud and clear.

"I'd love to see your shelves someday, Harry," Jack said with a slightly flirtatious inflection, as though it contained a double meaning.

Harry grinned guilelessly and said, "I'm sure that could be arranged."

"I'm not doing anything right now."

Harry laughed, as though not quite able to believe this was happening to him. "Well, I myself am working now," he said. "I own a gallery just across the street." He jerked his thumb over his shoulder.

Jack glanced that way and said, "I'll have to stop by. I'm in the market for a new place, and once I've got one I'll need to fill the walls."

"I can definitely help you there."

A small, electric pause followed. "Well," said Jack, "what are you doing *after* work?"

Harry said, "Uh . . . look, I don't want to be weird or

anything but, I . . . God, this is embarrassing." He blushed. "Are we . . . are we, like, *flirting* here?"

"I can only speak for myself," said Jack. "But yes, I am definitely flirting."

Harry seemed momentarily stunned by his candor; he blushed again and said, "I only ask, because, well, I'm seeing someone, and I—"

"Oh, I'm sorry," said Jack, putting his hands up, "I didn't know you had a lover. I should've realized, though—guy like you . . ."

Harry laughed again and said, "Well, he's not a *lover,* exactly, we've just been dating a few months, and . . ." He shrugged. "You know how it goes."

Jack nodded. "Right. You've got the monogamy thing going on."

Harry cocked his head and said, "I suppose. I mean, we've never really discussed it, but . . ."

"But you see each other every night, so it's, like implied. I get it."

Harry's laughter was growing nervous. "Well, not *every* night, but . . ."

"But tonight. You're seeing him tonight."

Harry's laughter died completely. "I don't think so, no. I mean . . . we haven't made any plans."

Jack stared at him for a moment, as though amused by him. "Soooo, let me get this straight: you're not living with anyone, you don't have a lover, you're dating someone not exactly monogamously, and you don't have plans tonight . . ." He arched an eyebrow in mild censure. ". . . and you're telling me I can't come examine your shelves?"

He locked onto Harry's eyes and wouldn't let him look away. The rest of the coffee bar seemed to go quiet.

Finally Harry said, "Can you come by the gallery at six?"

"Yes I can."

"We'll have a drink first."

"Great." Jack sat back and smiled, and Harry, now smiling too, got up and said, "Well, all right then, I'll see you late*eerrk*—" He'd hooked his foot around the table leg and almost fallen; now he righted himself and said, "I meant to do that," and Jack laughed.

"Till six," Harry said.

"Till six," said Jack.

And as Harry retreated, Jack thought, *Sayonara, Brian Isley.*

Chapter 40

Several hours later, they stumbled through the door to Harry's apartment, somewhat the worse for drink, and Harry switched on the light.

Jack looked around, and was surprised by what he saw. What he recollected best about living with Harry was his unrepentant slovenliness; they'd spent a fortune renovating and then decorating their home to make it a showplace, then Harry had blithely begun allowing the debris of his life to encroach on every nook and cranny. Dirty laundry . . . clean laundry . . . grooming products . . . magazines . . . junk mail . . . empty soda cans . . . they collected as though they had volition, as though the environment's pristine condition created a vulnerability they could sense, and which had provoked them to hostile invasion.

But here—in an apartment where Harry lived alone, with no Jack to nag him about his messes or guilt him into token gestures at tidiness—there wasn't a thing out of place. Jack wondered if perhaps Harry had a cleaning lady; or maybe he'd run home during the lunch hour and tidied the place up himself, knowing he'd have a guest that evening . . .

. . . or maybe, he concluded, Harry's sloppiness had been a subconscious rebellion against Jack that served no further purpose now that Jack was no longer around.

Harry opened a liquor cabinet and said, "Get you any-thing?"

Jack shook his head. "Thanks, I think I've had more than enough."

Harry looked over his shoulder. "Oh," he said. "Well . . . probably me too, then." He shut the cabinet, then turned and said, "Come on, then, I'll show you around." He put his arm around Jack's shoulder and, smiling, said, "We'll start with those shelves you've heard so much about."

He led Jack across the room to a bookcase that covered an entire wall. Jack pretended to listen as Harry pointed out the prizes of his collection—really, what did any sane person need with a biography of Mrs. Grover Cleveland?—but his senses were actually attuned to the rest of the apartment. It was so odd, to see familiar furniture in so strange a setting. Like he'd walked into a parallel universe. Even odder to be with Harry, a little drunk, his guard down—and to have to remember, to have to remind himself constantly, *I am not me, I am not who I was*—lest he betray some casual familiarity, make some reference to something Corey Szaslow couldn't possibly know.

There was a small grand piano, its lid littered with photo-graphs in silver frames. Feigning idle curiosity, he ambled over to these and scanned them.

A wave of nostalgia engulfed him by surprise. So many of the photos he had taken himself; there was Harry, shirtless and lobster-red, fishing off the back of a friend's yacht; Harry and his sisters on his fortieth birthday; Harry and Nelly. The other photographs were of friends, dear friends, some of them the very people Jack had so callously just deposited into Corey's life, without even a thought about abandoning them forever. His heart lurched.

There was a signal omission, though: no photo of Jack himself.

Alcohol had made him bold; he turned and said, "Which one's your ex?"

Harry, dimming the lights now, said, "I don't think he's up there."

"Really? . . . What was he like?"

Harry slipped off his shoes and padded over to him. "Oh . . . you know. Older." He came up behind Jack and started kneading his shoulders.

"Handsome?" he asked.

Harry made an unenthusiastic but affirmative noise.

"Ah," said Jack. "But not hot?"

"Not like you," he said, and he kissed Jack's neck.

To be kissed by Harry again! . . . Jack was surprised at the surge of feeling it stirred in him. He'd had so much sex the past few months, yet he'd forgotten the power of a single kiss—the potent, irresistible brew of carnality mixed with love.

And he *did* love Harry; he'd never stopped. So much had gotten in the way of that; blocked them both from seeing it, feeling it, going on together any longer. Now, all that was stripped away. Here he was, back with Harry, prepared to begin anew—to make Harry and Corey the success Harry and Jack had ultimately failed to be.

Why, *why* then, was Jack so fixated on obtaining some acknowledgment of Harry's regard for the old him—the man he could never be again? . . . Why was he striving to rekindle an affection that, if revived, could do him no earthly good?

The old Jack was gone. Harry-and-Jack was gone. Everything from this point, had to be new and fresh . . . Who knew? This time around, Jack might even strive to learn enthusiasm for the minutiae of the lives of presidential wives.

He relaxed, slipped free the bonds of memory, and succumbed to Harry's repeated kisses. Harry led him to the bedroom, and they put the seal on their new intimacy.

There was just one final, desperate moment, some time later, after Harry had fallen asleep, when Jack reached gingerly across him and opened the drawer of his nightstand—

thinking, absurdly, he might find a photo of his old self, which Harry had hidden to prepare for Corey's arrival.

He found none, and berated himself for having even looked.

He drifted off to sleep, still feeling a lingering, irrational discontent.

Chapter 41

Jack saw Harry every night after that; and he began to resent Frida's approaching dinner party, since it would prevent him seeing Harry on Saturday as well. But on Friday, he made a serious faux pas: he let slip the words "I love you" during sex, and the change in Harry was immediate—a sudden stiffening (and not in the good way), an aura of wariness, that put them both off their stride and caused them to fumble to an unsatisfactory finish. Neither said anything about it afterwards, but Jack now thought it just as well he was booked the following evening; he had a hunch Harry would've made some nervous excuse about "needing a night to himself," and he couldn't have borne that. This way, Harry would have time alone to reflect on how much he missed him.

If he missed him. Jack had to remind himself that he was already much farther along in this relationship than Harry—that he even called it "a relationship" was evidence of that. It had been so easy to let that "I love you" slip out; he had, after all, said it countless times before, under precisely the same circumstances. Well—maybe not precisely; he'd been in another body then, but why quibble?

Jack thought he might also benefit from a night away from Harry, to clear all these doubts from his head. Maybe they'd seem smaller afterwards, and he'd be able to put them in some perspective.

Frida had told him to come by around seven, so he felt safe arriving at 7:45. He was surprised to find himself the first arrival, and his hostess still not dressed. "Zip me, will you?" she said as she met him at the door, and immediately turned her naked back to him, the flaps of her dress hanging open as though exhausted. "Sorry," she said, holding her hair away from her nape, "running late as usual, you know me."

No, I don't, actually, he wanted to say, but he obliged her by zipping her up, then followed her into the apartment. Though his acquaintance with her was far shorter than she imagined, he knew her well enough to comment on her greatly improved appearance. "You look wonderful," he said, "very clean. Fresh."

She smiled, and in truth her face, now freed of its thick cosmetic façade, looked younger and quite pretty. "Thanks," she said. "Wouldn't have risked it if it hadn't been for you." She gestured towards the interior of the apartment and said, "This, either."

Most of the furniture was gone, and Jack was surprised to find himself in a fairly bright, pleasant room, with plenty of space to mill about and mingle. There was something else missing, as well; he sniffed to be certain.

"I gave it up," she said as she placed mismatched cutlery around the old oak dining table. "Costing me an arm and a leg, plus, what the fuck, you gotta grow up sometime."

"I agree," said Jack. "Speaking of which . . . what are we listening to?"

She looked up, surprised. "Scissor Sisters," she said. "Our favorite."

"It is?" he said, slightly appalled. "Well, in any case, it's not dinner music." He went over to her stereo and flipped through her little rack of CDs. "Don't you have anything but disco?"

She shrugged. "I like to dance. You never complained before."

"Music's not just for dancing," he said. "It has all sorts of purposes. You want to get something to relax by, for nights like tonight." He paused. "Oh, here's Celine Dion."

"Someone gave me that," she insisted, a little too readily.

"Never mind; she's not really what we're looking for either. Woman's voice can slice through cast iron. Ah!" he said triumphantly. "Here we go. The *Walk the Line* soundtrack."

"Oh, I just got that 'cause Joaquin Phoenix is *hot*."

"Then the DVD might've been a better use of your entertainment dollar," he said, opening the jewel case. "Never mind, it'll get us through tonight." He switched the discs, and in the interim silence said, "What time is everyone else due?"

"Eight-thirty," she said.

"Eight . . . what?" He got to his feet to the twang of guitars. "Why'd you ask me to come at seven, then?"

"To keep me company," she said, placing napkins at each place setting; these were mismatched as well. "You don't mind, do you?"

"No, no," he said in a way that implied yes, yes. "But . . . Frida, eight-thirty? . . . When are you planning on serving dinner?"

She shrugged again. "Eight forty-five? . . . Nine? Depends when the food is done."

"But . . . that doesn't leave any time for cocktails."

"It doesn't?"

"No." He made his way towards her kitchen. "Have you even *got* anything for cocktails?"

"Oh," she said, scurrying after him, "don't worry, I've got it *all*—gin, vodka, whiskey, all the mixers, the lot. I really went all out."

He reached the kitchen and saw that all the counter space had been filled with bottles of booze. "No, I mean, hors d'oeuvres." She didn't answer, and he turned to look at her; her face was frozen in a kind of guilty shock. "You don't have anything, do you?"

"No," she said. "I didn't think of it."

"You're just going to have everyone come in here, kiss them on the cheek, then slam them into a chair at the table?"

"I . . . no?"

"No," he said. "You need an hour or so in which everyone just chills out with some drinks and some nibbles. Gets to know each other, or if they already do, catch up on all their news. Build up some drama for the moment you usher them all in to dinner. It's all about pacing; it's theater, really."

Tears brimmed in her eyes. "I didn't know! I've never done this before!"

He turned his head and sighed. How was it possible for someone to have grown to adulthood without knowing the first thing about entertaining? . . . He checked his watch and said, "Look, we've still got half an hour. I'll run out and get some cheese and crackers, things like that."

She was starting to blubber a bit. "I'm such an idiot," she said.

"No, no, you're not, you're . . . you're very brave for plunging in like this. Only way to learn."

"Thanks," she said, snuffling up some phlegm. "How come gay guys know everything?"

"We don't know ev—" He caught sight of something bubbling on the stove. "What," he said fearfully, "is *that?*"

"Ratatouille," she said proudly. (She pronounced it *rat-a-tooly.*) "It's what I'm serving. One of the guests is vegetarian, see."

He looked into pot, at the viscous, oily substance simmering there. "Frida . . . why is there rice in it?"

"Well, the recipe said to serve it with rice."

"Ah. So . . . you just dumped it right in there. Along with the tomatoes and the eggplant and the peppers and everything else."

"Mm-hm," she said. "So I could free up counter space for the liquor. Smart, huh?"

He made some noncommittal noise that might be construed as affirmative. Then, "It . . . it looks about done."

"Already?" she said, amazed. "I'm a faster cook than I knew!"

"The problem is, it's ready now, but we won't be eating it for another hour."

She thought a moment, then said, "I'll just turn down the heat to the minimum, to keep it warm."

Jack forced himself to smile, then said, "All right," and jerked his thumb towards the door. "Go get those crackers now, shall I?"

"You're a sweetheart," she said. "What would I do without you?"

You'd have a lot less to eat, that's for sure, he thought as he hurried back down to Clark Street.

In the end, he bought three kinds of crackers, six different cheeses, assorted olives, a bunch of fresh basil to help salvage the ratatouille, a loaf of bread, and enough Gala apples to fill a basket. After a moment's consideration, he bought the basket too.

Chapter 42

Dinner went off much as Jack feared. The last of the guests didn't arrive till after nine, and by the time the group could tear itself away from cocktails, which was close to 10:30, the rice had turned to glue and rendered the ratatouille a brick-like mass. With the liberal use of olive oil, Jack was able to pound it into a kind of ratatouille paste, which he advised the diners to spread on their hunks of bread. It wasn't exactly a feast, but by that time everyone was too toasted to care—including the hostess herself.

There were only two other guests. The first was Frida's surprise: a new boyfriend, Patrick. He lived in the same building, and she had been eyeing him appreciatively for months but been too afraid to introduce herself. Again, she gave Jack credit for her courage. "After our fight, remember?" she told him later, as they were clearing away plates. "My first thought was to really kill myself, just to show you? . . . Well, after that, I saw him in the lobby, and I figured, heck, I just looked death in the face, this guy's not so scary, so I went up and said hi, and he said hi back, and . . . here we are!"

Patrick was a big, strapping Irish boy, a real Chicago type—with a few welcome quirks (he was, for instance, the previously announced vegetarian). He was also, Jack was glad to see, unmistakably heterosexual. His clothes alone told the tale: completely lacking in any style or color, and so ill-fitting he might have dropped into them from above as they hung on a clothesline, the way cartoon characters sometimes did. "You'll have to do something about his wardrobe," Jack had whispered, and Frida surprised him by saying, quite rightly, "Nuh-uh. I'm taking him as I find him. If he wants to improve, I'll help him, but it has to be his idea."

Despite his rock-solid heterosexuality, Patrick was completely at home with Frida's gay guests. At one point he said, "Frida told me not to bring anything, but come on, I couldn't show up empty handed, so I figured, I'll bring the lady some flowers. Then I remembered she said you boys would be here, and I panicked, I told the florist, 'Hey, make me up somethin' special, I'm gonna get judged by gay guys on this!'"

The remaining guest constituted the other "gay guy." His name was David; he was short, balding, and bearded, but with broad shoulders and a trim waist. He was a frequent customer of Frida's salon; he liked to come in every few weeks for a pedicure (it was amusing to Jack, the idea of this fuzzy, bearish man being addicted to foot spas) and he and Frida had fallen into an easy rapport. "He reminds me of you," she told Jack, back in the kitchen; "you have the same sense of humor."

For the first part of the evening the focus was all on Patrick, as he strove to impress Frida's friends with his charm and gregariousness. But after dinner, when the guests had retired to the living room for grappa and apples, Jack found himself seated next to David. And when Frida and Patrick went off together to fetch the coffee, the two men were left alone.

"So, what do you do?" asked Jack, hating himself for the banality of the question.

"I'm a Realtor," David said, appearing a bit pained at having to admit this.

"You don't seem too keen on it," said Jack.

"Very observant. I'm actually a chef, see; I went to culinary school and everything. My dream is to open a catering service, and then someday my own restaurant. But it's a long time coming. First I need to find a partner, someone who can provide the financing."

Jack leaned in and said, "Well, when you get there? . . . You just say the word, and I'll make sure to get you the recipe for the ratatouille paste."

David snorted into his shot glass and grappa came out his nose.

Later, once again in the kitchen, Frida asked, "So, what do you think of David?"

"I like him," said Jack. "A tad quiet, but he's a sweetheart."

"I'm just asking, 'cause you usually turn your nose up at guys who look like him."

"Do I?" asked Jack, rinsing the wine glasses under the sink. "Well, maybe I did. No, I actually find him attractive. He has lovely eyes. And very white teeth."

"But . . . not your type, though, right?" she asked, clearly probing for more as she hung a dishrag over a drawer handle to dry.

"Oh, I wouldn't say that." In fact, he'd always had a thing for strong Semitic features: the noble, prominent nose, the high cheekbones, the full lips. And in fact, David looked remarkably like an Israeli soldier who'd appeared on the cover of *Newsweek* back when Jack was a teenager—a soldier who, despite the desperation of the cover scene (something about the occupied territories, so far as he could remember) was so smolderingly sexy that Jack had spent the ensuing weeks masturbating while gazing at him; to this day he remained burned into his memory.

But he wasn't about to admit this to Frida.

Soon the party came to an abrupt halt; it became clear to

both Jack and David that their hostess was eager to be alone with her boyfriend, to celebrate her first social triumph, and that he was a hundred percent in accord with her. In fact he was so very much in accord that he was almost on top of her. She managed to shrug him off long enough to say goodbye to Jack.

"Thank you for everything, baby," she said. "Don't think I don't know how this all would've turned out if not for you. And . . . I gotta say, it's just amazing how you've changed. All of a sudden you're so smart, so capable, you know all about cheeses and you're so confident and you make decisions and have opinions about politics and . . ." She shook her head at the wonder of it. "I guess I just remember how not too long ago, you were the one who was in awe of *me,* because you thought I was so grown up. And now the tables have turned. I think you're my new hero."

Jack smiled and kissed her on the cheek, and said, "You're fine, and you're going to be superfine," but he was thinking, *Corey actually looked up to this poor sweet thing? . . . He must really have been a needy soul.*

As she showed him and David out the door, David said, "Uh, Jack, can I offer you a ride?"

"Thanks," said Jack, smiling, "that's sweet, but I drove."

"You drove?" said Frida. "You have a *car? . . . You?*" She shook her head again. "*Definitely* my hero!" Then Patrick appeared behind her, grinning lewdly, and made her close the door.

It was only after they'd descended together, said goodbye in front of the building, and gone their separate ways, that Jack realized he and David had been set up. Frida had been matchmaking! . . . And by the moist longing in David's eyes as they parted, she'd at least succeeded brilliantly with him.

But Jack, still flush with ecstasy over his renewed happiness with Harry, hadn't even been able to see David as anything but Frida's friend. Even now, he was having a little trouble remembering what he looked like.

But then, with Harry in his thoughts, even the Israeli soldier became a curiously hazy apparition.

Chapter 43

Harry didn't call on Sunday. Obviously, "I love you" had freaked him out more than Jack had supposed.

Never mind; knowing Harry as well as he did, it was no trouble at all to arrange another "accidental" meeting. He knew, for instance, that while Harry ordinarily shunned gay bars, he wouldn't miss Monday nights at Side Track, because that was "Show Tune Night," when the overhead monitors pumped out clip after clip from Hollywood musicals, Tony Awards broadcasts, and other marginalia of the kind only gay men could bear to watch even while drinking. Jack had always made a point of avoiding Show Tune Night, having once suffered a near aneurysm when he had foolishly agreed to accompany Harry and then was forced to endure an endless fifteen minutes of Ethel Merman numbers played at a volume usually reserved only for the most soulless techno tracks.

But now, he would gladly brave such agony again, if it meant reclaiming Harry. And so, on Monday evening, he showered, put on his most flattering couture, and headed to Halsted Street.

He entered the bar to the strains of Betty Buckley singing "Children Will Listen," which made him stop in his tracks and nearly turn around, but he clenched his fists and forged ahead. The bar was, of course, packed, and almost everyone was singing, completely unironically, which for gay men, he felt, was really a kind of miracle.

He bought himself a beer as the monitor switched to The Andrews Sisters warbling "Beat Me Daddy Eight to the Bar," and he felt his shoulders relax. The video appeared not to be a favorite, as many of the patrons now turned to each other and began (or resumed) talking. Jack, clutching his bottle, made his way through the dizzyingly thick crowd, in search of his man.

He found Harry just as the number changed to Brian Stokes Mitchell crooning "The Impossible Dream." Jack decided not to take it as an omen; though he was more than a little surprised to see that Harry wasn't with his usual crowd of show-tune cronies . . .

. . . No, he was with Brian Isley.

There was no reason, he now realized, to have supposed that Harry would stop seeing Brian. They'd apparently been dating for a few months, and even a brief fling with another young stud wouldn't immediately dent that; not even if the young stud in question *were* reading a biography of Grace Coolidge. In Harry's place, Jack would have done the same thing. And Harry must be congratulating himself right about now; by keeping his regular boyfriend while he frolicked with a potential new one, he was able to ease right back into normality after the potential had erred by trotting out the L-word.

All right, then. The thing to do was to appear casual, easygoing, carefree. Jack waited till he'd caught Harry's eye (he smiled; Harry went white) then made his way over to him and, to Harry's increasing discomfort, gave him a hug.

"Harry!" he said. "Didn't know you were a show queen!"

"I could say the same," said Harry, his smile far too wide to be genuine. "I've never seen *you* here before." The implication being, *So you have no business being here now.*

"Oh, I sometimes drop in," was all Jack said, before turning to Brian Isley and saying, "Hi! Corey Szaslow."

"Brian Isley," came the reply, as they shook hands. "You're a friend of Harry's?"

"Oh, Harry and I share a very special passion." Harry appeared to lift two inches off the floor, then Jack leaned into Brian and said, just loudly enough for Harry to hear, "We're both obsessed with the wives of our Chief Executives."

"God, not another First Ladies faggot," said Brian with a good-natured laugh. "There can't possibly be two of you!" He was friendly, outgoing, and handsomer than Jack remembered. He loathed him utterly.

"Oh, we're everywhere," said Jack. "Harry and I are just the tip of the iceberg."

"I've got a brother who's nuts about *Star Wars,*" Brian said. "When he gets together with his friends, they dress up like the characters." He turned pointedly to Harry. "Just in case there's anything you want to tell me."

"Frankly," said Jack, "I think Harry'd make a bitchin' Mamie Eisenhower." Brian laughed, and Jack decided he'd made just enough of an impression; anything more would be overkill. He said, "Nice meeting you, Brian," then turned to Harry and said, "Good seeing you. Let's stay in touch." And still smiling, he turned and made his way back to the front of the bar, just as Kay Thompson barked out the chorus to "Think Pink!" and was accompanied by nearly three dozen slightly drunken baritones.

Jack knew he had executed his salvage mission perfectly; the glancing nature of his contact with Harry had eradicated the three little words he'd so unwisely uttered, and as if in confirmation of this, Harry called him on Tuesday and asked when he might be free.

"Be nice to see you again," he said. "Get to know you a little better." This was a very subtle reference to the "I love you" gaffe; *We're not well enough acquainted for any weird emotional pledges,* is what he was telling him. Jack heard him loud and clear.

They agreed to meet for drinks. That's all Harry said, and, by implication, all he would commit to. He was obviously still a little unnerved. Jack, knowing Harry almost better than he knew himself (certainly these days, anyway) again knew exactly how to play this meeting. Above all, he knew he must not mention Brian Isley, not even in passing. He must show no curiosity whatsoever about who he was or what his relationship to Harry might be. He strongly suspected that Brian had made some further inquiries about the nature and longevity of Harry's acquaintance with *him,* and Jack wanted to show Harry that he was, by contrast, devoid of anything resembling jealousy or covetousness. He liked Harry, liked him a lot; enjoyed being with him; would gladly be with him much more frequently; that, and that alone, was what he would put across.

He put it across so well that, while drinks never did actually segue into dinner, they managed to segue into bed. As they lay together afterwards, the sheets tangled around their ankles, Harry turned and propped himself on his elbow and said, "So what do you do, anyway?"

Jack said, "Hm?" He hadn't expected that. Harry wasn't the kind of guy who asked questions like that. He was far more likely to ask someone's ethnicity or religious affiliation, than anything so prosaic as this.

"I mean," Harry said, chuckling, "what do you do for *money?* Sorry to be nosy, just trying to get the full picture here."

"Oh, well, I . . . investments, mostly," Jack said, stammering a bit. It was true, after all.

"But you need money to get into investing," Harry insisted. "Where's yours come from? Wealthy family, Internet startup . . . what?"

Jack blushed. He couldn't really tell him the truth; couldn't tell him Jack's story when he was meant to be Corey. Finally, in desperation, he grasped at a lie: "Mainly these days it comes from a catering business I run with a friend of mine, who's a chef."

Harry nodded. "I see," he said. "You'll have to give me one of your cards. I do a fair bit of entertaining. Maybe I'll use you someday."

Jack made a mental note to have some cards printed up. But taking priority over that would be the matter of starting the actual business . . .

Chapter 44

. . . and so Jack found himself in a car with Frida's friend David, being escorted around the North Side, looking at houses. He'd put this off for too long; he'd only intended to stay in the apartment a few weeks, and he'd been there more than two months. Time to find more suitable digs for the long run.

His idea had been to kill two birds with one stone. Since David was a real estate agent, he could take Jack around the available properties; and this would also give Jack time to observe David more closely, and gauge whether he really was someone with whom he wanted to go into business. He'd had David in mind when he boasted to Harry of having a partner in catering, so it seemed only natural that David be the first choice to fill that role.

At first, their time together passed awkwardly, with great gaping silences as David drove up and down the streets of Edgewater. It was probably to be expected, Jack thought; parties, especially ones at which wine flowed like water, often created bubble-like intimacies between people who'd only just met, intimacies that couldn't survive sobriety, sunlight, and the passage of a few short days.

Still, David conducted himself very professionally, betraying no signs of flakiness, incompetence, or scattered concentration. He knew what he was doing, and did it with quiet confidence.

It wasn't his fault that the houses he'd arranged for Jack weren't to his taste. He didn't necessarily want a big house, but he wanted big rooms, and in most of the properties David showed him they were tiny and boxlike, connected by harrowingly narrow corridors. Jack couldn't imagine breathing in a house like that, much less living in one.

David seemed embarrassed by his inability to show him what he wanted; clearly, he'd meant to make a good impression. Jack kept consoling him with repeated refrains of "Never mind, it's just our first day, who finds a house on the first day?"—but he could tell that David wasn't entirely convinced there'd be a second day.

The ice between them started to thaw later in the morning, as they came to the less desirable houses on David's list—the ones that had been on the market forever and seemed likely to remain there. The first was appealing enough from the street, but inside it was a shambles, with warped floors, sagging ceilings, even a visible crack in the foundation. But its most unsettling feature was a virtual cavalcade of pest strips, hung from the ceiling in every room, each one choked with houseflies.

"Surely they knew a prospective buyer was coming," Jack whispered to David as the selling agent led them through the kitchen, the gluey abbatoirs waving gently above them as they breezed past. "And yet they didn't think to take them *down?*" David was so horrified he couldn't even look at them, but he was also visibly suppressing laughter.

The house after that was equally dumpy, but was notable for its dark, cramped attic, in which six Korean women hunched over sewing machines, not even glancing up when David and Jack climbed the stairs and peered in. "Did we just see . . . a sweatshop?" Jack asked when they were safely back in David's car.

David shook his head and laughed. "More like a sweat-shop wannabe."

"A sweatshop starter kit," Jack quipped. They laughed again, and Jack said, "Seriously, should we . . . I don't know. Call somebody about it?"

"I'll handle it," said David, turning the key and starting the engine. "No need for the valued customer to be inconvenienced."

"It is right and proper that you put my comfort first," said Jack in an equally pompous tone. The ice was thoroughly broken.

But it was the next house that shattered all remaining reserve between them. A pleasant little four-square, in which a father and son lived together. The selling agent took them through it, pointing out its features as she read them from the listing sheet; it seemed that she herself was visiting for the first time.

They started upstairs, with the master bedroom. It was a fair size, nothing special; but Jack was astonished to see that one entire wall was stacked with porn videos. The lurid titles blared out at him: *Naughty Nurses, Bang In There Baby, To Snatch a Thief,* and so on. The listing agent—a rather prim woman—looked a bit taken aback herself; but she apparently had decided to respond by pretending not to see them.

Jack whispered to David, "Why didn't someone just put those in the closet?"—a question answered when the listing agent opened said closet for them. It was piled, floor to ceiling, with even more videos: *Flirty and Dirty, Betty Blows Babylon, Gag Me With Some Poon.*

And so it went, all through the house—even in the son's room, where a stack of X-rated tapes was topped by a plastic Bart Simpson figure; for some reason, this single detail brought home the utter depravity of the place. Jack whispered to David, "Let's get out of here," but David said,

"Please, let's just see the cellar," and when Jack asked why his eyes sparkled, and he said, "I just have a feeling . . ."

And sure enough, when they descended the stairs to the "finished basement, with pine paneling and a wet bar," as the listing agent recited it to them, they discovered the place old pornography went to die. Jack had to gasp; he hadn't realized so much porn existed in the universe. There was a ping-pong table buckling beneath the weight of it; the wet bar was completely obscured by it; and Jack, on taking a tour of the space, even found, stored atop a small refrigerator, a sub-collection devoted to bisexual three-ways, and a single gay epic titled *Hammerhead.* Jack wondered what made it sufficiently special to have the honor of representing its entire genre, but was too self-conscious to take it down and have a look.

The listing agent, her face now bright crimson, was still maintaining the polite fiction that there was nothing here out of the ordinary. The veritable archive of filth was the elephant in the room that no one would talk about.

Of course, back in the car, Jack and David could talk of nothing else. They spent most of the return drive comparing the titles they'd seen, rocking with laughter; at one point David actually had to stop the car and pull himself together.

". . . *Thar She Blows* . . ."

". . . *Sleaze It to Beaver* . . ."

". . . *Cunt-Tastic Voyage* . . ."

". . . *Tinkle Tinkle Little Twat* . . ."

Eventually, wearied by too much mirth, Jack suggested they stop and have lunch. There was a brief flicker of hesitation on David's face, so he quickly added, "On me," to show that this was to be a social activity, separate from business.

They found themselves at a local bistro that had an outdoor garden; Jack ordered blackened tilapia, David a croque monsieur. It was the perfect segue into talking about catering. Jack asked David about his proposed business; he looked flabbergasted that Jack would even remember this.

"Oh, sure," said Jack. "I'm very interested. Tell me, do you have some kind of specialty, or theme? . . . Some kind of angle that would set you apart, give you your own little piece of the market?"

"Well," said David as he dumped a packet of sugar into his iced tea, "I have this idea of mixing the exotic with the familiar. 'Nouveau comfort food,' I call it." He swirled the sugar around the glass, then licked the spoon and continued. "For instance, I think risotto is maybe the next big comfort food craze. It's creamy and starchy and warm and delicious, and it's infinitely adaptable; I've got two dozen variations in my own repertoire right now, including the classics, like Milanese, but also beet root, black truffle, primavera, pesto, porcini, lemon and cream—you get the idea. But it's also a bitch to make; very time-consuming, with all that stirring. So most people don't bother. So it's got the lure of exoticism and the warmth of the familiar. Now imagine a caterer who could provide a buffet of four or five very different risottos. I could see people going back again and again to sample each one." He shrugged. "Beats the hell out of macaroni and cheese, anyway."

Jack raised an eyebrow; so far, he was impressed. And as he continued to coax David into revealing more of his aspirations, he grew increasingly more so. After lunch, as they strapped themselves back into David's car, Jack said, "Listen, I've got a proposition for you."

David turned to him, on sudden alert, and said, "Yes?"

"If you can show me a business plan, I think—well, I'm pretty sure I'd be interested in partnering with you. Being your tawdry money man, I mean."

David's brow slightly furrowed. "You've got that kind of cash? . . . I'm sorry, but from what Frida's told me about you . . ."

"She's known me a long time," he said quickly. "She still

thinks of me the way I was when we first met, back when we were just reckless kids. I've come a long way since then."

"You're serious about this." David seemed reluctant to trust his own hearing.

"I'm very serious about it," Jack said. "Why wouldn't I be?"

Impulsively, David leaned over, grabbed Jack's head, and pulled him into a kiss.

When they broke the lip-lock, David didn't release him; he held him in place, and Jack found himself staring into David's beautiful, olive-black eyes.

They kissed again, this time more passionately.

Finally Jack got hold of himself and pulled away.

"Sorry," he said. "Sorry, that was . . ."

"No, no, I'm sorry," said David, now quickly resettling himself in his seat and starting the car.

"It's just, I'm seeing someone," Jack said. And just like that, he realized his hypocrisy. *I'm seeing someone who's seeing someone else. So that's no excuse at all.*

But he couldn't help it; he wanted Harry, and his intention was soon to have him exclusively. It was the sole objective of his life, now. It was the only reason he'd even thought of partnering with David; he needed some profession in order to hold Harry's respect.

The drive back to Jack's was more awkward and uncomfortable than before. When Jack got out of the car, he made David promise to send him a business plan, and David agreed, but it was clear all he wanted now was drive away very fast, and put as much road as possible between the two of them.

Chapter 45

David did send Jack a business plan; Jack read and ap-
proved it, and had a lawyer draw up a contract for
their partnership. The soul-deadening sonorities of legal lingo
sapped some of the tension between them, to the point where
they even felt comfortable going out to look at houses again.

In the meantime, Jack's affair with Harry continued apace.
He made it a point to be always alert around him, lest he
make another slip of the "I love you" variety; in fact, he played
things so cool that he had yet to mention Brian Isley, or
make any inquiry about the other side of Harry's romantic
life. Of course, he was secretly dying to know the status of
Harry and Brian's relationship.

After one of their frantic bed sessions, Harry had gone to
take a shower. Jack then scrambled over to Harry's side of
the bed, took the telephone from the nightstand, and scrolled
through the recent Caller I.D. listings. Brian's name showed
up twice over the past five days. Jack felt a lurch in his
stomach; but of course, the fact that he called didn't mean
anything. Harry had left his cell phone on his desk, in the
adjoining room; Jack could go and examine that for *outgoing*
calls, to see if Harry was still calling Brian . . .

But, no, no. That way lay madness. He knew better than
to feed his own jealousy. Far better to continue as he was—

not *pretending* to be free and easy, but actually, honestly *being* that way. No subterfuge, nothing clandestine; Harry deserved nothing less.

It was a noble sentiment; but it soon came up against its equivalent to the acid test.

Harry called Jack to make another date, and this time surprised him by suggesting that he stay the night. Jack was thrilled; it was exactly the kind of breakthrough he'd been hoping for, and he attributed it directly to his unswerving commitment to his plan of attack.

He hated to leave Nelly for the night, especially since she seemed, finally, to be bonding with him in his new body; but her health had been holding steady, so there was no cause to hover over her. He arranged for Frida and her boyfriend to give her her evening walk (Patrick had, on hearing that Jack had a dog, enthusiastically volunteered to watch her "anytime you want, buddy"), then packed a small overnight bag and headed over to Harry's.

It was a quiet night—just dinner out, at a new fusion restaurant Harry's receptionist had been babbling on about, then back home for some snuggling over after-dinner drinks, and finally bed, glorious bed. It couldn't have gone better, though Jack did virtually have to bite his tongue to keep from blurting *I love you, I love you, goddamn son of a bitch, I love you.*

In the morning he woke up alone; but the aroma of coffee wafted through the door. Jack grinned, stretched, then rolled out of bed (he still hadn't grown used to how easily these young joints responded), wrapped himself in a towel, and padded out to the kitchen.

Harry was there, in a terrycloth robe, seated at his breakfast counter and poring over the morning paper. He looked up at Jack and smiled, and Jack felt the sun rise all over again.

He went over and kissed him and said, "Gonna grab a shower."

"Fine," said Harry. "You want any breakfast?"

"Nah. Breakfast is for kids and cattle."

Harry cocked his head. "Funny. I used to know someone who said exactly that."

Jack grew flustered; *he* was the one who used to say that. Stupid of him to let it come tumbling out of Corey's mouth.

He scurried off to the guest shower and luxuriated in Harry's truly state-of-the-art plumbing—all brass, Harry had bragged—and was nearly beet red by the time he stepped out. He hummed tunelessly as he dried himself . . .

. . . then stopped at the sound of the doorbell. Was Harry expecting company?

Well, no matter. He could be discreet.

Except . . . his clothes were still in the bedroom.

He listened as Harry crossed the apartment to the front door, waiting to judge just the right time to dart from the bathroom back to where he could dress and make himself presentable.

He heard Harry say, "Oh, hi—wasn't expecting you," and decided this was the moment. He sprang forth from the bathroom, again clad only in a towel, and headed towards the bedroom at a sprint.

But he was stopped in his tracks by what came next: a loud bass voice saying, "What do you mean you weren't expecting me? Didn't you invite me over for *feinkochen* before racquetball? So let me in already, I'm *shvitsting* like an animal, here."

Walt? . . . *Walt* was here?

As if in confirmation, Harry now said, "Walt, I called you yesterday to cancel. I'm busy this morning."

"Yeah, you look real busy. Which number did you call? . . . Not 4114. I told you I changed that, *shoyn fargessen?*"

Jack heard the door close and two sets of feet now padding his way. It was too late to turn back for the guest bathroom, he'd never make it in time; nor could he bolt for the master bedroom without darting right in front of them.

Desperate, he looked for someplace he might hide; there

was a large upholstered chair just to his left. He ducked behind it and fell into a crouch. *Look at me,* he thought in disbelief; *I'm in a goddamn opera buffa. I'm in a French bedroom farce.*

"I can't keep track of all your phone numbers," Harry was saying as he led Walt into the apartment. "Why the hell are you always changing, anyway?"

"*Oy,*" said Walt, "you give it out to the wrong person, suddenly you've got an *ongetshepter,* right? . . . A stalker."

Jack could hear Walt pouring coffee. "Well, if you wouldn't insist on picking up hoodlums . . ."

"*Shoyn genug!* I don't criticize what you like, don't you do it to me. Speaking of which . . . what's the *tararam* today, you have to cancel? You can't leave Brian for one morning, *paskudnik?*"

A small silence.

"*Oy, shkandal!* . . . It's not Brian, is it?"

"None of your business, Walt."

"Didn't say it was. And . . . he's still here?"

"Walt!"

"*Hob nit kain deiges,* I won't tell anyone."

"I'm not asking you to lie. Just . . . respect my privacy."

"*Tahkeh,* I respect it, I respect it! . . . In fact, I wish your ex could be the *hulyen* you are."

"Walt . . ."

"A real *klogmuter,* that one. Sitting at home like an *onge-blozzener,* moaning about his lost youth . . . *oy,* he gives me a headache! He should be more like you."

"Jack's not me, Walt. More coffee?"

"Mm, *biteh.* But seriously, I mean it, Harry. If you want youth, you have to grab it, like you do. Did I tell you about Jack's sad-sack cocktail party . . . ?"

"Yes, Walt, you did."

"Hottest little *shaigitz* there, serving appetizers—really, you'd have gone *meshuggah* to see him—and your Jack . . ."

"He's not my Jack."

". . . your Jack doesn't even look twice at him. I figured, *Well, if Jack doesn't want him, here's an alter kucker who does.*" He sighed. "But he escaped me on his bicycle, the little *yungatsh.* Lost him on a one-way street."

Jack closed his eyes in relief. He'd instinctively known he shouldn't let Walt see him. He shuddered at the idea of Walt telling Harry that his new young boy toy had been a waiter at his ex's party. He wanted nothing to connect him, in Harry's mind, with the old Jack.

"Poor, poor Jack," Walt continued. "Last time I saw him, he wasn't even making sense. Babbling like his mind was gone. *Klemt beim hartz,* I tell you."

There was a pause. "Interest you in some danish?" Harry asked. "I just had some sent up fresh, and my . . . friend doesn't want any."

"*Biteh,*" said Walt. Then, probingly, "So . . . where is he?"

"In the shower. Let it be, Walt."

"I don't hear any water running."

"*Walt!*"

They began negotiating a new date for racquetball, and soon Harry had to go to his office to check his calendar. Walt followed him.

Jack stood up and peered after them. The office was just off the bedroom, so his clothes were still off-limits to him.

But really . . . that seemed almost insignificant now. The knowledge that Walt—his old friend Walt, to whom he'd remained loyal through so much that would have cost him anyone else's good will—was badmouthing him to Harry! . . . Just as he'd badmouthed Harry to *him.* The poisonous, two-faced little snake!

And worse . . . Harry had listened. Oh, he'd tossed out a few token objections, but there'd been a note of glee in his voice when he did so; possibly no one who didn't know him as well as Jack would've heard it.

The betrayal was almost overwhelming. It was the kind of thing that wasn't to be borne.

Certainly Jack Ackerly wasn't going to bear it.

Fortunately, he'd left his cell phone on the table next to Harry's front door. He fetched it now, then sucked his chest in, tightened the towel around his waist, and left the apartment.

He was in such a white fury that he soon found himself outside the building with little recollection of how he got there.

He flipped open his phone and dialed Frida's number, which fortunately was still saved from the days when the phone had belonged to Corey.

"Hello?" Her voice was thick with sleep.

"Sorry to wake you," he said. "Emergency. I need you to get in your car and come get me."

"Emer'ncy?" she said through a yawn.

"Yes. Come right now, please."

"Awright . . . where?"

Jack was about to give her the address, then thought better of it; he didn't want to be standing in front of the building when Walt came back out—especially wearing nothing but a towel. "Fullerton and Orchard," he said, naming an intersection safely four blocks away. "And please, hurry."

It was still fairly early; despite it being the weekend, not many people were up and about. Also, the day was very warm already, so the sight of someone clad in only a towel wouldn't necessarily be too outlandish.

Even so, he didn't want to brazen out the four blocks to his rendezvous point . . . not when he could creep there unseen. He ducked behind a row of townhouses and began to make his way up the alley. Unfortunately, the pavement here was far less amenable to bare feet than the sidewalk he'd just left; it was strewn with gravel, broken glass, shredded plastic, all manner of debris. He had to pick his way through it carefully, and with every step he cursed Walt, cursed Harry, cursed fate and the world and the universe and the God who

made it—till at last his anger became quite literally blinding, and he stepped on an old rusted nail.

"Shit! Shit fuck crap fuck fuck fuck!" He hopped over to
a gate, the entrance to someone's sumptuous backyard, and
leaned against it to examine his foot. The injured spot was
red, but the skin had not been broken.

His relief was cut short by a sudden tugging at his waist.

He turned to find a large Doberman—or rather, its snout—
protruding through the slats in the gate; its vice-like jaws
were clenched around his towel.

"Oh, no, you don't," Jack said, pulling back. "Let *go,*
you fucking agent of Satan!"

A tug-of-war of some intensity ensued; alarmingly, Jack
found the Doberman was easily his match. It snarled ferociously and wouldn't give an inch, any more than Jack would.

The towel, however, wasn't quite as tough as either of them,
and ended up coming apart with a spectacular rip that almost sent Jack back onto his rump. He managed to keep his
balance by grabbing onto a big red Dumpster.

He was, however, now left with only a narrow strip of
fabric, about four inches wide. The Doberman had the rest,
and Jack could see it now, through the slats, shaking it as
though trying to break its neck.

"This is fine," said Jack with scalding sarcasm. "This is
just great! In fact, this is how I hoped today would go. This
is the realization of my dream for today."

He looked at the scrap of towel, wondering if it were any
good at all to him. He tried to wear it sumo style, a narrow
band covering his genitals and the rest winding around his
waist like a sash. But it wasn't long enough.

He felt like crying. How had this happened? . . . Wasn't it
just an hour ago he'd been in the cool, crisp bed of the man
he loved, the aroma of coffee enticing him, the promise of
hours of indolent leisure ahead of him? . . . How, how was
it possible that he was now standing naked, dirty, and lame,
surrounded by garbage? Was Fate having a good laugh? A

real knee-slapper at his expense? . . . Well, screw Fate too! Screw it with a *chain saw.*

He forced himself to get ahold of himself. He was about two blocks from where he needed to meet Frida. Once he connected with her, everything would be fine. It was just a matter of getting there without getting arrested first.

He turned and looked at the Dumpster, took a deep breath, and opened it. A warm, fungal wave rose up to greet him. He scrunched up his nose, and from the top of the damp, dirty detritus he plucked a relatively untouched newspaper.

Fortunately, it was the *Tribune,* and thus a broadsheet; much better for his purposes. He pulled it apart, spread by spread, and made a little skirt for himself, then belted it into place with his strip of towel. It was perfectly hideous and he'd be humiliated if he ran into anyone he knew, but at least it kept him legal.

And—finding what solace he could in this desperate situation—he'd taken some pleasure in arranging a page with a story on the Vatican, so that the Pope Benedict's photo rode quite low on his ass.

"There now," he said, proud of himself. "Ackerly ingenuity at work."

But Fate, insulted, was not finished with him; and three minutes later, it began to rain.

A quarter-hour later Frida pulled up to the prearranged corner, her windshield wipers working hard against what had become a fully fledged downpour. When she saw Jack, by now a mass of wet grey pulp, her jaw dropped.

He got into the car and, putting on a brave face, said, "Thanks, honey, I appreciate it."

"No problem, but—"

"How's Nelly?"

"She's fine, but—"

"You brought my keys?"

"Yes, yes—look, will you shut up for a minute?" She shook

her head as though it might wake her from some crazy dream. "Corey, what's going on? You ask Patrick and me to walk your dog, and when we show up at the address—Corey, your *apartment!* That *furniture!* All those *things!* And I'm, like, wondering, how did he ever *pay* for all this? . . . Then I get a call telling me to pick you up in this swanky neighborhood, it's some freaking big emergency, and I get here and you're waiting on the street, in the pouring rain, wearing nothing but *wet newspapers*. And . . . I'm afraid to put two and two together, because—because I don't even *know* what I'll get." She looked at him searchingly and said, "Baby, are you involved in something? . . . Are you in over your head?"

He stared into his lap—his soggy, pulpy lap—and after a long, glum pause, he said, barely audibly, "I don't even know whose head it *is,* anymore."

Chapter 46

Despite his travails—or maybe because of them—Jack's anger remained hot; it kept him flushed, his forehead burning. And yet he was also torn by confusion. Why had he cared *so much* what Walt had said? . . . It was nothing he hadn't said about himself. It was the reason he'd gone through all he had, done all he had, to become young again. And why did he feel so viciously stung by the betrayal? . . . The Jack who Walt and Harry laughed about didn't even exist anymore; Jack himself had seen to that.

Or . . . *did* he exist? To what extent was this new life really new? . . . He was in a young body, sure, but what was he doing with it? Pursuing his ex-lover, trying to rebuild a relationship that had run its course once before? . . . With a world of opportunity before him, why was he sifting through the ashes of his past?

Predictably, Harry called within a few hours. Jack almost didn't take the call, but knew he had to face it sooner or later; and Jack—old Jack, new Jack, *any* Jack—had never been shy about facing his fears.

"So . . . you're home?" Harry said.

"Let's see," said Jack frostily. "You called my home number, and I answered; yep, I guess I'm home."

"What happened to you?"

He sighed. It was no use trying to tell the truth; there was no comprehensible way even to start. "I felt sick," he said. "I decided to go home."

"You felt sick?"

"Mm-hm," said Jack. He sat down on his couch, sensing this might take a while. "I think it's the flu."

"You left your clothes," Harry said. "You left your *pants*."

"I . . . was feverish, I guess. Disoriented. Plus, I don't like people seeing me when I'm not well. It's just this thing I have. And your friend was there."

A long pause. "You felt suddenly sick, so you just left without saying goodbye."

"Mm-hm."

"Naked."

"I had a towel."

"What, did you walk home?"

"I don't see that that's any of your business."

Another pause. "This is . . . not adding up. What's going on? You sound pissed off. Did I do something? Are you mad at me for something?"

"*I. Have. The. Flu,*" said Jack with finality.

Harry sighed again. "Fine. You have the flu. And I have your clothes, your bag, and your car keys."

"I'll send someone over for them."

"You do that."

"Is that all?"

"Yes, Corey. By the sound of your voice, I do believe that is all."

They hung up, and for a while Jack remained slouched on the sofa, rerunning the conversation in his head. He couldn't say he was pleased with his performance. He couldn't say he was proud of *anything* he'd done that day. He'd allowed Walt—*Walt,* of all people, whose toxic troublemaking he knew full well—to throw him into a kind of derangement. And because of it, he'd completely scuttled his budding romance with Harry, and got Frida thinking he was some kind of high-priced prostitute.

Well, there was a lesson to be learned here, surely. He wasn't able to determine what it might be, not at the moment; he was still reeling from too many outrages, hurts, and regrets. The only thing to do was to grab what was left of his life, and forge ahead.

To that end, he called David and asked if he were free to show him some houses that afternoon. David readily agreed.

"Glad to hear it," said Jack. "And, listen, on your way over, could you do me a favor?"

"Happy to," said David.

"I need you to stop by someone's house and pick up a few things for me. It's on your way."

"Fine, sure."

"His name's Harry McGann. You got a pen handy? I'll give you the address . . ."

When David showed up later, he handed Jack his overnight bag. Jack dug his wallet and keys out of the pants pockets, and sighed. He'd almost been hoping there'd be a note somewhere. But Harry clearly had nothing to say to him.

In the car, David tried to bring him up to date on his progress setting up their catering business, but the subject depressed him. He'd only sought out the partnership so that Harry wouldn't think him some kind of slacker; now that Harry was out of the picture, what was the point of having a business? What was the point of anything?

Still, he supposed he had to have some kind of occupation, not to mention income; he'd taken quite a bit of money with him when he switched over to being Corey, but it wouldn't last forever. And he did seem to have forever, now; though it was a less felicitous thought than it had been two months ago.

He tried hard to listen to David's news, but it must have been clear that his mind was elsewhere, because David soon trailed off, then fell entirely silent.

After looking at a few nondescript houses, they were driving back to Jack's place, when David said, "So, the guy you sent me to today. The one with your bag and stuff."

"Harry," said Jack, suddenly on guard.

"Yeah, him." His eyes remained fix on the road ahead. "He didn't know I was coming."

"I *told* him I was sending somebody."

"You didn't tell him you were sending *me*." Pause. "He gave me kind of a hard time."

Jack felt his heart drop in his chest. "Oh, Christ," he said. "I'm sorry. Guy's an asshole."

David drove on, still looking ahead. Then he said, "So, is he the guy you've been seeing?"

Jack realized that David had feelings for him, and that this question was therefore a matter of some weight to him. He didn't dare shrug it off. "Yes," he said.

He hoped, hoped dearly, that David's next question wouldn't be, *Is it over between you?* Because Jack would have to say yes, and he didn't want David to know that. He didn't want David to think he was available, that David had a chance.

But . . . *why* didn't he want that? What was wrong with David? He was lovely, sweet, and in his own furry way, more than a little hot. What could possibly be wrong with starting something with him?

As soon as he'd asked himself this, the answers came rushing in, each more disturbing than the last:

Because I've been hurt, and I don't want to be hurt again.

Because I like David, and I don't want to hurt him either.

Because . . . I still love Harry.

Fortunately, David asked him nothing further, and Jack had the small comfort that the only pain he'd caused today was to himself.

He found it difficult to get up the next morning. Nelly was content to sleep in, and since she appeared to feel no urgent need for a walk, he felt no urgent need to force her into one. He remained in bed till the piercing sunlight wouldn't let him anymore, then he dragged himself to the kitchen and made some coffee, and sat staring at nothing, in his bathrobe.

A little later his doorbell rang. All his nerve endings came warily alive. He was expecting no one.

He looked out the window and saw Harry standing patiently below.

His first thought was to pretend not to be home; but he knew the rest of the day would then be agony for him, not knowing why he'd come—or what was in the paper bag he was carrying.

So Jack buzzed him in.

His heart pounding, he went to the door and opened it; he could hear Harry's tread on the stairs, light at first, then heavier as the climb took its toll on him. At last he appeared on the landing.

"Hi," he said, smiling.

Jack wasn't ready to smile back. "What are you doing here?"

Harry held up the bag. "I figured you might still be sick, so I brought chicken soup."

"How do you even know where I live?"

"You left your wallet at my house, remember?"

"You went through my *wallet?*" He was trying to feel outrage, but he couldn't; he was just too glad to see him.

"Yup." He reached the door, then leaned in and kissed him. "Was that okay?"

Jack smiled. "It was . . . fine."

"I don't quite get you, Corey Szaslow. You come on like a freight train the moment I meet you, then three weeks later walk out on me without even bothering to dress. I gotta admit I'm intrigued."

Jack shrugged. "What can I say? . . . I'm a complicated man."

"Like *that's* a bulletin." He lifted Jack's chin so that they were eye to eye. "Seriously, kid—I don't know what happened, what made you do what you did . . . but I don't care. I just want it to be over."

"So do I."

They stared at each other happily for a moment. Then Harry said, "You gonna invite me in, or what?"

Jack balked. "The place is a mess."

"You've been sick. No worries." He breezed past him.

Jack felt something rise within him; a new hope, and new worth, a second chance—if not technically a third—to make it right, to make everything right.

And then it all came crashing down.

The buzzer had roused Nelly, who had quietly followed him to the door. At the sight of Harry, she went slightly wild, wagging her tail and jumping up on him. Harry was stooping now, petting her and saying, "Well, hello there, beautiful! You remind me of someone I know . . . in fact, if you aren't just the spitting image of . . . of . . ." His voice grew cold. "Oh. Oh, my God . . . *Nelly?*"

Jack stood at the door, which still hung open, and felt the entire universe constrict around him, suffocating him.

Harry turned and gave him a look of searing anger. "What are you doing with my dog?"

Jack hadn't anticipated this—couldn't think of anything to say.

Harry got up and grabbed him by his collar. "I said, *what are you doing with my dog?*"

"M-my dog," was all Jack could muster.

Harry's face twisted into what looked like a fist. "We'll *see* about that," he said, and he stormed out of the apartment and clattered down the stairs deafeningly, his footsteps like the report of a machine gun.

Chapter 47

The silence that followed was deafening.

Whatever Jack had expected to happen next—some explosive scene involving accusations, denials, reprisals, and so on—never came to pass. The next day dawned, then wound down to dusk, and there were no calls, no letters, no injunctions, no news of any kind.

Jack had immediately called Corey and left a message warning him that Harry might come to see him, demanding to know why a stranger now had Nelly; but Corey had never called back. He was extremely perturbed by this; he'd resisted, all these months, the impulse to phone Corey and ask for clarifications, explanations, advice on minor matters; he felt it best to handle things on his own, and to divorce himself as completely as possible from the man who used to lead the life that was now his. Apparently, Corey felt the same, for he'd never contacted Jack, either. Perhaps he resented Jack calling even about this present matter; perhaps he thought Jack an alarmist, and didn't want to encourage him to bother him with even more mountains-in-a-molehill by responding to this one.

But it didn't seem like so minor a matter to Jack. It involved the man he loved, and the dog he loved, and his uncertain hold over both. He'd even been tempted to call Harry himself, to try to explain; but he'd yet to come up with any remotely credible story, and was very afraid that if he again inserted himself in Harry's field of vision, he'd start the whole crazy thing over again, and this time possibly lose his dog.

So he waited, on tenterhooks; and as the second day passed glacially—

—so did Nelly. Quietly, in her sleep.

Jack's grief was titanic. This was, after all, more than a dog; she was his last tether to the life he'd lived for so long; and just recently, she was the wedge that had finally made returning to that life impossible.

More than that, she was a friend. A beloved companion, for almost fourteen years.

After he'd made arrangements for her cremation, he returned to the apartment, which, without her, now seemed so large, so empty, so devoid of all warmth. He paced its length like a tiger in a cage, but even so he felt unreal himself, as though he were a kind of phantom, and might walk through the furniture.

Who am I, what am I, he repeated to himself, like a mantra. *I'm a man in another man's body. I'm a man in another man's life. One doesn't mean the other; they're separate things, and I'm lousy at both.*

Something coiled up inside him like a spring, and he felt it needed immediate release, or the result would be something awful, possibly even violent.

And so he found himself at Bar Sharona, dancing shirtless on the platform with two go-go dancers grinding their hips into him. He was drunk, high on poppers, and clean out of control. He was also making a spectacle of himself; it wasn't unheard of for patrons to climb up and dance with the strippers, but the unwritten rule was that you climbed down again after a few bars. Jack wouldn't get down, so that even the dancers themselves grew uncomfortable and inched as far away from him as the tiny platform would allow.

Eventually the manager came over, grabbed his wrist and firmly invited him to descend. Jack was about to put up a fight when a smattering of applause went up in response. So, popular opinion was against him? . . . Fine, fine, fuck 'em all.

"You can let go now," Jack said to the manager, who hadn't released his wrist even as he clambered down from the platform. "I won't go back up. I won't offend the rest of the crowd by daring to expose my less than perfect flesh."

He looked for his shirt, which seemed to have disappeared; but what did he care? Who needed a shirt when there were newspapers? He let out a whooping laugh, and lurched toward the door; but found his way blocked by a tall, sober-faced man with jug ears.

"Hello, Corey," he said.

Jack looked up at him, but couldn't quite focus in on the face. Never mind; it was obviously someone he hadn't met—another on Corey's list of former friends.

"Which one are you?" he burbled.

The man shook his head. "Frida told me you'd changed," he said. "She didn't mention it was for the worse."

Jack said, "What's that supposed to mean?"

Someone next to him said, "Come on, Tyler. Waste of your time."

Tyler. Jack tried to remember why this mattered, but his memory was a greasy smear.

Tyler turned to go, but looked back at Jack and said, "We've been friends a long, long time, you know. I've seen you through a lot of bad shit. So believe me when I tell you: right now—sweaty, hopped up, ruining the night for everyone else in the place—*this* is rock bottom. You've finally reached it. And there's not one goddamn thing I can do about it. Or care to."

And then he was gone—swallowed up by the crowd as though sinking into a body of water. Jack tried to follow him but his eyes wouldn't work in tandem—the lights kept distracting him, people pushing up against him, bits of conversation pummelling his ears—sensation piled on sensation, his pulse thrumming, his throat dry and raspy, his heart careening about his ribcage like a wild animal—

By some stroke of luck he found the door and stumbled out into the cool night. The sweat on his bare chest immediately chilled, and he started to shiver.

He couldn't remember how he got here—in what direction home was—

Lurching toward the curb, he sat down and put his head between his knees. It was difficult to breathe—reminding him of his old lungs, in his old, allergy-battered body. So now he'd even lost *that* advantage.

I hate this life, he thought. *I hate what I've done to it. Corey gave it up because he thought he'd run it into the ground, but it took me to do that.*

Crumpled on a side street, alone, friendless, half-dressed and shivering in the dark, Jack reached an epiphany:

I don't want this anymore.

I want to be Jack Ackerly again.

Chapter 48

Jack phoned Francesca as soon as the sun came up.

"I'm just on my way to work," she said. "Is something the matter?"

"I'd really like to speak to you. Privately."

"Oh, cripes. Yowza. Let me put on my thinking cap."

"Today, if possible."

"Well, I work all day, and I've got my bowling league tonight—"

"You're a witch, and you're in bowling league?"

"It's an all-witch league," she said defensively. "Well . . . there are a couple of shamans, Santerians, and Asatruars, but let's not be persnickety."

"Well, could I come to the bowling alley?"

"Oh, sweetums. Not a good idea. They're not all as nice as I am. You don't want to go home with an extra appendage somewhere inconvenient."

Jack grimaced. "Come on, Francesca. They can't do that."

"No, I was just making a funny." He could actually hear her slap her knee.

"All right, do you have any time between your job and your league? . . . When you'll be home for just, I don't know, ten minutes?"

"Well-lll . . . I do have to feed the gang. And that does

take a fair amount of time, especially since I have to chop flatleaf parsley for Osiris, who won't touch his Meow Mix without it."

"Six o'clock-ish?"

"Six o'clock-ish what?"

He gritted his teeth in frustration. "Is six o'clock a good time for me to come over?"

"Yes, yes. I'll be feeding the gang."

"Thank you. I'll see you then."

"Well, I'm disappointed," said Francesca, as she stood in her kitchen scooping cat food into fourteen separate bowls, two of them with names on the side—MISTY and DASHER— that to Jack's best recollection belonged to none of her brood. "Especially after the actual transference worked so well." Her cats writhed all around the kitchen in anticipation, weaving between her legs, padding across the countertops, one even hunched precariously on her shoulder; she ignored them all equally.

"I'm not ungrateful," he said, seated at the small breakfast nook, where another cat eyed him suspiciously.

"I was actually even thinking I might ask you and Corey for testimonials," she said, as her wooden spoon continued its staccato operation from bag to bowl, bag to bowl, bag to bowl. "I mean, I was sure I was going to get a special citation for the super way it all came off, but that big fat Druid battle-ax Pansy Wetherall couldn't have that, oh no, so she invented some ridiculous story about how there was a terrorist attack on Wrigley Field and she actually *rolled back time* to prevent it. I ask you." She finished filling the bowls and started placing them on the floor. Jack had often heard the phrase *feeding frenzy* but had never had a visual image to accompany it, till now.

"Anyway," she continued, "Pansy was very clever, she had a very detailed explanation about *how* she made time go backwards—lots of phrases like 'inverting the chronal envelope' and the like—but then someone asked her how she stopped the terrorists, and her face went blank; she hadn't figured out that part. I suppose we were all to assume she just stormed in with her own personal SWAT team." The bowls were all on the floor now, and Francesca concluded by tipping a little dish of chopped parsley into one of them—to please the finicky Osiris, who, it turns out, was the feline who'd been keeping an eye on Jack. He now reluctantly gave up that vigil in favor of his dinner.

Francesca wiped her hands on a dishtowel and said, "Even so, Pansy is *insisting* that we acknowledge what she claims she did, though by the very nature of it there *can't* be any proof of it. That's why I thought, if you and Corey came in and gave a brief testimonial in *my* favor . . ."

Jack looked sheepish. "I'm sorry, Francesca. I really am."

She shrugged. "Oh, never mind. I always said I'm not in this for the glory." She sat across the table from him. "But I am sorry it hasn't worked out for you. Sometimes the things we most want are the most disappointing when we finally get them. Still, I betcha it's gonna get better, and probably in ways you can't even imagine right now."

Jack shook his head. "But I don't want it to."

"Well, now, if that's your attitude, it *won't*. Come on, now! Chin up, bucky! It could be worse!"

He looked up into her eyes. "I want to reverse the spell, Francesca."

She took a moment to realize what he was saying; then she slapped her forehead and said, "Yumpin' Yiminy! Do you realize what you're asking?"

"You told me it was possible. I distinctly recall it."

"I did, but . . . it's horrible. *Horrible.*"

"How horrible? What do I have to do?"

"You and Corey both. Oh, Jack, don't make me say it."

"Francesca, come on. You're a pro. Put the squeamishness aside and just *tell me.*"

Her face grew crimson with embarrassment, and for a

few moments she sat in silence, apparently searching for just the right words. Jack waited patiently; the only sound was the swish of fourteen erect cat tails, swaying gently like shafts of wheat.

"It's like this," she said at last. "You and Corey can go back to being your original selves. But it involves connecting with him on a different plane . . . what I mean is, there can be no barriers, you . . . oh, for cryin' out loud," she blurted, "you have to get jiggy with him!"

Jack cocked his head. "You mean—have sex with him?"

She balled her fists and buried her face in them, then nodded.

Jack sat back. "That . . . that's *all?*"

She glanced up, as though not believing what she was hearing.

"I mean," he said, backpedaling, "that's—uh—that's terrible, but I . . . well, I guess if it has to be done, I have no choice."

"I'm so sorry," Francesca said, as though she'd just condemned him to an unspeakable fate.

He rose, and patted her on the shoulder. "It's all right. None of this is your fault. Don't worry."

She leapt to her feet. "Oh, don't go yet," she said, and she raced over to a bureau, pulled open a drawer, and after a bit of rummaging produced a small crystal. "Break this at the height of the . . . you know. What you have to do. It'll help promote the transference."

Jack put the crystal in his pocket, and said, "Thanks."

"Also," said Francesca, "let me just check something." She opened a small leather binder and began flipping through its pages.

Jack was becoming impatient to leave. "What now?" he asked, trying not to sound irritated.

"If you recall, I told you the spell was only reversible up to the Fall Equinox. I think you're cutting it pretty close here . . . let me just find out the exact date."

He sighed in exasperation. "Shouldn't a witch already *know* the date of the Equinox?"

"Well, yes," she said, still turning pages, "a witch in the truest sense, meaning a real Wiccan. I'm not that; I'm closer to a geomancer, though I really try to be more interdisciplinary. It's a matter of semantics more than anyth—ah, here it is!" She'd found the page she wanted and ran her finger down its contents.

Her face blanched; then she looked up at him and said, "Oh, mercy."

His heart did a little somersault. "Oh mercy, *what?*"

"It's tonight, Jack. The Equinox is tonight."

Chapter 49

It had been nearly three months since Jack had left his old apartment, never to return. Or rather *intending* never to return, because here he was, back again, outside the gate and looking in. The effect was disorienting; as though no time at all had passed, and nothing had changed. Except that the cherry blossoms were gone, replaced by tiny black fruit. And his reflection in the glass was that of a twenty-six-year-old.

Even more disconcerting was his inability to get in. Up to now, this gate, this fence, had never been a barrier to him; now, lacking the key, he noticed for the first time how imposing it was, how daunting; there was no scaling it, no squeezing between its bars. It could only be passed with permission.

And Jack wasn't being permitted. Corey wasn't answering the buzzer.

Jack buzzed again and again, panic rising in him like a crescendo. He had only a few hours in which to find Corey and convince him to undo the spell. He didn't think it would take much convincing; having spent a few months as a wheezing, stiff-kneed fiftysomething, Corey would certainly jump at the chance to get back his own firm young flesh. But this depended on Jack actually *finding* him. If the deadline passed before he could track him down, it wouldn't matter how much either or both of them wanted to undo what they'd done; they'd be stuck in each other's bodies till the crack of doom.

Jack checked the time on his cell phone; 7:30, for God's sake. The sun was already low in the sky; soon it would be dark.

He'd called his old attorney Judith Addison-Madison, but her office hours were long over, and he couldn't remember her cellular number. Besides, even if he'd reached her, he knew for certain she wouldn't give her client's whereabouts to a stranger; not over the phone. And not in response to so desperate a plea. Only Fancy might have done that; but he couldn't remember her number, either. He'd tried Directory Assistance, but she was unlisted. His frustration was very near critical mass.

He pressed the buzzer again. And again and again and again.

If only he had some clue as to where Corey might be, where he might have gone; but he couldn't even begin to imagine. What Corey had made of his Jack's old life—in what direction he had taken it—was beyond Jack's ability to conjecture. Until he arrived here and saw his name still on the buzzer, he hadn't even been sure Corey hadn't just up and moved.

Restless as he was, he could think of no better plan than to remain right here, in the hope that Corey might return. This was the only place in the world that he could with reasonable certainty conclude Corey would appear, sooner or later.

He wondered whether he might be better off waiting in the alley behind the building; that's where Corey would enter the garage, presuming he was out in the Porsche. But if he weren't in the Porsche . . . if he were traveling by taxi . . . then he'd return through the front of the building and Jack, in the alley, would never know it.

No, no; best to stay put, and watch the windows. It was

getting dark enough now that if Corey returned home he'd have to turn on the lights; and that would give Jack his cue to buzz again, this time with the assurance of being answered.

Time crawled. It moved achingly forward, gasping, on its belly. Jack had never known such agony. The streetlights flickered on. He felt as though he might cry. This body— this young, strong, passionate, hot-blooded body—was strangely more prone to things like crying jags. Jack was still getting used to that. Except, he no longer wished to get used to it. Not anymore. He wanted to be rid of it, to shirk this flesh, this life, because it wasn't his, it wasn't him.

Finally, the tears came. Jack blubbered like a child, unselfconscious and unashamed.

A taxi pulled up and for a moment his heart climbed high in his chest; then it plummeted again when a woman clambered out. He turned away from her, to hide his tear-stained, snot-streaked face; and as the taxi rolled away the woman came up behind him and inserted a key into the gate.

Jack realized he could slip in behind her. He could follow her into the building, then make his way to his old apartment and wait in the hallway. He'd be out of the cold—for indeed a chill had now settled over the night—and if by chance Corey came in from the garage, he'd hear him through the door.

He turned and positioned himself to be ready for the moment the woman swung open the gate; but she was having trouble with the key, as though not accustomed to using it. *"Damn,"* she muttered.

Something about the timbre of her voice made Jack look at her more closely.

"Oh my God," he said. *"Sharon?"*

She turned and looked at him. Her own eyes were puffy, as though she'd been crying too. "Sorry," she said, "do I know you?"

Do you know me? he wanted to say. *We grew up to-*

gether! But of course he was no longer her older brother; he'd become someone else—had abandoned her along with his old life, in the grip of the madness that had claimed him so completely. He couldn't even hug her now, as he—to his surprise—so much wanted to.

"Um, I'm a friend of . . . of your brother's," he said. "Jack's told me a lot about you."

She looked at him a bit dubiously. "He must've described me pretty goddamn well if you could recognize me in the dark."

"He, uh, showed me pictures," he added. "What are you doing here?"

She took a step back. "I'm not sure that's really any business of yours."

Of course it wasn't. He'd long since forsaken any relationship with her. He made an effort to get hold of himself. "I'm sorry," he said. "But listen, do you know where Co—where Jack is? It's absolutely vital that I find him. A matter of life and death."

She let out a bitter chuckle. "Yeah, well, what isn't these days?"

He cocked his head. "Sorry?"

"You say you're a friend of Jack's? . . . But you obviously haven't heard the news."

Jack felt the abyss widen; he was afraid to hear more, lest he fall in—but what else could he do? He'd come this far . . .

"What news?" he asked, his voice hoarse, little more than a whisper. "Please, please, tell me where he is."

She regarded him with a measure of distrust, then looked at the door to the building, as though assessing her chances if she made a run for it. In the end she shrugged and said, "Hell with it. I guess there's no harm in telling you . . ."

One of the things Jack had learned, early in his life, was that it really didn't matter what you did, as long as you did it with an air of unimpeachable authority. Look sufficiently secure in your own sense of purpose, and no one will think to question you.

He put that to work now, as he strode the brightly lit corridors. Visiting hours had long been over, he knew that; and yet he passed any number of official personnel, not one of whom cared to arrest his determined, confident stride. He was even so bold as to stop one of them and ask directions. And was given them, no questions asked.

He arrived now at the designated room. The light inside was low, but not extinguished completely. He could just see the end of the bed, and the feet beneath the pale green blanket. They looked so small, so frail, those feet—*his* feet.

He took a deep breath, summoned all his courage, and entered.

Corey was awake, but not looking very alert. He was watching the television bolted high on the far wall, though the sound seemed to have been muted. Jack looked at him—at his own former face, drawn and haggard; at the pale arms, one of them pierced by an I.V. feed; at the slow, rhythmic rasping as he breathed. He remembered how hard it had been to breathe in that body; he'd never really known what it was to inhale freely till he'd left those lungs behind.

"God forgive me," he said, thinking of the sweet, trusting, sad young man, trapped in that wreck of a body. "What've I done to you?"

At the sound of his voice, Corey turned and saw him. He smiled. "Hey, boss!" he said weakly. "Wasn't expecting *you*."

"I'm sorry," Jack said, approaching. "I can't tell you. So very sorry." He sat on the bed and took Corey's hand in his.

"'S'not your fault," said Corey. "I just had a little heart attack, is all."

Jack shook his head. "Listen," he said. "This is wrong. I've learned a lot, in the past few months. I . . . this is going to sound silly, but I've *grown up*. I've learned what it means to be a man."

"Cool," said Corey. "Is it a secret, or can you tell?"

"It's not a secret," he said. "Being a man means accepting with grace and dignity the consequences of your actions. It's that simple." He grimaced. "I mean, it's simply put; not so simple to do. Me, I've never done it, ever. Least of all with you. I dumped all the consequences of my actions onto *you*. And look at you now."

Corey shook his head. "It was mutual. You got all my crap, too. Plus, we agreed."

"No, no. *You* agreed. This was my idea, this whole crazy, stupid, selfish plan was mine, designed to serve me. You were at a point in your life where you almost had to go along with it. Because, see, that's the only option I offered you. I'm a bad man, Corey. A very sad, stunted, stupid man. But I'm going to make it up to you." He got up, shut the door, turned off the TV monitor, then came back and kissed Corey on the lips and said, "I'm going to put us back where we belong. I'll be as gentle as possible. Just trust me. Go with me."

He kissed Corey again, and then Corey raised a hand and stopped him. "Wait," he said. "What are—are you telling me, you want to switch us back?"

"That's right," said Jack. "I'll be Jack again, you'll be Corey again. I'll be where you are, and you'll be free to walk out of here." He caressed Corey's hair. *My hair*, he thought. He felt surprisingly maternal; as though he were about to give birth to himself.

But Corey interrupted him. "Whoa, there," he said. "Shouldn't you, like, *ask* me first?"

Jack was taken aback. "I—I didn't think I had to." He laughed, as though surprised at having to say something so ridiculous. "I mean . . . I'm the goddamn cavalry, here."

"Well, you *do* have to ask," said Corey. "And the answer is no."

"What?" Jack said. "What are you saying?"

"I'm saying no, Jack. I don't *want* to change back."

Jack's jaw went slack. "But . . . in God's name . . . *why?*"

He smiled. "'Cause I'm happy."

Jack stared at him, open-mouthed.

"I'm *happy,* Jack," he repeated. "Thanks for your visit. But you can go now. Just go, and please—*leave me alone.*"

Part Five

Corey (Jack)

Chapter 50

Corey had several times tried to imagine how it would feel to find himself in someone else's body. He'd wondered whether it was something he would always be intensely aware of—the additional weight under his belt, the sound of a strange voice issuing from his lips, the feeling of different teeth under his tongue, and so on, all too insistently *present* to forget for even a moment—or whether he'd settle in so comfortably, as though wearing someone else's old coat, that it would only be when he caught sight of himself in a storefront or car window that he'd be reminded, *Oh, yeah; that's me now.*

But these were all speculations on how the change would impinge on his consciousness; he hadn't anticipated that there would be a sudden and dramatic impact on his primal condition, his very reflexes. Yet as he staggered away from Francesca's, nearly blinded by tears, gasping for air from nasal passages swollen almost shut, he was effectively reduced to the level of instinct. There wasn't a coherent thought in his head; he was lurching from moment to moment, striving only for the next breath, the next step, and endeavoring not to fall down.

He had begun with a destination in mind—Jack's car—*his* car—and somehow that early imperative remained in place as everywhere else in him, survival took precedence. There was, it seemed, just enough sentience available to keep it clear that he wasn't just stumbling, lunging, and floundering; he was stumbling, lunging, and floundering *towards* something.

When he reached the Porsche, his relief was so great that he laughed aloud, and maniacally groped himself for the keys. He fumbled the door open, tumbled into the driver's seat as though being shoved from behind, and slammed himself in. There: the world was shut out, its motes, flecks and particles unable to assail him further. With a slightly clearer head, he recalled Jack telling him there were allergy pills in the glove compartment. He reached over to open it, and ended up swinging his hand past it, hitting the passenger door and grazing his knuckles. Apparently he'd have to gesture with greater care, till he became more familiar with how this body responded to the demands he made of it.

He found the plastic vial of pills and tried, as calmly as possible, to screw off its cap. But his fingers felt strange, and he was still shaking from the ordeal of the walk, and the cap ended up popping like a cork, with pills erupting everywhere.

He picked two capsules off his lap and placed them on his tongue, then noticed that the label directed only one should be taken at a time. Muttering an expletive, he forced himself to swallow both, which with his dry throat took a full sixteen seconds; they almost got caught in behind his Adam's apple, but he refused to die in so undignified a manner, having inhabited this body not half an hour, and somehow got them all the way down by sheer force of will. It was only then that he noticed the bottle of water in the door pocket.

He started the engine, turned the air conditioner on high, then sat and waited for the beating of his new heart to return to normal. He was just realizing that he didn't know what normal was when someone tapped on the window; it was a meter maid.

He rolled down the window, and she said, "Sir, this meter has expired."

"I am having an allergy attack," he said, in the same tones someone else might say *I am having a baby.*

"You need to move on, or feed the meter."

"I am having an allergy attack," he repeated, more shrilly, and he rolled the window back up. He sat as still as possible and concentrated on breathing while the dreadful woman wrote out a ticket and stuck it under his windshield wiper, mere inches from his beleaguered nose.

Eventually he felt sufficiently in possession of his new self to shift the car into gear and drive home. His eyes still itched and watered a little, and his vision was just that much impaired that he had to pay very close attention to the road on the way home, lest he cough or sneeze and suddenly find himself sailing through someone's picture window.

When he was safely in the garage, he turned off the ignition, got out of the car, then leaned back in and picked up all the loose pills. *Definitely don't want to lose these,* he told himself. His hands were still shaking, so that he would occasionally deposit a pill back onto the seat even though he'd aimed for the vial.

He stopped on his way up to the apartment to pick up Jack's mail—*his* mail, now. He was astonished by how much there was. Magazines, catalogs, prospectuses from investment firms, special offers, pleas for tax-deductible donations, invitations to join, appeals for help, statements, invoices, bills, bills, bills. Jack had shown him where to file most of these things, but he suspected about two-thirds of them could be safely relegated to the trash.

He dropped the mail onto the table inside the front door and headed straight across the apartment *(his* apartment now) to the bar cart. He poured himself a very large vodka and tonic and sat down in one of the remaining custom-made chairs (he'd have to order some new ones; what was the name of that designer?), and proceeded, sip by sip, to drink the whole thing down.

Seated among Jack's things, surrounded by their loveliness, the burnished quality he had so admired in them at first, he began to feel better about the choice he had made. For additional comfort, he reached up and patted the breast pocket of his jacket, where Jack's leather wallet rested comfortably against his chest. It was a slim thing, not the credit-card-choked monstrosity he'd expected.

He took it out with some curiosity. Funny, Jack had never thought to show him its contents, and he'd never thought to ask. He opened it; and sure enough, it contained only Jack's driver's license (handsome photo, too; Corey was impressed), an insurance card, a platinum AmEx card, and six crisp fifty-dollar bills. Jack Ackerly apparently liked to travel light. Corey would have to learn that trick.

He replaced the wallet and finished off his drink with greater calm than he'd started it. Despite the seeming precariousness of his physical state, he felt safe. For the first time in his life, he could look to the future without fear or panic. He was set. *More* than set. After years of hanging onto solvency by his fingernails, he could ease his grip and *relax*.

As for the allergies . . . the more he thought about it, the more certain he was that they were something he could handle. No doubt they were exacerbated by this body's slight corpulence. A strict new diet and exercise regimen would fix that.

But for now . . . he poured himself another drink. His head was feeling funny; it had been an eventful, confounding, and ultimately harrowing day. And he'd also taken twice the prescribed dose of Jack's pills; so he went into the adjoining media room and watched the flat-screen TV for a while, to dull his turbulent thoughts. Meantime, the vodka reacted with the allergy pills, and in combination with his physical and emotional fatigue, helped knock him out like a prize-fighter's punch. He awoke hours later, still fully dressed, with *My Name Is Earl* blaring in his face, and it took him several moments to remember where he was.

And who he was.

Chapter 51

Because he'd dozed through the dinner hour, Corey couldn't fall asleep the rest of the night. He felt mildly intoxicated—could this middle-aged body really not handle a cocktail and some pills?—and he'd eaten nothing except a toaster waffle from Jack's freezer, so his stomach gnawed at him as well. Worse, in the dark, he kept forgetting, drifting away to some hazy half-dreamland—then he'd snap back and remember everything that had happened, everything he'd done that day, and be crushed anew by the awesome weight of all it meant for him.

The thing to do, he decided, was splurge; the delicious novelty of heedlessly spending money would shock him out of these doldrums and into an appreciation of his new identity. His first thought, of course, was new clothes; but Jack already had such an expansive wardrobe. And his taste seemed impeccable. Corey didn't really yet trust himself to dress this body; he was afraid he'd skew too young and make himself look ridiculous. Also, shopping for clothes wasn't nearly grand enough to have the desired effect. Shopping for a new *car* might do it—but he rather liked the Porsche. It made him feel aristocratic, like a character in a Merchant & Ivory film that lived in an enormous house with an actual name, like Ash Manor or Larksworth, and spent Saturdays on horseback, surrounded by baying hounds. The exoticism tickled him.

Then he hit on it: *travel*. The entire world was open to him now. He could go anywhere he liked, stay in the finest hotels, dine at four-star restaurants . . .

. . . but alone. There was no one to join him. His old friends were forever lost to him, of course, and he couldn't see traveling with anyone from Jack's circle; the effort of pretending to be who he wasn't would exhaust him after a day, if not less. Besides, they all seemed more business associates than friends.

All the same, he thought he'd at least look up the number of Jack's travel agent—Rita something; he remembered her from the cocktail party; the cosmetic surgery victim—just to have it on hand. Something might occur to him. Perhaps a long weekend in London. He might do that on his own. There was no language barrier, and he'd be free to act any way he liked, since presumably no one there would know Jack Ackerly.

He went to the desk, where Jack kept his leather address book. He looked under 'T' for Travel but found no entry, and was thus forced to go back to A and start combing the entire book for the agent's number. Fortunately, her name was Danilov, so he stumbled onto it sooner than later. He picked up the phone to call her—might as well get her checking out fares for him now—and heard the stutter-tone that indicated there were messages waiting on voice mail.

He had forgotten the password, but fortunately Jack had programmed it into speed dial. Within seconds, he was hearing the neutral tones of the recorded operator telling him *"You have—sixty-one—new messages."* Corey's jaw dropped. Sixty-one messages in *one day?* He doubted that, in his old life, he'd ever had that many in a whole month.

They started coming at him, fast and furious. He listened to each to the point at which it caused him panic, then pressed the pound key to skip forward.

"Hello, Jack, it's Milt. I just got a call about some code violations at 1386 Armitage, if you could give me a call back to authorize—" *Skip*.

"Jack, it's Judith. Listen, we're looking at some capital gains trouble ahead if you don't find some kind of shelter or—" *Skip*.

"Mr. Ackerly? It's Linda Sproat from Literacy Now? We're having our annual fundraiser this year at the Four Seasons and if you recall last year you committed verbally to buying a table again, but if you could just call and confirm I'd really apprecia—" *Skip*.

"Jack, hi, it's Robyn. Listen, I've just been asked to join the board of a new center for disadvantaged youth, I'm very excited, it's—you should see these kids, break your heart, they're so—anyway I was wondering with your—well, given our history together, it seemed like you'd be—" *Skip*.

"Hello? . . . Mr. Ackerly? . . . Todd Mannix from the Park District. We haven't heard from you yet regarding your slip at Diversey Harbor; if you're going to renew, please let us know as soon as possible. If we don't hear from you by the end of the week we'll have to let it go to someone else, my number is—" *Skip*.

Corey slammed down the phone. His head was spinning; he wasn't ready to deal with *any* of these calls. There were already more decisions being asked of him all at once than he'd ever had to make in the course of a year. And there were fifty-odd calls still *waiting*.

He sat down and put his head in his hands. If this was what it was going to be like to be Jack Ackerly, he didn't know if he could do it. Jack had made it sound so easy, as though an entire staff of worker bees was waiting to handle all his responsibilities. But it seemed the worker bees still had to look to him for direction, and he just wasn't equipped to provide it.

Jack's final advice to him had been, "If it gets too much for you, call in Fancy. Technically she's retired, but she's a busybody by nature, can't bear to be inactive, and she's very fond of me. She'll handle *anything* you throw at her. Done a few things for me only recently and hasn't even asked to be paid for it. I think she just likes to get out of the house."

But Corey's understanding was that Fancy had been Jack's assistant for many years. As such, she probably knew him as well as anyone alive. He was afraid to let someone like that too close to him. He'd also observed Fancy at the cocktail party; the woman was sharp as razor wire. *Nothing* escaped her. No, no—he couldn't have her around. The idea actually frightened him.

He sat back with a sigh. A whole day lay before him—his first as Jack Ackerly—and already he'd been beaten into paralyzed submission. He really didn't have the slightest idea how to live this life.

And just like that, he knew what he must do: get out, and get sweaty. *Work* this body. There was no cure for stress like physical activity; and hadn't he decided his priority was to whip this new self into shape? . . . After a good, solid hour or two at the gym, his head would be clearer, his blood humming, and he'd be capable of anything. He was sure of it.

He packed Jack's gym bag—correction: *his* gym bag (this was going to take some getting used to). Then, after downing a few more allergy pills, to defend himself against the hostile outdoors, he headed off to Jack's fancy health club.

Chapter 52

Several men in the locker room saluted Corey and asked how it was going, and it seemed to satisfy them when he said, "Same old, same old." One older guy, stark naked except for black stretch socks and leather loafers, came over to chat while flossing his teeth, and Corey—who at that point was pulling on his workout trunks and was thus at his most vulnerable—felt an onrush of panic, because he had no idea who this fashion plate might be. But after a few moments it became clear that, whoever he was, he was more interested in talking than listening, and after a bite-sized eternity he trundled off, having told Corey all about his asthma, his new Lamborghini, his plans to winter in Scottsdale, and his affair with his sister-in-law.

Corey decided a new gym was in order . . . one with fewer members acquainted with Jack Ackerly.

He decided to start his workout with a brisk, five-mile run, then spend half an hour on the rowing machines before finishing with some free weights. He grabbed a towel on his way out of the locker room, then paused before the adjacent mirror. He hadn't allowed himself to have a good look at his new body yet . . . the kind of up-close scrutiny he hadn't been able to make when it belonged to Jack, because it felt too funny. But now that he was on the brink of reshaping that body for the better, he felt sufficiently optimistic to risk it. He stepped up to the mirror and confronted himself at close range, and again marveled at the inky depths of Jack's dark eyes. When he'd first entertained the idea of inhabiting Jack's body, he'd been unable to shake the silly idea that those black eyes would be harder to see through than his own ice-blue ones. He noticed, too, that the eyes were bloodshot; but that might simply be from allergies, and the past day's scattershot diet.

Lowering the eyes now, he now examined the teeth. They felt funny; he'd fallen into the habit, without realizing it, of probing the lower left incisors with his tongue. He pulled back his cheek now and had a look; it appeared that there was a dental bridge there—it wasn't even the same color as the rest of the teeth. Corey felt a slow rise to irritation. Jack hadn't mentioned *this*.

Next he examined closely the texture of the skin. There were wrinkles aplenty; no crevasses visible from across the room, certainly, but at this range he could clearly see a tiny web of chicken scratches. No real sagging beneath the eyes, which was a comfort; and the laugh lines rather added to the face's charm than detracted from it.

He stepped back and took in the rest of the picture. Well . . . nothing had vastly improved since he'd seen Jack in the raw a few days earlier. The general impression was still one of youthful vigor slowly giving way to decrepitude. There were muscles, yes, and in places where fat didn't tend to dwell (the pectorals, the calves, the forearms) the flesh was as firm as teak. But the midsection was soft and doughy, the thighs a bit thick, and what he could see of the rump didn't tempt him to try to see more.

Still—all that was fixable. And with a burst of positivity he bounded up the stairs to the running track, dropped his towel over the bar overlooking the racquetball court, and set off at a trot.

He knew, of course, not to push himself. This body had,

after all, passed the half-century mark. He figured he'd work it at two-thirds his usual energy level. That sounded about right.

And indeed, a few hours later, when he emerged, showered and dressed, he felt newly invigorated, and drove home in the highest of spirits. He entertained a fantasy of a time, some weeks hence, when Jack would run into him in the street and be stunned by the transformation he'd effected on his former physique. Perhaps he might even ask for it back.

En route home, he stopped and picked up a falafel for lunch; but by the time he got back to his flat his appetite was curiously abated.

He put the falafel on the counter for later, kicked off his shoes, and sat down before the TV to relax till he felt up to eating. He put his feet up on the coffee table and gazed at the screen, on which an anchorwoman was reporting a fire at a South Side paper plant. He couldn't quite get a bead on her; she kept drifting in and out of focus. Hadn't Jack told him he sometimes needed reading glasses to watch television? . . . Corey seemed to remember having seen a pair on Jack's desk. But the idea of now getting up and fetching them was curiously daunting. It was just down the hallway. What was the big deal . . . ?

And yet he remained supine, knitting his brow in an effort to make the anchorwoman coalesce; but the more he strove, the more he felt as though he were floating in a warm bath. Gentle waves of fatigue washed over him. It was an effort to keep his eyes open . . .

. . . He turned a bit and poked himself in the eye, then sat up with a start in a now-darkened apartment. There was a slick of drool over his chin, and a rerun of *The Cosby Show* on the screen. He fumbled for the floor lamp and almost knocked it over; when he'd turned on the light, he saw that the clock read 6:18. Once again, he'd slept away the entire afternoon.

He got up from the couch and his legs almost gave way. They actually *hurt*. But . . . he'd only run seven miles! How was it possible?

He staggered into the kitchen. The falafel had gone cold. He reheated it in the microwave and snarfed it down, then sat back on the couch with a beer, with which he washed down another two allergy pills.

The compulsion to close his eyes settled over him again. He fought it bravely until half past eight, when he shambled into the bedroom, toppled onto the mattress like a felled tree, and gratefully let himself succumb to slumber.

Chapter 53

Twelve hours later he woke up with a start to the sound of the telephone.

He rolled out of bed, and when his feet hit the floor he felt a jolt of searing pain that traveled like an electric current up his shins and into his thighs.

"Ow, ow, ow," he whined as he hobbled to the phone. He grabbed it from the cradle and brusquely said, *"Hello."*

"Oh, hi, Jack? . . . It's Robyn, listen I didn't wake you, did I? Because I . . . well, it's almost nine, I figured . . . Anyway, I was wondering, I've left a few messages for you, probably you didn't—well, maybe you did, but—I mean, if you did and you just weren't interested, I'd—well, let me just tell you again, it's this board I've just joined, I've been telling them about you and they'd be really happy to—I mean, if you'd still even consider that after the way we were—Although you seemed fine with it—not fine, okay, but better than me is what I—"

"Hello?" Corey repeated, rubbing his eyes. He couldn't believe how stiff and sore he was. After one day at the gym! *One.*

"Oh, sorry—let me just get straight to the point, which is—I know I said that before, but—oh, God, sorry, I'm just flustered, you have that effect on me, I'm sorry, it's just didn't realize I'd be waking you, I—"

"Who are you calling, please?" said Corey, the mist clearing from his head.

"Um . . . it's *Robyn*, Jack. I'm just, uh, following up on my earlier—I already said that, I—look, do you want me to just start over?"

"Do I know you?" The pain in his legs—arms, too!—was making him cranky.

There was a small, fearful pause. *"Robyn Vivin,"* she said. "We were on the Tealight Board together." With a touch more bravado: "You invited me to your cocktail party."

"Oh, *that* Robyn." Corey sat down and massaged his left leg with his free hand. "Sorry. Um . . . what can I do for you?"

Another pause. "Um . . . I've left you some messages. A new board. Non-profit youth center." She paused. "Is this a bad time?"

"I just don't know what you're talking about."

"Well, I thought you—I mean, if you're interested—you could be on the board with me. Like before, only—well, obviously better this time, because—well, I don't even have to tell you."

Yes, you do, thought Corey. "All right," he said. "What would I have to do?"

The longest pause yet. "Pardon?"

"If I were on this . . . thing with you. What'd you call it?"

"The . . . you mean, the board?"

"Uh-huh." He switched the receiver to his other hand and began massaging his right leg. "What's it all about?"

"Well . . . raising money. For the organization." She was speaking slowly, as if to someone newly brain-damaged.

"Okay. That sounds fun." *Something to do, anyway,* he thought. "Yeah, I could help you out."

"Oh, *great,*" she said, obviously relieved. "Only, the board meets at the end of the week, I'm sorry, I've left messages for you the past couple of days, I was hoping—well, I know this is a bit last-minute, it's just, the way this has all just happened so suddenly—"

"End of the week works for me," he said.

"It does?"

"Just tell me when and where."

"Oh, it's really convenient for you," she assured him. "It's not far from where you—well, maybe a *little* bit far, but you've got a car right? . . . What am I saying, of *course* you have a car, you've probably got a totally gorgeous import job or someth—"

"Why don't you just e-mail me the specs?" Corey said. He'd placed her now; the jittery Amazon in the kitchen who couldn't finish a sentence, and who'd roused Fancy's ire by smoking.

"Fine, I can do that," she said. "In fact, I'll do it right now. If you have any trouble getting it, call me?"

"Sure," he said, leaning back in the chair to ease his smarting back. "You said this is a non-profit organization, right? . . . So, it's about, like, helping people?"

Another pause. "Well, this one is. It's a center for disadvantaged youth. Didn't I tell you this alrea—Well, maybe you haven't checked your messages, or—"

"I haven't," said Corey. "I'll go do that now." And with only a little more conversational wriggling, he managed to untangle himself from Robyn and hang up the phone.

He then got up and limped to the office, dropped into the chair, and dialed voice mail.

"You have . . . one-hundred and . . . eighteen . . . new messages."

Corey felt himself swoon. Nearly twice as many as when he checked yesterday! . . . What the hell kind of man was Jack Ackerly, that he had people calling him in this quantity? What did everybody *want* from him? . . .

He'd resolved to spend the morning going through the calls and making a list of which he felt sufficiently confident to return. But now that they'd doubled in number, the idea was too daunting; there were just so freakin' *many* of them. And besides, if they were really important, they'd call back, like Robyn did.

Except . . . he wouldn't be here. He had to go back to the gym, and work out the kinks in these long-unused muscles, or the soreness would get even worse. He wouldn't let mere pain defeat him. He'd get this body in shape, and that was *that*.

It was while he was on the track, shuffling along at about a third the speed he'd run yesterday, that he realized he'd have to break down and ask Fancy for help.

Chapter 54

"Well, Jack," said Fancy with what Corey could only read as a hint of smugness, "I've been expecting your call."

"You have?"

"Mm-hm. There was something . . . I don't know . . . *valedictory* about that cocktail party. Gathering together all the old troops. I said to myself, 'He's going to make an announcement.' You didn't, then, but I figured it wouldn't be long in coming."

"Well . . . I really don't have anything major to say."

"Oh, come on now. I know you."

"No, you don't," he said; and he instantly regretted it. Worst thing of all would be to put this woman on alert. He shifted on the couch, where he was lying with hot compresses on his legs. "What I mean is . . . well, I *have* sort of made some changes in my life."

"Mm-hm. *What* a surprise."

"But they're more . . . I guess you could say, internal. Nothing like, 'Oh, I'm going to join the priesthood,' or anything like that."

"Internal, huh?" She giggled. "Oh, Jack, you are a treat."

"Anyway, listen," he said, growing apprehensive about the intimate tone this call was taking. Hadn't Jack said this woman used to be his secretary? . . . Well, he'd also said she'd functioned as his "professional mom," so maybe some familiarity went with the territory. "It's just, I'm going to try to be, uh, appreciating life more, seeing more of it, if you know what I mean . . ."

"Not exactly."

"I . . . it doesn't matter. The point is, I'm going to have less time to do things like, y'know, handle my phone calls, sort through my mail, stuff like that."

"Mm-hm."

"And I've been thinking of getting someone to come in, twice a week, maybe three times, to do that for me. I thought maybe you might know of someone."

"You mean, will I do it?"

"No, no—I know you're retired, I was just thinking you might—"

"You were thinking you could get me to do it without asking me outright," she said. "Save you feeling guilty for yanking an old woman away from her well-earned rest." Corey felt himself go red. She really *did* know him . . . and he wasn't even him anymore! "Never mind, I'd be happy to. Getting a little bored around here, to tell the truth. I almost joined a sewing circle yesterday, if you can believe it. Was *this close*. Then I thought, no, if I'm meant to die, I'll just wait for the real thing."

Corey laughed.

"Also," she said in a more confidential tone, "Mickey is driving me *mad*. He's retired too, you know, and the only thing he's found to fill the time, is trying to teach his lousy mynah bird to recite the whole of *Hiawatha*. All day long it's, '*By the shores of Gitche Gumee . . . By the shores of Gitche Gumee, goddamn you!*' If I don't get away from him, I may actually have to kill him. And the bird right after."

He laughed again. "Well, then—a suitable arrangement for us both."

"Seems like it, yes."

"One small thing," Corey said as he moved one of the compresses up his leg. It had gotten lukewarm; he'd have to reheat it after he hung up. "The whole matter of . . . you know. Money."

"Mm-hm. Well, what are you looking at?"

"Honestly, I hadn't really thought about it. What would you consider fair?"

She giggled again. "Oh, here we go, classic Jack Ackerly! 'Never be the first party to put a number on the table.' Really, you'll never change."

Corey thought, *You'd be surprised.*

"Let me come 'round tomorrow," she said. "Have a look at what the workload is, exactly. We can come to terms then."

"That sounds fine," he said. But suddenly, at the idea of laser-eyed Fancy hanging around, picking up on every subtle alteration in his behavior, he grew uneasy again. "I'll run through it with you and then I'll give you a key to the place. And, and you can just get to work in my absence."

"Oh, are you going somewhere?"

"Yes. Just for a day or two."

"Where?"

Corey had thought about checking into a hotel, but of course that was ridiculous. As long as he was getting out of Fancy's way, he might as well make it some real distance. "London," he said.

"Oh, how nice! Will you be seeing Mr. Powers and Mr. Blevins while you're there?"

Who? "Uh . . . no."

"'Cause I'd be happy to ring them and set up dinner for you."

"No, no, I won't be seeing Mr. Pony and, uh, Mr. Beavers."

"What about Barbara Everly?"

"No, no one, actually, I'll just—uh, just be conducting some private business."

"Ah," said Fancy, and give her credit, she knew not to pry.

After he'd got her off the phone, Corey felt a little dispirited. He'd been thinking of London as a kind of refuge—a place where he could go to shake the burden of having to be Jack Ackerly. But now it turned out that the city was crawling with people who *knew* Jack Ackerly. He'd just have to do his best to keep a low profile. Accordingly, when he phoned Rita Danilov to make the arrangements, and she asked if he'd like to stay at Claridge's as usual, he said no, and made her find a hotel in a different part of town.

Once that was taken care of, he had nothing left to do with his day except go back to the gym. His legs were in agony from his first two visits, but he told himself that was merely a sign his program was working.

The trouble was, he was also so *tired*. He felt as though he'd just run back-to-back marathons. But he was determined to work through his pain, his fatigue, everything. He couldn't very well give up on the single activity he'd yet found for this new life.

And so the gym it was.

But first, just a *very* short nap . . .

Chapter 55

It really was amazing, the difference in the way people treated you when you were middle-aged and had money. Limousine service to the airport, followed by a comfortable wait in the private lounge—someone actually came and tapped his shoulder to let him know his flight was boarding!—and then there was First Class. Corey had never done anything first-class in his life, but if it was all like the airline version—constant, smiling attendants, instant gratification of every whim, a surfeit of drinks, pillows, movies, and all with more room to stretch out than Frida had in her entire apartment—he was all in favor of it. He crossed the Atlantic in a near-purring state of contentment.

Then there was the taxi to the hotel, during which his Cockney driver had actually called him "guv'nor," and the almost fawning service at the spectacular One Aldwych Hotel, which appeared to be simply thrilled to have his business, although they couldn't have heard of Jack Ackerly prior to this . . . could they?

But it must be said . . . after all of that, London was a little disappointing. Corey had never been out of the country before, and he supposed he'd come to believe that other parts of the world had . . . what, a different texture? Different laws of physics? A greater, or lesser, pull of gravity? . . . There was a light rain when he set out on his first walk, and it felt just like light rains in Chicago, and the people looked like people generally did, they put up umbrellas like people everywhere. The quality of light was the same, the faint scent of ozone in the air, the way the water beaded on his shoes, so that he had to rub them against his calves lest they spot.

But once he grew accustomed to the disappointing sameness of London, the exoticism began to trickle in. The streets were all a-jumble, with wide, broad avenues bisecting little Victorian lanes where all the buildings trod on each other's feet. There were plaques everywhere commemorating this and that epochal event in seventeen-this or eighteen-that, and he began to wonder whether there was a half-mile stretch anywhere in the city that hadn't witnessed a turning point in history.

He went to the British Museum but the line was too long so he decided to have a kidney pie from a street vendor, which made him feel like a character from Dickens, except that he didn't like it at all and ended up tossing it in the bin (which is, he learned, what Londoners called wastebaskets). The rain grew more intense so he bought an umbrella and decided to go to the National Gallery, got lost, and ended up in the National Portrait Gallery instead, which was probably more fun. After an hour or so there he went to the West End, had lunch at an Indian restaurant (a curry dish that made his hair go damp and limp), then picked up some theatre tickets: Felicity Kendal in a play called *Happy Days,* which was supposedly a classic.

After that, back to his hotel for a drink at the bar, then a nap. Jet lag sank its claws into him so that he barely awakened in time to make the play, which, to his consternation, was about a woman who was buried up to her waist in dirt. She had a surly husband in the background but mainly she just spoke to herself, or addressed the audience outright. At intermission he had another drink and observed the crowd, trying to spot the ways in which they were different from

Americans, till he overheard enough conversation to realize they all *were* Americans. In Act Two, the play's heroine was buried up to her chin. She talked to herself some more and then the play ended. Corey didn't get it, but everyone else had laughed all the way through and applauded generously.

Perhaps it was a consequence of all the wandering alone, the drinking alone, and of being alone in a theatre filled with people who were seeing something he couldn't, but Corey felt a sudden ache of loneliness. Seated at a Japanese restaurant, having some really remarkable sushi, he imagined how much fun he'd be having if Tyler were here, dishing all the other diners and making fun of the play. Corey, who'd never minded being on his own before, suddenly minded it very much. Possibly because, as every stray glance at a reflective surface reminded him, he no longer really even had himself for company.

The loneliness triggered desire; perhaps that was only natural. But it was one of the unexpected consequences of his switch with Jack that Corey hadn't really felt any such stirrings till now. He'd imagined that giving up his sex life would involve a terrible withdrawal; but in fact, he seldom now even thought along those lines. Was this what it meant to be fifty-three? . . . He'd never realized, till his first few mornings as Jack Ackerly, that it was even possible to wake up without an erection. That it was equally possibly to go through an entire *day* without one had startled and upset him.

But Jack's body was old, not dead, and now, in London, it wanted what it wanted. This suited Corey. If this had happened in Chicago, he didn't know if he could have faced going back to his old haunts; he knew only too well what was said behind the backs of "men of a certain age" when they dared to trespass on the playgrounds of youth. Also, he didn't know if he could bear to look back on what he'd left behind; even after a few days, he felt such a poignant tug of nostalgia just thinking about it.

But here in London, everything was new, nothing had any resonance or affiliations for him. He hopped in a cab and boldly asked the driver to take him to the city's biggest gay bar, and God bless the cabbie, he didn't even flinch. "Well," he said, "I believe that's a bit farther afield than an out-of-towner might care to go, but I tell you what, there's a fair-sized one near Charing Cross, just the ticket, see, and you'll still be in the city center."

"Deal," said Corey.

"Beg pardon?"

"Uh, I mean, that's fine."

The bar was called Heaven, and it was a very loud, active, welcoming sort of place, with a series of interconnecting rooms and two expansive dance floors. Corey wandered the place for a while, enjoying the sights and sounds, and renewing his appreciation for a well-sculpted slab of male flesh; and before long his skin started prickling in a way that could only mean he was being followed.

Casually he turned, and his keenly honed senses picked up his pursuer at once. Youngish—mid-twenties at most—lithe, lean, dirty-blond hair. Nothing exceptional about his looks, but he was possessed of an attractive swagger. He met Jack's eyes and grinned lewdly. *Obviously* a hustler.

Well, that was fine. Corey had money now, and he had no moral or ethical objections to paying for sexual companionship. He approached the boy and said, "Hi."

"Evening," the boy said, extending his hand. "I'm Vic."

"Hello, Vic, I'm Cor—Jack," he said. Too late, he realized that here—now—there was no need to have corrected himself. He could be Corey if he wanted to.

"American, yeh?" said Vic.

"Is it that obvious?"

"Only Americans say, '*Hi!*'" And here he put on a bright, wide-eyed face and raised his hand in a wave. Corey laughed.

"So," Vic continued, "what are you in the mood for tonight?" He took Corey by the arm and gently pulled him aside, as though moving him out of the flow of traffic; but a quick glance revealed there was no one trying to pass him. *Oh, this guy's good,* thought Corey.

"I'm not sure," said Corey. "Persuade me."

"You're open to persuasion, then?" Vic said, setting aside the tumbler he'd been sipping from.

"That's for you to find out," said Corey.

Within minutes they were deep into a surprisingly energetic snogging session. Corey felt himself come to full mast, and managed a little triumphant grin somewhere between the ferocious kisses.

Soon they were into groping, and then into rubbing, and Corey thought, *We'd better move this somewhere else or it'll all go down right here.* He extricated himself from Vic and straightened his jacket and pants, and Vic winked at him and said, "C'mon, 's'get us a taxi."

Corey felt a peculiar floating sensation as Vic led him by the hand towards the entrance. People drifted by him like balloons, their faces in various states of ecstasy, lust, or dismay. And then he was distracted by a familiar face—an older face, cruelly revealed in the light, a face twisted by craving into a horrid Halloween mask—and a moment after it was gone, he realized with a start that he'd passed a mirror, and the face had been his own.

He dug in his heels and stopped short.

Vic—his young face unlined, unseasoned, untouched by time or trouble—turned and looked at him quizzically, as if to say, Is something the matter?

And he wanted to reply: *Yes, there is; I am a grotesque old man in my fifties and I am debasing myself. I am making a fool of myself.* But it was too loud to say anything at all, so he just sadly shook his head, and melted back into the crowd.

Vic was momentarily disappointed, but when Corey looked back over his shoulder he could see that the boy had already found a new quarry.

Corey took a cab back to the hotel. He wanted to have a drink in the bar before bed, but his clothes stank of smoke and sweat and he realized he couldn't sit among polite people without offending them.

He rode the elevator up to his room in glum silence, and when he entered there was a red light flashing on his phone. He had a message.

It was Fancy. Did he realize he had a board meeting with the Edgewater Youth Center the day after tomorrow? . . . Corey said, aloud, "No, I don't," and wondered what the hell Fancy had been smoking.

Then he remembered, and smacked himself in the forehead. The Robyn thing. The "board." That he'd said yes to without even thinking twice.

The next morning, he checked out of the hotel and flew home.

Chapter 56

Corey was still nervous about using Jack's passport; it felt as though he were trying to get away with something, and might get caught. But that was ridiculous; he wasn't passing as Jack Ackerly . . . for all practical purposes, he *was* Jack Ackerly now. It just hadn't fully sunk in yet. He wondered if it ever would.

He'd arrived at LaGuardia, where he had a forty-minute layover before his connecting flight to Chicago. It wasn't pleasant, but he'd had to agree to it; the first available direct flight wouldn't have got him back in time for the board meeting.

Here, as in Chicago, he was able to escape the Third World atmosphere of the open terminal by slipping through a glass door and into the quieter and swankier environment of the Admirals' Club. He tried not to look like a first-timer as he pulled his carry-on behind him, wandering from enclosure to enclosure, trying to find the most private nook in which to plop down and zone out.

He found a leather chair by a window overlooking the tarmac, where a pair of pleasantly burly airline employees were loading luggage into the belly of a jet. They looked like fearful primitives, feeding a vengeful god to appease its wrath. Corey settled in, lowered the handle of his bag and stowed it next to him, then from its outer pocket slid the copy of *Maxim* he'd just bought and perched it on his knee, ready for a nice, long wallow in shallow materialism.

As luck would have it, he'd no sooner immersed himself in an article about recent advances in manscaping, when someone approached and said, "Well! Here's a *haimish ponem.*"

Corey looked up and saw the horny Yiddish-spouting guy from Jack's party, smiling inscrutably at him. "Oh, hi," he said. He couldn't seem to remember his name.

The man peered into his lap. "Well, well, well," he said. "Jack Ackerly reading a lifestyle magazine? . . . I believe that's one of the signs of the Apocalypse."

Corey slapped shut the magazine and forced a smile, though he feared the effort must have shown. "So, what're you doing here, uh . . . buddy?"

"'Sit down, Walt?' Why thanks, don't mind if I do," he said with a little vocal flourish, and he lowered himself into the chair across from Corey. This was pretty much the last thing Corey wanted: to be trapped for a half-hour or more with one of Jack's old cronies. But at least he knew his name, now.

"To answer your *frageh,*" said Walt, draping his suit coat over the arm of the chair and signaling for a waitress, "I'm on my way to Frankfurt. Checking out a potential new acquisition. You?"

"Just getting back from London," said Corey.

"Brandy Alexander," said Walt to the waitress who'd just appeared. He turned expectantly to Corey.

"Oh," said Corey. "Uh—just a Coke, thanks." Walt looked at him oddly and he nervously added, "A bit early for me. Still on London time." As soon as he said this he remembered it was six hours *later* in London, but fortunately Walt had paid no attention.

"A Coke, huh?" he said with keen interest.

"*Diet Coke,*" Corey called over his shoulder to the retreating waitress. "I meant Diet Coke."

Walt sat back and raised one eyebrow, as if examining him

for a structural flaw. "Jack Ackerly, turning down a cocktail," he said. "Jack Ackerly, reading *Maxim* instead of Milton. Jack Ackerly, ordering Coke instead of Pepsi."

Corey silently cursed himself; he'd forgotten that quirk of Jack's. "I don't think they have Pepsi here," he said.

"No, of course not," said Walt with oozing insincerity. "So," he added, how was London? You see Oscar and Paul?"

"Nnn-no," said Jack. "Didn't have time."

Walt seemed surprised. "What about Barbara Everly?"

Corey shook his head.

Walt raised an eyebrow. "But . . . surely you saw Colin and Nancy."

Something in his voice put Corey on alert, and he shifted uncomfortably in his seat. "Um, no," he said with some trepidation.

"You didn't even see Colin and Nancy?"

He was growing warm with discomfort; any moment now he'd start sweating. "We couldn't make our schedules work," he said.

"I can't believe you'd go to London without seeing Colin and Nancy."

Corey shrugged, as nonchalantly as he could manage.

"Can I ask you a question, Jack?"

"Um . . . sure."

"Who are Colin and Nancy?"

Corey's heart stumbled over a beat. Walt was smiling at him, as though he'd trapped him in a corner; which of course he had. "What do you mean?" he asked.

Walt put his hands up. *"Ich vais nit,"* he said. "I just made them up, sitting here, but apparently they're real people, and friends of yours."

Here came the sweat. "Why would you do a thing like that?"

"Only because you're not acting like yourself."

"What do you mean?"

"You're not acting like Jack Ackerly."

Corey forced himself to laugh. "Well, now, that's plain crazy. You can *see* I'm Jack Ackerly."

"Then why are you pretending to know people who don't exist?"

"I . . . just presumed they were acquaintances I forgot about. I meet lots of people, Walt."

"*Lokshen,*" said Walt with derision, and Corey didn't need to know Yiddish to understand what that meant. "What's going on with you, Jack? *Mitten derinnen,* you're like a different man. Is it something medical? You can tell me."

Corey laughed again. "What, because of a fashion magazine and a Coke, suddenly I'm supposedly not myself?"

"You're *not* yourself. I've known you for twenty years, Jack. Even the way you're tilting your head is off. What's happened? . . . You might as well tell me, I'll find out eventually. *Gloib mir.* You know I will."

Corey stuffed the magazine back in its pocket. "This is crazy talk," he said. "And anyway, I've got to board my plane."

"Which flight?" asked Walt pointedly.

"*My* flight," said Corey, scrambling to his feet and grabbing his carry-on.

"What airline?"

Corey wasn't about to tell him. He'd check the Departures schedule and see that Corey was lying. "What's it matter, Walt?"

"Just making conversation. What are you so nervous about?"

"*I'm not nervous,*" Corey snarled at him.

Walt sat back, a little startled, and held his hands up in a gesture of defeat. "*Nisht do gedacht,*" he said. "Sorry I said anything."

"Forget about it," said Corey as he started rolling his bag away. And he really meant it: *Forget about all of this!*

Walt said, "Safe travels. Oh, and don't forget my birthday next week! I'm counting on you."

"Fine, fine, I'll be there," said Corey, not meaning it.

For a brief moment there was no sound but the clatter of Corey's wheels; then Walt called after him, *"My birthday's in February."*

Corey ran all the way to his gate.

Chapter 57

"Thank God you're here," said Robyn, and she gripped his arm like she was afraid he might turn and bolt. "I was afraid you wouldn't make it. Your assistant said—well, never mind, you're here, it's—Jack, I have a confession to make." She leaned into him as she led him to the back room of the restaurant, where the board members were holding their meeting.

"What's that?" said Corey, a bit woozily. Jet lag had hit him even harder on the way home. It seemed scarcely fair that he should have it both coming and going. True, he hadn't spent much more than a day in London, but he wasn't really in the mood to be rational.

"It's just—well, the real reason I wanted to get you on this board with me—not that I don't respect your abilities, you know how I—anyway, it's just, I don't think I could do it without you." She stopped and said, "How do I look?"

Corey gave her the once over. "Fine."

"Just fine?" She looked down at her female-gladiator ensemble.

"No, great. You look great."

Her shoulders sagged as though he'd just told her her hair was lank and her blouse stained. "Anyway," she said, as they headed down the corridor to the private room, "the thing is, you always know what to say, you always know how to handle a situation."

"Right," said Corey, a bit annoyed. *That's me, Jack Ackerly. Mister Perfect.* How was he ever supposed to live up to this guy?

And then they plunged into the room, in which five other people were already seated around a table. They were engaged in muted conversation, but at the sight of Robyn and Corey they got up and smiled and extended their hands, and made much of how pleased they were to be finally meeting "the Jack Ackerly they'd heard so much about," and then there was a flurry of introductions, most of which went right over Corey's head. He could only recall that one woman's name was Portia, which stuck with him because it wasn't something you heard every day, and one of the men's name was Nate, which stuck with him because he was kind of a hottie.

"As you know," Robyn said in conclusion, as she and Corey sat down, "Jack—well, some of you already know this—he founded and ran his own public relations agency, Ackerly & Associates, for—what was it? I don't remember how many years—anyway, he has relationships with everybody who's *anybody* in town."

Corey blushed on hearing this; not out of false pride, but because he really *didn't* deserve it. He wasn't the man who had done those things, and he felt a little guilty posing as him. Still, that had been the deal, and Jack himself clearly didn't mind.

There was a breakfast spread already on the table, which included a platter of Swedish pancakes with lingonberries, Corey's favorite. He grabbed a plate, piled half a dozen pancakes onto it, and then sugared them for good measure. He tucked right in and had devoured half the stack before he looked up and saw everyone else looking at him with a kind of alarmed perplexity.

"What?" he asked. He glanced down at his plate, then up again. "It's not for us?"

"No, no, it's for us," said Portia, in a tone that implied a rather large *but*.

Robyn, grinning nervously, said, "Jack just flew in from London, just for this meeting," and then she looked at him with naked anxiety on her face and said, "Didn't you, Jack?"

"Mm-hm," Corey replied, his mouth full.

Tentatively, the conversation resumed. Robyn bravely put a cinnamon roll on her plate, and occasionally picked at it, as though making a half-hearted attempt at common cause with Corey, but the others ignored the food entirely. One of the women did at one point reach over and help herself to a few grapes, but that was it.

Corey thought, *Well, those cinnamon rolls do look good,* and was going to show them all he wasn't intimidated by having one, when he recalled that he was fifty-three years old and that any decent fat-burning workout condemned him to a two-hour nap in the afternoon; and so he thought better of it.

The others were engaged in some earnest talk about the operating budget of the Edgewater Youth Center, and of its vital importance in giving kids who might otherwise be drawn into gangs a place to go where there were structured activities that could lead them to make better life choices and blah blah blah, and Corey was having a hell of a time paying attention, especially since he really *really* wanted a cinnamon roll, when suddenly he had the most wonderful epiphany:

Hadn't he promised his mother he was going to be the kind of man who helped people? . . . And wasn't it one of the sole benefits of becoming Jack Ackerly that he was now in a position to do so? . . . And wasn't this exact moment the absolutely *perfect* opportunity to start?

Accordingly, he extended a hand, stopping one of the women in midsentence, and said, "Hey, maybe I can save us all a lot of time. Why don't I just donate the whole operating budget myself?"

They all looked at him, stunned, Robyn most of all. She said, "Um . . . Jack?"

But he wasn't prepared to yield the spotlight. He said, "No, seriously. I mean, what's the annual damage for a place like that, anyway? A hundred grand? Two hundred? Half a million? . . . I mean, big deal, I'm good for it. I'm sure Robyn told you."

Nate flashed Robyn a questioning look, then turned to him and said, "Jack, we certainly appreciate that. And naturally we encourage some level of financial support from our board members themselves. But our ideal scenario is to engage the kind of ongoing corporate support for the center that will not only see it through the coming year, but the years following."

"We're looking to build corporate *relationships,* Jack," said Portia in the kind of tone she might have used on a four-year-old. "So that we have plenty of resources not only for operations, but for growth."

Their condescension only angered him. "So, what? . . . You're saying no? You're telling me I'm an idiot because I want to help?" He shoved his empty plate away in disgust. "I mean, how fucked is that? It's not like I'm asking for anything in return. I'm not, like, 'Yeah, and let's name the place after me too,' or anything." Then, before anyone could reply, he had another spectacular idea: "Although, if you wanted to show some gratitude, you *could* rename it the Lucille Szaslow Youth Center." A grin erupted onto his face. His mom's name on an actual building! . . . It was like he couldn't stop his brain from spewing genius today.

But for some reason, no one else seemed as impressed as he did. After an ungainly pause, Nate said, "Who's Lucille Szaslow?"

Corey modestly shrugged. "Someone who had a big influence on me." When they stared at him blankly, he added,

"When I was a kid," as though that might make it more relevant to the case at hand.

"But who was she?"

Corey grew exasperated and threw his hands in the air. "Look, does it matter? I'm offering you half a million bucks and just saying *maybe* in return you might *consider* naming the center after someone I choose."

They all looked at each other, clearly closing ranks.

"But, who is she?" repeated Nate.

"Why does it *matter?*" He was almost shouting.

"I rather think that's what we're asking you. Why *does* it matter?"

"It *doesn't!*" He stood up and said, "Christ on a joystick! I mean, what the fuck?" He headed for the door. "I've gotta use the john. When I get back, maybe you'll let me know what you've decided, huh?" He caught his foot on Portia's chair and almost fell on top of her, but fortunately righted himself in time and managed to escape the room without any further damage to his dignity.

In the men's room, he threw cold water on his face and stared in the mirror. Black eyes and wrinkles stared back at him. He moved in to look closer, as though he might find some tiny fleck of his old self somewhere in the mix, but instead the whole visage went blurry. He took his reading glasses from his pocket and donned them, but it didn't help. There was only Jack Ackerly, down to the molecules.

Except where it counted. Except for the part of Jack Ackerly that always knew what to say, and how to act in any situation. How would *he* have conducted himself in this meeting? . . . It was impossible to know, because for the life of him, Corey still couldn't understand what he had done wrong.

He was about to find out. When he exited the men's room, Robyn was waiting for him, her face rigid with mortification. "What was *that* all about?" she growled at him.

"You tell me," he said, taken aback by her ferocity. "I thought I was being totally generous."

"You *completely* embarrassed me in there," she said. "I talked you up, I—well, I've already told you—and I wasn't lying, you've always been so good, such a *natural* at this kind of—But now, today, when I was counting on you, you indulge in this kind of childish *grandstanding*—"

"Hey," said Corey, raising a hand to silence her, "I don't need to stand here and be insulted like this." He turned away from her. "Good luck raising your precious operating budget. This is half a million bucks walking out the door."

He was pretty proud of that, as an exit line. He replayed it in his head again and again on his way home. But the pleasure he took in it was tainted by the distressing suspicion that Lucille Szaslow, looking down at him from some celestial vantage point, was shaking her head in dismay.

Chapter 58

Corey suffered a severe sinus attack later that morning. Oddly, Jack's allergies (he still thought of them as Jack's, as though reluctant to claim them as his own) hadn't bothered him at all in London. He'd even forgotten about them. But for whatever reason—the stale, pressurized air on the plane? The emotional upset of the morning meeting?— he found himself now in a terrible state, barely able to breathe, his eyes watering, his head pounding. He took a long, hot bath, which relieved the symptoms somewhat, then spent the rest of the day in the cool of his apartment with the shades drawn, listening to the most soothing music he could find. Since almost all Jack's CDs seemed, to him, like elevator music, it wasn't hard to choose. The one that seemed to work best for him was called *Clifford Brown With Strings*.

He was feeling marginally better by midafternoon, but didn't dare venture out of doors again. Instead, he watched television until he couldn't stand it anymore, and then— bored, lonely, and desperate for distraction—he broke down and called Robyn to apologize. Fortunately, he got her machine; a few minutes of her constantly self-derailing conversation might have caused him a relapse. He said, "Hi, Robyn, it's Jack. Listen, I'm very sorry about this morning. I still don't really get what went wrong, but I'll take your word for it that I'm to blame. The thing is, I've reached a point in my life where I, uh, well, I guess I just don't fit in professionally with, y'know, professionals, anymore. Been through some changes, I guess. Sorry I had to upset you so much before I could realize that. Anyway, uh, sorry. Good luck with everything and . . . uh, yeah. Bye."

He ordered Chinese food for dinner, but by the time it arrived he didn't feel like eating it. He was ailing again, but this time it was a kind of soul sickness. He'd meant what he said to Robyn; he'd tried being Jack Ackerly in a Jack Ackerly situation, and found himself wanting. He wouldn't attempt it again. Whatever he was going to do with the rest of his life, it wouldn't—*couldn't*—involve being in that sphere. He just didn't understand the kind of people who inhabited it. They had meetings with food but you weren't supposed to eat it. They developed strategies for raising money but you weren't supposed to offer them any. Possibly in bed they put their heads under the covers and their feet on the pillows; at this point, it wouldn't have surprised Corey one bit.

He wanted to sleep in the next morning, but, typically, he was, with the sun, invincibly awake. He had nothing in the world to do, but apparently he was to be denied the pleasure of being unconscious while not doing it. He sighed, got up, showered, dressed, and fed himself, then sat in his living room and stared out the window at the toxic breeze rustling through the trees.

Things got a little more interesting when his cell phone rang. He didn't even care if it was someone wanting something he couldn't supply; it would be a relief even to feel the frustration of having to disappoint them.

"Hi, Jack; didn't wake you, did I?" Corey assured the caller he hadn't, while trying to brighten the dullness in his voice that had given this impression. He asked who was speaking. "It's Marty."

Marty, Marty. Corey thought frantically back to Jack's list, which he'd tried to memorize before going to London so that he could hide it from Fancy. *Martin Raice, invest-ment banker.* That was it. "Morning, Marty," he said, "how's the financial world treating you?" He winced at how awkwardly that had come out.

After a slight pause, Marty said, "Well enough. Say, Jack, if you want to bump up your charitable giving, why don't we meet and talk about it? I'm sure I can help you out, and make sure you're covering your ass for tax time as well."

Corey's felt his face burn. That goddamned Robyn! She'd been talking about him! "Listen, Marty," he said, "I don't know what Robyn told you, but—"

"Who?" said Marty. "I don't know any Robyn. Listen, Jack, I'm just concerned about the way you—"

At that moment there was a knock on the door, then the door itself swung open a few inches and Fancy peered in. "All right if I come in?" she stage-whispered.

Corey nodded, then said, "Marty, I'll call you back," and hung up.

Fancy entered, and as soon as Corey got a good look at her face he knew that she, too, had heard the news. "Well, this is just great," he said.

She put down her purse and took off her little sun hat. "I thought you might need me today," she said, bravely maintaining her cover story.

"No, you didn't," he said. "You came to check up on me, because you've been talking behind my back."

She took the chair opposite his. "Don't be silly," she said. "You know I'd never do that." She paused. "I have, however, been *listening* behind your back."

"Robyn, right?" he said acidly.

"She's concerned about you. And from what I heard, she has reason to be."

Suddenly Corey felt like crying. His face screwed up like a fist and his throat closed up. "*What did I do that was so wrong?*" he said, and there was an alarming wail in his voice.

Fancy was momentarily stunned into silence. Then she

said, carefully, evenly, "As I understand it, Jack, you didn't *listen*. Didn't, and wouldn't. That's really what it comes down to. Please tell me if I've been misled."

He sniffed up some dangerously loosened mucous. "I don't know."

"That means you agree," she said. She leaned forward and touched his knee. "Jack. Jack, my dear. I'm worried about you, too."

He blinked to hold back the tears. "You are?"

She nodded. "I'm not *really* so keen to give up my retirement, you know. Though I did mean it about the damn mynah bird." In spite of himself, Corey laughed. She sat back and continued. "Ever since you called me that night, much the worse for drink, and asked me to help you find someone who could magically restore lost youth, I've been a little concerned. And since then, you've been acting less and less like yourself."

"I'm *not* myself," said Corey, with ringing truthfulness.

"I've noticed." She smiled. "I can understand it, dear. You've been through a lot of tumultuous change recently. Selling the agency, separating from Harry, moving to this new place . . . and by her absence, I take it poor Nelly's no longer in the picture."

He looked at his hands. "No. She's not."

Fancy frowned. "I'm sorry, Jack."

"It's all right. Really."

She got up. "I'm going to leave you now. I really just wanted to make sure you're all right." As she lowered her sun hat back onto her little round head, she said, "The one thing I'll always remember best about you, Jack—the reason for your success, in my opinion—is what a good listener you are. That's all I'm going to say. What you do from here is up to you."

She blew him a little kiss, and then she was gone.

Chapter 59

Fancy's parting words lodged themselves in Corey's skull, but their effect wasn't positive. All that occupied his thoughts was that Jack was somewhere, in Corey's young body, enjoying himself to the hilt, while Corey was stuck in Jack's life and making a mess of it. What on earth had led him to think that having money was the answer to all his problems? . . . Certainly there was security in being wealthy, but *only* security. He was walled up in a virtual prison of security—"a maximum-security prison," he said aloud, and chuckled in spite of himself—and his attempts to break out of it were ill-conceived and ultimately failed. And all because he didn't know how to *listen?* . . . What did that even mean? He'd listened to Fancy, hadn't he? If he hadn't, he wouldn't be thinking about it right now.

He spent the day weeping intermittently. He couldn't really even say why; after each crying jag he'd wash his face and think, *Well, I must have needed that, I feel better having gotten it out of my system,* and then an hour later he'd be back in bed, wracked with sobs. Everything seemed so utterly desolate. For the first time in his life, he thought—fleetingly, only fleetingly—about suicide. He might've been tempted to consider it more seriously, had he not got immediately hung up on semantics: since he wasn't really Jack Ackerly, would killing Jack Ackerly's body really be suicide, or just plain murder?

In late afternoon his cell phone rang again; it was Fancy. "How are you feeling?' she asked.

"Better," he lied.

"Listen," she said, "I have a message for you. Gary called."

"Who?"

"Gary Mahlanki." Corey tried to conjure up Jack's list of names, but his head was so addled by distress it wouldn't come to him. "He wants to know if you'll come by the office tomorrow."

"The office?" None of this was making sense to him. Jack had no office.

"The *agency*," Fancy said, allowing the merest hint of exasperation to slip into her voice. "He said he has a proposal for you. I thought you'd want to know that."

"If the proposal's for me, why did he call you?"

"Jack, haven't you noticed that your phone hasn't been ringing?" Now that Corey thought about it, he realized it hadn't. "When you were in London, I had all your calls forwarded to my number. Given the way things have been since you got back, I haven't reverted the service yet. I thought you could use the space."

He grimaced. "That can't be right. Marty Raice called yesterday."

"He called your cell, remember? I told him to." A pause. "He's an old friend and an ally, Jack. Don't mind it."

"I don't." In fact, he was too tired to mind anything.

"So I'll leave it to you to call Gary, and either accept or decline as you see fit."

"Thanks, Fancy." He almost asked for Gary's number, but didn't want to raise her suspicions any more than he already had. Certainly it would be in Jack's phone book.

"Do you want me to keep monitoring your calls a while longer?"

"If you wouldn't mind."

"Don't be silly."

"Thank you, Fancy. Really . . . I mean it. You're the tits."

She giggled and hung up.

At a little after eleven the next morning, Corey entered the building that housed Mahlanki & Mahlanki Public Relations, just off Michigan Avenue in the north Loop. Streams of confident, driven people flowed by him, making him feel even more lost and purposeless. He'd put on one of Jack's finest Italian suits for the occasion, but it felt like drag to him; he couldn't fake the ambition, the vim, the invulnerable resolve of these people of affairs.

He rode the elevator to the nineteenth floor, then found his way to the M&M offices. Meekly he entered, and was about to give the gangly, blonde receptionist his name when she leapt from her chair, rushed around her desk, and came flying at him, her flailing arms and legs making her look like a praying mantis on a rampage. Jack stumbled backward in alarm, but soon found himself engulfed him in a bony hug.

"Hello, stranger!" she trilled in his ear. "Holy cats, it's good to see you!" She stood back and looked at him. "You haven't changed a *hair*. Still the dashing young executive who first hired me in eighty-eight."

Ah, thought Corey; *one of Jack's old employees, now resettled with Gary Mahlanki.* He smiled and said, "Lovely to see you too, hon. You look younger than ever, if that's even possible."

She hooted with laughter and said, "Well, look who's developed a silver tongue in his old age! Never thought I'd see the day!" She winked at him, then went back behind her desk and said, "I'll let Gary know you're here."

Apparently Gary had hired several more of Jack's old team, because when news of his arrival spread, Corey found himself accosted by even more strange faces, all beaming warmth and welcome at him. His hand was shaken like a piston and much was said of the "old days" that meant nothing to him, but he laughed and smiled as agreeably as he could, yes, yes, wasn't that a time, yes.

Finally he was ushered into Gary's office. Corey knew Gary had been at Jack's cocktail party, but hadn't quite been able to place a face to the name; his heart sank a little when he saw him now, and realized he was the heavy-set man with the lethal halitosis.

"Jack," he said heartily as he gave his hand to Corey. "Thank you for coming." Corey leaned back, extending his arm to its full length so as to be out of the way of the worst of the nearly visible fumes, and shook hands with him.

Gary gestured towards the chairs before his desk, and as Corey seated himself he moved back to his own chair on the opposite side. "Carol's in Wisconsin, visiting her family," he said. "She'll be sorry she missed you."

Carol, thought Corey. *That's the wife. The other Mahlanki in Mahlanki & Mahlanki.* "Well, be sure to give her my love."

"It's a difficult time for her. Her mother has cancer—the uterine kind."

"I'm sorry to hear that."

"I'm just sorry it isn't cancer of the mouth," said Gary, and he laughed bitterly.

Corey was momentarily shocked, then figured *Mother-in-law, I get it,* and laughed along.

Gary leaned back in his chair. "How've you been, Jack?"

"Oh . . . you know." Corey had no idea what to say. "Pretty good. Just got back from London."

Gary nodded. "Business or pleasure?"

"Just pleasure," Corey assured him.

"Good town for that."

"*Great* town for that." Except, of course, when you're middle-aged and alone and horny.

"So you're managing to keep busy?"

Corey shrugged, as if to say, Busy enough.

Gary shook his head. "Never thought it'd last, honestly.

When you sold A&A and 'retired'"—and here he hooked
his two index fingers in the air, to emphasize that he was using
the word with more than a little irony—"I never thought
it'd take. I thought, 'The guy's only just past fifty. He'll be
bored out of his mind in no time."

Corey laughed, but couldn't think of a response.

Gary stared at him for an uncomfortably long while, then
said, "Let's go to lunch, buddy."

"Um . . . sure."

He got up and came around the desk. "The Samovar? . . .
Be like old times."

This sounded a little dubious to Corey, but he felt obliged
to agree.

Within half an hour he found himself on the far west
side, seated at a table in a small, noisy, and—astonishingly
for this day and age—smoky eastern European restaurant.
Everyone around them looked like Leonid Brezhnev. Even
the women. *Especially* the women. Gary ordered them both
bowls of borscht—"Bet you've been craving it all these
months," he said—and then a round of vodka-and-tonics.

By the time the borscht arrived, Gary was on his second
drink, and Corey, who was distressed to note that the alcohol hadn't burned away any of the foulness of Gary's breath,
was glad to taste a fair amount of garlic in the soup. Maybe
it would mask the other odors in Gary's radioactive mouth.
Such was the severity of Gary's problem; even garlic breath
would be an improvement.

But Gary seemed uninterested in the borscht; he barely
touched it. Instead he nattered on, mainly gossip about people he and Jack both knew, though to Corey they were only
names. Corey, however, was feeling famished, and so finished
off his own borscht in record time, and with enormous satisfaction. Funny thing, he'd never liked borscht before; he
wondered if this particular restaurant prepared it especially
well, or whether it was simply a matter of experiencing it
through a different set of taste buds.

He was still hungry, and so worked his way through the bread dish while Gary downed a third and then a fourth drink. Corey realized the man was trying to embolden himself for something, and before long, out it came:

"Listen, Jack, there's a reason I asked to see you now, while Carol's out of town. She wouldn't like me talking to you. She still thinks we can make it on our own. Back in the A&A days, she was always nagging me, telling me I was in your shadow, I oughtta step up and be my own man. Well, that's what I've been doing the last two years, and Jack . . ." He rubbed his hand over his forehead in an explicit gesture of despair. "It's not working out so well."

"Ah," said Corey, and he put down his rye crisp.

"The thing is, we've been holding our own, we've got basically the same slate of clients we started with," and here he tossed down his last swig of vodka and signaled the waiter for another one. "Minus one or two we've lost along the way. No tragedy there, you have to expect some attrition in this game. But we haven't signed on any *new* accounts. I just don't have the gift for it, I guess. I pound the pavement, I work the events, I network, I schmooze . . ." He shrugged. "I get nothing for it. And meanwhile the cost of doing business just keeps going up and up and up . . ."

Corey, uncomfortable, drew little outlines in the condensation on his glass; he'd only taken a few sips, and the drink itself was now warm and clammy.

"I need a rainmaker, Jack," said Gary. "And you're so damn good at that. You're a people person. I was hoping— you'll tell me if this is out of line—but I was hoping you were bored with retirement. What I'm offering you here is a full partnership. We'd be Mahlanki & Ackerly—hell, Ackerly & Mahlanki, if you want—and all I'm asking from you is a day or two a week. I just want you to bring in new accounts. That's *all.*"

Corey felt a surge of panic, but he quelled it. His initial urge was to refuse, apologize, and bolt; but he kept hearing

Fancy in his head: *You're a good listener, Jack . . . it's the reason for your success . . .*

"What do you say?" asked Gary, open pleading in his voice.

Corey shook his head. "I'm sorry," he said. "I'm really not fit for business anymore." And that was the truth. He couldn't pretend otherwise.

Gary grabbed his arm. "As a favor, then," he said. "You know I wouldn't ask it things weren't . . . well, if they weren't *bad*. Let's just leave it at that."

It was hard to listen objectively to someone who was physically clamped to you, like a barnacle, but Corey forced himself. *This isn't about me,* he thought; *this isn't about Jack. What is it this guy wants? . . .*

And then he listened to the despair behind the words, and it hit him. Gary was a drowning man. He'd grab at any life-line that came his way. So why not toss him one . . . ?

Corey took a deep breath. "Look," he said. "Buddy."

Gary's eyes gleamed hopefully.

"You've got this idea," Corey continued, "that I can do something you can't. That I've got some special gift with people that you don't have."

"You *do*," Gary insisted. "I've seen it. People are *drawn* to you."

Corey forced himself to lean in a little closer, unpleasant though that was. "Gary, I'm gonna give you some advice, and you're not gonna like it at all."

Gary looked a little taken aback, but he said, "It's all right. Go ahead."

"No, seriously. This is the kind of advice that ends friendships. But you have to hear it. So just know, I'm saying it for your own good."

Gary gulped. He had no idea what was coming.

"It's your breath," said Corey.

"My . . . what?"

"Your *breath*. I'm telling you, Gary . . . it stinks."

Gary looked at him as though this were some kind of joke. "Come on," he said.

"I'm not kidding. And I'm sure—I mean, I'm *beyond* sure—that it's what's messing up your sales pitch. Haven't you ever noticed the way people back away from you?"

Gary released his grip on Corey's arm and sat back in his chair. He looked as though he'd been hit in the stomach. "It can't be *that* bad."

"Believe me, buddy: it's the worst. It's paint-peeling bad. It's canary-in-a-coal-mine bad. It's *Chernobyl* bad. It's probably got something to do with your diet. Or maybe your dentist can help."

"I . . . I don't have a dentist."

"Well, there you go. Step One in resolving the problem. Listen, guy, I'm sorry to be the one to have to tell you this. It should've been, like, your wife, or something."

Gary had gone quite pale. "Actually," he said, "Carol was in a car accident when she was nineteen. Massive head trauma. Ever since, she's had no sense of smell."

"Ah," said Corey.

"All through my thirties, she was the only woman who'd go out with me."

"Two and two make four," said Corey.

Gary put his face in his hands and kept it there a very long time. Corey didn't know what to do. Should he just quietly get up and go, and let Gary salvage what was left of his dignity? . . . Or should he stay put, in case there was any more listening to do? . . . Their waitress came by twice during this awkward interval; the first time Corey silently gestured for her to please go away. The second time he asked for more rye crisp.

At long last Gary removed his hands and looked up. There was a ghastly sunkenness to his features, but also the beginnings of a kind of resolve. "Thank you, Jack," he said. "I realize that can't have been easy to say."

Easier than it is to smell, thought Corey. But he said,

"You deserved to know. And, honestly, I do think it's gonna make a huge difference in the way you interact with people."

Gary turned towards him, without quite meeting his eye. "Listen, I really feel like I just need to get out and take a walk. Would you mind very much taking care of the check?"

"Not at all. You sure you're all right?"

"Yes. Yes, I'm fine. I'm better than fine. There's a lot that's suddenly so clear to me." He rose from his chair, still unable to look Corey in the face. "I'll thank you properly later, honestly, Jack . . . but right now I really need some fresh air."

"I understand. Go ahead. Talk to you later."

A brisk, quick handshake—and then Gary slipped away.

Now that it was safe to do so, Corey took a deep breath, then signaled to his waitress. But by the time she arrived he'd changed his mind; instead of the check, he asked for another bowl of borscht.

Chapter 60

The lunch with Gary sufficiently raised Corey's spirits, that he was able to instruct Fancy to put all his calls back through to him—though he reassured her he'd still appreciate her help in dealing with the bulk of them. And she was only too happy to comply; she had a real genius for management, and had all of his various commitments and obligations sorted into digestible chunks for him in no time.

He began making decisions, financial and otherwise, and while this usually involved listening to the counsel of his representatives and then saying "Okay," he found he really *was* listening, and even more surprisingly, understanding. Fancy, in providing him the key to Jack's success, had given him the key to his own.

If he needed any confirmation of this, it came a week later, when Gary called to thank him again. "I can't tell you how bitterly I resent all the years when no one said a *word* to me about this," he said; "but I can't dwell on it, I have to just move on. Even so, Jack, you can't imagine how grateful I am to you for having had the courage to help me out."

"It was nothing," said Corey. "Really."

"It was *everything*," he insisted. "Anyway, I've since seen a dentist and a nutritionist and I'm working on clearing things up. I've also hired a young hotshot account executive away from PDM, and she's brought two new clients with her. So that'll tide us over till I've got my confidence back up, and the minty freshness to go with it."

"Glad to hear it."

"But," Gary added, more conspiratorially, "I'd really appreciate it if you didn't say anything about this to anyone. I know I don't have to ask you that, I know you wouldn't anyway, but I'm compelled to say it all the same. It's just the embarrassment, you know? I can just take it, between the two of us, but . . . well, you understand."

"Totally," said Corey. "Not a problem." *Besides,* he added to himself, *who would I tell?*

"Not even Carol," Gary added. "I don't want her to know about this."

"Your own wife?"

"She thinks I'm a hero. Always has. I don't want her to find out she's been married to a liability all this time."

"That's being a little harsh on yourself . . . but never mind, I get it. My lips are sealed."

Corey didn't hear from him after that, and it slowly dawned on him that however grateful Gary might be to him, he now associated him with the worst humiliation of his life. He'd probably take pains to avoid him henceforth. It was sad, really; but it wasn't as though Corey had anything invested in the relationship. Jack might have; but then, Jack had given it up pretty quickly too, for reasons of his own, so all things considered there was no harm, no foul.

A few weeks later, as Fancy was taking Corey through his calendar, they came across the Literacy Now benefit ball. "I didn't say yes to that," he told her.

"You don't have to. You buy a table every year, smartypants. It's one of your pets."

Jack hadn't mentioned this; Corey wondered what the other "pets" might be. "Do I have to rent a tuxedo?" he groaned.

Fancy leaned back and gave him a quick once-over. "I

wouldn't think so," she said. "You don't appear to have gained any weight."

This confused Corey, until he realized, *Ah! I must already have one in the closet.*

"I bought the table for you, like I always used to," Fancy continued, "and took the liberty of filling it as well. I presumed you wouldn't mind."

"Who'd you invite?"

"Lois and Jeremy"—this must be Lois Kohr, his insurance broker; Corey would double-check this against Jack's list later—"Milt and Penny"—Milt Gonzago, who managed Jack's real estate holdings—"then there's Mickey and me. And you. Oh, and that Robyn you've been tight with recently."

Corey blanched. *"She* agreed to come?"

"Jumped at the chance."

Corey felt a chill of apprehension. Fancy must have invited her before the calamity of the Edgewater Youth Center meeting. He wondered if she still intended to show up . . .

The day of the event arrived; Corey showered and shaved, then carefully took the tuxedo from the canvas garment hanger in which he'd found it. It was a gorgeous thing, and it fit him beautiful; in fact it managed to make even Jack's less than ideal body look smokin' hot.

He put on the equally fabulous cummerbund—Versace, a dark rose pattern, flecked with gold—then fell into a panic because he didn't know how to knot the bowtie. What had he been thinking? That Jack Ackerly would wear a clip-on? . . . Cursing himself, he called Fancy. "I don't know how to—I mean, I can't remember how to do this!"

"Go look on the Internet," she said. "There's sure to be a Web site that will refresh your memory."

He did as she advised and found a site with step-by-step instructions and even diagrams, but it was no good; he couldn't get it to work. And now his heart was pounding and he was beginning to sweat. He put in another call to Fancy.

She sighed. "I'll be right over."

She appeared twenty minutes later, bearing a clip-on. "It's Mickey's," she said.

Jack took it from her gratefully. "Won't he be needing it?"

"Oh, he's not coming," she said, dusting off the back of his jacket. "Decided yesterday he couldn't bear it. I've invited my acupuncturist instead. You'll like him, nice boy."

Corey sighed. Everything seemed to be going wrong . . . Well, almost everything. At least Mickey's tie was solid black, so he could still wear his gorgeous cummerbund without clashing.

Chapter 61

The ball was held at the Four Seasons; Corey hadn't been here since his disorienting meeting with Jack. Now, he was back, *as* Jack, and in Versace to boot. This felt curiously like full circle, and he allowed himself a sly, triumphal smile.

The enormous ballroom was choked with tables festooned with floral centerpieces, each incorporating a literary theme. Corey's table's display was made up of white and purple irises and artfully appliquéd pages of *The Mill On the Floss*. As he and Fancy reached it, a middle-aged couple stood up and greeted them; he recalled the woman from Jack's cocktail party—Lois Kohr. She kissed him on the cheek and thanked him for inviting them, then said, "You remember my husband, Jeremy?"

Not at all, thought Corey, but he shook the impish little man's hand and said, "Good to see you again."

Jeremy said, "You too, Jack, and what a wonderful cause. You know, Lois is a great reader."

"Is she, now," said Corey.

"Oh, yeah. Every day she reads me the riot act."

Lois laughed her shrill, joy-killing laugh, then gave him a little faux punch in the shoulder and said, "You *stop!*"

"She's *always* telling me to stop," Jeremy said, not missing a beat. "Last time I said, 'But honey, I haven't even un-buckled my belt yet!'"

Lois howled again and balled her fists and pounded him, then turned to Corey and said, "Don't mind him, he's *terrible*," while Jeremy grinned with pride.

Corey smiled, then did a quarter-turn towards Fancy and said out of the corner of his mouth, "It's gonna be a long night, isn't it?"

Milt and Penny Gonzago showed up soon after. Milt hadn't been at Jack's cocktail party, so Corey was at a slight disadvantage; but there was nothing in Milt's demeanor—sullen, jowly, and taciturn—to derail him. Also there was dandruff on his jacket shoulders, which made Corey feel comfortably superior. "Jack," was all he said as she shook Corey's hand; then he took a seat at the table—at Fancy's place, which required an annoyed Fancy to hastily gather and redistribute the name cards.

Milt's wife was a small, drab woman with wide eyes and a nervous smile, whose fairy-princess gown was covered by a hideous flesh-toned shawl she'd almost certainly knitted herself. Corey didn't know where they lived, but it must have been somewhere forbiddingly far away, given the comments she continually made about how exciting it was to be "in the big city." She kept looking around her in wonder, as though at any moment the whole building might just launch into space.

Fancy, having got the seating arrangements in order again, now plopped into her chair. Jack remained standing a moment longer, in case Robyn arrived; he scanned the crowd for her, but there were so many distractingly gorgeous people in the room, he couldn't help being half-hearted about it. At one point he spotted a strikingly handsome man, tall and lean, with auburn hair and long sideburns, and Jack, enchanted, followed him with his eyes until it became apparent he was coming to their table.

When Fancy saw him she said, "Oh, there you are, Preston," and turning to the others at the table said, "Everybody, this is my wonderful acupuncturist, Preston Frye. I can't even begin to tell you how he's helped my sciatica."

"Pleasure to meet you all," said Preston after Fancy had run down all their names for him.

"What did she say you do?" asked Jeremy. "What kind of puncture?"

"Acu," said Preston Frye.

"*Gesundheit,*" said Jeremy, and his wife bayed in delight and hit him.

"Is it all right to have a bread roll?" Penny said, hungrily eyeing the only food yet on the table. "Not everyone's seated, I know . . . I'm not sure how things are done here in the big city."

Corey realized this was a plea for him to sit, so he sat, and Preston Frye took the place next to him. He'd have to thank Fancy later for that. He was trying to think up some opening gambit for small talk, when he noticed the cover of the program. "*Fancy,*" he said, "you didn't tell me Janis Ian was the headliner tonight!"

"Didn't I?" said Fancy.

"No, no, I'd have remembered. God, I *love* her!" In fact, he'd grown up on her music; his mother had had all her LPs. But he quickly remembered he was now fifty-three years old and that such enthusiastic outbursts weren't really in his best interest, so he added, as soberly as possible, "A very fine songwriter, and a distinguished body of work."

Preston turned and smiled, as though amused by him . . . though in a good way. Corey noticed for the first time that his ears stuck out a little; not enough to be freakish, really, just enough to be endearing and adorable.

Suddenly Robyn appeared, wearing a skintight take-no-prisoners black dress and carrying a leather purse overrun with massive belt buckles that looked like it might contain a semi-automatic weapon. All the men jumped to their feet as if their lives depended on it. Corey said, "Oh, hi, Robyn—everybody, this is Robyn Vivin, an old colleague of mine," and he flashed her a smile which she did not return. He made the round of introductions for her and when he finished she said hello to everyone but him, then took her place beside Penny, who sheepishly eyed her dress and said, "So, is this what's all the rage in the big city?"

A waiter loomed over them with a pair of wine bottles. "Red or white?" he asked, and the ladies invariably chose white. Corey had a momentary quandary; he didn't know if he'd look girlish if he asked for white as well. Stalling for time, he asked to see the label. The waiter, a little taken aback, showed it to him; of course it meant nothing to him, the only word he recognized was Chardonnay, but he decided, *What the hell,* and said yes to it.

To his relief, Preston Frye chose the white as well, though after he had a sip he scowled and said, "Awful stuff."

"Is it?" Corey said. "We can call him back and get you the red instead."

"No, no, that's sure to be worse," he said. "Nothing but swill ever gets served at these things, I'm sure you know that. But at least the Chard won't turn your teeth blue."

"Chard," thought Corey. *That must be what real wine aficionados call it.*

The waiter had come to Jeremy Kohr. "Red or white?"

"Half-breed, actually," said Jeremy. "Just call me Big Chief Running Late For Supper." His wife shrieked with mock horror and hurled a napkin at him.

Corey looked over his shoulder at the stage, anxious to see Janis Ian. "When's the show start?" he wondered aloud.

Preston flapped open his napkin and placed it in his lap. "Oh, you know how these work. First we have to sit through all the tiresome self-congratulatory speeches while we eat our bland, tasteless meals. Then they clear the dance floor and bring out the performer and you get to hear all your favorite songs over a really disastrous sound system."

Corey gazed at Preston with open admiration. He was obviously a man of he world, and had much to teach.

"In fact," Preston said, "I might not be able to stay for the show."

"Oh," said Corey, a bit too much disappointment coloring his voice; "that's a shame!"

"Can't be helped; prior engagement. I really only came to fill a chair, so Fancy wouldn't be embarrassed by an empty place at the table." He gave Jack a meaningful look. "Or, rather, so she didn't embarrass *you*. She thinks the world of you, you know."

Corey blushed. "It's mutual."

The salad course arrived. Corey, indiscriminate with regard to food, inhaled his; Preston barely touched it, as did most everybody else at the table except for Penny, who chomped on a green onion and said, "I'm hoping to pick up some pointers from all this big-city cooking!"

At one point Corey caught Robyn looking at him, but as soon as their eyes met she turned away from him and launched into conversation with Jeremy.

Preston, who witnessed this, said, "Detecting a little friction," in a low voice.

Corey shrugged. "Business related. What can I say, I've already apologized."

"Ah, well, you know women."

"Actually, I don't," said Corey.

Preston chuckled. "Neither do I."

They giggled together, and Corey caught Fancy beaming at them. This was, he now realized, a set-up. He wondered if she'd ever intended to bring Mickey at all.

With the arrival of the dinner course, which consisted of a lump of lukewarm penne tossed in acrid pesto, and a burned filet that had no flavor whatsoever, Preston launched into a wistful narration of his recent travels in Italy, where by God, people knew how to *eat,* and if anyone in Florence or

Bologna tried to serve this kind of fare to a room full of *cittadini*, they'd rise up in a fury and burn the place to the ground.

Corey listened, rapt, as he rambled on; he had such a wonderful, mellifluous voice, with a little ping at the top range that was like an exclamation point whenever he reached it. He could've easily been contented to listen to him talk all night. But soon, as Preston had predicted, the "self-congratulatory speeches" began, interrupted only by a short film about immigrants and underclass kids whose lives had been changed by the programs offered by Literacy Now. Corey heard barely a word of this; he was too busy envisioning himself traipsing across Europe on Preston Frye's arm, dining with gusto at outdoor cafes and then fucking gymnastically in olive groves, beneath the swelling moon.

When the speeches were finished and the dessert trays cleared away, Preston daubed his mouth with his napkin and said, "Well, this is my cue. Nice meeting you, everyone," and then to Corey, "Thank you for having me."

"Oh, say you're not going yet!" protested Penny.

"Yeah," said Jeremy, "the night is still young, which is more than I can say for the rest of us," which caused his wife to expel the better part of a mouthful of wine through her nostrils.

"Alas, it can't be helped," Preston said. "Enjoy the remainder of the evening."

Corey watched him turn and head for the door, and with him all possibility of any kind of romance. Then he thought, *Dammit, I haven't felt this way since I first got stuck with this tired old sack of skin,* so he dashed after Preston and said, "Thought I'd walk you out."

"That's nice," said Preston with a smile that wasn't at all discouraging.

Corey searched for what to say next. "Um . . . shame you can't stick around. I've really enjoyed talking to you."

Preston looked suddenly wily and said, "Well-ll, I could possibly spare the time for *one* more drink at the bar. Just to get the taste of that dinner out of my mouth."

Behind them, Janis Ian's band took the stage and started tuning up. Corey inadvertently looked over his shoulder, causing Preston to say, "But hey, I know you've been waiting to see the entertainer, so if you'd rather—"

"*No,*" said Corey emphatically. "No, I'd *love* a drink at the bar." He screwed up his nose. "Something to erase the taste of that Chard."

Chapter 62

Preston ordered a single-malt scotch, which inspired Corey to do the same. Which was a shame, because now he was faced with the herculean task of drinking it.

"Mm," said Preston appreciatively after he'd taken a sip. "Smooth, isn't it?"

"Yes," said Corey, who did in fact agree, it *was* smooth, but it also made the tiny hairs in his ear canal stand erect and quiver. When the bartender had poured him his glass, he'd thought, *That's all I get?* Now, he couldn't imagine finishing it without putting every one of his motor skills at serious risk.

Preston leaned back in the banquette and crossed his legs. "Fancy tells me literacy is one of the causes you champion," he said. "That's admirable, certainly, but I have to wonder—I'm sorry, I don't mean to offend you . . ."

"No, go ahead," said Corey, crossing his legs as well.

"It's just that I'm not certain how much good these nonprofit organizations really do the communities they seek to serve. Like this one: sure, a few kids are trotted out who've gone from functional illiteracy to gobbling up *Harry Potter,* but—I guess what I'm really questioning is the role literacy plays in society at large. Obviously, it *should* play a decisive one; but does it? . . . And if it doesn't, aren't we really doing these kids a disservice? I'd be interested in hearing your thoughts on that, because I'm not at all certain of mine. As I said, it's something I wrestle with."

"Uh," said Corey.

"What I mean is, take a serious look at the past fifteen years." He paused long enough to take another swig of scotch, then said, "I'm not sure what percentage of intellectual pursuit, or of cultural and political discourse, now occurs over the Internet, and possibly it still isn't much; but compared to middle of the last century, it's a huge increase. And this new medium, as you know, is an elastic and constantly evolving one; as it should be. I'm not arguing for any kind of controls or strictures over it. But doesn't it worry you that the way it's developing, it actually *encourages* nonlinear thought? . . . Because that's critical to literacy, isn't it? The whole idea of structure? And I'm telling you, there are times that I open a magazine today—say, *Harper's,* or the *Atlantic*—and I'm confronted with a solid page of text, and even *I* have a little moment where I have to switch gears to read it, because there aren't any words underlined in blue."

"Uh," said Corey.

"So you take kids thirty, forty years younger than we are, and you have to imagine how their minds are developing. When you have to set up nonprofit organizations just to help teach a handful of them how to navigate a conventional paragraph, aren't you fighting a battle that's already lost? . . . I think sometimes we're on the verge of a massive alteration in the very nature of consciousness itself. Possibly you and I are dinosaurs, and fifty years from now no one will have the desire, or even the skills, to read a conventional book. Instead of text you'll have 'hypertext' and the way each reader experiences it will be different from every other. The whole idea of *the author* will radically change if not disappear entirely."

"Uh," said Corey.

"Novels might end up as nothing more than a historical

fluke, have you ever considered that? . . . As a literary form, they're not much more than two hundred years old. A drop in the bucket, in the cultural chronology. If they disappeared tomorrow, they'd leave scarcely a mark on civilization. Whereas if you think of other literary forms—well, take theater, for instance, one of the oldest; *that* operated on a gestalt principle, didn't it? . . . Because each performance was really a collaboration between the playwright, the cast, and the audience. A single work could, as a result, alter dramatically from night to night, depending on the energy going back and forth from the stage to the stands. So possibly there's some precedent for the kind of transformation we're seeing now, this new concept of a collective 'idea space.' I'm just shooting off my mouth here, feel free to stop me at any time."

"No, no," said Corey. "Go on."

"Anyway, I'm sure you've done a lot more thinking on all this than I have. I'd really appreciate hearing your thoughts." He took another swallow of Scotch, then looked up and waited for Corey to reply.

And waited.

And waited.

But Corey couldn't think of a single coherent thing to say. The irony of Preston's barrage of words on the subject of literacy, was that he had, by his very volubility, rendered Corey more or less pre-verbal. He might bark, or snarl, or meow, but he was suddenly incapable of actual speech.

Each succeeding moment grew more and more uncomfortable, till Preston Frye finally said, "No thoughts, then?"

Corey emphatically shook his head.

Preston cocked his head and seemed to bridle with reserve; Corey could almost feel a chill waft off him. "Well, I don't blame you," he said. "I can be a bit of a blowhard, and who wants to mix it up with one of those?"

Corey found his voice again. "No," he said, "it's not that . . ."

But Preston Frye was on his feet; he polished off the last of his Scotch, bent over to place the empty glass on the table, and said, "Thanks for the drink, Jack. Enjoy the concert." And there seemed to be a little pinprick of mockery in this sendoff.

Humiliated, Corey sat for almost twenty full seconds before realizing he'd also been stuck with the bill.

His shoulders slumped. *I'm a complete fucking asswipe,* he thought. *I'm a socially and intellectually retarded twenty-six-year-old stuck in the body someone twice my age and three times my experience. I should be in the body of a seven-year-old. That's all I'm really ready for.*

He cringed now at the way he'd gazed adoringly at Preston during dinner and entertained such embarrassingly clichéd fantasies of frolicking through rural Europe with him. Shaking his head, he lifted his glass to his lips for another mouthful of Scotch, then thought, *Hell with it. I don't have to drink this now, so I won't.*

He plonked the glass on the table and looked around for someone who might bring him his bill. He could hear the bass beat of the band reverberating through the walls and ceiling; if he got back to the ballroom soon, he could still catch most of Janis Ian's set.

No waiter or waitress was in sight, so he got up and went up to the bar to pay. And that's where he found Robyn, seated alone on a stool and slumped over a sloe gin fizz.

"Oh, hey," he said. "Why aren't you watching the concert?"

"Why aren't *you?*" There was an edge of hostility in her voice.

He sighed, and said, "Come on, Robyn. I apologized for the whole board meeting fiasco. Cut me a little slack here."

She turned on him, naked pain on her face. "Why? Why do you even *need* my slack, hm? . . . Because you behave like that in the meeting—like some kind of . . . deranged . . . I mean, if *I* ever acted like that, I'd be lucky if anyone ever . . .

But never mind, Jack Ackerly can be a prize ass if he wants to, and still be king of his table at some benefit ball, and me who he embarrassed, *I* have to come crawling—" And that's where she broke down.

Corey sat down next to her, alarmed. "Hey," he said, "*Hey.* For God's sake. This is totally unnecessary."

"*Don't tell me what's necessary,*" she hissed through her tears.

Her ferocity startled him. "Where's this coming from?" he asked, unconsciously backing away from her.

"I'm *tired,*" she said, and a little rivulet of snot escaped her nose. She wiped it away with a soggy cocktail napkin. "Tired of nothing ever being easy, of having to scramble for every . . . for just the least little . . . while you just go on sailing through, the wind at your back." She blew her nose in the napkin, and it broke in two. "*Shit!*" she burbled.

Corey shook his head. "That's a complete fantasy," he said. "You've made the whole thing up, you realize that, don't you? . . . You should've seen what just happened to me here. Yeah, I sail through life, *right.*"

She sniffled. "What happened here?"

"That cute guy at our table, Preston? . . . I came here for a drink with him. Five, six minutes tops, and he's got my number. Like, 'Oh, I seem to have made a mistake.' He can't get away fast enough. *And he leaves me with the tab.*"

Robyn's face lightened, and after a moment she cupped her hand over her mouth and laughed.

"Yeah," said Corey. "Ha fucking ha."

"I'm sorry," she said. "It's just that kind of thing happens to me all the time."

"Sucks, doesn't it?"

"Yeah, but what can you do?" She turned back to her drink.

"Are you really asking me?"

She looked at him oddly. "What? Am I asking you what?"

"What you said. 'What can you do?'"

She smirked at him. "Oh, because you've got the answer, do you?"

"For you, maybe."

She narrowed her eyes at him. They both realized they were on rocky footing here. "Well, I already hate you," she said, "so you might as well go ahead."

He lowered his voice. "It's the way you dress."

Her hackles visibly rose. "What about it?"

"It gives the wrong impression of the kind of woman you are."

She shook her head. "I'm a businesswoman, I *have* to look strong."

"You do. It's the follow-through that's the problem."

"I don't want to hear anymore," she said, and she picked up her drink again.

Corey backed away and said, "I understand, sorry."

She whirled on him. "I really *try* to be tough," she said. "It's not easy, you know."

"Well, that's exactly my point. Why are you trying so hard to live up to your clothes? It's so much easier to get clothes that reflect who you already are."

"I can't come to the office dressed like Rebecca of Sunnybrook Farm."

"No, and you shouldn't, 'cause that's not you, either. But you do have a certain sweetness to you, Robyn, that's very disarming."

She made a little scoffing noise.

"No, it is. But by the time most people see it, they're all confused about who you are under all that . . ." He gestured at her gown. "The whole dominatrix thing."

She avoided meeting his eyes. "You think I should soften my look a little . . . ?"

"A lot, actually."

"I'm not all *that* soft, you know."

"Sure. But look at it this way: the little hard streak you have will be like your secret weapon. People who meet you for the first time won't know you have it, till you whip it out and use it. Take them totally by surprise."

She pursed her lips and was silent for a while. "I'll think about it."

"Up to you," he said, sliding off his stool.

"Don't go congratulating yourself, you might easily be full of . . . well, no, never mind, I don't want to . . . I'll think about it, that's all."

He decided to leave well enough alone, and headed quietly back to the ballroom.

His unsettling conversations with both Preston and Robyn preyed on him the rest of the night, so that he could barely take in the folky fabulousness of Janis Ian. Even later, when he was dancing with Fancy to the follow-up band, he was never quite in the moment. And after the ball concluded, and he had received everyone's warm thanks for having invited them and fed them and showed them such a lovely time in the big city, Corey waited in front of the hotel for the valet to bring him his car, and ran through everything that was said, in both encounters, yet one more time.

He was interrupted by a tall, distinguished man, who hovered briefly over his shoulder and said, "Jack?"

Corey turned; the face—reserved, aristocratic, young but not youthful—didn't register with him. He said, "Well, hey there, what a surprise," and shook the man's hand—his standard fall-back move when meeting someone whose name he didn't know.

"You've been to the benefit, as well?"

"Uh-huh." He fingered his bow tie. "What was your first clue?"

"Enjoy it?"

"Oh, yeah, sure."

"As did we." He made a glancing nod at a patrician-looking woman a few steps away. She smiled at him. "And a good cause."

"Yeah, that too."

The man hesitated, as if reluctant to speak, then made up his mind to forge ahead. "I got the message that you'd no longer be requiring my services, Jack," he said, "though I'm still a little mystified as to why."

Corey, who had no idea what he was talking about, could only shrug. "Well, what can I say?"

"Just reassure me that it's not due to dissatisfaction with me as a professional."

"No, of course not," he said emphatically, as he was thinking, *Who the hell is this guy?*

"I'm very glad to hear it," the man said. "And please, Jack, do let me know if you ever feel the inclination to resume our sessions. It probably goes without saying, but as your therapist, I care about you as more than just a source of billable hours."

Aha!, thought Corey, and he said, "I understand completely."

At that moment the Porsche rolled up, and Corey shook the therapist's hand and bid him goodnight.

On the way home, he thought, *Imagine ol' Jack having a therapist and not saying a word about it!*

And by the time he pulled into the garage, his spirits once more dampened by obsessive contemplation of his rejection by Preston Frye, he was seriously thinking, *Hmmm . . .*

Chapter 63

"**I** was little surprised to hear from you so soon," said Alan as he greeted Corey at the door to his office. "But pleasantly so. Come in, come in." Corey realized he was hanging back, as though requiring permission to enter a space he would—as Jack—have often entered before.

He strode in and said, "Well, y'know, I got to thinking, you bring your car in for periodic tune-ups, so why not your head?"

Alan nodded. "Well. I won't fault your logic, since it got you here." They stood facing each other for a moment, then Alan gestured toward a chair and said, "Please."

Corey, who thought he might be required to lie down on the couch, gratefully complied. Alan took the chair opposite him, on the same side of the desk. "So, tell me how it's been for you."

"How what's been for me?"

"The several weeks since I've seen you."

Corey sat back and made opened his arms expansively. "Hey, how *should* it be? I'm Jack Ackerly, king of the world, right?"

Alan cocked his head. "Picking up some irony there."

Corey laughed and said, "No, really. I mean, what could

be wrong? . . . I got money, friends, a great crib . . . it's all good."

"And yet . . . here you are."

"And yet, here I am." He sighed and averted his eyes from Alan. In doing so, his gaze fell on the metal sculpture kit on the desk. He immediately started fiddling with it.

"Even the king of the world can have troubles, Jack."

"Yeah, tell me something else I don't know." He piled the metal chips into two little mounds, and they actually stayed there. He built them even higher, to see how far the magnetic field reached.

"Do you want to tell me about it?"

The chips at the very top dribbled off to the side, like candle wax. Corey had found the outside limit of the magnetism. He wondered if he could build a little bridge from one mound to the other. "Well, I tell ya, Doc, it's this middle-age thing."

"I thought it might be," said Alan. "We never really resolved that the last time."

Corey looked up, surprised, and one end of his bridge collapsed. "Didn't we?"

Alan shook his head.

Corey turned back to the kit and commenced rebuilding. "How far did we get?"

"As I recall, we left it up to you to process what we talked about. So you're really the one to answer that."

"Huh," said Corey. "Yeah, that figures. As usual, I gotta be the guy with all the answers." The bridge collapsed again.

Alan said, "Not sure what you mean by that."

"I had a conversation a couple days ago," he said, piling up the chips again, "that really upset me. Another guy my age, you know? Potential B.F. material."

"B.F.?" asked Alan.

"Boyfriend. Anyway . . . I couldn't even talk to him. He made me feel like some kind of idiot kid."

Alan waited. "Go on."

"I don't have . . . any . . . opin . . . ions," Corey said carefully as he tried to get both ends of his bridge to meet in the middle.

"Everyone has opinions, Jack."

The chips collapsed. "Has anyone actually ever made a bridge out of this thing?" he asked.

Alan looked at him strangely. "Some," he said. "It's a question of scale. Like most things in life."

Corey nodded, and said, "So, I should try for a smaller one first? . . . It's like a lesson?" He remolded the chips so that the arch was more diminutive.

Alan cleared his throat. "You were saying you feel like you have no opinions."

"Not about anything that *matters*," he said as he contentedly sculpted away. "It's funny, y'know, lately I've been giving people advice? . . . And they've been, like, taking it? . . . And on the other hand, I can't figure out what to tell myself."

"That's an age-old quandary, Jack. You're far from the first to experience it."

Corey finished his bridge, and proudly displayed it to Alan. "Ta-daaa! Not bad, huh?"

Alan shifted in his chair. "Very nice."

He now flattened it with his hand, then examined the metallic pancake he'd made and said, "*Cool.*"

"What kind of advice have you been giving people?" asked Alan.

"Well, how to un-fuck-up their lives, basically."

"And that's the kind of advice you think *you* need?"

"No, I need advice on how to grow the fuck up."

Alan took a deep breath. "I'm a little confused, Jack. Last time we spoke, you were convinced you'd never really experienced youth. Now you seem to be telling me you don't feel sufficiently adult."

"I'm a complicated guy, I know." He smiled.

"We're all complicated. You can't use that as excuse for maintaining contradictory impulses."

"Huh?" said Corey.

Alan leaned forward and put his elbows on his knees. "These people you advised. Why do you think they came to you for help?"

"'Cause I'm Jack Ackerly, I've got a reputation, I've got money. I've got status."

"Is that really all?"

"Experience, too, maybe. Thing is, the advice I gave them doesn't have anything to do with all that. It's like, I thought having money would mean I could help people? . . . But when I've tried to do that, to help with actual money, I've been shot down. And the only help anyone will take from me is the kind you don't even need money for. Just, y'know, common sense. Ironic, huh?"

"Except, by your own admission, they wouldn't have come to you for common sense if you hadn't demonstrated a flair for prosperity."

Corey pursed his lips thoughtfully. "That's true . . . so what are you saying?"

"I'm not saying anything, Jack, I'm just helping you clarify the scenario."

"Is that what you usually do?"

Alan looked stumped for a moment. "In a sense, I suppose. Yes."

"'Cause, here's the thing, Doc . . ."

Alan raised his hand. "Please, Jack, I'd rather you didn't call me 'Doc.'"

Corey looked abashed. "Doctor, then?"

"Just Alan is as good as it ever was."

He heaved a big sigh and sat back. "Maybe it was a mistake to come here."

"That depends on what you wanted to accomplish."

"I just want to know how to act my age."

Alan shook his head. "That's simplicity itself, Jack. You can't help but act your age. You *are* your age."

That's what you think, Corey thought sadly.

"You don't look persuaded," said Alan.

Corey got to his feet. "I've taken enough of your time."

Alan looked a little surprised. "Well . . . I hope I've helped you put some things in perspective."

"Yes, you have," said Corey, shaking his hand. *Like, how there's no way I can actually succeed at being Jack Ackerly.*

And yet he was fated to remain Jack Ackerly till he died.

Chapter 64

. . . Or was he? If there'd been a way to switch Jack's mind for Corey's, possibly there was a way to switch back. He thought of calling Jack and feeling him out on the subject; but of course this was ridiculous. Jack was now young, hot, independently wealthy, and busily fucking like a mink; why on earth would he consider, even for a moment, giving that up? Even so, the possibility tormented Corey, and once he went so far as to dial Francesca's number, but lost his nerve and hung up before she could answer.

Alas, he'd forgotten about Caller I.D. She phoned back in an instant. "Is this Jack or Corey?" she asked.

"Um, well, that's the question, isn't it," he said with a nervous laugh.

"That's Jack's voice, so it's Corey, correct?"

"Yes, ma'am."

"Sorry, I couldn't remember whether you switched names too. Why did you call this number and then hang up, Corey?"

"I'm sorry about that, ma'am." Silly, this calling her *ma'am* when by some measures he was older than she was.

"It just burns my tail, darnit. *Lollipop, get down!*"

"I really totally apologize."

"Did you want something?"

"I . . . did, but at the last minute I changed my mind."

"Is everything all right there?"

"Mm-hm. I just thought I might ask you for a spell, uh, a good luck spell, for a . . . sort of game I'm competing in, but then I thought maybe that would be cheating."

"Well, the Rules and Ethics Committee is divided on that, because, for instance, Christians pray, and if that's not cheating, why should a spell be any different? But *some* people, including yours truly, say it's all right for Christians to pray because they're leaving the decision on whether to answer the prayer to a Supreme Being who *presumably* has an ethical sense and can therefore choose to intervene or not, whereas one of my spells is pretty much a sure thing. You see the difference? *I said down! Down before Mommy zaps!*"

"Yeah, I do," said Corey. "That's how I see it, I guess. Thanks anyway, Francesca. Have a good night."

"You too, angel cake. Ta-tah. *All right, Mommy warned you—*"

After hanging up, he realized he'd blown it. He'd not only lied to Francesca, which would make it all the more difficult to approach her again, he'd also managed to make himself a little bit afraid of her. Glumly, he resolved to forget the entire hopeless matter.

As if his mood weren't sufficiently low, he once again ran into Walt . . . and, as before, in a place where he couldn't make a quick getaway. This time, it was the steam room at the club.

Walt was already within when Corey entered; so for Corey to turn around and walk out again would be a clear admission that he was avoiding him. And Walt would have every right to ask the reason.

While Corey stood fixed inside the door, Walt waved his hand before his face, to clear the steam and make sure he was seeing who he was seeing; then he smiled and said, *"This* is a good sign."

"What do you mean?" asked Corey.

"You, coming to sweat out all your toxins."

"Uh, right," said Corey, and he took a seat neither too far from nor too near Walt, as if to show himself utterly neutral.

Walt looked across the room at the only other patron in the place: a white-haired, sunken-chested old man with a wet towel draped over his head, making him look bizarrely like Mother Theresa. Walt looked back at Corey and said, "I know him. Deaf as a post. We can speak freely."

"Oookay," said Corey, looking longingly at the door.

"You know him, too, actually," said Walt. "Or you used to, anyway."

Corey looked at him with suspicion. Was this another trap? . . . If he pretended to recognize the old man with the terrycloth wimple, Walt might swoop in with a revelation that'd he'd only invented their acquaintance; and besides, he couldn't even name the guy, so why bother bluffing? He decided the best course of action was simply to say nothing.

Walt, whose own chest was smooth, plump, and lobster-pink, took a limp towel and mopped the sweat from where it had collected under his chin. "I know what's going on with you, you know," he said.

'Do you?" said Corey warily.

"Please! I've known you for twenty years. Watched you become a *choshever mentsch,* a real pillar of the community. Suddenly, overnight, you're a hopeless *draikop,* you don't know your ass from your elbow. Everything about you is just off-kilter, wrong. And worse?" he added, daubing the towel behind his ears. "You completely cut off your closest friend and ally. I have feelings, you know."

Corey sighed. "It's nothing to do with you."

"Oh, I know," said Walt. "I may be a loudmouth and a *plyotkenitzeh,* I may whisper behind people's backs, but I'm loyal in my way. And you know it." He leaned meaningfully toward Corey, a large drop of sweat swinging menacingly from his nose. "Or rather, the *real* Jack Ackerly knows it."

Corey felt himself go suddenly, terribly still. "What are you saying?"

"I'm saying you can't hide what's going on. I can see it, in your eyes I can *see* it."

"Y-you can?"

"Mm-hm. It couldn't be more evident. *Deigeh nisht,* I won't tell anybody."

"Um . . . tell them what?"

"Don't be coy, my dear. I'm not stupid. And it's not the first time I've seen this happen."

Corey arched an eyebrow. "It's not?"

Walt shook his head. "One of my exes. You met him, but I doubt you'll remember; not now, anyway. Dean Junger? . . . No, I didn't think so. Anyway, we stayed close after we broke up. And I saw it happen to him: the drawing away from his nearest and dearest . . . the lapses of memory . . . the complete shift in his personality . . . all the same."

Corey wrinkled his brow. What was this guy getting at?

Walt scooted over to him and, despite the only possible eavesdropper being hard of hearing, he lowered his voice as he said urgently: "What is it, anyway? Pills? . . . Vicodin, Oxycontin? . . . Or something more purely lethal? Meth? Let me see your teeth . . ."

He reached for Corey's face, and Corey bolted got up and pulled away from him. "It's not any of that," he said. "For God's sake, dude!"

Walt looked at him sadly. "Oh, no? . . . Well, then, my good friend Jack, suppose you tell me what it *is.*"

Maybe it was the suffocating closeness, the heat, or the fear that Walt might try to touch him again; or maybe the burden of shouldering his secret was taking its toll on him, and Walt's appeal to friendship in some way touched a nerve. For whatever reason or reasons—and Corey himself was unable to untangle it later—he looked Walt in the eye and said, "It's a transference spell. That's what. I'm actually a twenty-six-year-old who traded bodies with Jack Ackerly.

He got mine, and I've got his. Now he gets to live the youth he never had, and I get to have the wealth and comfort I never *would've* had. So it's a good solution for both of us, though there are drawbacks, like me not remembering you or," with a quick glance at wimple man, "anybody else."

Walt stared at him for what seemed a very long time. Corey could hear his own breath, feel his heart galumphing in his chest, as he waited for a response.

Finally, Walt said, "All right, Jack. Fine. *Don't* tell me." With a great show of dignity he got up, tightened the towel around his waist, and said, "*Es macht mir nit oys.* It doesn't matter to me."

He grandly exited the steam room.

As the door swung shut behind Walt, the old man with the towel on his head looked up at Corey and said, "Hm? . . . Someone say something?"

Chapter 65

A nd so Corey's life meandered in a meaningless manner
for several weeks more. Bored beyond imagining, he
began planning a trip to Italy—that much of his fantasy about
Preston Frye lingered on—but half-heartedly, since he still
had no one he might conceivably invite along in Preston's
place.

One day while he was frying eggs and rehearsing trav-
eler's Italian with a CD, the phone rang.

"Hello?" he said, taking the pan off the griddle.

"Jack, it's Sharon."

"*I prefer the one on the left. 'Preferisco quello al sin-
istro.'*"

"Hello? What?"

"Sorry," he said. "Hold on, let me turn it off."

"*May I see the one in the window? 'Posso vedere quello
nella finestra?'*"

"Hello, hello? What?"

"Just a sec—"

"*Let go of my purse or I will scream. 'Rilasci la mia
borsa o urlerò.'*"

As he flipped off the stereo he mouthed the name *Sharon,
Sharon,* but couldn't place it. It sounded faintly familiar, but

he was certain it wasn't on the list Jack had left him, which he had now committed to memory.

"There," he said, picking up the phone again. "That's better."

"I've left Bert."

Corey blinked. "All right. Sorry. We're going to have to rewind a bit. Who is this?"

"For God's sake, Jack. *Sharon.*"

Still no enlightenment. "Hi, Sharon!" he said brightly.

"I've left Bert and I'm at O'Hare and I need you to come pick me up."

"You've . . . uh . . . left Bert?" *Bert who?*

"Yes. For God's sake, just come and get me, please. I'm at the American terminal. I just got off the plane, I still have to get my luggage . . ."

"You—you want me to come and *get* you?" Who was this woman that she felt she could order him around like this?

"*Christ,*" she snapped, "if it's too goddamn inconvenient to come and get your own goddamn sister in her moment of crisis, never mind, I'll just take a goddamn cab!"

Sister! thought Corey. Jack *had* mentioned a sister and brother-in-law; supposedly they were safely tucked away in North Carolina and unlikely to intrude on him.

Not any more.

"All right, all right," he said. "I'll be there in half an hour." He almost said, *How will I know you?,* but caught himself in time.

In the end, he nearly ran her down. He was cruising the lower level of the terminal, where arriving travelers were disgorged, and for lack of any better means of distinguishing her, was looking for someone who might resemble Jack in a wig. Remarkably, he spotted someone who seemed to fill the bill, and at the moment he stepped on the accelerator to take him to her, a much younger, prettier woman, with long, coal-black hair, grabbed onto the passenger door handle, and was thus pulled bodily into the car with a big WHOOMPF.

"Oh, shit," Corey muttered, and he rolled down the passenger window and said, "Are you all right?"

"*Idiot*," she barked, as she rubbed her upper arm and flexed her fingers. "Were you trying to kill me?"

"I didn't see you there," he said lamely.

"Goddammit, I *waved*." She opened the back door and hefted her suitcase into it. "Thanks for the help," she said acidly, as he sat at the wheel looking over his shoulder at her, semi-stunned. All he could manage to think was, *This is Sharon?* . . . She looked like—and apparently was—one tough bitch.

She hopped into the car and shut the door behind her, did a quick check of her makeup in the visor mirror, then turned and said, "Sorry for snapping, I know it was an accident, I'm just at my wit's end right now. It's sweet of you to come to my rescue." She leaned over and gave him a kiss on the cheek.

"Hey, what are big brothers for?" he asked, smiling as genuinely as he could.

A moment or two drifted by, then she said, "Okay, you can drive now."

"Oh. Right." He shifted gears and pulled into the lane leading to the city. "Where am I taking you, by the way?"

When she didn't reply, he turned to look at her. Her jaw was hanging open. "Are you kidding?" she said. "You mean, you're, like, expecting to drop me at some *hotel?*"

"I—I just didn't know what you, what your plans might—"

"Jack, for fuck's sake, what is *with* you? . . . You've had your finger up your ass ever since I called. Are you high or something?"

"Well, I, I am on a lot of allergy medications. It's the season, you know." The reality was more prosaic: he'd just never had a little sister—or a sister of any kind. He had no idea how such a person would expect to be treated.

"Well, you're not sneezing your way out of hosting me," she said. "This is a family emergency, dammit. I'll be staying at your apartment, sleeping in your guest room, and raiding your refrigerator if I goddamn well feel like it, and you'll be kind and understanding and sit quietly and listen when I rail away for hours about what a schmuck I married."

Corey detected a hint of self-mockery in all this . . . or hoped he did. "What happened, anyway?" he asked, with what he imagined was suitable fraternal solicitousness.

"What usually happens? A cheap little affair with some tramp in his office. My God, you'd think the guy might be original, at least. But I'm beginning to realize I never really knew him at all. I thought he was some amazing fucking renaissance man, and it turns out he's just an ordinary, nothing-special, run-of-the-mill adulterous asshole."

Corey didn't know how to respond to this. "Remind me how long you were married?" he asked tentatively.

She made a *psssh* sound, as though the question meant nothing, and said, "Twenty-one years."

"And . . . you're just now realizing the guy was a loser?" He couldn't help it. He had to speak up to her now, or he risked becoming afraid of her.

Again she didn't reply, and he could tell she was looking at him; but he kept his eyes on the road. Finally, she said, "So what are you saying, you knew that all along?"

"That's not what I said."

"You knew it and you didn't tell me?"

"Would you have believed me if I did?"

"Seriously, Jack: you've never liked Bert? . . . Ever?"

Well, now he'd stepped in it. He didn't know the first thing about Bert, or Bert's past relationship with Jack. After hemming and hawing, he said, "Well, let's just say no one would've been good enough for my little sister."

"But . . . you used to say you'd pity any man who married me, even the Antichrist."

Corey laughed. "I said that?"

"More than once."

He laughed again, even harder. Apparently Jack hadn't been afraid of her either; it helped to know that.

When he caught his breath, he said, "The Antichrist wouldn't have a tawdry affair with some cheap coworker."

She looked contemplative for a few moments. "I don't know where you're going with that."

"I don't either. Let's just get you home."

Chapter 66

Several hours later, Corey was seated in one of his designer chairs, listening for what seemed the dozenth time to Sharon's story about How She Found Out, What She Said to Him, What He Said Back, and How Sorry He's Going to Be He Ever Fucked With Her. And even though they were into the second bottle of a very soothing Cabernet Sauvignon from Jack's wine cellar, Sharon showed no signs of mellowing out, or of lessening in any way her almost Medean lust for vengeance. Corey found himself staring longingly out the window behind her, thinking, *There's a whole world out there, and I'm trapped in here,* which was a complete reversal from his usual habit, which was to eye the outdoors with suspicion and distrust, on account of its fury of allergens.

Finally—*finally*—the wine seemed to kick in, and Sharon lazily stretched her arms above her head and smiled. "Thanks for listening to all my garbage," she said. "You're very sweet. And you're sweet to put me up, too." She brought her arms down on her head and ruffled her hair. "I'm feeling much better now." She pulled a throw pillow onto her lap and said, "You haven't asked why I'm not staying with Kari."

"Why aren't you staying with Kari?" *And who's Kari?*

"Well, obviously, she's the first one I turned to, and you'd think she would've been only too happy to have me, right? . . . I mean, she's been complaining that the baby's running her ragged. Well, hello, live-in help right here! But no, she's always been Daddy's little girl, and I swear she's taking his side in this. She hasn't actually said so, but she *did* say she thought I was overreacting."

"Well, aren't you?"

She looked shocked by the question. "You don't mean that."

"'Fraid I do."

"So—you think it's all right that Bert plugs his pecker into the office floozy?"

"Of course it's not all right. It's not the end of the world either."

Her nostrils flared. "You don't know the details."

"And you're too *hung up* on the details. What's the big picture, here? . . . Is Bert in love with this tramp? Does he want to be with her?"

"No, but—"

"He wants to work things out with you?"

"Of course he does, he's got a good gig with me."

"And you've got a good gig with him."

"Apparently not as good as all that."

"It's not going to get any better if you walk out." He stretched his legs out before him. "I mean, my mom walked out on my dad for just this kind of thing. I grew up without him, and he died without my ever knowing him. And it's not like Mom was happy without him. She had to struggle to make ends meet till the day *she* died. Helluva price to pay for pride, you know what I'm saying?"

Sharon looked at him, bewildered. "What are you talking about? Mom never left Dad."

He suddenly remembered who he was and swiftly drew his legs in. "Oh, I—uh—I was just, uh, pretending to be a,

what do you call it—a *hypothetical* character. Just for the
sake of argument, y'know?"

She shook her head. "That's just weird, Jack. I mean . . .
what next, a puppet show?"

"No, I was just—"

"If you're going to talk to me, talk to me as yourself.
Jesus!"

"Fine," he said. "All right. Then here's the way I see it:
monogamy? . . . Well, monogamy is like world peace. You're
never really going to achieve it, but that doesn't mean you
don't stop trying."

"So, that's not what broke up you and Harry? . . . Because you never did say."

He shook his head. "Gay men don't break up over stuff
like that. Neither would straight men, if they weren't married to women." In reality, he didn't know why Jack and
Harry had split, but he felt certain it wasn't over infidelity.

For the first time, Sharon edged out from the confines of
her own consuming psychodrama. "So . . . what was it,
then? Because you two seemed so solid to me. I actually
used to envy you."

Corey balked. He might feel free to say why Jack and
Harry *didn't* break up; but he wouldn't dream of inventing
the reason they did.

Instead, he decided that he'd given up enough of his day
to being a supporting character in a Lifetime Original
Movie, and it was time for him to take the situation into his
own manly hands. "Nearly time for dinner," he said. "Let's
go grab a bite, and then I'll take you out and cheer you up."

"Take me 'out'?" she said, suddenly wary. "You mean,
like—to a bar or something?"

"Mm-hm."

"I can't go out to bars, Jack! I'm a fucking *grandmother.*"

He took her by the hand and pulled her to her feet. "That
doesn't matter. My therapist told me, you can't helping acting your age, because you *are* your age."

"What the hell's that supposed to mean?"

"Near as I can tell, it means if you go on a pub crawl, then it must be because that's what grandmothers do."

She snorted. "Why don't I have a therapist like that?"

"Go put your shoes on, Grandma. You're on my turf now."

It had been several months since Corey had been to Radius, the dance bar on Clark Street, and in fact he hadn't expected to return—not in Jack Ackerly's weary old flesh, certainly. That would smack of delusion and desperation. But somehow it seemed a different matter to show up with a woman on his arm—and a middle-class, middle-aged woman to boot. It removed him from any suspicion of thinking he might fit in, and placed him squarely in the tourist camp; or rather, tour guide, for it was his job tonight to bring Sharon out of her doldrums.

She seemed at first a bit intimidated by the hordes of shirtless muscle hunks and leather-lashed bears, but by a blessed whim of fate it happened to be Eighties Night, and every song that pumped from the speakers was a siren call to her, drawing her back to what she called her "scandalously misspent youth." She grew more visibly involved by the minute, and after tossing down a quick succession of mojitos—which Corey had to admit was an impressive feat after all the wine they'd consumed—she was sufficiently divested of sorrow to drag Corey onto the dance floor for the Human League's *Don't You Want Me,* to which she bumped and ground like a woman half her age.

It was the first time Corey had danced in Jack's body, and certainly it didn't respond as readily as he'd have liked to the call for abandon inherent in the music; all the same he pushed the envelope, though he knew he'd pay for it the next day. So wild, in fact, were he and Sharon that a little space cleared around them, the younger dancers making room to accommodate them, and watching them in what must have been sardonic glee as they got increasingly down and ever more funky.

When the song ended, Sharon fell on Corey's shoulder and said, "God, that brings back memories! You wouldn't *believe* how many of the Ten Commandments I broke while listening to that song!"

"You were a bad girl, huh?" Jack had never really said much about her, but he was beginning to infer a lot.

"I was one hot mama," she said, as they hauled their panting carcasses back to the bar. "Don't tell me you don't remember. You spent half your life wagging your finger in my face."

"I was a bit of a buzz-kill, I bet." They found a single stool open; Corey allowed her to mount it, then squeezed in next to her and leaned on the counter.

"You were a black hole," she said merrily. "Joy got sucked into you and never came out again. *Oi!*" she barked over her shoulder. "A little service here, bucky!" The bartender's eyes flicked back and forth, as though he were seeking some avenue of escape; but in the end he gave up and meekly obeyed. Sharon seemed to have that effect on people.

"But let me tell you, Jack," she said once she was happily resupplied with drink, "I never thought I'd see *you* making moves like you did out there. Where'd you learn to dance?"

"All gay men know how to dance."

"Well, maybe it was always *in* you," she said, "but you sure as hell never let it *out* before. Even at my wedding, which come to think of it was probably the last time we danced together, you moved like the hangers were still in your clothes."

They both laughed at this; but Corey could tell Sharon's attention wasn't fully directed at him. She'd been darting her eyes over his shoulder every few seconds, and now she leaned into him and said, "All right, it's been a long time since I've seen him, but . . . isn't the guy at the end of the bar Harry?"

Corey now of course had to turn and pretend to look,

though he had no real idea what Harry looked like. He'd only seen one picture, a framed shot on Jack's desk before he moved out; it was of the two of them on a fishing boat, with most of Harry's face in the shadow of his hat. Fortunately, most of the guys lined up at the bar were in their twenties, so the sole fortysomething had to be the one Sharon meant.

He turned back. "It could be," he said.

"Course it's him!" She gave him a shove. "Go and say hello. I mean it, Jack. Be civilized."

"I don't want to," he whined.

"Stop being so silly. He was my brother-in-law—well, *ish*—for, like, twenty-whatever years. I'm not going to sit here and ignore him."

"Then *you* go say hello."

"If you force me to do that, I'll tell him you were too afraid to do it yourself."

Corey sighed. Acquainting himself with Jack's discarded lover was the last thing he wanted out of life, but he knew he was defeated. He squeezed back into the crowd and dragged his heels over to where Harry was engaged in heated conversation with another, younger man.

"I keep telling you," Harry was saying, "there's nothing in it. We just have a particular interest in common, that's all."

"If that's all it is, then it shouldn't make any difference if you don't see him again."

"But that's the whole point. The only reason you've given me for not seeing him again is your silly jealousy—"

Corey cleared his throat. "Excuse me . . . Harry?"

Harry turned and, at the sight of Corey, broke into a wide-eyed smile. "Good God—*Jack!* . . . You're about the last person I'd ever expect to see at *Radius*."

Yeah, well fuck you, too, thought Corey, but he said, "Just came in for a drink." He was surprised to find that Harry was in fact noticeably younger than Jack.

Harry put his hand on his companion's shoulder. "You remember Brian Isley."

Corey, not quite hearing him, shook Brian's hand and said, "Nice to meet you."

Brian chuckled nervously and said pointedly, "Good to see you again."

Corey looked back at Harry. "I'm here with Jack's—uh, my sister, Sharon," and he pointed her out; when Harry looked her way, Sharon waved. "She'd like to say hello."

"Oh, my God," Harry said, "little devil girl's in town?" He turned to Brian. "Excuse me, I *have* to pay my respects."

Corey followed Harry as he made a beeline for Sharon, then stood behind him as he kissed her on the cheek. "It is *so* good to see you," he said. "You look absolutely gorgeous. What kind of trouble you getting into these days?"

"Too old for trouble, Harry," she said. "Didn't Jack tell you? I'm a grandmother now."

Harry gave her a playful shove. "No way!"

She shoved him back. "Way!"

"And Bert's a grandfather?"

"Bert's an asshole."

They both hooted at this, and Corey felt a surprising twinge of jealousy.

"How long's it been, anyway?" asked Harry.

"I can tell you exactly," said Sharon. "The family reunion in '93 . . . The one right before Mom died?"

"Down in Fort Lauderdale, right," said Harry. "That's when we stayed on the beach all night drinking that horrible rotgut your Dad liked, then went skinny-dipping in the ocean."

"Except for Jack, who refused to bare his ass in front of his baby sister," said Sharon merrily. "And we were all like, 'Fine, then you can sit here and watch our wallets.'"

They shrieked with laughter at the memory, and Corey had the unusual sensation of going crimson with embarrassment over something he hadn't even done.

After a few more minutes of small talk, The Go-Gos' "Head Over Heels" burst through the speakers. Sharon grabbed Harry's arm and said, "Oh, God, I *totally* have to dance to this one; Jack, do you mind if Harry steals me for a few minutes?"

"Yes," said Corey, "as a matter of fact I do," and he hauled Sharon off the stool and, without a backward glance, forced her to dance with him instead.

Several minutes later, after the last crashing chord, they returned to the bar. Harry and Brian Isley were gone.

Chapter 67

The next morning Corey awakened in agony, a punishing hangover working in tandem with a sinus attack to send him lurching for the coffeemaker, a groan on his lips.

Sharon was already up, wearing one of his terrycloth robes and skimming over his morning *Tribune*. "You look like hell," she said.

He made some guttural response, and she laughed.

"You should behave with more dignity when you go out, and this wouldn't happen."

"Fuck you," he growled.

She lowered the newspaper. "That's the first time you've ever said that to me! . . . This and the dancing? . . . Seriously, who are you and what have you done with my real brother?"

She was only joking, of course, but Corey couldn't help feeling a momentary thrill of exposure, on par with what he'd experienced with Walt.

He burned his thumb pouring out the coffee, then sat down and plucked the front page from under Sharon's elbow. He flapped it open and looked at it; everything but the headline was a sea of murk. Well, of course, he'd left his reading glasses on the bed stand. He refolded the paper and shoved it back at Sharon.

She took a sip from her own cup. "Didn't you used to have a . . . some kind of animal, or something?"

"Hm?" Oh, she meant Jack's dog. "Yeah. I did."

"Not anymore?"

"No. I couldn't take care of her, so I . . . well, gave her away, basically."

"Sorry to hear it. I know how much you like those, y'know . . . pet things."

"Not a fan yourself, I take it."

"Are you kidding? . . . Don't you remember me dousing the parakeet in Chanel Number Five?"

Corey almost spit out a mouthful of coffee.

"I can't believe you don't remember that! My God, it's family legend. Mom never let me live that down. She actually mentioned it on her deathbed! I swear, she looked right at me and mouthed the words, *Poor, poor Eekie.* It may actually have been the last coherent thing she ever said."

Corey wiped his chin with a napkin, and said, "You really *were* a devil girl, weren't you?"

"You're the last person I'd expect to need reminding of that." She got up and opened one of the cabinets. "Got any cereal or anything?"

"In the pantry, next to the refrigerator."

The phone rang, and he went into the next room to answer it.

"Hi," said a caller, without identifying himself. "Hope I'm not waking you."

"No," said Corey. He was trying to place the voice; it was very familiar.

"It's not a bad time to call?"

"No. Who is thi—"

"Listen, I just wanted to say how good it was to see you and Sharon last night. Reminded me of old times."

Oh; this was *Harry.* "Yeah," he said, unsure of what else to say.

"It made me realize . . . I've sort of missed you."

"Mm," Corey said as noncommittally as possible.

"Why don't we have lunch and catch up?"

Take more than a lunch to catch you up on me, thought Corey, but he said, "Fine. Maybe next week sometime." *Or the week after. Or never.*

"I was thinking more like today," said Harry. "You wouldn't happen to be free, would you?"

"I . . ." He couldn't think of an excuse quickly enough. "I might be. I guess." Shit! Why did he say that?

"Could you come by the gallery at noon? I'll meet you outside, you don't have to come in, or anything."

"The gallery," said Corey. *What gallery? . . . Where?* "Um, I'd rather not."

"All right, I understand. How about, say . . . Frank's Tavern at twelve-thirty?"

"Okay." He knew no Frank's Tavern, but presumably it was in the phone book.

"Great! I look forward to it. See you then. And . . . thanks, Jack."

"Uh-huh."

He hung up the phone and returned to the kitchen, where Sharon was pouring herself a bowl of Product 19. "Why is all your cereal so boring?" she asked.

"Don't look at me, I didn't buy it." He picked up his coffee cup and took another revivifying sip from it.

"Well, if you didn't, who did?"

He was about to say *Jack, of course,* but caught himself and said, "Houseguests."

Sharon nodded and said, "Oh, right, I forgot. 'Breakfast is for kids and cattle.'" She picked up the box and examined it. "I should check the date on this, shouldn't I? Don't want to end up chowing down on some relic from the Clinton presidency."

"There's a Monica Lewinsky joke in there somewhere, but I'm too tired to find it."

She fetched a bottle of two-percent milk from the refrigerator. "Who called?"

"No one."

"I see." She splashed the milk over the cereal, sending a little lactose tsunami over the rim of the bowl. "And are you going?"

Corey raised an eyebrow. "Going where?"

"To lunch." She was trying to keep a wicked smile from her face.

"What the fuck," he said angrily. "Were you listening in?"

"Course not," she said, with mock affrontery. "I'm many things, but not sneaky. No, last night Harry told me he was going to call and ask you. He wanted my opinion on whether you'd say yes." She took the sugar bowl and removed the lid, only to discover it was empty. "Honestly, Jack," she whined.

"And what did you tell him?"

"I said you'd absolutely say yes. Do you have any honey, or something?"

"Brown sugar, above the stove." Corey dropped his head into his hands and ran his fingers through his hair. "I wish you'd just mind your own business. For God's sake, I don't even know the guy," he said, then hastily added, "anymore. And I don't *want* to know him. All I want is to be left alone. I mean, what the hell?"

"What we want isn't necessarily what we need, Jack." She stood on her toes and plucked the carton of brown sugar from a high shelf.

"Yeah, well you could just as easily apply that to yourself."

This set off a little flurry of sniping at each other, which resulted in each retiring to a separate corner after breakfast. And in fact Corey still hadn't seen her when, reluctantly, and still somewhat hungover, he left the house for lunch.

Chapter 68

There was almost no one else in the tavern, which only made things worse. In a bustling, noisy environment, Corey could have pretended that lunch was just lunch; but in the echoing, oaken room with its high-backed banquettes, every whisper carried weight. It was impossible to hide from intimacy. And intimacy was clearly Harry's goal.

"I have to tell you," he said, crumbling some oyster crackers over his gumbo, "it was the sight of you actually dancing that gobsmacked me. I say dancing, I should say, getting *down*." He smiled for emphasis, and Corey smiled too, but only because he had never heard the phrase sound so very, very white. "You were just burnin' up the floor out there. Even old devil girl couldn't keep up with you."

"Could you pass the salt?" asked Corey.

"And I thought to myself, what a goddamn fool I've been. You know—running around chasing these young guys, these twentysomethings—trying to, what, reconnect myself with youth, I guess. And really all I've been doing is making myself ridiculous. You don't reconnect with youth by fucking it. I mean, seeing you out there on the dance floor—you were younger in that moment than I've managed to feel this past year! Completely in the moment, completely unself-conscious . . . it made me think I never knew you."

"Butter?" requested Corey.

"And you know what else?" He leaned across the table as he handed Corey the butter tray. "The way you didn't remember having met Brian. I mean, the Jack Ackerly I thought I knew would've *obsessed* about Brian after seeing him with me. But it turns out that's not you at all. You *didn't even remember him.*"

Corey put down his fork, his appetite rapidly going south. What could be more off-putting than an attempted reconciliation from someone you never were involved with in the first place? "Look," he said bravely, "that was all an act. Of course I remember meeting him. I was only pretending to be cool about it."

Harry smiled knowingly. "Oh, is that a fact?"

"It is."

"Then tell me: *where* did you meet him?"

"What?"

"Tell me the circumstances. Since you remember it so well. Where was it, what time of day, what were we all doing?"

Corey narrowed his eyes. He was busted.

"I thought so," Harry concluded with a maddening smugness. "You can't hide the fact that you've changed. The breakup has obviously been good for you. Like it's been good for me. It's given us both some much-needed perspective. But now I think it's time we considered treating it like the temporary aberration it is."

Corey sighed and looked down at his BLT. He'd only taken two bites, and it was very good, but he knew he was destined not to finish it. "Don't I get any say in this decision?" he asked.

"What's to say?" Harry said with a shrug, trawling his spoon though his bowl. "You came here today. That already speaks volumes."

"I came for *lunch*. I came to *catch up.*"

Harry gave him a "fine-have-it-your-way" look. "All right, then. Let's catch up. Are you seeing anyone?"

Corey openly sighed. "None of your goddamn business."

"That means no. Had a serious boyfriend since we broke up?"

"Define 'serious.'"

"That means no." He grinned, then swallowed a spoonful of gumbo.

Corey turned his head, counted to ten, then turned back. "I'm going to go now," he said.

"You can run, but you can't hide."

"If I run fast enough I won't have to hide." He plucked the napkin from his lap and balled it up. "Bye." He got to his feet.

"I love you," said Harry.

Corey looked down at him and said, gently, "Look, sorry. It's just not mutual."

"It used to be."

"Everything's changed."

"I know it has. But wonderfully! . . . I finally saw the boy in you, Jack. I know he's in there now. And knowing that, I can love you till you're a hundred. I'm sure of it."

"Fine," Corey said. "Love me till I'm a hundred. Just do it *over there.*" He jerked his thumb in the opposite direction and walked out.

Harry got up and followed him. *Oh, Jesus,* he thought, as he picked up his pace, *he really is gonna make me run!* He managed to make it through the door to the street, but then Harry was next to him, grabbing his arm and drawing him in for a kiss.

At first Corey resisted; then he saw, from the corner of his eye, a trio of what looked like young street toughs, and he thought, *No way am I gonna let them think they're intimidating me,* so he allowed it; he allowed Harry to wrap him in his arms and bury his tongue in his mouth.

After a judicious moment he then gently pushed him away and said, "You take care, now," then made a deliberate point of walking right past the three toughs, to show them he wasn't afraid.

When he was just parallel, one of them sneered, "Get a room, grandma," and the others screamed like seal pups.

Corey shook his head in dismay. He couldn't even tell who was gay anymore. Maybe he was actually *becoming* fifty-three.

He continued on his way, each step leaving Harry farther behind.

Chapter 69

And yet . . . the kiss lingered.

As did what Harry had said. "I've seen the boy in you . . ." No one else had. No one else who'd known Jack had come so close to the truth of the matter. Not even his shrink. Not even his sister. Walt, of all people, had come closest; he'd seen that Jack was not Jack. But he'd only seen dysfunction; he hadn't seen *Corey*.

And hadn't he realized, after his disastrous flirtation with Preston Frye, that he couldn't be a fifty-three-year-old in a fifty-three-year-old body? . . . He could only be what he was: a twenty-six-year-old in a fifty-three-year-old body. And Harry not only saw that, he *liked* it. He'd broken up with middle-aged Jack, not because Jack's flesh was no longer young; Harry had said it, he could love Jack to the age of a hundred as long as he knew there was a boy inside. Well, wasn't that an almost exact description of the kind of man Corey was now?

And, yes . . . that kiss. It hadn't felt like much at the time, but in memory it warmed and thrilled him. There'd been an almost ideal balance of familiarity and passion in it . . . truly, Corey had never had one like it. It bore the stamp of ownership; it was like a brand. And yet it was hungry; it pleaded.

He tried to make himself stop thinking about it, but inevitably, as the days passed, and Sharon ran through repeated recitations of what now seemed to be a polished monologue—Part One: *The Wronged Wife*, Part Two: *The Jerk Will Be Sorry*—Corey felt his mind slipping more frequently into contemplation of Harry.

It was a little silly, of course; he didn't know much of anything about the man, other than that he was Jack's ex. He was handsome enough, for his age; had a lovely cleft chin, though his eyes were a little watery. And he had charm; he had it, he knew it, and he used it to get what he wanted. Well . . . Corey could respect that. He'd had it, himself, in his previous life.

But it was impossible that he should become involved in any way with him. Half a lunch and a quick grope was about the extent of what his masquerade could endure. Any significant time spent with him, and Harry would have to see that something was deeply wrong; that Jack didn't just possess a boyish aspect, it was the only aspect he had left. All the others had set up shop elsewhere.

Still . . . *that kiss.*

Since Corey, like Sharon, now had something he wanted to purge from his mind, their nighttime excursions became more frequent and more frantic. On this particular night, Corey was particularly bereft. He'd been deliberately ignoring Harry's incessant phone calls, till today; today, no call had come. He had an immediate sense that something irrevocable had happened, but couldn't put his finger on what, nor did he know what, if anything, he should do about it.

Accordingly, both he and Sharon had begun drinking early and in earnest, and now sat at a drag bar called Halo Street, swilling Cosmopolitans while harpy-like transvestites swooped and dove around them. She had been adamant about coming here; Corey wondered what it was about drag that so intrigued straight people. They couldn't seem to get enough of it.

He'd just bought another round at the bar and brought the drinks back to the corner he and Sharon had claimed, only to find her smoking. "Well, this is new," he said.

"I can have *one*," she said, a little too defensively, as though she'd been expecting a more direct attack.

"I don't care what you do," he said, setting down the drinks. He winced as a pain in his lower back flared up.

"I just felt like having one, is all," she continued. "So I borrowed one from Lola Falafel over there." She gave a little wave to a mocha-colored drag queen in an enormous red wig, who waved back with frighteningly long press-on nails.

Corey sat back down with an "*Ooof.*"

Sharon looked at him with concern. "Are you all right? . . . You seem a little messed up. Don't think you're getting out of dancing."

"I just went for a run today," he said. "It always beats the crap out of me. But I have to stay in shape, so . . ." He trailed off into a shrug.

She blew some smoke in the opposite direction, then turned and said, "You should swim, instead. That's what I do. It's a full-body workout, and you don't pound the shit out of yourself. You're too old to take that kind of beating."

"That's a good idea," he said, meaning it. "Really, really good. I mean, it may be the perfect solution for this body."

She snorted. "I like the way you put that—'*this* body.' What, have you got another one hanging up somewhere?"

Used to, he thought.

He reached over for his drink, then grimaced in pain again, and Sharon said, "Right. Time for emergency measures." She got up, a bit drunkenly.

"Where are you going?"

"I want to dance, and you're not dancing material yet," she said. "We're gonna fix that." She disappeared into the crowd.

A moment after she left, a slim, pouty-lipped drag queen in a beaded cocktail dress and an electric-blue Cleopatra wig sidled up to him and said, "Hey there, baby. All alone and lonely?"

"Neither, actually."

"If you ask nice, I could make your wildest fantasy come true."

"Right now, that would be a hot bath with Epsom salts, but thanks for the offer."

The queen gave him an even more pronounced pout and sauntered off. Corey took a few deep breaths and then wiped some sweat from his brow with his sleeve. He really shouldn't be out; he didn't feel at all well.

A few minutes later Sharon returned with a large smile and a small vial.

He squinted closely at it. "Poppers? . . . You bought *poppers?* You're a grandmother, for God's sake!"

"Then buying poppers must be what grandmothers do." She sat next to him and snapped open the vial. "Here."

He knew he shouldn't indulge. He'd long ago sworn off party drugs of any kind. Also, he was run down, emotionally upset, and loaded with allergy medicine. And he was fifty-three years old. But he wanted to feel good, he wanted to dance; and, he might as well admit it, he was feeling intense peer pressure from Sharon. So he inhaled a snootful of amyl nitrate.

The effect was immediate and glorious. Excitement overwhelmed him. The rush extended even to his fingers and toes. He could feel himself giving off sparks.

And so he found himself dancing. In fact, he couldn't seem to stop. He felt the bass beat in his solar plexus; the lights stabbed and prodded him, urging him on; and Sharon, her arms snaking over her head, writhed in and out of his line of sight, sometimes disappearing entirely in the press of other bodies.

And then . . . there was Harry!

At the sight of him, Corey went rigid, though everything around him continued to writhe and gyrate.

Sharon found her way over to him and shouted in his ear, "Don't be mad! I told him we'd be here tonight! He really, really wanted to see you!"

Corey had to fight for breath. This was silly—he didn't even *know* this man—but here he was, approaching him across the dance floor, like something from a goddamn Hollywood movie—and his heart skipped and skittered and somersaulted . . .

. . . But something wasn't right. Something didn't fit. It was the look on Harry's face. Even Sharon noticed it. She said, "Harry?" and tried to pull Corey away from him.

But it was too late. Harry grabbed him, taking both arms in his hands, his grip like pincers, and screamed in his face. *"Who do you think you are? Who the fuck do you think you are?"*

Corey reeled; Sharon tried to intervene, but couldn't wedge herself between them.

"That was my dog too!" Harry was unrelenting, his face screwed up in terrifying rage. *"How dare you give my dog away?"*

Corey searched for words, and finding none, searched for breath with no better result. He felt a sharp, sudden pain in his chest, and then another in his arm, and then he realized that Harry's grip was all that was holding him up—and then he was on the floor, and everyone was looking at him—Sharon, and Harry, and dozens of drag queens—and he looked up at them too, and tried to say something, but the music was too loud, and he couldn't tell if he'd said anything, or if he had, whether anyone had heard him.

Chapter 70

He opened his eyes, but there was nothing to see except hooks and clamps and tubes and monitors. So he shut them again.

The next time he opened them, he was someplace else, and Sharon and Fancy were standing over him. He attempted to say hello, but it took four separate tries, and that's when he knew he was on some serious drugs.

With difficulty, he focused on the feed in his wrist, and followed it up to the I.V. drip. "Whassin there?" he asked, his tongue lolling a bit over the words.

"Whatever it is," said Fancy sternly, "it's been prescribed by a medical professional, not administered by some thoughtless know-it-all who thinks rules only exist for her to break." She shot Sharon a withering glance, and Sharon actually cringed.

Whoa, thought Corey. *Who'd have thought round little Fancy could intimidate the devil girl?*

Tears streamed down Sharon's face. "I'm so sorry, Jack," she said, her voice cracking in at least three places.

"'S'allright," he said, smiling weakly. "Big boy. Made my own deshishions."

"You're tired," said Fancy, and she stroked the hair from his forehead. "We should let you rest."

"Happen' to me?" he asked.

"You had a heart attack, dear," she said, and in the background Sharon burst into open sobbing. Fancy cast her an impatient glance, then said, "A small one. No reason you shouldn't make a full recovery, though of course you'll have to take better care of yourself afterwards."

"Gon' start shwimming," he said. "Sharon's idea." He had to stick up for the poor girl; he could only imagine how hard Fancy had come down on her.

"That's fine," said Fancy. "But for the moment, just concentrate on getting some rest and letting your doctors repair the damage."

"'Kay," he said, and he shut his eyes.

He opened them again, and Sharon was there on her own, her face buried in a celebrity magazine.

"Hi," he said, and he smacked his lips; they were very dry.

She looked up, smiled, and closed the magazine. "How you feeling?"

"A lot better. Can you help me sit up?"

She looked dubious. "I'd better not. As many, many people have been telling me, I've done enough already."

"I can't imagine you taking that from them."

"Well, seeing your brother flopping around like a fish on the filthy floor of a drag bar can be a little humbling."

"You want to talk humbling? Try being the one doing the flopping."

They both laughed, and he said, "Seriously, I'd love to sit. There's a stitch in my side from all this lying down."

She shook her head. "No. With my luck, I'll try to prop you up and dislocate your arm or something."

He sighed. "Well, at least I can talk again. Must be different drugs."

"I don't know. No one will tell me anything. I'm the villain of the piece, or haven't you heard?"

He shook his head. "That's ridiculous. I'm fifty-three years old. I don't do anything I don't want to do."

"I know. But I can't really tell them that. It'd look like I'm shirking responsibility." She sighed. "I already tried pointing out that Dad had *two* heart attacks by the time he was your age. That went over like a lead balloon."

He sighed, then turned to the window. "Is it raining?"

"Just windy."

He watched as a treetop swayed violently back and forth. It was almost hypnotic. Eventually he said, "When can I go home?"

"Not sure."

"I feel perfectly fine."

"Just take it easy, Superman. It'll happen when it happens."

He lifted his wrist and scowled at the I.V. feed. "This thing hurts."

"Be a man about it."

"If I was a man about it, I'd just rip it out and tell the doctor to go fuck himself." He sat back and sighed. "I'm bored."

She tossed the celebrity magazine onto his lap.

"Not *that* bored."

They laughed.

"Can I get you anything?" she asked.

"A Coke would be great."

She squinted at him. "Don't you mean Pepsi?"

"Coke, Pepsi . . . whatever they've got."

She rose out of the chair. "See what I can find."

While he was waiting for her to return, the inertia of his situation crept over him again. And his eyes fell shut.

He opened them again, and Harry was there.

"Oh," he said warily. "Hey."

Harry raised his palms in a gesture of truce. "Don't get upset, I'm not here to yell at you."

"Okay. Good start."

"I just came to apologize. I feel terrible about what happened."

Corey sank back into his pillow. "Bet I feel worse."

"No, seriously . . . the insane way I went off on you . . ."

"Well . . . you had cause, I guess."

He shook his head. "No, honestly . . . it wasn't even really about Nelly. I mean, I was never all *that* crazy about her, we both know that. That's why I let you keep her in the first place. I've been thinking about it, and I realize now, it was the idea of you having given her away—what that *symbolized* . . . that's what made me snap. I mean, sure, you'd been keeping me at arm's length, not answering my calls, but I figured sooner or later our history had to mean something, all the years we'd invested in each other, the life we built. But when I found out that you gave Nelly away? . . . It was like you'd given all that away with her. Like you'd just wiped the slate clean. And I was shocked; still am. I couldn't believe you'd done that, that you'd *ever* do that. It made me realize you really, truly *have* changed."

"Yeah, I have," said Corey quietly.

"And . . . I confess, I've been playing a game with you, Jack. I wanted you back, but on my terms. I've been phoning you, cajoling you, but still seeing other guys while I was doing it. Hedging my bets, you know." He shook his head sadly. "It's only this," and here he gestured at the hospital bed, "that's brought me to my senses. The idea of a world without you in it . . ."

"I'm not real fond of the concept myself."

"Please don't joke." He reached over and took Corey's hand. "I'm going to make a commitment to you, right here and now: let me back in, and it'll be a fresh start. A hundred percent us. Just you and me."

"A fresh start, huh?" Corey asked, intrigued.

"Right. A new you, a new me, a whole new life together. Starting from day one. No past, only future. How does that sound?"

Corey's damaged heart started making itself heard: *thump, thump, thump,* a little tom-tom within his breast. "It sounds pretty good."

Harry's face lit up like a marquee, and Corey couldn't help smiling; couldn't help rejoicing that he—he, of all people!—had actually made someone that happy.

Had actually made *himself* that happy.

Harry leaned over and kissed him—a kiss, if possible, even more spine-tingling than the first. He drew back, smiled, then descended for another one; Corey put a hand on his chest and said, "Hold on, there, tiger."

He laughed and said, "Sorry. Carried away." He pointedly smoothed out his pants, then said, "Get some sleep. I'll be back tomorrow."

"I love you," said Corey, and he was amazed he was the first to say it.

Harry beamed at him. "I love you, too." He smiled at him all the way out the door.

A few minutes later, Sharon came in. "Visiting hours are over," she said, and she fetched her purse from one of the chairs. "They're kicking me out."

"Where's my Coke?" he asked.

She looked at him. "What?"

"You were supposed to get me a Coke."

"That was seven hours ago, Jack. I came back with one, but you were asleep. So I drank it myself."

"You drank my Coke?"

"Well, it'd hardly be worth drinking now, would it? And anyway, it was Seven-Up."

He grinned at her. "Never mind. The mood I'm in, I forgive you. And I forgive you for plying me with poppers, and I forgive you for telling Harry I gave the dog away."

She pulled the purse strap over her arm. "I didn't tell him that."

He furrowed his brow. "Didn't you?"

"Uh-uh." She primped in the mirror over the sink.

"You sure?"

"Honestly, Jack," she said, turning to go. "It's not the kind of thing I talk about."

She kissed him goodbye, and after she left he thought, *Then how'd he find out?* . . . But he was apparently still on just enough medication to make any kind of conjecture difficult, so he turned on the TV instead and tried to lull his brain into a comforting torpor.

He must have nodded off, because suddenly he was in the middle of a crime show he couldn't remember having started. He followed it just long enough for the flurry of details and plot points to hurt his head, then he dialed the volume all the way down and just let the characters dash across the screen to amuse him.

Several minutes later he heard someone muttering at the door. He turned and saw . . . good God, he saw himself! No—it was his *former* self . . . it was *Jack*. Jack Ackerly, in his old body!

He smiled. "Hey, boss! Wasn't expecting *you*."

"I'm sorry," Jack said, entering tentatively. "I can't tell you. So very sorry." He sat on the bed and took Corey's hand in his.

"'S'not your fault," said Corey. "I just had a little heart attack, is all."

Jack shook his head. "Listen," he said. "This is wrong. I've learned a lot, in the past few months. I . . . this is going to sound silly, but I've *grown up*. I've learned what it means to be a man."

"Cool," said Corey. "Is it a secret, or can you tell?"

"It's not a secret. Being a man means accepting with grace and dignity the consequences of your actions. It's that

simple." He grimaced. "I mean, it's simply put; not so simple to do. Me, I've never done it, ever. Least of all with you.
I dumped all the consequences of my actions onto *you*. And
look at you now."

Corey shook his head. "It was mutual. You got all my
crap, too. Plus, we agreed."

"No, no. *You* agreed. This was my idea, this whole crazy,
stupid, selfish plan was mine, designed to serve me. You were
at a point in your life where you almost had to go along with
it. Because, see, that's the only option I offered you. I'm a bad
man, Corey. A very sad, stunted, stupid man. But I'm going
to make it up to you." He got up, shut the door, turned off
the TV monitor, then came back and kissed Corey on the lips
and said, "I'm going to put us back where we belong. I'll be
as gentle as possible. Just trust me. Go with me."

He kissed Corey again, and Corey thought, *What is it
with everyone trying to mash with me in my hospital bed?*
He raised a hand and stopped him. "Wait," he said. "What
are—are you telling me, you want to switch us back?"

"That's right. I'll be Jack again, you'll be Corey again. I'll
be where you are, and you'll be free to walk out of here."

Corey was struck momentarily dumb. Couldn't Jack hear
himself? . . . He was apologizing for having unilaterally
made the decision to switch bodies; yet here he was trying
to make up for it by unilaterally making the decision to
switch back. "Whoa, there," Corey said. "Shouldn't you,
like, *ask* me first?"

Jack seemed taken aback. "I—I didn't think I had to. I
mean . . . I'm the goddamn cavalry, here."

"Well, you *do* have to ask. And the answer is no."

"What?" Jack said. "What are you saying? "

"I'm saying no, Jack. I don't *want* to change back."

Jack's jaw went slack. "But . . . in God's name . . . *why?*"

Corey almost told him. He *almost* told him. But he quickly
realized he didn't dare to. The complications that might
ensue, if Jack learned Corey had "reunited" with his own

ex . . . ? No, best just keep it to himself. He owed Jack no explanation, anyway. So in the end, he just smiled and said, "'Cause I'm happy."

Jack stared at him, open-mouthed.

"I'm *happy*, Jack," Corey repeated. "Thanks for your visit. But you can go now. Just go, and please—*leave me alone.*"

Looking thoroughly defeated, Jack turned toward the door and headed out.

Chapter 71

B ut he stopped.
At the door, he stopped, and turned back.

Shit, thought Corey, *I thought that went a little too easy.*

"Just one thing," he said.

Corey said, "Jack, you've already made your big speech, and I'm tired."

"It won't take a moment." He came back in and sat on the side of the bed. "I see that my sister's in town."

"Sharon? . . . Yeah, she is."

"Just tell me how she is, and I'll go." His face was strangely unreadable.

Corey shrugged. "She's fine. We've been having fun, painting the town red . . ."

Jack looked surprised. "Oh—I thought she came in because . . ."

Corey gestured to his I.V. feed. "'Cause of this? . . . No, she was already here when my ticker went tilt. Had a ringside seat, matter of fact."

"Then . . . why is she here? She never goes *anywhere.*"

"Oh, she split up with her old man. Turns out he was corkin' a coworker. So she came running to big brother to lick her wounds."

Corey expected some indignation on Jack's part; maybe

even an empty vow to punch Bert's lights out, or something similar. What he hadn't expected was the way Jack's face contorted in grief. What he hadn't expected was to see emotions cross that face, that Corey had never known it capable of expressing, even when it belonged to him. What he hadn't expected was to see Jack Ackerly cry.

"It's all right," Corey said. "She's fine. I've been taking her out on the town, getting her mind off it."

Jack couldn't speak for a few moments; then he rallied, pulled himself together, and said, "Well, yes, fine, till you had a heart attack and collapsed at her feet." Distractedly, he ran his fingers through his hair. "I can't even imagine what she's going through right now."

"She was just here a while ago. She's fine."

Jack looked at him as though he were stupid, or crazy. "She's been betrayed, she's all alone, she's running away from herself, and the man she came to for protection almost died right in front of her." He shook his head. "She's *not* fine. She's putting up a brave front, but she's scared and she needs my help."

"I just told you, boss, I've *been* helping her."

"*You don't know her.*" There was something in his voice that frightened Corey. A sarcastic comeback died in his throat.

"Tell me what I should do," he said instead.

"Love her," said Jack. "That's what it's going to take. Can you do that? Can you love my sister?"

And Corey realized: *I can't.* He liked Sharon well enough; he might even like her a lot. But if she disappeared from his life tomorrow, she'd leave no trace. He didn't love her; couldn't, after so short a time with her. Might never love her, even *with* time.

And yet, he was supposed to be Jack Ackerly now. He was supposed to assume Jack Ackerly's duties. What was it Jack had just been saying about accepting responsibility? . . .

He'd accepted Sharon. He'd taken her into his home, become her confidante. But if she needed more . . .

"You can't, can you?" Jack said. "No matter how hard you pretend to be me, there are some things you just can't fake."

"You should have thought about that, then, before you abandoned your family to me," said Corey acidly.

"Yes, I should've! That's exactly what I'm saying. I was unfair to them, I was unfair to you. I've been wrong all around. I can't expect you to take my place. I can't expect you to return the love of people you meet for the first time—love that's taken years to blossom and ripen." And suddenly Corey thought of Harry. A *fresh start,* he'd promised; *no past, only future.* But how likely was that . . . ? A lifetime with no reference to anything that had ever happened to them before? All of their common cast of characters, their shared traumas and triumphs, their in-jokes and their anecdotes, all set aside forever? . . . It was crazy to pin his hopes on that.

Corey realized that he'd allowed himself to take a spell of flirtation and a few passionate kisses for love; capital-L *love.* It was a kind of madness; he saw that now. Certainly, he might have a wonderful few weeks with Harry; and yes, Harry did want to be with him because he'd seen some of Corey in the man he thought was Jack. But if he wanted a Corey, he could have had a Corey; seemed to have one already, in fact, in Brian Isley. But he was coming back to Jack. He wanted *Jack.* And Corey, in whatever body, was just Corey.

He turned and looked outside. The wind had died down.

"Tell me what you're thinking," said Jack.

"I'm thinking," said Corey, "that if you have one more big speech, it might put me over."

Jack took his hand. "Maybe a small one," he said. "Corey, being you these past months . . . it's been an honor. One of the things I've learned is that you're a better man than you know. You undersold yourself to me. You're loved far more than you realize. You have friends who care deeply for you, and who want and need you in their lives. And you deserve their love. You deserve to follow through with those relationships, to reap the benefits of all that you've invested in the life I stole from you. You deserve a thirtieth birthday, Corey. You deserve a fortieth, and a fiftieth. You deserve to look in the mirror and see the things that you do, the choices you make, the love that you share, etch themselves on your face. You deserve to grow old in your own time, in your own way. Don't let me take that from you. Especially now that I'm willing to give it back."

Corey sighed. "Yep," he said. "That was the speech."

Jack squeezed his hand.

"What now?"

Jack kissed him.

And kissed him again.

And then Corey kissed him back.

He couldn't resist opening his eyes a little; this was an experience he couldn't easily categorize. Making out with himself? . . . Freud could've written nine or ten monographs on this alone.

It touched Corey to see that Jack's fingers trembled as he pulled the hospital gown from his shoulders, then doffed his own shirt. Corey noted that Jack had stopped shaving his old chest; there was a spray of dirty blonde hair across it now. It seemed . . . more welcoming. Like a comfortable old bed, inviting him to come and lie down.

A bit more fumbling, and they were naked. Corey pulled the intrusive I.V. needle from his arm and cast it aside. They embraced; kisses spilled into kisses; their erections pressed into each other's bellies; and then they found a rhythm, and worked it, first this way, then that—reacquainting themselves with their former bodies, as well as the men who now occupied them—and if they occasionally lost track of which was who, and whose body was giving pleasure to whom, well, wasn't that the point?

And so it went, with increasing vigor and excitement, and cries and whispers, and sweat and snot, and then, and then Corey felt it coming on, oh yes, coming up fast, coming up *fast*—"I'm close," he gasped, and it was still Jack's voice.

"Me too," Jack said, "but hold on—just ride it for a moment—"

"I don't know if I can wait—"

Jack reached down around his ankles, and from his discarded cargo shorts pulled something—it caught the light . . . a crystal? What the hell?

Panting with his approaching climax, he said, "From Francesca—supposed to break it—at the critical moment—"

"God, *now*," cried Corey. *"Break it now!"*

Jack let out a strangled groan, thrust himself forward, and in the same motion slammed the crystal on the adjacent table . . .

Interlude

Francesca

The book was titled *Occult Uses Of the Astrolabe* and it was very interesting indeed, with all sorts of nifty ideas for utilizing the ancient instrument to calibrate probability; and as Francesca knew well enough, probability, when accurately measured, could be manipulated. In fact, this was her speciality.

She shooed Pantagruel off the page so that she could flip to the next one, then shifted the lampshade so that it threw more light on the text. As she read, she nibbled a Lorna Doone, which crumbled into the gutter between the pages. Clicking her tongue at her sloppiness, she flicked the crumbs away with her forefinger, then picked up reading where she'd left off in mid-paragraph.

Twenty minutes passed in silent study before a new idea occurred to her; she wondered if she might detect altered probability in the ether itself, by a change in pitch. It was worth a try. Hadn't she a tuning fork somewhere? . . . She got up (prompting a momentary scramble by Razor and Osiris, who had fallen asleep on her feet) and headed for the bureau where she kept her artifacts and talismans. She began searching the drawers, one by one.

As she rummaged through the third drawer down, she dislodged a tissue envelope of dried lavender, which revealed a crystal hidden beneath it. She plucked it up and examined it. Surely it shouldn't be here. Surely she'd given it to Jack just a few hours earlier. Had he mistakenly left without it? . . . No, even if he'd done that, it wouldn't have ended up back in the drawer.

Had she mistakenly given him a *different* crystal? . . . She tried to remember how many she'd had on hand, and with what energies each was imbued.

She sorted through the rest of the drawer till she'd found the others. Four in all. That was fine, she'd thought she had five. So Jack *had* left with one of them. But which?

She frowned. She was always promising herself to work up a nice, tidy inventory of her stock, with each item listed by category, potency, and place, so that she'd know exactly where to go for what she needed and wouldn't have to be always rooting through everything like a madwoman. But so far, she'd never actually got around to doing this.

Winkle and Ashtoreth wove between her ankles as she tried to recall which crystal she'd handed Jack. She wasn't certain it was even a problem. Probably any crystal she gave him would serve as well, since all that was intended was an amplification of the unbinding equation. Any crystal except, of course . . .

She opened her hands and took another look at the four remaining.

"Uh-oh," she said.

Part Six

JACK O'CORCERY

Chapter 72

The crystal shattered into fragments, one of which jabbed Jack's hand; the pain traveled up Corey's arm to Jack's brain, and Corey yelped. Ecstasy, ephemeral at best, now opened onto something different; pleasure burst at the seams, unraveling the delicate hemwork of reality. Jack was flooded by memories, loud and rude: of birthday parties, hobby kits, acne outbreaks, terrible report cards . . . all the fits and sulks and disappointments, the quotidian and the epochal events, of a life—but not of his own. . . . *Corey's.* Likewise Corey, still beneath him (atop him? . . . how to tell anymore?) writhed under the onslaught of a lifetime's worth of business agreements, fraternal obligations, regrets, triumphs, heartbreaks, and ambitions, all the myriad moments that made up Jack Ackerly.

Jack stood over Lucille Szaslow's open casket, weeping uncontrollably. They hadn't got her face right, they hadn't got it right at all. The left cheek was flat, like she'd been hit with an iron, and Jack kept complaining through his tears, but Aunt Ginger could only tell him, "They did their best, honey . . . they did their best . . ."

Corey lay on sweat-soaked sheets, his small frame ablaze with measles. The room was dark, and his brother Jimmy held his hand and told him a story that made no sense to him, but he listened raptly all the same. He felt that he might fall through the center of the earth, were it not for Jimmy's reassuring voice; the voice he idolized, from the brother he hero-worshipped. A brother who abandoned him when he came out, who never wrote, never called, would only speak to him through Sharon . . .

Jack passed a joint to Tyler at a concert at Grant Park. The weather was sultry, the sun hung just over the horizon as though exhausted, but still cast its bloody glow over Patti LaBelle, who looked appropriately like an Aztec priestess. Tyler passed the joint on to Frida, who took a deep toke and passed it on to Perry, and from there it went to Steven, and to Kevin, and as he watched it travel down the row of those he loved best Jack was overcome by emotion, and he fell onto their laps, shouting over the music, *"This is one of the happiest nights of my life,"* and everyone laughed and told him he was high, and he said, *"No, honestly, it really is,"* and it really was, even now, it still was . . .

Corey dove off the high platform board at the hotel pool in San Diego, having taken a dare from his fellow convention-eers, and he felt light and free and immortal in the air, but then he suddenly felt the pull of gravity and he panicked and twisted and hit his temple on the way down, and everything was confusion when he hit the water, he couldn't see, he couldn't think; and then there were hands on him, tugging at him, and he endured a kind of mock rebirth, being pulled from a warm, fluid womb and onto cold concrete, where he gasped for air and someone said, "Are you okay? Are you all right?" and it was Harry's voice. And he opened his eyes and there was Harry's face, dripping onto his, and he said, "How do you feel?" and Corey wanted to say, *Safe, I feel safe,* but his colleagues were clustered around him and he was too embarrassed so he said nothing . . .

In the hospital room, Jack grabbed Corey's hand—or Corey grabbed Jack's—and asked, "What's happening?," and Jack replied—or Corey did—"I don't know, just hold on"—

And Jack had his first kiss, from a man twice his age, in the back of a seedy bar in Milwaukee, where he'd run away from Aunt Ginger for just this purpose, and the kiss tasted black and foul, curdled with bitterness, but he took another one all the same . . .

And Corey stood before his employees and announced that he was retiring and selling the agency to a media conglomerate and Iris from Accounting started to cry, till he brought up the severance packages he'd negotiated for them . . .

And Ignacio stood before a mirror examining the knife wound behind his left ear; it had healed but was still so ghastly it might as well still be fresh, and he knew from then on that whatever fashion might dictate he would have to wear his hair long . . .

What—what are you doing here? . . . What are you doing in my head? Who the hell are you? . . .

And Kent the bartender brought his mother her cigarettes and her first beer of the evening while she watched wrestling on TV, and didn't dare complain because she didn't ask for rent but my God, when would the old battle-ax finally just die? . . .

Who—who's there? . . . What is this? . . .

And Harry stood by helplessly while his best friend, Trevor Probst, chased the soccer ball into the road and was hit by a car and flew into the air like a rag doll, and nothing, nothing, nothing would ever make sense again, and he staggered back, his eyes rimmed with tears, and he turned and fled, fled without conscious thought, until he stopped abruptly and looked up, and said—

J-Jack? . . . Is that you? . . . Corey? . . .

And in the hospital room Corey and Jack clung to each other as more minds opened up to them, as men they had never known before, connected to them only through Ignacio, or Kent, or Harry, or through any of *their* other lovers, blossomed in their heads—a constellation of a thousand consciousnesses twinkling into being, all of them linked by

a decades-long chain of mutual embraces, crossing the world over and over again, a latticework of powerful male love . . .
. . . and not just for them alone.

In Kansas, a senile octogenarian, ending his days in a third-rate nursing home, found himself strong and blond and happy as he crouched atop a bright blue board and surfed an ocean he had never even seen . . .

And in Siena, a Catholic priest who had been celibate since the age of twenty, was able to recall with loving accuracy the texture and aroma of the chest hair of his lover of thirty-one years . . .

And in Bangkok, a fourteen-year-old dancer in a hustler bar nearly fell off the stage from the overpowering but impossible memory of holding his first-born child . . .

And in Buenos Aires a young transvestite paused while painting his toenails to recall with uncanny vividness the loss of his virginity to a fellow soldier in the dense Korean jungle in 1954 . . .

And in South Africa, a bookkeeper, profoundly deaf since birth, was overwhelmed by a memory of playing the trumpet in a Mozart's *Jupiter* Symphony . . .

And in rural China, a middle-aged farmer who had only twice in his life dared to act on his forbidden desires was to his astonishment able to recall a whole string of one-night stands from when he toured Europe with his modern dance company . . .

"It's too much," gasped Corey/Jack, on the verge of hyperventilating; and Jack/Corey said, "Hold on, I'm here, hold on . . ."

And every sacred kiss, every back-alley blowjob, every perfunctory fuck, every single act of male-male desire, driven by whatever impulse, from self-loathing to selfless adoration, opened the door to every life, every mind, every mine of memories, of every man who partook of it, and then raced on to do the same for all the lives and memories of every other man who had ever shared sexual passion with him . . . and all of these countless, incandescent lives blazed in unison, coalescing into a vortex of gay experience, an endless, swirling whirlpool of love and death, pain and pleasure, decadence and despair, grace and glory—the full gamut of what life offered men who love men, and the chilling range of what it inflicted on them . . .

And at the center of it all, their minds forming the hub about which this potent brew eddied and gushed, were a man named Jack and another named Corey.

"Hold on," one said to the other, "there has to be an end-point—we can't be infinite . . ."

"I'm *trying,*" said the other, "but it just gets faster and faster and I'm pulling away from you—"

"No, hold on!—"

"—pulling away from *us*—"

"Hold on—"

But he could feel himself, metaphorically, losing his grip— his essential self, *their* essential selves, slipping, slipping away into the maelstrom; it was inevitable, it was imminent, it was—

"Ex*cuse* me, what the *hell* do you think you're doing?"

And, just like that, the spell was broken.

The vortex dissipated, the turbulent surge of memory ceased as though switched off.

Lying entwined, panting, Corey and Jack now separated— broke the epoxy that their sweat had become, sat up, and turned toward the door to the room, where a truly massive nurse glared at them with shafts of lightning in her eyes.

"Do you *realize,*" she snarled, "that this man is recover-ing from a *heart attack?*"

"Yes," said Corey and Jack in unison; then they looked at each other and laughed.

"Oh, so it's *funny?*" she barked. "You find this kind of disgusting lewdness, putting a *life* at risk, a real knee-slapper? Because I'm telling you right *now*—"

"It's all right, it's all right!" cried a handsome, chocolate-colored orderly, who darted in front of her and bravely put a soothing hand on her shoulder. "It's not what it looks like."

"What the hell else can it be?" she snapped, resisting any attempt to placate her.

"It's a long story, and it's not that interesting," he said. "Just leave it to me, I'll see that they stop."

The nurse looked at him, then at Corey and Jack, and with a snort she turned and left the room.

The orderly turned and smiled, and said, "Sorry, gentlemen; I'll just give you back your privacy now."

"Thanks, Lewis," said Jack.

"Yeah, thanks," Corey added. "Give our love to Jermaine."

"I rather think you just did that," Lewis said with a wink. And then he shut the door, leaving them alone again.

Corey and Jack looked at each other. Their chests still heaved for breath; the last few minutes had pushed them both to exhaustion. But they felt wonderfully, dizzyingly, dazzlingly alive.

Corey, still straddling Jack, tapped his own, original head and said, "You're still in here, you know. But I think I'm the one at the wheel."

"Same here," said Jack, back in the body he was born with. Then he made a face and said, "So, you really honestly like Clay Aiken?"

Corey blushed and said, "Um, yeah. But unless I miss my guess, so do you, now."

Jack reflected a moment, then frowned. "Oh my God. I *do.*"

They both laughed; they couldn't help themselves, it bubbled out of them like foam. Then Corey's face went suddenly taut, and he said, "Jack . . . *Jack.*"

"What's the matter?"

"Your *eyes,* Jack." They had turned Arctic blue.

Jack reached up and brushed the flap of hair out of Corey's face. "Yours, too," he said. For Corey's were now as black as jet.

Chapter 73

The eradication of the boundaries between all gay lives connected by sex had lasted but briefly; and across the globe, the men thus affected shook themselves back into the present tense and convinced themselves it had been some kind of momentary derangement, or a freakish kind of migraine. Most declined to talk about it; those who did speak of it found when comparing notes that the details receded from memory even as they verbalized them.

For those closer to Jack and Corey in the great chain of loving, the effects lasted longer; so that, by simple mathematics, there were more men in Chicago than anywhere else whose lives were suddenly open books to one another. Walt Neurath was giddy with glee at suddenly having so much wonderful material for gossip; but his delight evaporated when he realized that anything he might whisper or insinuate, everybody else already knew. Just as they knew the tawdry details of his *own* private life. But eventually, even for these men, the knowledge became hazy and indistinct, and then eluded them completely, like a dream upon waking.

For those whom Jack and Corey had loved personally, the effects endured longest of all. They were joined in a joyously awkward fellowship, tumbling around in each other's heads, sharing each other's vast store of experiences and stories; and even after all this dwindled away some weeks later, they retained for each other an inescapable affection, and whenever two or more of them met thereafter, they met as brothers.

For Jack and Corey, the effects eventually faded as well, with one signal exception: each was now permanently embedded in the mind of the other. But they had already walked in each other's shoes, so this dual occupancy felt almost natural to them. Each moment of each one's life was now part of the other's as well, so any friction that might have been engendered by such inescapable intimacy was smoothed over by the increasing confusion about where one man left off and the other began.

Immediately after the incident, Francesca left a rambling apology on Jack's voice mail, the gist of which was, "Jack, I'm so sorry. I'm so, so, so, so sorry. I'm just really so sorry. I just can't say how sorry I am."

After his discharge from the hospital, he phoned her back and said, "Don't worry, it all turned out fine. Though it was a helluva ride . . . a real E ticket."

Inside his head, Corey asked, *What's an E ticket?*

"*You* know," said Jack.

Corey thought for a moment, then said, *Hey, yeah! I do.*

Sharon flew home and reunited with Bert. She'd essentially reconciled with him already, by phone; he'd been so kind to her, so consoling, during her panic and guilt over Jack's brush with death. Now Jack was well again . . . though, it had to be said, behaving very oddly. Harry was suddenly back in the picture, but so was that young man, Corey; and the way Harry looked at both of them—the way they looked at each *other*—made her increasingly uncomfortable. She wasn't quite certain what dynamic was at work there, and was only too happy to leave before she found out.

She was also strangely unsettled by the blue contact lenses Jack had inexplicably taken to wearing. Sometimes, when he turned his gaze on her, it was like being looked at by somebody else.

Ten months later, the Lucille Szaslow Literacy Project opened in Andersonville. Corey was there, of course; and where Corey went, David was never far behind. Jack and Harry showed up just in time for the opening festivities to get under way.

Gary and Carol Mahlanki were on hand, as the project's public relations representatives, thus sparing Jack and Corey the tedium of having to speak to reporters. Not that many actually showed up; this wasn't big news, and certainly not mainstream fare. Even so, Corey and Jack were called on to pose for innumerable photos with community and civic leaders. Corey was mildly annoyed by the way his friends made a game of trying to get in every picture, and was surprised that Tyler was far more shameless in this regard than Frida. *You've grown up, that's all,* said Jack, inside his head.

As co-founders, Jack and Corey were much occupied by accepting the greetings and congratulations of the many attendees. These included Aunt Ginger, whom Corey had flown in just for the occasion, and who cried openly on his shoulder and told him his mother would have been "so terribly proud." At roughly the same time, Jack was cornered by Robyn, who was looking positively virginal in Laura Ashley, and who wanted to discuss the possibility of sharing resources with the Edgewater Youth Center, of which she was now board president.

Because of all this well-wishing, Jack and Corey had little chance to speak to each other during the event; but due to the ongoing conversation in their heads, neither did they feel so strong a need. Still, it had been several weeks since they'd actually seen each other, so when the celebration had wound down to the dregs of the guests, the ones who'd have to be removed with a crowbar, Jack took a seat next to Corey and said, "Hey."

"Hey, boss," Corey replied with an inviting smile.

Behind them, Harry crooked a finger at David. "C'mon, I'll buy you a drink. You know you won't understand a word these two say to each other anyway."

"Thanks," said David, who knew only too well the kind of verbal shorthand Harry was referring to. "I'll join you right after I check on my team." His company had catered the event, and he wanted to make sure it had all gone well . . . though with Fancy overseeing his staff, there was little doubt of it.

Left alone, Corey and Jack gazed at each other in blissful silence. Each was appraising the other with pride and affection. There was more between them than could easily be summarized; in tandem they had lived more lives than they could even remember, though none more precious to them than the pair they now shared between them. The enormity of their bond crowded out easy sentiments. In perfect accord, they sat and basked in their proximity.

Finally, it came time to part.

"It's all good?" asked Jack, knowing the answer.

"It's all good," said Corey.

And they rejoined their husbands as the lights flickered out.